Praise for Kate Morton

'Kate Morton excels in this enthralling novel about
desires and divided loyalties'
Good Housekeeping

'A fascinating family saga . . . I adored this book – and
was – literally – unable to put it down. There were
echoes of Daphne du Maurier, of Victorian novels,
and of Ian McEwan's *Atonement*'
Irish Examiner

'A nuanced exploration of family secrets and
betrayal, Morton's latest is captivating'
People

'Atmosphere, intrigue and intelligence'
Metro

'A dilapidated castle, aristocratic twins, a troubled
sister and a series of dark secrets cast a whispery spell
in Morton's third book'
Marie Claire

'A haunting story . . . packed with memorable characters
and evocative settings. Cleverly constructed and beautifully
written, this is the perfect summer read'
Choice

'A beautifully written and satisfying novel'
Daily Express

THE SECRET KEEPER

Kate Morton grew up in the mountains of south-east Queensland and now lives with her husband and young sons in Brisbane. She has degrees in dramatic art and English literature, specializing in nineteenth-century tragedy and contemporary gothic novels.

Kate Morton has sold over 7 million copies in 26 languages, across 38 countries. *The Shifting Fog*, published internationally as *The House at Riverton*, *The Forgotten Garden* and *The Distant Hours* have all been number one bestsellers around the world. Each novel won the Australian Book Industry award for General Fiction Book of the Year.

You can find more information about Kate Morton and her books at katemorton.com or facebook.com/KateMortonAuthor

THE SECRET KEEPER

KATE MORTON

PAN BOOKS

For Selwa
friend, agent, champion

First published 2012 by Mantle

This paperback edition published 2013 by Pan Books
an imprint of Pan Macmillan, a division of Macmillan Publishers Limited
Pan Macmillan, 20 New Wharf Road, London N1 9RR
Basingstoke and Oxford
Associated companies throughout the world
www.panmacmillan.com

ISBN 978-1-4472-3107-3

1 3 5 7 9 8 6 4 2

A CIP catalogue record for this book is available from the British Library.

Typeset by Ellipsis Digital Limited, Glasgow
Printed and bound by CPI Group (UK) Ltd, Croydon CR0 4YY

Visit **www.panmacmillan.com** to read more about all our books
and to buy them. You will also find features, author interviews and
news of any author events, and you can sign up for e-newsletters
so that you're always first to hear about our new releases.

PART ONE

LAUREL

$\mathcal{O}$ne

Rural England, a farmhouse in the middle of nowhere, a summer's day at the start of the nineteen sixties. The house is unassuming: half-timbered, with white paint peeling gently on the western side and clematis scrambling up the plaster. The chimney pots are steaming and you know, just by looking, that there's something tasty simmering on the stove top beneath. It's something in the way the vegetable patch has been laid out, just so, at the back of the house; the proud gleam of the leadlight windows; the careful patching of the roofing tiles.

A rustic fence hems the house and a wooden gate separates the tame garden from the meadows on either side, the copse beyond. Through the knotted trees a stream trickles lightly over stones, flitting between sunlight and shadow as it has done for centuries; but it can't be heard from here. It's too far away. The house is quite alone, sitting at the end of a long dusty driveway, invisible from the country lane whose name it shares.

Apart from an occasional breeze, all is still, all is quiet. A pair of white hula hoops, last year's craze, stand propped against the wisteria arch. A teddy bear with an eye patch and a look of dignified tolerance keeps watch from his vantage point in the peg basket of a green laundry trolley. A wheelbarrow loaded with pots waits patiently by the shed.

Despite its stillness, perhaps because of it, the whole scene has an expectant, charged feeling, like a theatre stage in the moments before the actors walk out from the wings. When every possibility stretches ahead and fate has not yet been sealed by circumstance, and then –

'Laurel!' A child's impatient voice, some distance off. 'Lau-*rel*, where are you?'

And it's as if a spell has been broken. The house lights dim; the curtain lifts.

A clutch of hens appears from nowhere to peck between the bricks of the garden path, a jay drags his shadow across the garden, a tractor in the nearby meadow putters to life. And high above it all, lying on her back on the floor of a wooden tree house, a girl of sixteen pushes the lemon Spangle she's been sucking hard against the roof of her mouth and sighs.

It was cruel, she supposed, just to let them keep hunting for her, but with the heatwave and the secret she was nursing, the effort of games – childish games at that – was just too much to muster. Besides, it was all part of the challenge and, as Daddy was always saying, fair was fair and they'd never learn if they didn't try. It wasn't Laurel's fault she was better at finding hiding places. They were younger than her, it was true, but it wasn't as if they were babies.

And anyway, she didn't particularly want to be found. Not today. Not now. All she wanted to do was lie here and let the thin cotton of her dress flutter against her bare legs, while thoughts of him filled her mind.

Billy.

She closed her eyes and his name sketched itself with

cursive flair across the blackened lids. Neon, hot pink neon. Her skin prickled and she flipped the Spangle so its hollow centre balanced on the tip of her tongue.

Billy Baxter.

The way he stared at her over the top of his black sunglasses, the jagged lopsided smile, his dark teddy-boy hair . . .

It had been instant, just as she'd known real love would be. She and Shirley had stepped off the bus five Saturdays ago to find Billy and his friends smoking cigarettes on the dance hall steps. Their eyes had met and Laurel had thanked God she'd decided a weekend's pay was fair exchange for a new pair of nylons—

'Come *on*, Laurel.' This was Iris, voice sagging with the day's heat. 'Play fair, why don't you?'

Laurel closed her eyes tighter.

They'd danced each dance together. The band had skiffled faster, her hair had loosened from the French roll she'd copied carefully from the cover of *Bunty*, her feet had ached, but still she'd kept on dancing. Not until Shirley, miffed at having been ignored, arrived aunt-like by her side and said the last bus home was leaving if Laurel cared to make her curfew (she, Shirley, was sure she didn't mind either way) had she finally stopped. And then, as Shirley tapped her foot and Laurel said a flushed goodbye, Billy had grabbed her hand and pulled her towards him and something deep inside of Laurel had known with blinding clarity that this moment, this beautiful, starry moment, had been waiting for her all her life—

'Oh, suit yourself.' Iris's tone was clipped now, cross. 'But don't blame me when there's no birthday cake left.'

The sun had slipped past noon and a slice of heat fell through the tree-house window, firing Laurel's inner eyelids cherry cola. She sat up but made no further move to leave her hiding spot. It was a decent threat – Laurel's weakness for her mother's Victoria sponge was legendary – but an idle one. Laurel knew very well that the cake knife lay forgotten on the kitchen table, missed amid the earlier chaos as the family gathered picnic baskets, rugs, fizzy lemonade, swimming towels, the new transistor, and burst, stream-bound, from the house. She knew because when she'd doubled back under the guise of hide-and-seek and sneaked inside the cool, dim house to fetch the package, she'd seen the knife glinting by the fruit bowl, red bow tied around its handle.

The knife was a tradition – it had cut every birthday cake, every Christmas cake, every Somebody-Needs-Cheering-Up cake in the Nicolson family's history – and their mother was a stickler for tradition. Ergo, until someone was dispatched to retrieve the knife, Laurel knew she was free. And why not? In a household like theirs, where quiet minutes were rarer than hen's teeth, where someone was always coming through one door or slamming another, to squander privacy was akin to sacrilege.

Today, especially, she needed time to herself.

The package had arrived for Laurel with last Thursday's post, and in a stroke of good fortune Rose had been the one to meet the postman, not Iris or Daphne or – God help her – Ma. Laurel had known immediately who it was from. Her cheeks had burned crimson, but she'd managed somehow to stutter words about Shirley and a band and an EP she was borrowing. The effort of obfuscation was lost on Rose, whose attention, unreliable at best, had already shifted to a butterfly resting on the fence post.

Later that evening, when they were piled in front of the television watching *Juke Box Jury*, and Iris and Daphne were debating the comparative merits of Cliff Richard and Adam Faith and their father was bemoaning the latter's false American accent and the broader wastage of the entire British Empire, Laurel had slipped away. She'd fastened the bathroom lock and slid to the floor, back pressed firm against the door.

Fingers trembling, she'd torn the end of the package.

A small book wrapped in tissue had dropped into her lap. She'd read its title through the paper – *The Birthday Party* by Harold Pinter – and a thrill had shot along her spine. Laurel had been unable to keep from squealing.

She'd been sleeping with it inside her pillowcase ever since. Not the most comfortable arrangement, but she liked to keep it close. She *needed* to keep it close. It was important.

There were moments, Laurel solemnly believed, in which a person reached a crossroads; when something happened, out of the blue, to change the course of life's events. The premiere of Pinter's play had been just such a moment. She'd read about it in the newspaper and felt an inexplicable urge to attend. She'd told her parents she was visiting Shirley and had sworn Shirley to deepest secrecy, and then caught the bus into Cambridge.

It had been her first trip anywhere alone, and as she sat in the darkened Arts Theatre watching Stanley's birthday party descend into nightmare, she'd experienced an elevation of spirits the likes of which she'd never felt before. It

was the sort of revelation the flush-faced Misses Buxton
seemed to enjoy at church each Sunday morning, and while
Laurel suspected their enthusiasm had more to do with the
new young rector than the word of God, sitting on the edge
of her cheap seat as the lifeblood of the onstage drama
reached inside her chest and plugged into her own, she'd felt
her face heat blissfully and she'd *known*. She wasn't sure
what exactly, but she'd known it absolutely: there was more
to life and it was waiting for her.

She'd nursed her secret to herself, not entirely sure what
to do with it, not *remotely* sure how to go about explaining
it to someone else, until the other evening, with his arm
around her and her cheek pressed firmly against his leather
jacket, she'd confessed it all to Billy . . .

Laurel took his letter from inside the book and read it
again. It was brief, saying only that he'd be waiting for her
with his motorcycle at the end of the lane on Saturday afternoon at two thirty – there was this little place he wanted to
show her, his favourite spot along the coast.

Laurel checked her wristwatch. Less than two hours
to go.

He'd nodded when she told him about the performance of *The Birthday Party* and how it made her feel; he'd
spoken about London and theatre and the bands he'd seen
in nameless nightclubs, and Laurel had glimpsed gleaming
possibilities. And then he'd kissed her, her first proper kiss,
and the electric bulb inside her head had exploded so that
everything burned white.

She shifted to where Daphne had propped the little
hand mirror from her vanity set and stared at herself, comparing the black flicks she'd drawn with painstaking care at

the corner of each eye. Satisfied they were even, she smoothed her fringe and tried to quell the dull sick-making sense that she'd forgotten something important. She'd remembered a beach towel; she wore her swimsuit already beneath her dress; she'd told her parents that Mrs Hodgkins needed her for some extra hours in the salon, sweeping and cleaning.

Laurel turned from the mirror and nibbled a snag of fingernail. It wasn't in her nature to sneak about, not really; she was a good girl, everybody said so – her teachers, the mothers of friends, Mrs Hodgkins – but what choice did she have? How could she ever explain it to her mother and father?

She knew quite certainly that her parents had never felt love; no matter the stories they liked to tell about the way they met. Oh, they *loved* each other well enough, but it was a safe old-person's love, the sort expressed in shoulder rubs and endless cups of tea. No – Laurel sighed heatedly. It was safe to say that neither had ever known the *other* sort of love, the sort with fireworks and racing hearts and physical – she blushed – desires.

A warm gust brought with it the distant sound of her mother's laughter, and awareness, however vague, that she stood at a precipice in her life made Laurel fond. Dear Ma. It wasn't her fault her youth had been wasted on the war. That she'd been practically twenty-five when she met and married Daddy; that she still trotted out her paper boat-making skills when any of them needed cheering up; that the highlight of her summer had been winning the village Gardening Club prize and having her picture in the paper. (Not just the local paper, either – the article had been syndicated in the London press, in a big special about regional happenings. Shirley's barrister father had taken great pleasure in trimming it out of his newspaper and bringing it round to show them.)

Ma had played at embarrassment and protested when Daddy stuck the clipping on the new refrigerator, but only half-heartedly, and she hadn't taken it down. No, she was proud of her extra-long runner beans, *really* proud, and that was just the sort of thing that Laurel meant. She spat out a fine shard of fingernail. In some indescribable way it seemed kinder to deceive a person who took pride in runner beans than it was to force her to accept the world had changed.

Laurel hadn't much experience with deceit. They were a close family – all of her friends remarked upon it. To her face and, she knew, behind her back. As far as outsiders were concerned, the Nicolsons had committed the deeply suspicious sin of seeming genuinely to like one another. But lately things had been different. Though Laurel went through all the usual motions, she'd been aware of a strange new distance. She frowned slightly as the summer breeze dragged strands of hair across her cheek. At night, when they sat around the dinner table and her father made his sweet unfunny jokes and they all laughed anyway, she felt as if she were on the outside looking in; as if the others were on a train carriage, sharing the same old family rhythms, and she alone stood at the station watching as they pulled away.

Except that it was *she* who would be leaving them, and soon. She'd done her research: the Central School of Speech and Drama was where she needed to go. What, she wondered, would her parents say when she told them that she

wanted to leave? Neither of them was particularly worldly –
her mother hadn't even been as far as London since Laurel
was born – and the mere suggestion that their eldest daughter was considering a move there, let alone a shadowy
existence in the theatre, was likely to send them into a state
of apoplexy.

Below her, the washing shrugged wetly on the line. A leg
of the denim jeans Grandma Nicolson hated so much ('You
look cheap, Laurel – there's nothing worse than a girl who
throws herself around') flapped against the other, frightening the one-winged hen into squawking and turning circles.
Laurel slid her white-rimmed sunglasses onto her nose and
slumped against the tree-house wall.

The problem was the war. It had been over for sixteen
years – all her life – and the world had moved on.
Everything was different now; gas masks, uniforms, ration
cards and all the rest of it belonged only in the big old khaki
trunk her father kept in the attic. Sadly, though, some
people didn't seem to realize it; namely, the entire popula-
tion over the age of twenty-five.

Billy said she wasn't ever going to find the words to
make them understand. He said it was called the 'generation
gap' and that trying to explain herself was pointless; that it
was like it said in the Alan Sillitoe book he carried everywhere in his pocket, adults weren't supposed to understand
their children and you were doing something wrong if they
did.

A habitual streak in Laurel – the good girl, loyal to her
parents – had leapt to disagree with him, but she hadn't.
Her thoughts had fallen instead to the evenings lately when
she managed to creep away from her sisters, when she

stepped out into the balmy dusk, transistor radio tucked beneath her blouse, and climbed with a racing heart into the tree house. There, alone, she'd hurry the tuning dial to Radio Luxembourg and lie back in the dark, letting the music surround her. And as it seeped into the still country air, blanketing the ancient landscape with the newest songs, Laurel's skin would prickle with the sublime intoxication of knowing herself to be part of something bigger: a world-wide conspiracy, a secret group. A new generation of people, all listening at the very same moment, who understood that life, the world, the future, were out there waiting for them . . .

Laurel opened her eyes and the memory fled. Its warmth lingered though, and with a satisfied stretch she followed the path of a rook casting across a graze of cloud. *Fly little birdie, fly.* That would be her, just as soon as she finished school. She continued to watch, allowing herself to blink only when the bird was a pinprick in the far-off blue, telling herself that if she managed this feat her parents would be made to see things her way and the future would unfurl cleanly.

Her eyes watered triumphantly and she let her gaze drop back towards the house: the window of her bedroom, the Michaelmas daisy she and Ma had planted over the poor, dead body of Constable the cat, the chink in the bricks where, embarrassingly, she used to leave notes for the fairies.

There were faint memories of a time before, of being a very small child, collecting winkles from a pool by the seashore, of dining each night in the front room of her grandmother's seaside boarding house, but they were like a dream. The farmhouse was the only home she'd ever known. And although she didn't want a matching armchair of her own, she liked seeing her parents in theirs each night; knowing as she fell asleep that they were murmuring together on the other side of the thin wall; that she only had to reach out an arm to bother one of her sisters.

She would miss them when she went.

Laurel blinked. She would *miss* them. The certainty was swift and heavy. It sat in her stomach like a stone. They borrowed her clothes, broke her lipsticks, scratched her records, but she would miss them. The noise and heat of them, the movement and squabbles and crushing joy. They were like a litter of puppies, tumbling together in their shared bedroom. They overwhelmed outsiders and this pleased them. They were the Nicolson girls: Laurel, Rose, Iris and Daphne; a garden of daughters, as Daddy rhapsodized when he'd had a pint too many. Unholy terrors, as Grandma proclaimed after their holiday visits.

She could hear the distant whoops and squeals now, the faraway watery sounds of summer by the stream. Something inside her tightened as if a rope had been pulled. She could picture them, like a tableau from a long-ago painting. Skirts tucked into the sides of their knickers, chasing one another through the shallows; Rose escaped to safety on the rocks, thin ankles dangling in the water as she sketched with a wet stick; Iris, drenched somehow and furious about it; Daphne, with her corkscrew ringlets, doubled over laughing.

The plaid picnic rug would be laid out flat on the grassy bank and their mother would be standing nearby, knee-deep in the bend where the water ran fastest, setting her latest boat to sail. Daddy would be watching from the side, trousers rolled up and a cigarette balanced on his lip. On his face – Laurel could picture him so clearly – he'd be wearing that customary look of mild bemusement, as if he couldn't quite believe his luck that life had brought him to this very place, this very time.

Splashing at their father's feet, squealing and laughing as his fat little hands reached out for Mummy's boat, would be the baby. Light of all their lives . . .

The baby. He had a name, of course, it was Gerald, but no one ever called him that. It was a grown-up name and he was just such a *baby*. Two years old today, but his face was still round and rich with dimples, his eyes shone with mischief, and then there were those deliciously fat white legs. Sometimes it was all Laurel could do not to squeeze them too hard. They all fought to be his favourite and they all claimed victory, but Laurel knew his face lit up most for her.

Unthinkable, then, that she should miss even a second of his birthday party. What had she been playing at, hiding in the tree house so long, particularly when she planned to sneak away with Billy later?

Laurel frowned and weathered a hot wave of recriminations that cooled quickly to resolution. She would make amends: climb back to the ground, fetch the birthday knife from the kitchen table and take it straight down to the stream. She'd be a model daughter, the perfect big sister. If she completed the task before her wristwatch ticked away ten minutes, she would accrue bonus points on the imagined score sheet she carried inside her always. The breeze blew warm against her bare sun-browned foot as she stepped quickly onto the top rung.

Later, Laurel would wonder if it all might have turned out differently had she gone a little more slowly. If, perhaps, the whole terrible thing might even have been averted had she taken greater care. But she didn't, and it wasn't. She was rushing and thus she would always blame herself in some way for what followed. At the time, though, she hadn't been able to help herself. As intensely as she'd earlier craved to be alone, the need now to be in the thick of things pressed upon her with an urgency that was breathtaking.

It had been happening this way a lot lately. She was like the weather vane on the peak of the Greenacres roof, her emotions swinging suddenly from one direction to the other at the whim of the wind. It was strange, and frightening at times, but also somehow thrilling. Like being on a lurching ride at the seaside.

In this instance, it was injurious, too. For in her desperate hurry to join the party by the stream, she caught her knee against the wooden floor of the tree house. The graze stung and she winced, glancing down to see a rise of fresh blood, surprisingly red. Rather than continue to the ground, she climbed back into the tree house to inspect the damage.

She was still sitting there watching her knee weep, cursing her haste and wondering if Billy would notice the ugly big scab, how she might mask it, when she became aware of a noise coming from the direction of the copse. A rustling noise, natural and yet separate enough from the other afternoon sounds to draw her attention. She glanced through the tree-house window and saw Barnaby lolloping over the long grass, silky ears flapping like velvet wings. Her mother wasn't far behind, striding across the meadow towards the garden in her summery home-made dress. The baby was wedged comfortably on her hip, legs bare beneath his play-suit in deference to the day's heat.

Although they were still a way off, through some odd quirk of the wind current Laurel could hear quite clearly the tune her mother was singing. It was a song she'd sung to each of them in turn, and the baby laughed with pleasure, shouting, 'More! More!' (though it sounded like 'Mo! Mo!') as Ma crept her fingers up his tummy to tickle his chin. Their focus on one another was so complete, their appearance together in the sun-drenched meadow so idyllic, that Laurel was torn between joy at having observed the private interaction and envy at being outside it.

As her mother unlatched the gate and started for the house, Laurel realized with sinking spirit that she'd come for the cake knife herself.

With every step Laurel's opportunity for redemption receded further. She grew sulky, and her sulkiness stopped her from calling out or climbing down, rooting her instead to the tree-house floor. There she sat, stewing darkly in a strangely pleasant manner, as her mother reached and entered the house.

One of the hula hoops fell silently to hit the ground, and Laurel took the action as a show of solidarity. She decided to stay where she was. Let them miss her a while longer; she'd get to the stream when she was good and ready. In the meantime, she was going to read *The Birthday Party* again and imagine a future far away from here, a life where she was beautiful and sophisticated, grown-up and scab free.

The man, when he first appeared, was little more than a hazy smudge on the horizon, right down at the furthest reach of the driveway. Laurel was never sure, later, what it was that made her look up then. For one awful second when she first noticed him walking towards the back of the farmhouse, Laurel thought it was Billy, arrived early and coming to fetch her. Only as his outline clarified and she realized he was dressed all wrong – dark trousers, shirt sleeves and a black hat with an old-fashioned brim – did she let herself exhale.

Curiosity arrived hot on the heels of relief. Visitors were rare at the farmhouse, those on foot rarer still, though there was a vague memory at the back of Laurel's mind as she watched the man come closer, an odd sense of déjà vu that she couldn't place no matter how hard she tried. Laurel forgot that she was sulking and with the luxury of conceal-ment surrendered herself to staring.

She leaned her elbows on the windowsill, her chin on her hands. He wasn't bad looking for an older man and something in his posture suggested a confidence of purpose. Here was a man who didn't need to rush. Certainly, he was not someone she recognized, not one of her father's friends from the village or any of the farmhands. There was always the possibility he was a lost traveller seeking directions, but the farmhouse was an unlikely choice, tucked away as it was so far from the road. Perhaps he was a gypsy or a drifter? One of those men who chanced by occasionally, down on their luck and grateful for whatever work Daddy

had to give them. Or – Laurel thrilled at the terrible idea –
he might be the man she'd read about in the local newspaper, the one the adults spoke of in nervous strains, who'd
been disturbing picnickers and frightening women who
walked alone along the hidden bend downriver.

Laurel shivered, scaring herself briefly, and then she
yawned. The man was no fiend; she could see his leather
satchel now. He was a salesman come to tell her mother
about the newest encyclopedia set they couldn't live without.

And so she looked away.

Minutes passed, not many, and the next thing she heard was
Barnaby's low growl at the base of the tree. Laurel scrambled to the window, peering over the sill to see the spaniel
standing to attention in the middle of the brick path. He
was facing the driveway, watching as the man – much closer
now – fiddled with the iron gate that led into the garden.

'Hush, Barnaby,' her mother called from inside. 'We
won't be long now.' She emerged from the dark hall, pausing at the open door to whisper something in the baby's ear,
to kiss his plump cheek and make him giggle.

Behind the house, the gate near the hen yard creaked –
the hinge that always needed oiling – and the dog growled
again. His hair ridged along his spine.

'That's enough, Barnaby,' Ma said. 'What's got into
you?'

The man came round the corner and she glanced sideways. The smile slipped from her face.

'Hello there,' said the stranger, pausing to press his
handkerchief to each temple. 'Fine weather we're having.'

The baby's face broadened in delight at the newcomer and he reached out his chubby hands, opening and closing them in excited greeting. It was an invitation no one could refuse, and the man tucked the handkerchief back into his pocket and stepped closer, raising his hand slightly, as if to anoint the little fellow.

Her mother moved then with startling haste. She wrested the baby away, depositing him roughly on the ground behind her. There was gravel beneath his bare legs and for a child who knew only tenderness and love the shock proved too much. Crestfallen, he began to cry.

Laurel's heart tugged, but she was frozen, unable to move. Hairs prickled on the back of her neck. She was watching her mother's face, an expression on it that she'd never seen before. Fear, she realized: Ma was frightened.

The effect on Laurel was instant. Certainties of a lifetime turned to smoke and blew away. Cold alarm moved in to take their place.

'Hello, Dorothy,' the man said. 'It's been a long time.'

He knew Ma's name. The man was no stranger.

He spoke again, too low for Laurel to hear, and her mother nodded slightly. She continued to listen, tilting her head to the side. Her face lifted to the sun and her eyes closed just for one second.

The next thing happened quickly.

It was the liquid silver flash Laurel would always remember. The way sunlight caught the metal blade, and the moment was very briefly beautiful.

Then the knife came down, the special knife, plunging deep into the man's chest. Time slowed; it raced. The man cried out and his face twisted with surprise and pain and horror; and Laurel stared as his hands went to the knife's bone handle, to where the blood was staining his shirt; as he fell to the ground; as the warm breeze dragged his hat over and over through the dust.

The dog was barking hard, the baby wailing in the gravel, his face red and glistening, his little heart breaking, but for Laurel these sounds were fading. She heard them through the watery gallop of her own blood pumping, the rasping of her own ragged breath.

The knife's bow had come undone, the ribbon's end trailed onto the rocks that bordered the garden bed. It was the last thing Laurel saw before her vision filled with tiny flickering stars and then everything went black.

Two

Suffolk, 2011

It was raining in Suffolk. In her memories of childhood it was never raining. The hospital was on the other side of town and the car went slowly along the puddle-pitted High Street before turning into the driveway and stopping at the top of the turning circle. Laurel pulled out her compact, opened it to look into the mirror, and pushed the skin of one cheek upwards, watching calmly as the wrinkles gathered and then fell when released. She repeated the action on the other side. People loved her lines. Her agent told her so, casting directors waxed lyrical, make-up artists crooned as they brandished their brushes and their startling youth. One of those Internet newspapers had run a poll some months ago inviting readers to vote for 'The Nation's Favourite Face', and Laurel had come second. Her lines, it was said, made people feel safe.

Which was all very well for them. They made Laurel feel old.

She *was* old, she thought, snapping the compact shut. And not in the Mrs Robinson sense. Twenty-five years now since she'd played in *The Graduate* at the National. How had that happened? Someone had speeded up the damn clock when she wasn't watching, that's how.

The driver opened the door and ushered her out beneath the cover of a large black umbrella.

'Thank you, Mark,' she said as they reached the awning. 'Do you have the pick-up address for Friday?'

He set down her overnight bag and shook out the umbrella. 'Farmhouse on the other side of town, narrow lane, driveway at the very end. Two o'clock still all right for you?'

She said that it was and he gave a nod, hurrying through the rain to the driver's door. The car started and she watched it go, aching suddenly for the warmth and pleasant dullness of a long commute to nowhere special along the wet motorway. To be going anywhere, really, that wasn't here.

Laurel sized up the entry doors but didn't go through. She took out her cigarettes instead and lit one, drawing on it with rather more relish than was dignified. She'd passed a dreadful night. She'd dreamed in scraps of her mother, and this place, and her sisters when they were small, and Gerry as a boy. A small and earnest boy, holding up a tin space shuttle, something he'd made, telling her that one day he was going to invent a time capsule and use it to go back and fix things. What sort of things? she'd said in the dream. Why, all the things that ever went wrong, of course – she could come with him if she wanted.

She did want.

The hospital doors opened with a whoosh and a pair of nurses burst through. One glanced at Laurel and her eyes widened in recognition. Laurel nodded a vague sort of greeting, dropping what was left of her cigarette as the nurse leaned in to whisper to her friend.

*

Rose was waiting on a bank of seats in the foyer and for a split second Laurel saw her as one might a stranger. She was wrapped in a purple crocheted shawl that gathered at the front in a pink bow, and her wild hair, silver now, was roped in a loose plait over one shoulder. Laurel suffered a pang of almost unbearable affection when she noticed the bread tie holding her sister's plait together. 'Rosie,' she said, hiding her emotion behind jolly-hockey-sticks, hale and hearty, hating herself just a little as she did so. 'God, it feels like ages. We've been ships in the night, you and I.'

They embraced and Laurel was struck by the lavender scent, familiar but out of place. It belonged to summer-holiday afternoons in the good room at Grandma Nicolson's Sea Blue boarding house, not to her little sister.

'I'm so glad you could come,' Rose said, squeezing Laurel's hands before leading her down the hallway.

'I wouldn't have missed it.'

'Of course you wouldn't.'

'I'd have come earlier but for the interview.'

'I know.'

'And I'd be staying longer if not for rehearsals. The film starts shooting in a fortnight.'

'I *know*.' Rose clenched Laurel's hand even tighter, as if for emphasis. 'Mummy will be thrilled to have you here at all. She's so proud of you, Lol. We all are.'

Praise within one's family was worrisome and Laurel ignored it. 'The others?'

'Not yet. Iris is caught in traffic and Daphne arrives this afternoon. She'll come straight to the house from the airport. She's going to call en route.'

'And Gerry? What time's he due?'

It was a joke and even Rose, the nice Nicolson, the only one who didn't as a rule go in for teasing, couldn't help but giggle. Their brother could construct cosmic-distance calendars to calculate the whereabouts of faraway galaxies, but ask him to estimate his arrival time and he was flummoxed.

They turned the corner and found the door labelled 'Dorothy Nicolson'. Rose reached for the knob then hesitated. 'I have to warn you, Lol,' she said, 'Mummy's gone downhill since you were here last. She's up and down. One minute she's quite her old self, the next . . .' Rose's lips quivered and she clutched at her long strand of beads. Her voice lowered as she continued. 'She gets confused, Lol, upset sometimes, saying things about the past, things I don't always understand. The nurses say it doesn't mean anything, that it happens often when people . . . when they're at Mummy's stage. The nurses have tablets they give her then; they settle her down, but they make her terribly groggy. I wouldn't expect too much today.'

Laurel nodded. The doctor had said as much when she rang last week to check. He'd used a litany of tedious euphemisms – *a race well run*, *time to answer the final summons*, *the long sleep* – his tone so cloying that Laurel had been unable to resist. 'Do you mean, Doctor, that my mother is dying?' She'd said it in a queenly voice, just for the satisfaction of hearing him splutter. The reward had been sweet but short-lived, lasting only until his answer came.

Yes.

That most treasonous of words.

Rose pushed open the door – 'Look who I found, Mummy!' – and Laurel realized she was holding her breath.

*

There was a time in Laurel's childhood when she'd been afraid. Of the dark, of zombies, of the strange men Grandma Nicolson warned were lurking behind corners to snatch up little girls and do unmentionable things to them. (What sort of things? Un-*men*-tionable things. Always like that, the threat more frightening for its lack of detail, its hazy suggestion of tobacco and sweat and hair in strange places.) So convincing had her grandmother been that Laurel had known it was only a matter of time before her fate found her and had its wicked way.

Sometimes her greatest fears had balled themselves together, so she woke in the night, screaming because the zombie in the dark cupboard was eyeing her through the keyhole, waiting to begin his dreaded deeds. 'Hush now, little wing,' her mother had soothed, 'It's just a dream. You must learn to tell the difference between what's real and what's pretend. It isn't always easy – it took me an awfully long time to work it out. Too long.' And then she'd climb in next to Laurel and say, 'Shall I tell you a story, about a little girl who ran away to join the circus?'

It was hard to believe that the woman whose enormous presence vanquished every night-time terror was this same pallid creature pinned beneath the hospital sheet. Laurel had thought herself prepared. She'd had friends die before, she knew what death looked like when it came, she'd received her BAFTA for playing a woman in the late stages of cancer. But this was different. This was Ma. She wanted to turn and run.

She didn't, though. Rose, who was standing by the bookshelf, nodded encouragement, and Laurel wrapped herself within the character of the dutiful visiting daughter. She moved swiftly to take her mother's frail hand. 'Hello there,' she said. 'Hello there, my love.'

Dorothy's eyes flickered open before closing again. Her breaths continued their soft pattern of rise and fall as Laurel brushed a light kiss on the paper of each cheek.

'I've brought you something. I couldn't wait for tomorrow.' She set down her things, withdrawing the small parcel from inside her handbag. Leaving a brief pause for convention's sake, she started to unwrap the gift. 'A hairbrush,' she said, turning the silver object over in her fingers. 'It has the softest bristles – boar, I think; I found it in an antiques shop in Knightsbridge. I've had it engraved, you see, right here – your initials. Would you like me to brush your hair?'

She hadn't expected an answer, not really, and none came. Laurel ran the brush lightly over the fine white strands that formed a corona on the pillow round her mother's face, hair that had once been thick, darkest brown, and was now dissolving into thin air. 'There,' she said, arranging the brush on the shelf so that light caught the flourish of the D. 'There now.'

Rose must have been satisfied in some way, because she handed over the album she'd taken from the shelf and motioned that she was going down the hall to make their tea.

There were roles in families; that was Rose's, this was hers. Laurel eased herself into a remedial-looking chair by her mother's pillow and carefully opened the old book. The first photograph was black and white, faded now with a colony of brown spots creeping across its surface. Beneath the foxing, a young woman with a scarf tied over her hair was caught forever in a moment of disruption. Looking up

from whatever she was doing, she'd lifted a hand as if to
shoo the photographer away. She was smiling slightly, her
annoyance mixed with amusement, her mouth open in the
articulation of some forgotten words. A joke, Laurel had
always liked to think, a witty aside for the person behind the
camera. Probably one of Grandma's many bygone guests: a
travelling salesman, a lone holidaymaker, some quiet bureau-
crat with polished shoes, sitting out the war in a protected
occupation. The line of a calm sea could be glimpsed behind
her by anyone who knew that it was there.

Laurel held the book across her mother's still body and
began. 'Here you are then, Ma, at Grandma Nicolson's
boarding house. It's 1944 and the war's nearing its end. Mrs
Nicolson's son hasn't come home yet, but he will. In less
than a month, she'll send you into town with the ration
cards and when you return with the groceries there'll be a
soldier sitting at the kitchen table, a man you've never met
before, but whom you recognize from the framed picture on
the mantel. He's older when you meet than he is in the picture, and sadder, but he's dressed the same way, in his army
khaki, and he smiles at you and you know, instantly, that
he's the one you've been waiting for.'

Laurel turned the page, using her thumb to flatten the
plastic corner of the yellowing protective sheet. Time had
made it crackly. 'You were married in a dress you stitched
yourself from a pair of lace curtains Grandma Nicolson was
induced to sacrifice from the upstairs guest room. Well
done, Ma dear – I can't imagine that was an easy sell. We all
know how Grandma felt about soft furnishings. There was
a storm the night before and you were worried it would rain
on your wedding day. It didn't, though. The sun rose and

the clouds were blown away and people said it was a good omen. Still, you hedged your bets; that's Mr Hatch, the chimney sweep, standing at the bottom of the church stairs for luck. He was all too happy to oblige – the fee Daddy paid bought new shoes for his eldest boy.'

She could never be sure, these past few months, that her mother was listening, though the kinder nurse said there was no reason to think otherwise, and sometimes as she went through the photo album Laurel allowed herself the liberty of invention – nothing too drastic, only that when her imagination led away from the main action and into the peripheries, she let it. Iris didn't approve, she said their mother's story was important to her and Laurel had no right to embellish, but the doctor had only shrugged when told of the transgression, and said it was the talking that mattered, not so much the truth of what was said. He'd turned to Laurel with a wink. 'You of all people shouldn't be expected to abide by truth, Miss Nicolson.'

Despite his having sided with her, Laurel had resented the assumed collusion. She'd considered pointing out the distinction between performance on stage and deception in life, telling the impertinent doctor with his too-black hair and too-white teeth that in either case truth mattered, but she'd known better than to argue philosophy with a man who carried a golf-stick novelty pen in his shirt pocket.

She moved on to the next page and found, as she always did, the series of her infant self. She narrated swiftly across her early years – baby Laurel sleeping in a crib with stars and fairies painted on the wall above; blinking dourly in her mother's arms; grown some and tottering plumply in the seaside shallows – before reaching the point where reciting ended and remembering began. She turned the page, unleashing the noise and laughter of the others. Was it a coincidence that her own memories were linked so strongly with their arrival, these stepping-stone sisters: tumbling in long grass; waving from the tree-house window; standing in line before Greenacres farmhouse – their home – brushed and pinned, polished and darned for some forgotten outing?

Laurel's nightmares had stopped after her sisters were born. Or rather, they'd changed. There were no more visits from zombies or monsters or strange men who lived by day in the cupboard; she started dreaming instead that a tidal wave was coming, or the world was ending, or another war had started, and she alone had to keep the younger ones safe. It was one of the things she could most clearly remember her mother saying to her as a girl: *Take care of your sisters. You're the eldest, don't you let them go.* It hadn't occurred to Laurel back then that her mother might be speaking from experience; that implicit in the warning was her decades-old grief for a younger brother, lost to a bomb in the Second World War. Children could be self-centred like that, especially the happy ones. And the Nicolson children had been happier than most.

'Here we are at Easter. That's Daphne in the highchair, which must make it 1956. Yes, it is. See – Rose has her arm in plaster, her left arm this time. Iris is playing the goat, grinning at the back, but she won't be for long. Do you remember? That's the afternoon she raided the fridge and sucked clean all the crab claws Daddy had brought home from his fishing trip the day before.' It was the only time Laurel had ever seen him really angry. He'd stumbled out after his nap, sun-touched and fancying a bit of sweet crabmeat, and all he'd found in the fridge were hollow shells. She could still picture Iris hiding behind the sofa – the one place their father couldn't reach her with his threats of a tanning (an empty threat, but no less frightening for it) – refusing to come out. Begging whoever would listen to take pity and *please, pretty please* slide her the copy of *Pippi Longstocking*. The memory made Laurel fond. She'd forgotten how funny Iris could be when she wasn't so damn busy being cross.

Something slipped from the back of the album and Laurel fetched it up from the floor. It was a photograph she'd never seen before, an old-fashioned black and white shot of two young women, their arms linked. They were laughing at her from within its white border, standing together in a room with bunting hanging above them and sunlight streaming in from an unseen window. She turned it over, looking for an annotation, but there was nothing written there except the date: May 1941. How peculiar. Laurel knew the family album inside out, and this photograph, these people, did not belong. The door opened and Rose appeared, two mismatched teacups jiggling on their saucers.

Laurel held up the photo. 'Have you seen this, Rosie?'

Rose set a cup down on the bedside table, squinted at the picture, and then smiled. 'Oh yes,' she said. 'It turned up a few months ago at Greenacres – I thought you'd be able to make a place for it in the album. Lovely, isn't she? So special to discover something new of her, particularly now.'

Laurel looked again at the photo. The young women with their hair in side-parted Victory rolls; skirts grazing their knees; one with a cigarette dangling from her hand. Of course it was their mother. Her make-up was different. *She* was different.

'Funny,' Rose said, 'I never thought of her like that.'

'Like what?'

'Young, I suppose. Having a laugh with a girlfriend.'

'Didn't you? I wonder why?' Though of course the same was true of Laurel. In her mind – in all of their minds, apparently – their mother had come into being when she'd answered Grandma's newspaper advertisement for a maid of all work and started at the boarding house. They knew the basics of before: that she'd been born and raised in Coventry, that she'd gone to London just before the war began, that her family had been killed in the bombings. Laurel knew, too, that the death of her mother's family had affected her deeply. Dorothy Nicolson had taken every opportunity to remind her own children that family was everything: it had been the mantra of their childhood. When Laurel was going through an especially painful teenage phase, her mother had taken her by the hands and said, with unusual sternness, 'Don't be like I was, Laurel. Don't wait too long to realize what's important. Your family might drive you mad sometimes, but they're worth more to you than you could ever imagine.'

As to the details of Dorothy's life before she met Stephen Nicolson, though, she'd never forced them on her children and they hadn't thought to ask. Nothing odd in that, Laurel supposed with mild discomfort. Children don't require of their parents a past and they find something faintly unbelievable, almost embarrassing, in parental claims to a prior existence. Now, though, looking at this wartime stranger, Laurel felt the lack of knowledge keenly.

When she was starting out as an actress, a well-known director had leaned over his script, straightened his Coke-bottle glasses and told Laurel she hadn't the looks to play leading roles. The advice had stung and she'd wailed and railed, and then spent hours catching herself accidentally-on-purpose in the mirror before hacking her long hair short in the grip of drunken bravura. But it had proven a 'moment' in her career. She was a character actress. The director cast her as the leading lady's sister and she garnered her first rave reviews. People marvelled at her ability to build characters from the inside out, to submerge herself and disappear beneath the skin of another person, but there was no trick to it; she merely bothered to learn the character's secrets. Laurel knew quite a bit about keeping secrets. She also knew that was where the real people were found, hiding behind their black spots.

'Do you realize it's the youngest we've ever seen her?' Rose perched on Laurel's armrest, her lavender fragrance stronger than before, as she took the photograph.

'Is it?' Laurel reached for her cigarettes, remembered she was in a hospital and took up her tea instead. 'I suppose it is.' So much of her mother's past was made up of black spots. Why had it never bothered her before? She glanced again at the picture, the two young women who seemed now to be laughing at her ignorance. She tried to sound casual. 'Where did you say you found it, Rosie?'

'Inside a book.'

'A book?'

'A play, actually – *Peter Pan*.'

'Ma was in a play?' Their mother had been a great one

for games of dressing up and 'Let's pretend', but Laurel couldn't remember her ever performing in a real play.

'I'm not sure about that. The book was a gift. There was an inscription in the front – you know, the way she liked us to do with presents when we were kids?'

'What did it say?'

'"For Dorothy."' Rose plaited her fingers together under the strain of recollection. '"A true friend is a light in the dark. Vivien."'

Vivien. The name did something strange to Laurel. Her skin went hot and cold, and she could feel her pulse beating in her temples. A dizzying series of images flashed across her brain – a glistening blade, her mother's frightened face, a red ribbon come loose. Old memories, ugly memories, that the unknown woman's name had somehow unleashed. 'Vivien,' she echoed, her voice louder than she intended. 'Who is Vivien?'

Rose looked up, surprised, but whatever she might have answered was lost when Iris came blasting through the door, parking ticket held aloft. Both sisters turned towards her mighty indignation and therefore neither noticed Dorothy's sharp intake of breath, the look of anguish that crossed her face at the mention of Vivien's name. By the time the three Nicolson sisters had gathered at their mother's side, Dorothy appeared to be sleeping calmly, her features giving no hint that she'd left behind the hospital, her weary body, and her grown daughters, slipping through time to the dark night of 1941.

Three

London, May 1941

Dorothy Smitham ran downstairs, calling goodnight to Mrs White as she shimmied into the sleeves of her coat. The landlady blinked through thick spectacles when she passed, anxious to continue her never-ending treatise on the neighbour's foibles, but Dolly didn't stop. She slowed sufficiently only to check herself in the hall mirror and pinch some colour into her cheeks. Happy enough with what she saw, she opened the door and darted out into the blackout. She was in a hurry, no time tonight for trouble with the warden; Jimmy would be at the restaurant already and she didn't want to keep him waiting. They had so much to discuss – what they should take, what they'd do when they got there, when they should finally go . . .

Dolly smiled eagerly, reaching into her deep coat pocket and rolling the carved figurine beneath her fingertips. She'd noticed it in the pawnbroker's window the other day; it was only a trifle, she knew, but it had made her think of him, and now more than ever, as London came down around them, it was important to let people know how much they meant. Dolly was longing to give it to him – she could just imagine his face when he saw it, the way he'd smile and reach for her and tell her, as he always did, how much he loved her. The little wooden Mr Punch might not be much, but it was perfect; Jimmy had always adored the seaside. They both had.

'Excuse me?'

It was a woman's voice and it was unexpected. 'Yes?' Dolly called back, her own voice catching with surprise. The woman must've noticed her when light spilled briefly through the opened door.

'Please – can you help me? I'm looking for number 24.'

Despite the blackout and the impossibility of being seen, Dolly gestured from habit towards the door behind her. 'You're in luck,' she said. 'It's right here. No rooms free at the moment, I'm afraid, but there will be soon.' Her very own room, in fact (if room it could be called). She slid a cigarette onto her lip and struck the match.

'Dolly?'

At that, Dolly squinted into the darkness. The owner of the voice was rushing towards her; she sensed a flurry of movement, and then the woman, close now, said, 'It *is* you, thank God. It's me, Dolly. It's—'

'Vivien?' She recognized the voice suddenly; she knew it so well, and yet there was something different about it.

'I thought I might've missed you, that I was too late.'

'Too late for what?' Dolly faltered; they'd had no plans to meet tonight. 'What is it?'

'Nothing . . .' Vivien started to laugh then, and the sound, metallic and unnerving, sent jangles up Dolly's spine. 'That is, everything.'

'Have you been drinking?' Dolly had never known Vivien to behave like this; gone was the usual veneer of elegance, the perfect self-control.

The other woman didn't answer, not exactly. The neighbour's cat bounded off a nearby wall, landing with a thud on Mrs White's rabbit hutch. Vivien jumped, and then whispered, 'We have to talk – *quickly*.'

Dolly stalled by drawing hard on her cigarette. Ordinarily she'd have loved for the pair of them to sit down and have a heart to heart, but not now, not tonight. She was impatient to be getting on. 'I can't,' she said. 'I was just—'

'Dolly, *please*.'

Dolly reached into her pocket and turned over the little wooden gift. Jimmy would be there already; he'd be wondering where she was, glancing at the door each time it opened, expecting to see her. She hated to keep him waiting, especially now. But here was Vivien, turned up on the doorstep, so serious, so nervy, glancing over her shoulder, pleading and saying how important it was that they talk . . . Dolly sighed in reluctant capitulation. She couldn't very well leave Vivien like this, not when she was so upset.

She told herself Jimmy would understand, that in a funny way he'd become fond of Vivien, too. And then she made the decision that would prove fateful for them all. 'Come on,' she said, extinguishing her cigarette and taking Vivien gently by a thin arm. 'Let's go back inside.'

It struck Dolly as they went into the house and up the stairs that Vivien might have come to apologize. It was all she could think of to explain the other woman's agitation, the loss of her usual composure; Vivien, with her wealth and class, wasn't the sort of woman much given to apologies. The thought made Dolly nervous. It was unnecessary – as far as she was concerned, the whole sorry episode was in the past. She'd have preferred never to mention it again.

They reached the end of the corridor and Dolly unlocked her bedroom door. The bare bulb flared dully when she flicked the switch, and the narrow bed, the small cabinet, the cracked sink with its dripping tap, all came into focus. Dolly felt a flash of embarrassment when she saw her room suddenly through Vivien's eyes. How meagre it must seem after the accommodation she was used to, that resplendent house on Campden Grove with its tubular glass chandeliers and zebra-skin throws.

She slipped off her old coat and turned to hang it on the hook behind the door. 'Sorry it's so hot in here,' she said, trying to sound breezy. 'No windows, more's the pity – makes the blackout easier but it's not so handy for ventilation.' She was joking, hoping to lighten the atmosphere, cajole herself into better spirits, but it didn't work. All she could think of was Vivien standing there behind her, looking for somewhere to sit down – oh dear. 'No chair, either, I'm afraid.' She'd been meaning to get one for weeks, but with times as tough as they were, and she and Jimmy resolved to save every penny, Dolly had decided just to make do.

She turned around and forgot the lack of furnishings when she saw Vivien's face. 'My God,' she said, eyes widening as she took in her friend's bruised cheek. 'What happened to you?'

'Nothing.' Vivien, who was pacing now, waved impatiently. 'An accident on the way. I ran into a lamp post. Stupid of me, rushing as usual.' It was true, Vivien always went too quickly. It was a quirk, and one that Dolly had always rather liked – it made her smile to see such a refined, well-dressed woman rushing about with the gait of a young girl. Tonight, though, everything felt different. Vivien's outfit was mismatched, there was a ladder in her stockings, her hair was a mess . . .

'Here,' said Dolly, guiding her friend to the bed, glad she'd made it so carefully that morning. 'Sit down.'

The air-raid siren began to wail then and she cursed beneath her breath. It was the last thing they needed. The shelter here was a nightmare: all of them packed together like sardines, the damp bedding, the putrid smell, Mrs White's hysterics; and now, with Vivien in this state—

'Ignore it,' Vivien said, as if reading Dolly's mind. Her voice was suddenly that of the lady of the house, used to giving orders. 'Stay. This is more important.'

More important than getting to the shelter? Dolly's heart fluttered. 'Is it the money?' she said in a low voice. 'Do you need it back?'

'No, no, forget about the money.'

The rise and fall of the siren was deafening and it spurred in Dolly a floating anxiety that refused to settle. She didn't know why exactly, but she knew she was afraid. She didn't want to be here, not even with Vivien. She wanted to be hurrying along the dark streets to where she knew Jimmy was waiting for her. 'Jimmy and I—' she began, before Vivien cut her off.

'Yes,' she said, her face lighting up as if she'd just remembered something. 'Yes, Jimmy.'

Dolly shook her head, confused. What about Jimmy? Vivien was making no sense. Perhaps she ought to take her, too – they could make a dash for it together while people were still scurrying to the shelters. They'd go straight to Jimmy – he'd know what to do.

'Jimmy,' Vivien said again loudly. 'Dolly, he's gone—'

The siren cut out just then, and the word 'gone' bounced around the room. Dolly waited for Vivien to say more, but before she could a frantic knock came at the door. 'Doll – are you in there?' It was Judith, one of the other residents, breathless having run from upstairs. 'We're going down to the Andy.'

Dolly didn't answer, and neither she nor Vivien made a move to leave. She waited until the footsteps receded down the corridor, and then hurried to sit beside the other woman. 'You've got it mixed up,' she said quickly. 'I saw him yesterday, and I'm seeing him again tonight. We're going together, he wouldn't have gone without me . . .' There was so much more she could have said, but she didn't. Vivien was looking at her, and something in her gaze allowed a sliver of doubt to creep through the cracks in Dolly's confidence. She fumbled a new cigarette from her bag, fingers shaking as she lit it.

Vivien started talking then, and as the first bomber of the night chugged overhead, Dolly began to wonder if there was even the tiniest possibility that the other woman was right. It seemed unthinkable, but the urgency in her voice, her strange manner and the things she was now saying . . . Dolly started to feel dizzy; it was hot in here, she couldn't manage to steady her breath.

She smoked hungrily, and fragments of Vivien's account mingled with her own racing thoughts. A bomb fell somewhere close, landing with a huge explosion, and a great swooshing sound filled the room, making Dolly's ears ache and every hair on her neck stand on end. There had been a time when she'd enjoyed being out in the Blitz – she'd found it exciting, not frightening at all. But she wasn't that silly young girl any more, and those carefree days seemed a long time ago. She glanced at the door, wishing Vivien would stop. They should get to the shelter or to Jimmy; they shouldn't just sit here, waiting. She wanted to run, to hide; she wanted to disappear.

As Dolly's own panic rose, Vivien's appeared to recede. She was speaking calmly now, low sentences that Dolly struggled to listen to, about a letter and a photograph, about bad men, dangerous men who'd set out to find Jimmy. The plan had all gone terribly wrong, Vivien said, he'd been humiliated; Jimmy hadn't been able to get to the restaurant; she'd waited for him and he hadn't come; that's when she'd known he was really gone.

And suddenly the disparate pieces came together through the haze and Dolly understood. 'It's my fault,' she said, her voice little more than a whisper. 'But I – I don't know how – the photograph – we agreed not to, that there wasn't any need, not any more.' The other woman knew what she meant; it was because of Vivien that the plans had been scrapped. Dolly reached for her friend's arm. 'None of this was meant to happen, and now Jimmy . . .'

Vivien was nodding, her face a study in compassion. 'Listen to me,' she said. 'It's very important that you listen. They know where you live, and they *will* come after you.'

Dolly didn't want to believe it; she was frightened. Tears ran hot down her cheeks. 'It's my fault,' she heard herself saying again. 'It's all my fault.'

'Dolly, please.' A new wave of bombers had arrived, and Vivien had to shout to be heard as she clasped Dolly's hands in hers. 'It's as much my fault as yours. None of that matters now anyway. They're coming. They're probably on their way already. That's why I'm here.'

'But I—'

'You need to leave London, you need to do it now, and you mustn't come back. They won't stop looking for you, not ever—'

A blast outside and the whole building juddered and shifted; the bombs were falling closer, and even though there were no windows an eerie flash of light came from somewhere, flooding the room, so much brighter than the glow of the dull single bulb.

'Is there any family you could go to?' Vivien pressed.

Dolly shook her head, even as a picture of her family came into her mind: her mother and father, her poor little brother, the way things used to be, before. A bomb whistled by and the guns fired back from the ground.

'Friends?' Vivien shouted over the blast.

Again Dolly shook her head. There was no one left, not that she could count on, no one except Vivien and Jimmy.

'Anywhere at all that you could go?' Another bomb, a Molotov bread basket by the sound of it, the impact so loud Dolly had to read Vivien's lips when she pleaded, 'Think, Dolly. You have to think.'

She closed her eyes. She could smell fire; an incendiary must have hit nearby; the ARP officers would be at it now with their stirrup pumps. Dolly heard someone yelling, but she screwed her eyes tighter and tried to focus. Her thoughts were scattered like debris, her mind a dark maze; she could see nothing. The ground was jagged underfoot, the air too thick to breathe.

'Dolly?'

There were more planes, fighters now, not just bombers, and Dolly pictured herself on the rooftop at Campden Grove, watching as they ducked and swooped across the sky, the green tracer lights that swept after them, the fires in the distance. It had all seemed so exciting once.

She remembered the night with Jimmy when they'd met at the 400 Club and danced and laughed; when they'd gone home through the Blitz, the two of them together. She'd have given anything now to be back there, lying side by side, whispering in the dark while the bombs fell, making plans for their future, the farmhouse, the children they'd have, the seaside. The seaside . . .

'I applied for a job,' she said suddenly, lifting her head. 'A few weeks ago. It was Jimmy who found it.' The letter from Mrs Nicolson of Sea Blue boarding house was sitting on the small table by her pillow and Dolly snatched it up, handing it shakily to Vivien.

'Yes.' Vivien scanned the offer. 'Perfect. That's where you must go.'

'I don't want to go by myself. We—'

'Dolly—'

'We were supposed to go *together*. It wasn't meant to be like this. He was going to wait for me.' Dolly was crying now. Vivien reached towards her, but the two women moved at the same time and the contact was unexpectedly sharp.

Vivien didn't apologize; her face was serious. She was frightened too, Dolly could tell, but she put her own fears aside, just as a big sister might, adopting the sort of stern loving voice Dolly most needed to hear right then. 'Dorothy

Smitham,' she said, 'you need to leave London, and you need to go quickly.'

'I don't think I can.'

'I *know* you can. You're a survivor.'

'But Jimmy—' Another bomb whooshed down and exploded. A terrified cry escaped Dolly's throat before she could stop it.

'That's enough.' Vivien cupped Dolly's face firmly between both hands, and this time it didn't hurt one bit. Her eyes were filled with kindness. 'You loved Jimmy, I know that; and he loved you, too – my God, I know that. But you have to listen to me.'

There was something eminently calming about the other woman's gaze and Dolly managed to block out the noise of a diving plane, the answering ack-ack fire, the horrible thoughts of buildings and people being crushed into pulp.

The pair of them huddled together and Dolly listened as Vivien said, 'Go to the railway station tonight and buy your-self a ticket. You're to—' A bomb landed nearby with a thundering crump and Vivien stiffened before continuing quickly, 'Get on that train and ride it all the way to the end of the line. Don't look back. Take the job, move again, live a good life.'

A good life. It was just what Dolly and Jimmy had talked about. The future, the farmhouse, the laughing chil-dren and the happy hens . . . Tears streamed down Dolly's cheeks as Vivien said, 'You have to go.' She was crying now, too, because of course she'd miss Dolly – they'd miss each other. 'Seize this second chance, Dolly: think of it as an opportunity. After everything you've been through, after everything you've lost . . .'

And Dolly knew then that, as hard as it was to accept, Vivien was right – she had to go. There was a part of her that wanted to scream 'No', to curl up in a ball and weep for the things she'd lost, for everything in her life that hadn't turned out the way she'd hoped, but she wouldn't do that. She couldn't.

Dolly was a survivor; Vivien said so and Vivien ought to know – just look at the way she'd recovered from her own early hardships to create a new life for herself. And if Vivien could do it, so would Dolly. She'd suffered so much, but she still had things to live for – she'd *find* things to live for. This was the time to be brave, to be better than she'd ever been before. Dolly had done things that made her ashamed to remember them; her grand ideas had been nothing but a young girl's silly dreams, they'd all turned to ash in her fingers; but everybody deserved a second chance, everybody was worthy of forgiveness, even her – Vivien said so. 'I will,' she said, as a series of bombs landed with heavy crashes. 'I'll do it.'

The light bulb flickered but didn't die. It swung on its cord, throwing shadows across the walls, and Dolly pulled out her little suitcase. She ignored the deafening noise outside, the smoke that was seeping in from the fires in the street, the haze that made her eyes sting.

There wasn't much she wanted to take. She'd never had many possessions of her own. The only thing she really wanted from this room she couldn't have. Dolly hesitated as she thought of leaving Vivien behind; she remembered what the other woman had written in *Peter Pan* – *a true friend is a light in the dark* – and tears threatened again.

But there was no choice; she had to go. The future stretched ahead: a second chance, a new life. All she had to do was take it, and never look back. Go to the seaside as they'd planned, and start again.

She barely heard the planes outside now, the falling bombs, the ack-acks firing their response. The earth trembled with each blast and plaster dust sifted down from the ceiling. The chain on the door rattled, but Dolly noticed none of it. Her case was packed – she was ready to go.

She stood, looking to Vivien, and despite her firm resolve she faltered. 'What about you?' Dolly said, and for a second it occurred to her that perhaps they *could* go together, that maybe Vivien would come with her after all. In some odd way, it seemed the perfect answer, the only thing to do – they'd each played their part, and none of it would have happened if Dolly and Vivien hadn't met.

It was a foolish thought, of course – Vivien didn't need a second chance. She had everything she could want right here. A lovely house, her own wealth, beauty to spare ... Sure enough, Vivien handed Dolly Mrs Nicolson's job offer and smiled a tearful farewell. Each woman knew in her heart it was the last time she'd see the other. 'Don't worry about me,' said Vivien, as a bomber thundered overhead. 'I'm going to be fine. I'm going home.'

Dolly held the letter tightly, and with a final nod of resolution, started towards her new life, no idea what the future might bring, but determined, suddenly, to meet it.

Four

The Nicolson sisters left the hospital in Iris's car. Although she was the eldest and traditionally favoured with front-seat privileges, Laurel sat in the back with the dog hairs. Her seniority was complicated by her celebrity and it didn't do to let the others think she was getting above herself. She preferred the back anyway. Absolved from conversational duties she was free to keep company with her own thoughts.

The rain had cleared and the sun was shining now. Laurel was itching to ask Rose about Vivien – she'd heard the name before, she was sure of it; more than that, she knew it was connected in some way to that awful day in 1961 – but she kept quiet. Iris's interest, once piqued, could be suffocating and Laurel wasn't ready to face the inquisition. While her sisters made small talk in the front, she watched the fields skim by. The windows were up but she could almost smell the fresh-cut grass and hear the jackdaw's call. The landscape of one's childhood was more vibrant than any other. It didn't matter where it was or what it looked like, the sights and sounds imprinted differently from those encountered later. They became part of a person, inescapable.

The past fifty years evaporated and Laurel saw a

ghosted version of herself flying alongside the hedgerows on her green Malvern Star, one of her sisters straddling the handlebars. Sun-browned skin, blonde leg hairs, scabbed knees. It was a long time ago. It was yesterday.

'Is it for television?'

Laurel looked up to find Iris blinking at her in the rear-view mirror. 'I'm sorry?' she said.

'The interview, the one that's been keeping you so busy.'

'Oh, that. It's a series of interviews really. I've still one more to shoot on Monday.'

'Yes, Rose said you were going back to London early. Is it for television?'

Laurel made a small noise of assent. 'One of those biopic things, an hour or so long. It'll include interviews with other people, too – directors, actors I've worked with – cut together with old footage, childhood stuff—'

'You hear that, Rose?' said Iris tartly. 'Childhood stuff.' She lifted herself off the car seat to scowl more fully at Laurel in the mirror. 'I'd thank you to hold back any of the family snaps in which I'm in a state of near or total undress.'

'What a shame,' said Laurel, picking a white hair off her black trousers. 'There goes all my best material. What-ever will I talk about now?'

'Point a camera at you and I'm sure you'll think of something.'

Laurel masked a smile. People paid her so much earnest respect these days; it was comforting to bicker with an expert.

Rose, however, who'd always preferred peace, was beginning to fret. 'Look, look,' she said, flapping both hands at a razed block on the edge of the town. 'The site for the new supermarket. Can you imagine? As if the other three weren't enough.'

'Well, of all the ridiculous . . . !'

With Iris's irritation gracefully redirected, Laurel was free to sit back and look out of the window again. They passed through the town, stuck to the High Street as it tapered into a country lane, and then followed its gentle bends. The sequence was so familiar that Laurel could have closed her eyes and known precisely where she was. Conversation in the front fell away as the lane narrowed and the trees overhead thickened, until finally Iris flicked the indicator and turned into the driveway signed Greenacres Farm.

The farmhouse sat where it always had at the top of the rise, looking out across the meadow. Naturally enough, houses had a habit of staying where they were put. Iris parked on the flat spot where Daddy's old Morris Minor had lived until their mother finally consented to sell it. 'Those eaves are rather the worse for wear,' she said.

Rose agreed. 'They make the house look sad, don't you think? Come and I'll show you the latest leaks.'

Laurel closed the car door but didn't follow her sisters through the gate. She planted her hands in her pockets and stood firm, taking in the entire picture – garden to cracked chimney pots and everything in between. The ledge over which they used to lower Daphne in the basket, the balcony where they'd hung the old bedroom curtains to form a proscenium arch, the attic room where Laurel taught herself to smoke.

The thought came suddenly: the house remembered her.

Laurel did not consider herself a romantic, but the sense was so strong that for a moment she had no trouble believing that the combination before her of wooden boards and red chimney bricks, of dappled roof tiles and gabled windows at odd angles, was capable of remembrance. It was watching her now, she could feel it, through each pane of glass; casting back over the years to marry this older woman in a designer suit to the young girl who'd mooned over pictures of James Dean. What did it think, she wondered, of the person she'd become?

Idiotic, of course – the house thought nothing. Houses did not remember people, they didn't remember much of anything. It was she who remembered the house and not the other way around. And why shouldn't she? It had been her home since she was two years old; she'd lived there until she was seventeen. True, it had been some time since she'd come to visit – even with her semi-regular trips to the hospital, she never seemed to make it back to Greenacres – but life was busy. Laurel glanced towards the tree house. She'd made sure to keep herself busy.

'It can't have been so long you've forgotten where the door is,' Iris called from the front hall. She'd disappeared inside the house, but her voice floated back behind her: 'Don't tell me – you're waiting for the butler to come and carry your bags!'

Laurel rolled her eyes like a teenager, collected her suitcase, and made her way up to the house. She followed the same stone path her mother had discovered on a bright summer's day sixty-odd years before . . .

*

Dorothy Nicolson recognized Greenacres as the place to raise her family the first instant she saw it. She wasn't supposed to be looking for a house. The war had only been over a few years, they'd no capital to speak of, and her mother-in-law had graciously consented to rent them a room in her own establishment (in exchange for ongoing duties, of course – she wasn't a charity!). Dorothy and Stephen were only supposed to be out for a picnic.

It was a rare free day in the middle of July – rarer still, Stephen's mother had offered to look after baby Laurel. They woke at the crack of dawn, tossed a basket and rug on the back seat, and then pointed the Morris Minor west, with no further plans than to follow whichever country lane took their fancy. This they did for some time – her hand on his leg, his arm slung round her shoulders, warm air flowing through the open windows – and so they might have continued had one of the tyres not sprung a leak.

But it did, and so they slowed the car, pulling onto the side of the road to inspect the damage. There it was, plain as day: a rogue nail protruding from the rubber, a comprehensive puncture.

They were young though, and in love, and they didn't often have free time together, so the day wasn't spoiled as it otherwise might have been. While her husband fixed the tyre, Dorothy wandered up the grassy hill, looking for a flat spot to spread the picnic rug. And that was when she crested the rise and saw Greenacres farmhouse.

None of this was supposition on Laurel's part. The Nicolson children all knew the story of Greenacres' acquisition by heart. The sceptical old farmer scratching his head when Dorothy knocked on his door, the birds nesting in the parlour fireplace as the farmer poured tea, the holes in the floor with planks laid across them like narrow bridges. Most importantly, no one was in any doubt as to their mother's immediate certainty that she must live in this place.

The house, she'd explained to them many times, had spoken to her, she'd listened, and it turned out they'd understood one another very well indeed. Greenacres was an imperious old lady, a little worn, to be sure, cranky in her own way – but who wouldn't be? The deterioration, Dorothy could tell, concealed a great former dignity. The house was proud and she was lonely, the sort of place that fed on children's laughter, and a family's love, and the smell of rosemary lamb roasting in the oven. She had good, honest bones and a willingness to look forwards rather than backwards, to welcome a new family and grow with them, to embrace their brand-new traditions. It struck Laurel now, as it hadn't before, that her mother's description of the house might have been a self-portrait.

Laurel wiped her feet on the mat and stepped inside. The floorboards creaked familiarly, the furniture was all where it should be, and yet the place felt different. The air was thick and there was a smell that wasn't usually there. It was stale, she realized, and that was understandable – the house had been closed up since Dorothy went into hospital. Rose came to take care of things whenever her grandchild-minding schedule allowed it, and her husband Phil did what he could, but nothing compared with the constancy of habitation. It was unsettling, Laurel thought, suppressing a shiver, how quickly a person's presence could be erased, how easily civilization gave way to wilderness.

She counselled herself not to be so bloody cheerless and added her bags, from habit, to the pile beneath the hall table. She went then unthinkingly to the kitchen. It was the place where homework had been done and sticking plasters applied and tears cried over broken hearts; the first place anyone ever went when they came home. Rose and Iris were already there.

Rose flicked the light switch by the fridge and the wiring hummed. She rubbed her hands together brightly. 'Shall I make us all some tea?'

'Can't think of anything better,' said Iris, slipping off her court shoes and stretching her black, stockinged toes back and forth like an impatient ballet dancer.

'I brought wine,' said Laurel.

'Except that. Forget the tea.'

While Laurel fetched a bottle from her suitcase, Iris took down glasses from the dresser. 'Rose?' She held one aloft, blinking sharply over the top of her cat's-eye frames. Her eyes were the same dark grey as her bobbed hair.

'Oh.' Rose worried her watch face back and forth. 'Oh, I don't know, it's only just gone five.'

'Come now, Rosie dear,' said Laurel, digging through a drawer of vaguely sticky cutlery for a bottle opener. 'It's full of antioxidants, you know.' She retrieved the opener and pressed her tacky fingertips together. 'Practically a health food.'

'Well . . . all right.'

Laurel drew out the cork and started pouring. Habit had her lining up the glasses to make sure the amount was even across all three. She smiled when she caught herself – talk about a reversion to childhood. Iris would be pleased, at any rate. Fairness might be the great sticking point for all siblings, but it was an obsession for those in the middle. *Stop counting, little flower,* their mother used to say. *Nobody likes a girl who always expects more than the others.*

'Just a tipple, Lol,' said Rose cautiously. 'I don't want to be on my ear before Daphne gets here.'

'You've heard from her, then?' Laurel handed the fullest glass to Iris.

'Just before we left the hospital – didn't I say? Honestly, my memory! She'll be here by six, traffic permitting.'

'I suppose I should think about putting something together for dinner if she's that close,' said Iris, opening the pantry and kneeling on a stool to inspect use-by dates. 'It'll be toast and tea if I leave it up to you two.'

'I'll help,' said Rose.

'No, no.' Iris waved her away without turning around. 'There's no need.'

Rose glanced at Laurel, who handed over a glass of wine and gestured towards the door. There was no point in arguing. It was enshrined in family lore: Iris always cooked, she always felt put upon, the others let her savour her martyrdom because that was the sort of small kindness accorded between sisters.

'Well, if you insist,' said Laurel, gurgling a tad more pinot into her own glass.

While Rose headed upstairs to check that Daphne's room was in order, Laurel took her wine outside. The earlier rain had washed the air clean and she drew a deep breath. The garden swing caught her eye and she sat down on its bench, using her heels to rock it slowly back and forth. The swing had been a gift from all of them on their mother's eightieth birthday and Dorothy had declared immediately that it must live beneath the big old oak. No one had pointed out that there were other places in the garden with prettier views. The outlook might have struck an outsider as little more than an empty meadow, but the Nicolsons all understood that its blandness was illusory. Somewhere out there among the shifting blades of grass was the spot upon which their father had dropped and died.

Memory was a slippery thing. Laurel's memory put her here in this very spot that afternoon, hand raised to block the sun from her eager teenage eyes as she scanned the meadow, waiting for a glimpse of him returning from a day's work; waiting to run down, hook her arm through his and walk with him back to the house. Her memory had her looking on as he strode across the grass; as he stopped to watch the setting sun, to register the pink lining of the clouds, to say, as he always did, *Red sky at night, shepherd's delight*; as his body stiffened and he gasped; as his hand went to his chest; as he stumbled and fell.

But it hadn't been like that. When it happened she'd been on the other side of the world, fifty-six rather than sixteen, and dressing for an awards ceremony in LA, wondering whether she'd be the only person there whose face hadn't been shored up with fillers and a good old dose of botulism. She'd been none the wiser about her father's death until Iris called and left a message on her phone.

No, it was another man she'd watched fall and die one sunny afternoon when she was sixteen.

Laurel struck a match and lit her cigarette, frowning at

the horizon as she fumbled the box back into her pocket. The house and garden were sunlit, but the distant fields, beyond the meadow and closer to the woods, were shadowing. She glanced upwards, past the wrought-iron top of the swing seat to where the tree-house floor was visible between patches of leaves. The ladder was still there too, pieces of wood nailed to the trunk, a few hanging crooked now. Someone had draped a strand of glittery pink and purple beads from the end of a rung; one of Rose's grandchildren, she supposed.

Laurel had climbed down very slowly that day.

She drew deeply on her cigarette, remembering. She'd come to with a gasp in the tree house and recalled at once the man, the knife, her mother's terrified face, and then she'd scrambled to the ladder.

When she'd reached the ground, she'd stood clutching the rung in front of her with both hands, resting her forehead against the tree's rough trunk, safe in the still quiet of the moment, unsure where to go or what to do next. Absurdly, the thought had come that she should head for the stream, catch up with her sisters and baby brother, her father with his clarinet and his bemused smile . . .

Perhaps that was when she noticed she could no longer hear them.

She'd headed for the house instead, eyes averted, bare feet picking along the hot stone path. There was an instant when her glance skittered sideways and she thought she noticed something large and white by the garden bed, something that shouldn't be there, but she bowed her head and glimpsed away and went faster, fuelled by the wildly childish hope that maybe if she didn't look and didn't see, she could reach the house, cross the threshold, and everything would continue on as normal.

She was in shock, of course, but it hadn't felt that way. She'd been buffered by a preternatural calm, as if she were wearing a cloak, a magic cloak that let her slip outside real life, like the person in a fairy tale who exists off the page and arrives to find the castle sleeping. She stopped to pick up the hoop from the ground before going inside.

The house was eerily quiet. The sun had slipped behind the roof and the entrance hall was dark. She waited by the open doorway for her eyes to adjust. There was a sputtering sound as the iron drainpipes cooled, a noise that signified summer and holidays and long warm twilights with moths fluttering around the lamps.

She looked up the carpeted staircase and knew somehow that her sisters weren't there. The hall clock ticked away the seconds and she wondered, briefly, whether they were all gone – Ma, Daddy, and the baby too – and she'd been left alone with whatever it was beneath that white sheet out there. The thought sent a tremor down her spine. And then a thump came from the sitting room, and she turned her head, and there was her father standing by the unlit fireplace. He was curiously rigid, one hand by his side, the other balled into a fist upon the wooden mantel, as he said, 'For God's sake, my wife is lucky to be alive.'

A man's voice came from off stage, somewhere beyond the doorway where Laurel couldn't see him: 'I appreciate that, Mr Nicolson, just as I hope you'll appreciate that we're only doing our job.'

Laurel tiptoed closer, stopping before she reached the light spilling through the open doorway. Her mother was in the armchair, cradling the baby in her arms. He was asleep; Laurel could see his cherubic profile, his plump cheek squashed up flat against her mother's shoulder.

There were two other men in the room, a balding fellow on the sofa and a young man by the window taking notes. Policemen, she realized. Of course they were policemen. Something terrible had happened. The white sheet in the sunny garden.

The older man said, 'Did you recognize him, Mrs Nicolson? Is he someone you've met before? Someone you've seen, even from a distance?'

Laurel's mother didn't answer, at least not so anyone could hear. She was whispering against the back of the baby's head, her lips moving softly against his fine hair. Daddy spoke loudly on her behalf. 'Of course not,' he said. 'As she told you before, she'd never laid eyes on him. If you ask me, you ought to be comparing his description to that fellow in the papers, the one who's been bothering picnickers.'

'We'll be following all leads, Mr Nicolson, you can be sure of that. But right now there's a dead body in your garden and only your wife's word as to how it got there.'

Daddy bristled. 'That man attacked my wife. It was self-defence.'

'Did you *see* it happen, Mr Nicolson?'

There was a note of impatience in the older policeman's voice and it made Laurel frightened. She took a step backwards. They didn't know she was there. There was no need for them to find out. She could creep away, keep on up the stairs, mind not to hit the creaky floorboard, curl up tightly on her bed. She could leave them to the mysterious machinations of the adult world and let them find her when they'd finished; let them tell her everything was fixed –

'I said, were you there, Mr Nicolson? Did you see it happen?'

– but Laurel was drawn to the room, its lamp-lit contrast to the darkened hall, its strange tableau, the aura of importance her father's tense voice, his stance, projected. There was a streak inside her, there always had been, that demanded inclusion, that sought to help when help had not been asked for, that loathed to sleep for fear of missing out.

She was in shock. She needed company. She couldn't help herself. Whatever the case, Laurel stepped from the wings and into the middle of the scene. 'I was there,' she said. 'I saw him.'

Daddy looked up, surprised. He glanced quickly at his wife and then back to Laurel. His voice sounded different when he spoke, husky and hurried and almost like a hiss. 'Laurel, that's enough.'

All eyes were upon her: Ma's, Daddy's, those of both the other men. The next lines, Laurel knew, were crucial. She avoided her father's gaze and started, 'The man came round the house. He tried to grab the baby.' He had, hadn't he? She was sure that's what she'd seen.

Daddy frowned. 'Laurel—'

She went faster now, determinedly. (And why not? She wasn't a child, slinking off to her bedroom and waiting for the adults to patch things up: she was one of them; she had a part to play; she was important.) The spotlight brightened and Laurel met the older man's eyes. 'There was a struggle. I saw it. The man attacked my mother and then . . . and then, he fell down.'

Nobody spoke for a minute. Laurel looked at her mother, who was no longer whispering to the baby but staring over his head at some point beyond Laurel's shoulder. Someone had made tea. Laurel would remember that detail through all the years to follow. Someone had made tea but no one had drunk it. The cups sat untouched on tables around the room, one on the windowsill too. The hall clock ticked.

Finally, the balding man shifted on the sofa and cleared his throat. 'Laurel, is it?'

'Yes, sir.'

Daddy breathed out, a great stream of air, the sound of a deflating balloon. His hand gestured in Laurel's direction and he said, 'My daughter.' He sounded defeated. 'My eldest.'

The man on the sofa regarded her, then his lips pulled into a smile that didn't reach his eyes. He said, 'I think you'd better come in, Laurel. Sit down and start from the beginning. Tell us everything you saw.'

Five

Laurel told the policeman the truth. She sat down cautiously on the other end of the sofa, waited for her father's reluctant encouragement, and then she began to recount her afternoon. Everything she'd seen, just as it had happened. She'd been reading in the tree house and then she'd stopped to watch the man's approach.

'Why were you watching him? Was there something unusual about him?' The policeman's tone and expression gave no hint as to his expectation.

Laurel frowned, anxious to remember every detail and prove herself a worthy witness. Yes, she thought perhaps there was. It wasn't that he'd run or shouted or behaved in an otherwise obvious way, but he'd nonetheless been – she glanced at the ceiling, trying to conjure just the right word – he'd been *sinister*. She said it again, pleased by the word's aptness. He'd been sinister and she'd been frightened. No, she couldn't have said why, precisely, she just was.

Did she think what happened later might have shaded her first impression? Made something ordinary seem more dangerous than it really was?

No, she was sure. There'd definitely been something scary about him.

The younger policeman scribbled in his notebook.

Laurel exhaled. She didn't dare look at her parents for fear she'd lose her nerve.

'And when he reached the house? What happened then?'

'He crept around the corner, much more carefully than an ordinary visitor would – *sneakily* – and then my mother came out with the baby.'

'Was she carrying him?'

'Yes.'

'Was she carrying anything else?'

'Yes.'

'What was it?'

Laurel bit the inside of her cheek, remembering the flash of silver. 'She was carrying the birthday knife.'

'You recognized the knife?'

'We use it for special occasions. It has a red ribbon tied around the handle.'

Still no change in the policeman's demeanour, though he waited a beat before continuing. 'And then what happened?'

Laurel was ready. 'Then the man attacked them.'

A small niggling doubt surfaced, like a shimmer of sunlight obscuring the detail in a photograph, as Laurel described the man lurching towards the baby. She hesitated a moment, gazing at her knees as she struggled to see the action in her mind. And then she went on. The man *had* reached for Gerry, she remembered that, and she was sure he'd had both hands out in front, making to snatch her brother from their mother's arms. That's when Ma had swung Gerry to safety. And then the man had grabbed at the knife, he'd tried to take it for himself and there'd been a struggle . . .

'And then?'

The young policeman's pen scratched against his note-book as he wrote down everything she'd said so far. The sound was loud and Laurel was hot, the room had grown warmer, surely. She wondered why Daddy didn't open a window.

'And then?'

Laurel swallowed. Her mouth was dry. 'And then my mother brought the knife down.'

The room was silent but for the racing pen. Laurel saw it all so clearly in her mind: the man, the awful man with his dark face and great big hands, grabbing at Ma, trying to hurt her, planning to harm the baby next—

'And did the man fall down straightaway?'

The pen had stopped its scratching. The young police-man by the window was looking at her over the top of his notebook.

'Did the man fall immediately to the ground?'

Laurel nodded haltingly. 'I think so.'

'You think so?'

'I don't remember anything else. That's when I fainted, I suppose. I woke up in the tree house.'

'When was that?'

'Just now. And then I came in here.'

The older policeman drew a slow breath, not quite silently, and then he let it out. 'Is there anything else you can think of that we ought to know? Anything you saw or heard?' He ran his hand over his bald pate. His eyes were a very light blue, almost grey. 'Take your time: the smallest thing could be important.'

Was there something she'd forgotten? Had she seen

or heard anything else? Laurel thought carefully before answering. She didn't think so. No, she was sure that was everything.

'Nothing at all?'

She said no. Daddy's hands were in his pockets and he glared from beneath his brows.

The two policemen exchanged a glance, the older one dipped his head slightly and the younger flicked his note-book shut. The interview was over.

Afterwards, Laurel sat on the window ledge in her bed-room, chewing her thumbnail and watching the three men outside by the gate. They didn't talk much, but occasionally the older policeman said something and Daddy answered, pointing at various objects on the darkening horizon. The conversation might have been about farming methods, or the warmth of the season, or the historical uses of Suffolk land, but Laurel doubted it was any of those topics they were discussing.

A van lumbered up the driveway and the younger policeman met it at the top, striding across the long grass and gesturing back towards the house. Laurel watched as a man emerged from the driver's seat, as a stretcher was pulled from the rear, as the sheet (not so white, she could see that now; stained with red that was almost black) fluttered on its way back through the garden. They loaded the stretcher and then the van drove away. The policemen left and Daddy came inside. The front door closed, she heard it through the floor. Boots were kicked off – one, two – and then a soft socked path was paced to her mother in the sitting room.

Laurel drew the curtains and turned her back on the window. The policemen were gone. She had told the truth; she'd described exactly what was in her mind, everything that happened. Why then did she feel this way? Strange and uncertain.

She lay down on her bed, curled up tightly with her hands, prayer-like, between her knees. She closed her eyes but opened them again so she'd stop seeing the silver flash, the white sheet, her mother's face when the man said her name—

Laurel stiffened. The man had said Ma's name.

She hadn't told the policeman that. He'd asked if there was anything more she remembered, anything else at all she'd seen or heard, and she'd said no, there was nothing. But there was, there had been—

The door opened and Laurel sat up quickly, half expecting to see the older officer, back to take her to task. But it was just her father, come to tell her he was off to fetch the others from next door. The baby had been put to bed and her mother was resting. He hesitated at the door, tapping his hand against the jamb. When he finally spoke again his voice was hoarse.

'That was a shock this afternoon, a terrible shock.'

Laurel bit her lip. Deep inside her, a sob she hadn't acknowledged threatened to break.

'Your mother's a brave woman.'

Laurel nodded.

'She's a survivor, and so are you. You did well with those policemen.'

She mumbled, fresh tears stinging, 'Thank you, Daddy.'

'The police say it's probably that man from the papers,

the one that's been causing trouble by the stream. The description matches, and there's no one else who'd come bothering your mother.'

It was as she'd thought. When she'd first seen the man, hadn't she wondered if it might not be the one from the papers? Laurel felt suddenly lighter.

'Now listen, Lol.' Her father drove his hands into his pockets, jiggling them about a moment before continuing. 'Your mother and I, we've had a word and we reckon it's a good idea not to tell the younger ones all that went on. There's no need, and it's far too much for them to understand. Give me the choice, I'd rather you'd been a hundred miles away yourself, but you weren't and that's as it is.'

'I'm sorry.'

'Nothing to be sorry for. Not your fault. You've helped out the police, your mother too, and it's over. A bad man came to the house but everything's all right now. Everything's going to be all right.'

It wasn't a question, not exactly, but it sounded like one and so Laurel answered, 'Yes, Daddy. Everything's going to be all right.'

He smiled a one-sided smile. 'You're a good girl, Laurel. I'm going to fetch your sisters now. We'll keep what happened to ourselves, eh? There's my girl.'

And they had. It became the great unspoken event in their family's history. The sisters weren't to be told and Gerry was certainly too young to remember, though they'd been wrong about that as things turned out.

The others realized, of course, that something unusual had occurred – they'd been bundled unceremoniously away from the birthday party and deposited in front of the neighbour's brand-new Decca television set; their parents were oddly sombre for weeks; and a pair of policemen started paying regular visits that involved closed doors and low serious voices – but everything made sense when Daddy told them about the poor homeless man who'd died in the meadow on Gerry's birthday. It was sad but, as he said, these things happened sometimes.

Laurel, meanwhile, took to nail-biting in earnest. The police investigation was concluded in a matter of weeks: the man's age and appearance matched descriptions of the picnic stalker, the police said it wasn't unusual in these cases for violence to escalate over time, and Laurel's eyewitness report made it clear her mother had acted in self-defence. A burglary gone wrong; a lucky escape; nothing to be gained from splashing the details across the newspapers. Happily it was a time when discretion was the norm and a gentleman's agreement could shift a headline to page three. The curtain dropped, the story ended.

And yet. While her family's lives had returned to regular programming, Laurel's remained in a fuzz of static. The sense that she was separate from the others deepened and she became unaccountably restless. The event itself played over in her mind, and the role she'd taken in the police investigation, the things she'd told them – worse, the thing she hadn't – made the panic so bad sometimes that she could hardly breathe. No matter where she went at Greenacres – inside the house or out in the garden – she felt trapped by what she'd seen and done. The memories were everywhere; they were inescapable; made worse because the event that caused them was utterly inexplicable.

When she auditioned for the Central School and won a place, Laurel ignored her parents' pleas to stay at home, to put it off a year and finish her A levels, to think of her sisters, the baby brother who loved her most of all. She packed instead, as little as she could, and she left them all behind. Her life's direction changed instantly, just as surely as a weather vane spun circles in an unexpected storm.

Laurel drained the last of her wine and watched a pair of rooks fly low over Daddy's meadow. Someone had turned the giant dimmer switch and the world was casting towards darkness. All actresses have favourite words, and 'gloaming' was one of Laurel's. It was a pleasure to articulate, the sense of falling gloom and helpless encompassment inherent within the word's sound, and yet it was so close to 'glowing' that some of the latter's shine rubbed off on it, too.

It was the time of day she associated especially with childhood, with her life before she left for London: her father's return to the house after a day spent working on the farm, her mother towelling Gerry dry by the stove, her sisters laughing upstairs as Iris cycled through her repertoire of impersonations (an irony, really, that Iris had grown up to become that most imitable of all childhood's figures, the headmistress), the transition point when the lights came on inside, and the house smelled of soap, and the big oak table was laid for dinner. Even now, Laurel sensed quite unconsciously the natural turn of the day. It was the closest she ever came to feeling homesick in her own place.

Something moved in the meadow out there, the path that Daddy used to walk each day, and Laurel tensed; but it was just a car, a white car – she could see it more clearly now – winding up the driveway. She stood, shaking out the last drips from her glass. It had turned cool and Laurel wrapped her arms around herself, walking slowly to the gate. The driver flickered the headlights with an energy that could only belong to Daphne, and Laurel raised a hand to wave.

Six

Laurel spent a large part of dinner observing her youngest sister's face. Something had been done to it, and done well, and the result was fascinating. 'A fabulous new moisturizer,' Daphne would say if asked, which, because Laurel didn't fancy being lied to, she refrained from doing. Instead she nodded along as Daphne tossed her blonde curls and enthralled them all with tales from the *LA Breakfast Show* set, where she read the weather and flirted with a newsreader named Chip each morning. Breaks in the garrulous monologue were rare, and when occasion finally presented, Rose and Laurel leapt at once.

'You first,' said Laurel, tilting her wine glass – empty again, she noticed – towards her sister.

'I was just going to say, perhaps we ought to talk a little about Mummy's party.'

'I should say so,' said Iris.

'I've some thoughts,' said Daphne.

'Certainly—'

'Obviously—'

'We—'

'I—'

'What were *you* thinking, Rosie?' said Laurel.

'Well – ' Rose, who'd always struggled in the sibling press, started with a cough – 'it will have to be in hospital, more's the pity, but I thought we could try to come up with ways to make it special for her. You know how she feels about birthdays.'

'Just what I was going to say,' said Daphne, catching a small hiccup behind baby-pink fingernails. 'And after all, this will be her last.'

Silence stretched between them, with the rude exception of the Swiss clock, until Iris broke it with a sniff. 'You're very ... *brash* now, aren't you?' she said, patting the blunt ends of her steel-grey bob. 'Since you moved stateside.'

'I was just saying—'

'I think we all know what you were just saying.'

'But it's true.'

'Precisely, some might argue, why you needn't have said it at all.'

Laurel regarded her tablemates. Iris glowering, Daphne blinking with blue-eyed chagrin, Rose twisting her plait with an angst that threatened to sever it. Squint a little and they could have been their childhood selves. She sighed into her glass. 'Perhaps we could take in some of Ma's favourite things,' she said, 'play some of the records from Daddy's collection. Is that the sort of thing you meant, Rosie?'

'Yes,' said Rose, with unnerving gratitude, 'yes, that's perfect. I thought we might even retell some of the stories she used to invent for us.'

'Like the one about the gate at the bottom of the garden that led to fairyland—'

'And the dragon eggs she found in the woods—'

'And the time she ran away to join the circus.'

'Do you remember,' said Iris suddenly, 'the circus we had here?'

'*My* circus,' said Daphne, beaming from behind her wine glass.

'Well, yes,' Iris interjected, 'but only because—'

'Because I'd had the horrid measles and missed the real circus when it came to town.' Daphne laughed with pleasure at the memory. 'She got Daddy to build a tent at the bottom of the meadow, remember, and organized all of you to be clowns. Laurel was a lion, and Mummy walked the tightrope.'

'She was rather good at that,' said Iris. 'Barely fell off the rope. She must've practised for weeks.'

'Or else her story was true and she really did spend time in the circus,' said Rose. 'I can almost believe it of Mummy.'

Daphne gave a contented sigh. 'We were lucky to have a mother like ours, weren't we? So playful, almost as if she hadn't fully grown up; not at all like other people's boring old mothers. I used to feel rather smug when I had friends home from school.'

'You? Smug?' Iris pretended surprise. 'Now that just doesn't seem—'

'With regard to Mummy's party,' Rose flapped a hand, desperate to avoid a new dip into argument, 'I thought I might bake a cake, Victoria sponge, her fav—'

'Do you remember,' said Daphne with sudden brightness, 'that knife, the one with the ribbon – '

'The red ribbon,' said Iris.

' – and the bone handle. She used to insist on it, every birthday.'

'She said it was magical, that it could grant wishes.'

'You know, I believed that for such a long time.' Daphne rested her chin on the back of her hand with a pretty sigh. 'I wonder what happened to that funny old knife.'

'It disappeared,' said Iris. 'I remember that now. One year it just wasn't there, and when I asked her she said it had been lost.'

'No doubt it took up with the thousand pens and kirby grips that went AWOL from this house,' said Laurel quickly. She cleared her throat. 'I'm parched. More wine, anyone?'

'Wouldn't it be something if we could find it . . .' she heard as she crossed the hall.

'What a splendid idea! We could take it in for her cake . . .'

Laurel reached the kitchen and was therefore spared excited preparations for the search party. ('How far could it have gone?' Daphne was enthusing.)

She flicked the switch and the room shuffled to life like a trusty old retainer who'd stuck around long past his use-by date. Empty of other people and with the fluorescent tube settling at a weak half-light, the kitchen looked sadder than Laurel remembered; the tile grouting was grey and the canister lids were dull with a film of greasy dust. She had the uncomfortable feeling that what she was seeing was the evidence of her mother's failing eyesight. She should have organized a cleaner. Why hadn't she thought to do that? And while she was self-castigating – why stop there? – she ought to have come to visit more often, cleaned the place herself.

The fridge, at least, was a new one; Laurel *had* seen to that. When the old Kelvinator finally gave up the ghost, she'd ordered a replacement over the phone from London:

energy-efficient and with a fancy ice-maker that her mother never used.

Laurel found the bottle of chablis she'd brought and swung the door closed. A little too hard, perhaps, for a magnet fell and a piece of paper swept to the floor. It disappeared beneath the fridge and she cursed. She got down on all fours to pat about among the dust bunnies. The newspaper clipping was from the *Sudbury Chronicle* and featured a photograph of Iris looking very headmistressy in brown tweed and black tights at the front of her school. It was none the worse for its adventure and Laurel sought a gap to reposition it in. The task was easier said than done. The Nicolson fridge had always been a busy place, even before someone, somewhere, got the idea of selling magnets for the express purpose of clutter creation: anything deemed worthy of attention had been Sellotaped to the big white door for family notice. Photographs, accolades, cards, and certainly any mention in the media.

From nowhere the memory came, a summer's morning in June 1961 – a month before Gerry's birthday party: the seven of them sitting around the breakfast table spooning strawberry jam onto buttery toast as Daddy cut the article from the local newspaper; the photograph of Dorothy, smiling as she held aloft her prize-winning runner bean; Daddy taping it to the fridge afterwards as the rest of them cleaned up.

'Are you all right?'

Laurel spun around to see Rose standing in the doorway.

'Fine. Why?'

'You've been gone a while.' She wrinkled her nose, regarding Laurel carefully. 'And, I must say, you're looking a little peaky.'

'That's just the light in here,' said Laurel. 'It gives one the most charming consumptive glow.' She busied herself with the corkscrew, turning her back so Rose couldn't read her expression. 'I trust plans for the Great Knife Hunt are coming along?'

'Oh yes. Really, when the two of them get together . . .'

'If we could only harness the power and use it for good.'

'Quite.'

There was a gust of steam as Rose opened the oven to check on the raspberry cobbler, their mother's trademark pudding. The sugary smell of warming fruit filled the air and Laurel closed her eyes.

It had taken her months to summon the courage to ask about the incident. Such was her parents' fierce determination to look onwards and upwards, to deny the whole event, that she might never have done so had she not begun dreaming of the man. But she had, each night the same. The man at the side of the house, calling her mother's name—

'Looks good,' said Rose, sliding out the oven rack. 'Not as good as hers, perhaps, but we mustn't expect miracles.'

Laurel had found her mother in the kitchen, on this very spot, a few days before she left for London. She'd asked her straight: 'How did that man know your name, Ma?' Her stomach had churned as the words left her lips, and a part of her, she realized as she waited, prayed that her mother would say she was mistaken. That she'd misheard and the man had said no such thing.

Dorothy hadn't answered right away. She'd gone to the fridge instead, opened the door and started riffling about inside. Laurel had watched her back for what seemed like forever, and she'd almost given up hope when her mother finally began to speak. 'The newspaper,' she said. 'The police say he must've read the article in the paper. There was a copy in his satchel. That's how he knew where to come.'

It had made perfect sense.

That is, Laurel had *wanted* it to make sense and therefore it had. The man had read the newspaper, seen her mother's picture and then set out to find her. And if a small voice in the back of Laurel's mind whispered *why?*, she waved it aside. He was a madman – who could say why for certain? And what did it matter anyway? It was over. So long as Laurel didn't pick too closely at its delicate threads, the tapestry hung together. The picture remained intact.

At least, it had done – until now. Incredible, really, that after fifty years all it took was the return of an old photograph and the utterance of a woman's name for the fabric of Laurel's fiction to begin unravelling.

The oven rack slid back with a clang and: 'Five more minutes,' said Rose.

Laurel glugged wine into her glass and strove for nonchalance. 'Rosie?'

'Mm?'

'That photograph today, the one at the hospital. The woman who gave the book to Ma—'

'Vivien.'

'Yes.' Laurel shuddered lightly as she set down the bottle. The name did something strange to her. 'Did Ma ever mention her to you?'

'A little,' said Rose. 'After I found the photo. They were friends.'

Laurel remembered the date on the photograph, 1941. 'During the war.'

Rose nodded, folding the tea towel into a neat rectangle. 'She didn't say much. Just that Vivien was Australian.'

'Australian?'

'She came here as a child, I'm not sure why exactly.'

'How did they meet?'

'She didn't say.'

'Why haven't we met her?'

'No idea.'

'Funny, isn't it, that she was never mentioned?' Laurel took a sip of wine. 'I wonder why not.'

The oven timer rang. 'Perhaps they had a bust-up. Drifted apart. I don't know.' Rose drew on the mitts. 'Why are you so interested, anyway?'

'I'm not. Not really.'

'Let's eat then,' said Rose, cupping the cobbler dish. 'This looks quite perf—'

'She died,' said Laurel with sudden conviction. 'Vivien died.'

'How do you know?'

'I mean – ' Laurel swallowed and backtracked swiftly – '*perhaps* she died. There was a war on. It's possible, don't you think?'

'Anything's possible.' Rose probed the crust with a fork.

'Take, for example, this really rather respectable glaze. Ready to brave the others?'

'Actually – ' the need to get upstairs, to check her flash of memory, was immediate and searing – 'you were right before. I *am* feeling poorly.'

'You don't want pudding?'

Laurel shook her head, halfway to the door. 'Early night for me, I'm afraid. Terrible to be ill tomorrow.'

'Can I get you something else – paracetamol, a cup of tea?'

'No,' said Laurel. 'No thanks. Except, Rose—'

'Yes?'

'The play.'

'Which play?'

'*Peter Pan* – the book the photo came from. Is it handy?'

'You are a funny thing,' said Rose with a lopsided smile. 'I'll have to dig it out for you.' She bobbed her head at the cobbler. 'Later all right?'

'Of course, no hurry, I'll just be resting. Enjoy your pudding. And Rosie?'

'Yes?'

'Sorry to send you back into the fray alone.'

It was the mention of Australia that had done it. As Rose recounted what she'd learned from their mother, a light bulb had fired in Laurel's mind and she'd known why Vivien was important. She remembered, too, where she'd first come across the name, all those years before.

While her sisters ate dessert and hunted for a knife they'd never find, Laurel braved the attic in search of her trunk. There was one for each of them; Dorothy had been strict in that regard. It was because of the war, Daddy had once confided in them – everything she loved had been lost when that bomb fell on her family home in Coventry and turned her past to rubble. She'd been determined her children would never suffer the same fate. She might not be able to spare them every heartache, but she could damn well make sure they knew where to find their class photo when they wanted it. Their mother's passion for *things*, for possessions – objects that could be held in one's hands and invested with deeper meaning – had verged on obsessive, her enthusiasm for collecting so great that it was hard not to fall into line. Everything was kept; nothing thrown away; traditions adhered to religiously. Case in point, the knife.

Laurel's trunk was tucked beside the broken radiator Daddy had never got around to fixing. She knew it was hers before she read her name stencilled on the top. The tan leather straps and broken buckle were a dead giveaway. Her heart fluttered when she saw it, anticipating the thing she knew she'd find inside. Funny the way an object she hadn't thought of in decades could arrive so precisely in her mind. She knew exactly what she was looking for, what it would feel like in her hand, the emotions its uncovering would cause to surface. A faint imprint of herself the last time she'd done so knelt beside her as she undid the straps.

The trunk smelled like dust and damp and an old cologne with a name she'd forgotten but a fragrance that made her feel sixteen again. It was full of paper: diaries, photographs, letters, school reports, a couple of sewing patterns for capri pants, but Laurel didn't pause to look them over. She pulled out one pile after another, scanning quickly.

Midway down on the far left-hand side she found what she'd come for. A thin book, totally unprepossessing, and yet, for Laurel, reverberating with memories.

She'd been offered the role of Meg in *The Birthday Party* some years back; it had been a chance to perform at the Lyttelton Theatre, but Laurel had said no. It was the only time she could think of that she'd put her personal life ahead of her career. She'd blamed it on her film schedule, which wasn't entirely improbable but wasn't the truth either. Obfuscation had been necessary. She couldn't have done it. The play was inextricably linked with the summer of 1961; she'd read it over and over after the boy – she couldn't remember his name; how ridiculous, she'd been mad about him – had given it to her. She'd memorized its lines, imbuing the scenes with all her pent-up anger and frustration. And then the man had walked up their driveway and the whole thing had become so muddled in her mind and heart that to contemplate the play in any detail made her physically ill.

Her skin was clammy even now, her pulse quickening. She was glad it wasn't the play she needed but what she'd tucked inside. They were still there, she could tell by the rough edges of paper jutting from between the pages. Two newspaper articles: the first a rather vague report from the local rag about a man's death during a Suffolk summer; the second an obituary from *The Times*, torn surreptitiously from the paper her friend's father brought home with him from London each day. 'Look at this,' he'd said one evening when Laurel was visiting Shirley. 'A piece about that fellow, the one who died out near your place, Laurel.' It was a lengthy article, for it turned out the man wasn't quite the

usual suspect; there'd been moments, long before he'd
turned up on the Greenacres doorstep, in which he'd distinguished himself and even been lauded. There were no sur-
viving children, but there'd once been a wife.

The single bulb swaying gently overhead wasn't bright
enough to read by, so Laurel closed the trunk and took the
book downstairs.

She'd been assigned their girlhood room to sleep in
(another given in the complex scale of sibling seniority) and
the bed was made up with fresh sheets. Someone – Rose, she
guessed – had brought her suitcase up already, but Laurel
didn't unpack. She opened the windows wide and sat on
the ledge.

A cigarette held between two fingers, Laurel slipped the
articles out from inside the book. She passed over the report
from the local paper, picking up the obituary instead. She
scanned the lines, waiting for her eye to alight on what she
knew was there.

A third of the way down, the name jumped out at her.
Vivien.

Laurel backtracked to read the whole sentence: *Jenkins
was married in 1938 to Miss Vivien Longmeyer, born in
Queensland, Australia, but raised by an uncle in Oxfordshire.* A little further down she found: *Vivien Jenkins was
killed in 1941 during a heavy air raid in Notting Hill.*

She drew heavily on her cigarette and noticed that her
fingers were trembling.

It was possible, of course, that there were two Viviens,
both Australian. It was possible that her mother's wartime
friend was unrelated to the Australian Vivien whose hus-

band had died on their doorstep. But it wasn't likely, was it?

And if her mother knew Vivien Jenkins, then surely she knew Henry Jenkins, too. 'Hello, Dorothy. It's been a long time,' he'd said, and then Laurel had seen fear on her mother's face.

The door opened and Rose was there. 'Feeling all right?' she said, wrinkling her nose at the tobacco smoke.

'Medicinal,' said Laurel, gesturing shakily with the cigarette before holding it out the window. 'Don't tell the parents – I'd hate to be grounded.'

'Secret's safe with me.' Rose came closer and held out a small book. 'It's rather tattered, I'm afraid.'

Tattered was an understatement. The book's front cover was hanging, literally, by threads, and the green cloth board beneath had been discoloured by dirt; perhaps, judging by the vaguely smoky smell, even soot. Laurel turned the pages carefully until she reached the title page. On the frontis-piece, handwritten in black ink, was the inscription: *For Dorothy, A true friend is a light in the dark. Vivien.*

'It must've been important to her,' said Rose. 'It wasn't on the bookshelf with the others; it was inside her trunk. She'd kept it up there all these years.'

'You saw inside her trunk?' Their mother had rather fixed ideas about privacy and its observation.

Rose blushed. 'No need to look at me like that, Lol; it's not as though I broke the padlock open with a nail file. She asked me to fetch the book for her a couple of months ago, just before she went into hospital.'

'She *gave* you the key?'

'Reluctantly, and only after I caught her trying to get up the ladder herself.'

'She wasn't.'

'She was.'

'She's incorrigible.'

'She's like you, Lol.'

Rose was being kind, but her words made Laurel flinch. A flash of memory came: the evening she'd told her parents she was going up to London to attend Central School. They'd been shocked and unhappy, hurt she'd gone behind their backs to audition, adamant she was too young to leave home, worried she wasn't going to finish school and get her A levels. They'd sat with her around the kitchen table, taking it in turns to make reasonable arguments in exaggeratedly calm voices. Laurel tried to look bored, and when they'd finally finished she said, 'I'm still going,' with all the sulky vehemence one might expect from a confused and resentful teenager. 'Nothing you say will change my mind. It's what I want.'

'You're too young to know what you really want,' her mother had said. 'People change, they grow up, they make better decisions. I *know* you, Laurel—'

'You don't.'

'I know you're headstrong. I know you're stubborn and determined to be different, that you're full of dreams, just like I was—'

'I'm not a *bit* like you,' Laurel had said then, her pointed words cutting like a blade through her mother's already shaky composure. 'I'd *never* do the things you do.'

'That's enough!' Stephen Nicolson put his arms around his wife. He signalled to Laurel that she should go upstairs to bed but warned her that the conversation was far from over.

Laurel lay in bed fuming as the hours passed; she wasn't sure where her sisters were, only that they'd been put somewhere else so as not to break her quarantine. It was the first time she could remember fighting with her parents and she was in equal parts exhilarated and crushed. It didn't feel as if life could ever go back to how it had been before.

She was still there, lying in the dark, when the door opened and someone walked quietly towards her. Laurel felt the edge of the bed depress when the person sat and then she heard Ma's voice. She'd been crying, Laurel could tell, and the realization, the knowledge that she was the cause, made her want to wrap her arms around her mother's neck and never let go.

'I'm sorry we fought,' said Dorothy, a wash of moonlight falling through the window to illuminate her face. 'It's funny how things turn out. I never thought I'd argue with my daughter. I used to get in trouble when I was young – I always felt different from my parents. I loved them, of course, but I'm not sure they knew quite what to make of me. I thought I knew best and I didn't listen to a word they said.'

Laurel smiled faintly, unsure where the conversation was headed, but glad her insides were no longer roiling like hot lava.

'We're similar, you and I,' her mother continued. 'I expect that's why I'm so anxious you shouldn't make the same mistakes I did.'

'I'm not making a mistake, though.' Laurel had sat up tall against her pillows. 'Can't you see that? I want to be an actress – drama school is the perfect place for someone like me.'

'Laurel—'

'Imagine you were seventeen, Ma, and your whole life was ahead of you. Can you think of anywhere else you'd rather go than London?' It was the wrong thing to say – Ma had never shown the least interest in going up to London.

There was a pause and a blackbird called to his friends outside. 'No,' Dorothy had said eventually, softly and a little sadly as she reached to stroke the ends of Laurel's hair. 'No, I don't suppose I can.'

It struck Laurel now that even then she'd been too self-absorbed to wonder or ask what her mother was actually like at seventeen, what it was she'd longed for, and what mistakes she'd made that she was so anxious her daughter should not repeat.

Laurel held up the book Rose had given her and said, more shakily than she'd have liked, 'It's strange to see something of hers from before, isn't it?'

'Before what?'

'Before us. Before this place. Before she was our mother. Just imagine, when she was given this book, when that photograph with Vivien was taken, she had no idea that we were out there somewhere waiting to exist.'

'No wonder she's beaming in the photo.'

Laurel didn't laugh. 'Do you ever think about her, Rose?'

'About Mummy? Of course—'

'Not about Ma, I mean that young woman. She was a different person back then, with a whole other life we know nothing about. Do you ever wonder about her, about what she wanted, how she felt about things – ' Laurel sneaked a glance at her sister – 'the sorts of secrets she kept?'

Rose smiled uncertainly and Laurel shook her head. 'Don't mind me. I'm a bit maudlin tonight. It's being back here, I guess. The old room.' She forced a cheeriness she didn't feel. 'Remember the way Iris used to snore?'

Rose laughed. 'Worse than Daddy, wasn't she? I wonder if she's improved.'

'I expect we're about to find out. You heading to bed now?'

'I thought I'd take a bath before the others finish up and I lose the mirror to Daphne.' She lowered her voice and lifted the skin above one eye. 'Has she . . . ?'

'It would appear so.'

Rose pulled a face that said, 'Aren't people strange?' and closed the door behind her.

Laurel's smile fell as her sister's footsteps retreated down the corridor. She turned to look at the night sky. The bathroom door clicked shut and the water pipes began to whistle in the wall behind her.

Fifty years ago, Laurel told a distant patch of stars, my mother killed a man. She called it self-defence, but I saw it. She raised the knife and brought it down and the man fell backwards onto the ground where the grass was worn and the violets were flowering. She knew him, she was frightened, and I've no idea why.

It suddenly seemed to Laurel that all the absences in her own life, every loss and sadness, every nightmare in the dark, every unexplained melancholy, took the shadowy form of the same unanswered question, something that had been there since she was sixteen years old – her mother's unspoken secret.

'Who are you, Dorothy?' she said beneath her breath. 'Who were you, before you became Ma?'

Seven

Dorothy Smitham was seventeen years old when she knew for certain she'd been stolen as a baby. It was the only explanation. The truth came to her, clear as day, on a Saturday morning around eleven as she watched her father roll his pencil between his fingers, run his tongue slowly over his bottom lip, and then mark down in his small black ledger book the precise amount (3s 5d) he'd paid the taxi driver to deliver the family and their trunk (an additional 3d) to the station. The list and its creation would occupy him for the better part of their stay at Bournemouth, and on the family's return to Coventry a gleeful evening would be spent, to which they would all be reluctant attendees, analysing its contents. Tables would be drawn, comparisons made with last year's results (and those stretching back a decade, if they were lucky), commitments undertaken to do better next time; before, refreshed from the annual break, he would return to his accountant's chair at H. G. Walker Ltd., Bicycle Manufacturers, and knuckle down to another year's work.

Dolly's mother sat in the corner of the carriage, fussing at her nostrils with a cotton handkerchief. It was a surreptitious dab, the hanky concealed for the most part within her hand, followed occasionally by a skittish glance at her husband to ensure he hadn't been disturbed and was still frowning with grim pleasure at his ledger. Really, only Janice Smitham could manage to catch a cold on the eve of the annual summer holiday with such astonishing regularity. The consistency was almost admirable and Dolly might've been able to salute her mother's commitment to habit if it weren't for the accompanying sniffle – so meek and apologetic – that made her want to jam Father's sharpened pencil through her own eardrums. Mother's fortnight by the sea would be spent as it was each year: making Father feel like King of the Sandcastle, fretting over Dolly's swimsuit cut, and worrying whether Cuthbert was making friends with 'the right kind of boys'.

Poor old Cuthbert. He'd been a glorious little baby, full of giggles and gummy smiles and with a rather fetching way of crying whenever Dolly left the room. The older he became, though, and the more he grew, the clearer it became to all that he was on a collision course with his fate: to become a doppelgänger of Mr Arthur Smitham. Which meant, sadly, that despite the affection between them, Dolly and Cuthbert couldn't possibly be flesh and blood, and begged the question: who were her real parents and how did she come to be mixed up with this sorry little group anyway?

Circus performers? A spectacular couple of high-wire walkers? It was possible – she glanced at her legs, relatively long and slender, both of them. She'd always been good at sports: Mr Anthony, the school sports master, made a point of selecting her for the first hockey team each year; and when she and Caitlin rolled back Caitlin's mother's parlour carpet and put Louis Armstrong on the gramophone, Dolly was quite sure she didn't just imagine herself to be the finer dancer. There — Dolly crossed her legs and smoothed her skirt — natural grace; that all but proved it.

'Can I have a sweet at the station, Father?'

'A sweet?'

'At the station? From the little shop.'

'I don't know about that, Cuthbert.'

'But Father—'

'There's the budget to think of.'

'But Mother, you said—'

'Now, now, Cuthbert. Father knows best.'

Dolly turned her attention to the fleeting fields outside. Circus performers — it felt about right. Spangles and sequins and late nights beneath the big top, empty but bathed still in the collective awe and adoration of the night's rapturous crowd. Glamour, excitement, romance — yes, that was far more like it.

Such entrancing origins would also explain the fierce admonishments meted out by her parents whenever Dolly's behaviour threatened to 'draw attention'. 'People will *look*, Dorothy,' her mother would hiss if her hem was too high, her laugh too loud, her lipstick too red. 'You're going to make them *look*. You know how your father feels about that.' Dolly did indeed. As Father was fond of reminding them, the apple didn't fall far from the tree, and thus he must've lived in fear that Bohemia would seep one day like spoiled fruit through the skin of propriety he and Mother had taken care to construct around their little stolen daughter.

Dolly sneaked a peppermint from the bag in her pocket, tongued it into her cheek and leaned her head against the window. How, precisely, the stealing might have been achieved was a rather more perplexing prospect. It didn't matter how she turned it, Arthur and Janice Smitham just weren't the thieving types. To imagine them creeping towards an unattended pram and snatching a sleeping babe was decidedly problematic. People who stole did so because, whether down to need or greed, they desired the item passionately. Arthur Smitham, by contrast, believed 'passion' should be removed from the English dictionary, if not the English soul, and that one might as well scratch 'desire' while one was at it. A trip to the circus? Well now, that just smacked of unnecessary fun.

Far more likely – the mint broke in two – Dolly had been discovered on the doorstep, and it was duty rather than desire that had brought her into the Smitham fold.

She leaned back further on the carriage seat and closed her eyes; she could see it clearly. The secret pregnancy, the ringmaster's threat, the circus train arriving in Coventry. For a time the young pair struggle bravely on their own, raising the child on a diet of love and hope; but alas, with no work (there being, after all, only so much call for high-wire skills) and no money for food, desperation sets in. One night as they pass through the centre of town, their baby too weak now to cry, a house catches their eye. A front step, cleaner and shinier than all the others, a light on inside, and the meaty aroma of Janice Smitham's (admittedly fine) pot roast brisket seeping out beneath the door. They know what they have to do—

'But I can't hold on. I can't!'

Dolly cracked an eye open sufficiently to observe her brother hopping from one leg to the other in the middle of the carriage.

'Come along, Cuthbert, we're almost—'

'But I need the lav *now*!'

Dolly closed her eyes again, tighter than before. It was true – not the bit about the tragic young couple, she didn't really believe that – but the part about being special. Dolly had always felt different, as if she were somehow more alive than other people, and the world, fate or destiny, whatever it was, had big plans for her. She had proof now, too – scientific proof. Caitlin's father, who was a doctor and ought to know about such things, had said as much when they played Blotto in Caitlin's parlour: he'd held up one ink-splotched card after another and Dolly had taken her turn, calling out the first thing that came to mind. 'Tremendous,' he'd mumbled around his pipe when they were midway through; and 'Fascinating,' with a small shake of the head; then, 'Well, I never,' and a light laugh that revealed him as rather too handsome for a friend's father. Only Caitlin's sour glare had kept Dolly from following him to his study when Dr Rufus declared her answers 'exceptional' and suggested – no, *urged* – further testing.

Exceptional. Dolly ran the word through her mind. Exceptional. She wasn't one of them, the ordinary Smithams, and she certainly wasn't going to become one. Her life was going to be bright and wonderful. She was going to dance outside the square of 'proper' behaviour within which Mother and Father were so eager to trap her. Perhaps she'd even run off to the circus herself and try her luck beneath the big top.

The train was slowing now as it drew nearer to Euston station. The houses of London appeared thickly through the window and Dolly felt a tremor of excitement. London! A great whirlpool of a city (or so it said in the introduction to the *Ward Lock & Co's Guide to London* she kept hidden in the drawer with her knickers), brimming with theatre and nightlife and truly grand people leading fabulous lives.

When Dolly was younger, her father used to go to London sometimes for work. She'd waited up those nights, watching through the banisters when her mother thought she was asleep, impatient just to get a glimpse of him. His key would sound in the lock, and she'd hold her breath, and then in he'd come. Mother would take his coat, and there'd be an air about him of having Been Somewhere, of being More Important than he had been before. Dolly never would have dreamed of asking him about his trip; even then she'd guessed that the truth would be a poor imitation of her imaginings. Still, she glanced at her father now, hoping he might meet her eyes, that she'd see in them evidence that he, too, felt the pull of the great city they were passing through.

He did not. Arthur Smitham had eyes only for his ledger book, the back page now, on which he'd made his careful notation of train times and platform numbers. The corners of his mouth twitched and Dolly's heart sank. She braced for the panic she knew was coming, that always came no matter how large a buffer they built into their travel time, no matter that they made the same trip every year, no matter that people everywhere caught trains from A to B and B to C and managed not to flap. Sure enough – she flinched pre-emptively – here it came, the rousing call to battle.

'Everybody stay together while we find a taxi.' A gallant attempt by their leader to radiate calm in the face of on-coming trial. He felt about on the baggage rack for his hat.

'Cuthbert,' Mother worried, 'take my hand.'

'I don't want to—'

'Everybody responsible for your own piece of luggage,' Father continued, his voice rising in a rare swell of feeling. 'Hold tight to your sticks and rackets. And avoid getting caught behind passengers with limps or canes. We mustn't allow ourselves to be slowed down.'

A well-dressed man who'd been sharing their carriage glanced askance at her father and Dolly wondered – not for the first time – if it was possible to disappear simply by wishing it badly enough.

The Smitham family had a habit, refined and cemented over years of identical seaside holidays, of heading down to the front straight after breakfast. Father had long ago ruled out hiring a bathing hut, declaring them unnecessary luxuries that encouraged show-offs, and early arrival was thus essential if they expected to secure a decent space before the crowds arrived. On this particular morning, Mrs Jennings had kept them in the Bellevue dining room a little later than usual, over-brewing the tea and then dithering dreadfully with the replacement pot. Father became increasingly twitchy – his white canvas shoes were calling to him, despite the sticking plasters he'd been forced to adhere to his heels after the previous day's exertions – but interrupting their host was unthinkable, and Arthur Smitham did not do unthinkable things. In the end it was Cuthbert who saved them all. He glanced at the ship's clock above the framed picture of the pier, swallowed a whole poached egg, and exclaimed, 'Golly! It's already gone half nine!'

Not even Mrs Jennings could argue with that, backing

towards the kitchen doors and wishing them all a lovely morning. 'And what a day you've got for it, what a perfect day!'

It *was* rather perfect, one of those heavenly summer days when the sky is clear and the breeze is light and warm, and you just know there's something exciting waiting round the corner. A charabanc was arriving as they reached the promenade and Mr Smitham hurried his family along, anxious to beat the hordes. With the proprietorial air of those who'd booked their fortnight in February and paid in full by March, Mr and Mrs Smitham took a dim view of day-trippers. They were impostors and imposers, decamping on *their* beach, crowding *their* pier, and making them queue for *their* ice creams.

Dorothy lingered a few steps behind as the rest of her family, marshalled by their fearless leader, sallied round the bandstand to cut off the invaders at the pass. They took the stairs with the majesty of victors and staked a spot right by the stone wall. Father set down the picnic basket and tucked his thumbs into the waistband of his trousers, gazing left and right before declaring the position 'just right'. He added, with a smile of self-satisfaction, 'And not one hundred steps from our front door. Not even a hundred steps.'

'We could wave hello to Mrs Jennings from here,' said Mother, always glad of the chance to please her husband.

Dorothy managed a faint, wincing smile, and then turned her attention to straightening the edges of her towel. Of course, they couldn't actually *see* Bellevue from where they were sitting. Contrary to the boarding house's name (imparted with uncharacteristic *joie de vivre* by the dour Mr Jennings, who'd once spent a 'fair' month in Paris), the building itself stood in the middle of Little Collins Street, which ran dog-legged off the promenade. The 'vue', therefore, wasn't particularly 'belle' – drab slices of the town centre from rooms at the front, the drainpipes of a twin house from those at the rear – but neither was the building French, so to quibble, it seemed to Dorothy, was rather pointless. Instead she rubbed Pond's cold cream into her shoulders and hid behind her magazine, sneaking glances over its pages at the richer, glossier people lounging and laughing on the balconies of the bathing huts.

There was one girl in particular. She had blonde hair, sun-kissed skin and cutie-pie dimples when she laughed, which was often. Dolly couldn't stop watching her. The way she moved like a cat on that balcony, warm and assured, reaching to stroke the arm of first this friend, then that one; the tilt of her chin, the bitten-lip smile reserved for the best-looking fellow; the light drift of her silver satin dress when the breeze brushed by. The breeze. Even nature knew the rules. While Dolly baked in the Smitham family camp, sweat beads colonizing her hairline and making her bathing suit stick, that silver dress fluttered tantalizingly from up on high.

'Who's for cricket?'

Dolly ducked lower behind her magazine.

'Me, me!' said Cuthbert, dancing from one foot (sun-burned already) to the other. 'I'll bowl, Dad, I'll bowl. Can't I? Can't I? *Please, please, PLEASE?*'

Father's shadow cast a brief respite from the heat. 'Dorothy? You always like to take first turn.'

Her gaze traversed the proffered bat, the rotundity of

her father's middle, the morsel of scrambled egg clinging to his moustache. And an image flashed across her mind of the beautiful laughing girl in the silver dress, joking and flirting with her friends – not a parent in sight.

'Might give it a miss, thanks Dad,' she said weakly. 'Headache coming on.'

Headaches carried the whiff of 'women's business' and Mr Smitham's lips tightened with awe and distaste. He nodded, backing away slowly. 'Rest up then, eh, don't exert yourself—'

'C'mon, Dad!' called Cuthbert. 'Bob Wyatt's stepping up to the fold. Show him how it's done, why don't you?'

In the face of such a rallying cry, Father was powerless but to act. He turned on his heel, strutting down the beach, bat slung over his shoulder, in the chipper manner of a much younger, far fitter man. The game began and Dolly shrank back even closer to the wall. Arthur Smitham's one-time cricketing prowess was part of the Great Family Story and the holiday game was thus a hallowed institution.

There was a part of Dolly that hated herself for the way she was acting – after all, it was probably the last time she'd come on the annual family holiday – but she couldn't seem to shake herself free of this ghastly mood. With every day that passed she felt the gulf between herself and the rest of her family widen. It wasn't that she didn't love them; it was just that they had a knack lately, even Cuthbert, of driving her crazy. She'd always felt herself to be different, there was nothing new in that, but recently things had taken a definite turn for the worse. Her father had started talking at the dinner table about what was going to happen when Dolly finished school. In September there was a junior position

opening up on the secretarial staff at the bicycle factory –
after thirty years of service he might just be able to pull a
few strings with the head secretary to make sure Dolly got
it. Father always smiled and winked when he said that,
about the strings, as if he were doing Dolly a huge favour
and she ought to be grateful. In reality the thought made her
want to scream like the heroine in a horror film. She couldn't
think of anything worse. More than that, she couldn't believe that after seventeen years, Arthur Smitham – her very
own father – could so misunderstand her.

From the sand there came a cry of 'Six!' and Dolly
glanced over the top of her *Woman's Weekly* to see her
father swing his bat over his shoulder like a musket and
begin the jog between makeshift wickets. Beside her, Janice
Smitham was emanating nervous encouragement, offering
tentative calls of 'Good show!' and 'Jolly well done!', coun-
tered quickly with desperate cries of 'Careful now,' or 'Not
so fast,' or, 'Breathe, Cuthbert, remember your asthma,'
as the boy chased his ball towards the water. Dolly took in
her mother's neat permanent wave, the sensible cut of her
bathing suit, the care she'd taken to present herself to the
world in a way that ensured she made the least possible
impact, and sighed with hot perplexity. It was her mother's
lack of understanding on the matter of Dolly's future that
vexed her most of all.

When she first realized that Father was serious about the
bicycle factory, she'd hoped Mother would smile fondly at
the suggestion before pointing out that *naturally* there were
far more exciting things in store for their daughter. Because,
although Dolly had fun sometimes imagining she'd been
swapped at birth, she didn't really believe it. Nobody who

saw her standing next to her mother could have thought such a thing for long. Janice and Dorothy Smitham had the same chocolate-brown hair, the same high cheekbones, and the same generous bust. As Dolly had recently learned, they had something more important in common, too.

She'd been searching the garage shelves for her hockey stick when she made the discovery: a powder-blue shoebox at the very back of the top shelf. The box was immediately familiar, but it took Dolly a few seconds to remember why. The memory came to her of her mother sitting on the edge of her twin bed in the room she shared with Father, the blue box on her lap and a wistfulness about her face as she went through its contents. It was a private moment, and Dolly had known instinctively to make herself scarce, but afterwards she'd wondered about that box, trying to imagine what it could possibly have held that made her mother look dreamy, and lost, and somehow both young and old at once.

That day, alone in the garage, Dolly had lifted the box's lid and all had been revealed. It was filled with bits and pieces of another life: programmes for singing performances, blue first-place ribbons from eisteddfods, certificates of merit proclaiming Janice Williams the singer with the Most Beautiful Voice. There was even a newspaper article with a picture of a bright young woman with starry eyes and a lovely figure and the look of someone who was going places, who wasn't going to follow the other girls in her school class into the dull ordinary lives expected of them.

Except that she had. Dolly stared at that picture for a long time. Her mother had once possessed a talent – a real one, that set her apart and made her special – yet, in seventeen years of living in the same house, Dolly had never heard Janice Smitham sing anything. What could possibly have happened to silence the young woman who'd once told a newspaper: 'Singing is my favourite thing in the whole world; it makes me feel that I could fly. One day I'd like to sing onstage before the king'?

Dolly had a feeling she knew the answer.

'Keep it up, boy,' Father called across the beach to Cuthbert. 'Look smart, eh. Don't slouch.'

Arthur Smitham: accountant extraordinaire, bicycle-factory stalwart, guardsman of all that was good and proper. Enemy to all that was exceptional.

Dolly sighed as she watched him jouncing backwards from the wicket, winding himself up to bowl the ball at Cuthbert. He might have won against her mother, convincing her to suppress everything that made her special, but he wasn't going to do the same to Dolly. She refused to let him. 'Mother,' she said suddenly, letting her magazine drop to her lap.

'Yes, dear? Would you like a sandwich? I've some shrimp paste here with me.'

Dolly drew breath. She couldn't quite believe she was going to say it, now, here, just like that, but the wind was with her and away she went. 'Mother, I don't want to go to work with Father at the bicycle factory.'

'Oh?'

'No.'

'Oh.'

'I don't think I could stand to do the same thing every day, typing up letters full of bicycles and order references and dreary *yours sincerelys*.'

Her mother blinked at her with a bland, unreadable expression on her face. 'I see.'

'Yes.'

'And what is it you propose to do instead?'

Dolly wasn't sure how to answer that. She hadn't thought about the specifics, she just knew there was *something* out there waiting for her. 'I don't know. I just . . . Well, the bicycle factory's hardly the right sort of place for someone like me, don't you think?'

'Why ever not?'

She didn't want to have to say it. She wanted her mother to know, to agree, to think it herself without being told. Dolly struggled to find the words, while the undertow of disappointment pulled hard against her hope.

'It's time to settle down now, Dorothy,' her mother said gently. 'You're almost a woman.'

'Yes, but that's exactly—'

'Put away childish notions. The time for all that has passed. He wanted to tell you himself, to surprise you, but your father's already spoken with Mrs Levene at the factory and organized an interview.'

'*What?*'

'I wasn't supposed to say anything, but they'll see you in the first week of September. You're a very lucky girl to have a father with such influence.'

'But I—'

'Father knows best.' Janice Smitham reached to tap Dolly's leg but didn't quite make contact. 'You'll see.' There was a hint of fear behind her painted-on smile, as if she knew she was betraying her daughter in some way, but didn't care to think about how.

Dolly burned inside; she wanted to shake her mother and remind her that she'd once been exceptional herself. She wanted to demand to know why she'd changed; tell her (though Dolly knew this bit was cruel) that she, Dolly, was frightened; that she couldn't bear to think the same thing might happen one day to her. But then –

'Watch out!'

A shriek came from the Bournemouth shoreline, drawing Dolly's attention to the water's edge and saving Janice Smitham from a conversation she didn't want to have.

There, in a bathing costume straight from *Vogue*, stood The Girl, previously of The Silver Dress. Her mouth was tightened to a pretty moue and she was rubbing her arm. The other beautiful people had clustered in a spectacle of tut-tutting and sympathetic posturing, and Dolly strained to understand what had happened. She watched as a boy of around her age stooped to scoop at the sand, as he righted himself and held aloft – Dolly's hand went gravely to her mouth – a cricket ball.

'So sorry, chaps,' Father said.

Dolly's eyes widened – what on earth was he doing now? Dear God, not making an approach, surely. But yes – her cheek burned – that's exactly what he was doing. Dolly wanted to disappear, to hide, but she couldn't look away. Father stopped when he reached the group and made a rudimentary mime of swinging the bat. The others nodded and listened, the boy with the ball said something and the girl touched her arm and then shrugged lightly and smiled those dimples at Father. Dolly exhaled; it seemed disaster had been averted.

But then, dazzled perhaps by the aura of glamour into

which he'd stumbled, Father forgot to leave, turning instead and pointing up the beach, directing the collective attention of the others to the patch where Dolly and her mother sat. Janice Smitham, with a deficit of grace that made her daughter cringe, started to stand before thinking better of it, failing to sit, and choosing instead to hover at a crouch. From this position she lifted a hand to wave.

Something inside Dolly curled up and died. Things could not have been worse.

Except that suddenly they were.

'Look here! Look at me!'

They looked. Cuthbert, with all the patience of a gnat, had grown tired of waiting. Cricket game forgotten, he'd wandered up the beach and made contact with one of the seaside donkeys. One foot already in a stirrup, he was struggling to hoist himself atop. It was awful to watch, but watch Dolly did; watch – a sneaking glance confirmed it – did everybody.

The spectacle of Cuthbert weighing that poor donkey down was the last straw. She knew she probably should have helped him, but Dolly couldn't, not this time. She muttered something about her headache and too much sun, swept up her magazine, and hurried back towards the grim solace of her tiny room with its stingy drainpipes view.

Back behind the bandstand, a young man with longish hair and a shabby suit had seen it all. He'd been dozing beneath his hat when the cry of 'Watch out!' cut through his dream and woke him. He'd rubbed his eyes with the heels of his hands and glanced about to pinpoint the source of the cry, and that's when he'd seen them by the foreshore, the father and son who'd been playing cricket all morning.

There'd been some sort of a kerfuffle and the father was waving at a group in the shallows – the rich young people, he realized, who'd been making so much of themselves at the nearby bathing hut. The hut was empty now, but for a swathe of silver fabric fluttering from the balcony rail. The dress. He'd noticed it earlier – it had been hard not to, which was no doubt the point. It wasn't a beach dress, that one; it belonged on a dance floor.

'Look here!' someone called. 'Look at me!' And the young man duly looked. The lad who'd been playing cricket was busy now making a donkey of himself, with, it would appear, a donkey. The rest of the crowd was watching the entertainment unfold.

Not him, though. He had other things to do. The pretty girl with heart-shaped lips and the sort of curves that made him ache with longing was by herself now, leaving her family and heading away from the beach. He stood up, swinging his haversack over his shoulder and pulling his hat down low. He'd been waiting for an opportunity like this one and he didn't intend to waste it.

Eight

Dolly didn't see him at first. She didn't see much of anything. She was far too busy blinking back tears of humiliation and despair as she trudged along the beach towards the promenade. Everything was a hot angry blur of sand and seagulls and hateful smiling faces. She knew they weren't laughing at her, not really, but it didn't matter one jot. Their jolliness was a personal blow; it made everything a hundred times worse. Dolly couldn't go to work at that bicycle factory, she just couldn't. Marry a younger version of her father and, bit by tiny bit, turn into her mother? It was inconceivable – oh, fine for the two of them, they were happy with their lot, but Dolly wanted more than that . . . she just didn't know yet what it was or where to find it.

She stopped short. A gust of wind, stronger than those that had come before it, chose the very moment of her arrival near the bathing huts to lift the satin dress, sweep it from the railing and send it scuttling across the sand. It came to rest right in front of her, a luxurious spill of silver. Why – she drew an incredulous breath – the blonde girl with the dimples mustn't have bothered to pin it down safely. But how could anybody care so little for such a beautiful piece of clothing? Dolly shook her head; a girl with such scant regard for her own possessions hardly deserved to have them. It was the sort of thing a princess might have worn – or an American film star, a fashion model in a magazine, an heiress on holidays in the French Riviera – and if Dolly hadn't come along right then it might've continued its flight across the dunes and been lost forever.

The wind returned and the dress rolled further up the beach, disappearing behind the bathing huts. Without another moment's hesitation, Dolly started after it: the girl had been foolish, it was true, but Dolly wasn't about to let that divine piece of silver come to harm.

She could just imagine how grateful the girl would be when the dress was returned. Dolly would explain what had happened – taking care not to make the girl feel worse than she already did – and the pair of them would start to laugh and say what a close call it was, and the girl would offer Dolly a glass of cold lemonade, real lemonade, not the watery substitute Mrs Jennings served at Bellevue. They'd get to talking and discover they had an awful lot in common, and then finally the sun would slip in the sky and Dolly would say she really ought to be going and the girl would smile disappointedly, before brightening and reaching to stroke Dolly's arm. 'What if you join us here tomorrow morning?' she'd ask. 'Some of us are going to get together and play a bit of tennis on the sand. It'll be *such* a lark – do say you'll come.'

Hurrying now, Dolly rounded the corner of the bathing hut after the silver dress, only to find as she did so that it had already stopped its tumble, having run straight into the ankles of somebody else. It was a man in a hat, bending down now to pick up the dress, and as his fingers grasped the fabric, as grains of sand slid from the satin, with them went all Dolly's hopes.

For an instant Dolly honestly felt she could've murdered the man in the hat, happily torn him limb from limb. Her pulse beat furiously, her skin tingled and her vision glazed. She glanced back towards the sea: at her father, marching stonily towards poor flummoxed Cuthbert; at her mother, frozen still in that attitude of pained supplication; at the others, those with the blonde girl, laughing now, slapping their knees as they pointed out the ridiculous scene.

The donkey let loose a perplexed and pitiful braying, echoing Dolly's feelings so entirely that before she knew what she was doing she'd spluttered at the man, 'Hey there!' He was about to steal the blonde girl's dress and it was up to Dolly to stop him. 'You. What do you think you're doing?'

The man looked up, surprised, and when Dolly saw the handsome face beneath the hat she was momentarily knocked off course. She stood, drawing quick breaths, wondering what to do next, but as the man's mouth started to pull up at the sides in a suggestive way, she suddenly knew.

'I said – ' Dolly was lightheaded, strangely excited – 'what do you think you're doing? That dress isn't yours.'

The young man opened his mouth to speak, and as he did so a policeman by the unfortunate name of Constable Suckling – who'd been making his portly progress down the beach – arrived beside them.

Constable Basil Suckling had been perambulating the promenade all morning, keeping an eye fixed firmly on his beach. He'd noticed the dark-haired girl as soon as she arrived, and had been watching her closely ever since. He'd turned away only briefly over that blasted business with the donkey, but when he looked back the girl was gone. It had taken Constable Suckling a tense few minutes to find her again, behind the bathing huts, engaged in what looked to him suspiciously like heated discussion. Her companion none other than the rough young man who'd been lurking beneath his hat at the back of the bandstand all morning.

Hand resting on his truncheon, Constable Suckling jostled across the beach. The sand made progress more ungainly than he'd have liked, but he did his best. As he drew near he heard her say, 'That dress isn't yours.'

'Everything all right, then?' said the constable now, holding his stomach in a little tighter as he came to a stop. She was even prettier up close than he'd imagined. Bowtie lips with upturned outer corners. Peachy skin – smooth, he could tell just by looking, yielding. Glossy curls around a love-heart face. He added, 'This fellow's not bothering you, is he, miss?'

'Oh. Oh no, sir. Not at all.' Her face was flushed and Constable Suckling realized she was blushing. Not every day she met a man in uniform, he supposed. She really was quite charming. 'This gentleman was just about to return something to me.'

'Is that right?' He frowned at the young man, taking in the insolent expression, the jaunty way he carried himself, the high cheekbones and arrogant black eyes. Those eyes gave the lad a distinctly foreign look, an Irish look, and Constable Suckling narrowed his own. The young man shifted his weight and made a small sighing noise, the plaintive nature of which made the constable disproportionately cross. Louder this time, he said again, 'Is that right?'

Still there came no answer, and Constable Suckling's grip closed on his truncheon. He tightened his fingers around its familiar shaft. It was, he sometimes thought, the best partner he'd ever had, certainly the most abiding. His fingertips itched with pleasant memories and it was almost a disappointment when the young man, cowed, gave a nod.

'Well then,' the constable said. 'Hurry it up. Return the young lady's item to her. '

'Thank you, Constable,' she said. 'It's so kind of you.' And then she smiled again, setting off a not unpleasant shifting sensation in the constable's trousers. 'It blew away, you see.'

Constable Suckling cleared his throat and adopted his most policeman-like expression. 'Right then, miss,' he said, 'let's get you home, shall we? Out of the wind and out of danger's way.'

Dolly managed to extricate herself from Constable Suckling's dutiful care when they reached the front door of Bellevue. It had looked a little hairy for a while – there'd been talk of walking her inside and fetching her a nice cup of tea to 'settle her nerves' – but Dolly, after no small effort, convinced him that his talents were wasted on such menial tasks and he really should be getting back to his beat. 'After all, Constable, you must have so many people needing you to rescue them.'

She thanked him profusely – he held her hand a little longer than was strictly necessary in parting – and then Dolly made a great show of opening the door and heading inside. She closed it almost but not quite completely and watched through the gap as he strutted back to the promenade. Only when he'd become a pinprick in the distance did she stow the silver dress beneath a cushion and sneak out again, doubling back the way they'd come along the prom.

The young man was loitering, waiting for her, leaning against the pillar outside one of the smartest guesthouses. Dolly didn't so much as glance sideways at him as she passed, only kept walking, shoulders back, head held high. He followed her down the road – she could tell he was there – and into a small laneway that zigzagged away from the beach. Dolly could feel her heartbeat speeding up and, as the sounds of the seaside deadened against the cold stone walls of the buildings, she could hear it too. She kept walking, faster than before. Her plimsolls were scuffing on the tarmac, her breaths were growing short, but she didn't stop and she didn't look behind her. There was a spot she knew, a dark juncture where she'd been lost once as a little girl, hidden from the world as her mother and father called her name and feared the worst.

Dolly stopped when she reached it, but she didn't turn around. She stood there, very still, listening, waiting until he was right behind her, until she could feel his breath on the back of her neck, his very closeness heating her skin.

He took her hand and she gasped. She let him turn her slowly to face him, and she waited, wordless, as he lifted her inner wrist to his mouth and brushed across it the sort of kiss that made her shiver from way down deep inside.

'What are you doing here?' she whispered.

His lips were still touching her skin. 'I missed you.'

'It's only been three days.'

He shrugged, and that lock of dark hair that refused to stay put fell forward across his forehead.

'You came by train?'

He gave a slow single nod.

'Just for the day?'

Another nod, half a smile.

'Jimmy! But it's such a long way.'

'I had to see you.'

'What if I'd stayed with my family on the beach? What if I hadn't headed back alone, what then?'

'I still would've seen you, wouldn't I?'

Dolly shook her head, pleased but pretending not to be. 'My father will kill you if he finds out.'

'I reckon I can take him.'

Dolly laughed; he always made her laugh. It was one of the things she liked best about him. 'You're mad.'

'About you.'

And then there was that. He was mad about her. Dolly's stomach turned a somersault. 'Come on then,' she said. 'There's a path through here that leads out into fields. No one will see us there.'

'You realize, of course, that you could've got me arrested?'

'Oh, Jimmy! Don't be silly.'

'You didn't see the look on that policeman's face – he was ready to lock me up and throw away the key. And don't get me started on the way he was looking at you.' Jimmy turned his head to face her, but she didn't meet his eyes. The grass was long and soft where they were lying and she was staring up at the sky, humming some dance tune beneath her breath and making diamond shapes with her fingers. Jimmy traced her profile with his gaze – the smooth arc of her forehead, the dip between her brow that rose again to form that determined nose, the sudden drop and then the full scoop of her top lip. God, she was beautiful. She made his whole body yearn and ache, and it took every bit of restraint he had not to jump on top of her, pin her arms behind her head and kiss her like a madman.

But he didn't, he never did, not like that. Jimmy kept it chaste even though it damn near killed him. She was still a schoolgirl, and he a grown man, nineteen years to her seventeen. Two years might not seem a lot, but they came from different worlds, the two of them. She lived in a nice clean house with her nice clean family; he'd been out of school since he was thirteen, taking care of his dad and working at whatever lousy job he could get to make ends meet. He'd been a lather boy at the barber's for five shillings a week, the baker's lad for seven and sixpence, a heavy lifter on the construction site out of town for whatever they would give him; then home each night to put the butcher's gristly odds and ends together for his dad's tea. It was a life, they did fine. He'd always had his photographs for pleasure; but now, somehow, for reasons Jimmy didn't understand and didn't want to unravel for fear of wrecking everything, he had Dolly too, and the world was a brighter place; he sure as hell wasn't going to move too fast and spoil things.

It was hard, though. From the first moment he'd seen her, sitting with her friends at a table in the street-corner cafe, he'd been a goner. He'd looked up from the delivery he was making for the grocer, and she'd smiled at him, just like they were old friends, and then she'd laughed and blushed into her cup of tea, and he'd known that if he lived to be a hundred years old he'd never see a more beautiful vision. It had been the electric thrill of love at first sight. That laugh of hers that made him feel the pure joy he remembered from being a kid; the way she smelled of warm sugar and baby oil; the swell of her breasts beneath her light cotton dress – Jimmy shifted his head with frustration, and concentrated on a noisy gull as it flew low overhead towards the sea.

The horizon was a faultless blue, the breeze was light, and the scent of summer was everywhere. He sighed and with it let the whole thing drift away – the silver dress, the policeman, the indignity he'd felt at being cast as some sort of threat to her. There was no point. The day was too perfect to argue, and no harm had come of it anyway, not really. No harm ever did. Dolly's games of 'Let's pretend' confused him, he didn't understand the urge she had to make believe and he didn't especially like it, but it made her happy so Jimmy went along with it.

As if to prove to Dolly that he'd put the whole thing behind him, Jimmy sat up suddenly and dug out his faithful Brownie from his haversack. 'How about a picture?' he said, winding on the spool of film. 'A little memento of your sea-side rendezvous, Miss Smitham?' She perked up, just as he'd hoped she would – Dolly loved having her photograph taken – and Jimmy glanced about for the sun's position. He walked to the far side of the small field in which they'd had their picnic.

Dolly had pushed herself up to sitting and was stretching like a cat. 'Like this?' she said. Her cheeks were flushed from the sun, and her bow lips plump and red from the strawberries he'd bought at a roadside stall.

'Perfect,' he said, and she really was. 'Nice light.'

'And what precisely would you like me to *do* in the nice light?'

Jimmy rubbed his chin and pretended to consider this deeply. 'What do I want you to do? Answer carefully now, Jimmy boy, this is your chance, don't blow it ... Think, damn it, think ... '

Dolly laughed, and he did too. And then he scratched his head and said, 'I want you to be you, Doll. I want to remember today just as it is. If I can't see you for another ten days, at least I can carry you round in my pocket.'

She smiled, a small enigmatic twitch of the lips, and then nodded. 'Something to remember me by.'

'Exactly,' he called. 'Won't be a minute now, I'll just fix the settings.' He dropped down the Diway lens and, because the sunshine was so bright, pulled up the lever for a smaller aperture. Better to be safe than sorry. By the same token, he took the lens cloth from his pocket and gave the glass a good rub.

'All right,' he said, closing one eye and looking down into the viewfinder. 'We're read—' Jimmy fumbled the camera box, but he didn't dare look up.

Dolly was staring at him from the middle of the viewfinder. Her hair fell in wind-loosened waves that kissed her neck, but beneath it she'd unbuttoned her dress and slipped it from her shoulders. Without taking her eyes from the camera she started peeling the strap of her bathing suit slowly down her arm.

Christ. Jimmy swallowed. He should say something; he knew he should say something. Make a joke, be witty, be clever. But in the face of Dolly, sitting there like that, her chin lifted, her eyes issuing him a challenge, the curve of her breast exposed – well, nineteen years of speech evaporated in an instant. Without his wit to help him, Jimmy did the one thing he could always rely on. He took his shot.

'Just make sure you develop them yourself,' said Dolly, buttoning up her dress with trembling fingers. Her heart was racing and she felt bright and alive, strangely powerful. Her own daring, the look on his face when he'd seen her, the way he was still having trouble meeting her eyes without blushing – it was intoxicating, all of it. More than that, it was proof. Proof that she, Dorothy Smitham, was exceptional, just as Dr Rufus had said. She wasn't destined for the bicycle factory, of course she wasn't; her life was going to be extraordinary.

'You think I'd let any other man see you that way?' said Jimmy, paying extravagant attention to the straps of his camera.

'Not on purpose.'

'I'd kill him first.' He said it softly, and his voice cracked slightly under a burden of possession that made Dolly swoon. She wondered if he would. Did such things really happen? They didn't where Dolly came from, the semi-detached mock Tudors standing proud in their soulless new suburbs. She couldn't imagine Arthur Smitham rolling up his sleeves to defend his wife's honour; but Jimmy wasn't like Dolly's father. He was the opposite: a working man with strong arms and an honest face and the sort of smile that came from nowhere to make her stomach turn back-flips. She pretended not to hear, taking the camera from him and staring at it with a show of thoughtfulness.

Holding it in one hand, she glanced up playfully from beneath her lashes and said, 'You know, *this* is a very dangerous piece of equipment you carry, Mr Metcalfe. Just think of all the things you could capture that people would rather you didn't.'

'Like what?'

'Why,' she lifted her shoulder, 'people doing things they shouldn't, an innocent young schoolgirl being led astray by a more experienced man – just think what the girl's poor father would say if he knew.' She bit her bottom lip, nervous but trying not to let him see it, and leaned closer, almost – but not quite – touching his firm, sun-browned forearm. Electricity pulsed between them. 'A person could get themselves into rather a lot of trouble if they got on the wrong side of you and your Box Brownie.'

'Better make sure you stay on my good side then, hadn't you?' He shot her a smile beneath his hair, but it disappeared as quickly as it came.

He didn't look away and Dolly felt her breaths lighten. The atmosphere had altered around them. In that moment, under the intensity of his stare, everything had changed. The scales of control had tipped and Dolly was spinning. She swallowed, uncertain, but excited too. Something was going to happen, something she had set in motion, and she was helpless to stop it. She didn't want to stop it.

A noise then, a small sigh from between his parted lips, and Dolly swooned.

His eyes were still fixed on hers and he reached to brush her hair behind her ear. He kept his hand where it was but tightened his grip, holding firmly to the back of her neck. She could feel his fingers shaking. The proximity made her feel young suddenly, out of her depth, and Dolly opened her mouth to say something (to say what?), but he shook his head, a single quick movement, and she shut it. A muscle in his jaw twitched; he drew breath; and then he pulled her towards him.

Dolly had imagined being kissed a thousand times, but she'd never dreamed of this. In the cinema, between Katharine Hepburn and Fred MacMurray, it looked pleasant enough, and Dolly and her girlfriend Caitlin had practised on their arms so they'd know what to do when the time came, but this was different. This had heat and weight and urgency; she could taste sun and strawberries, smell the salt on his skin, feel the press of heat as his body moved against her own. Most thrilling of all, she could tell how badly he wanted her, his ragged breaths, his strong muscled body, taller than hers, bigger, straining against its own desire.

He pulled back from the kiss and opened his eyes. He laughed then, in relief and surprise, a warm husky sound. 'I love you, Dorothy Smitham,' he said, resting his forehead against hers. He pulled gently at one of the buttons on her dress. 'I love you and I'm going to marry you one day.'

Dolly said nothing as they walked down the grassy hill, but her mind was racing. He was going to ask her to marry him: the trip to Bournemouth, the kiss, the strength of what she'd felt . . . What else could it all mean? The realization had come with overwhelming clarity, and now she yearned for him to say the words out loud, to make it official. Even her toes tingled with longing.

It was perfect. She was going to marry Jimmy. How had it not been the first thing she thought of when her mother asked her what she wanted to do instead of starting work at

Father's factory? It was the *only* thing she wanted to do. The very thing she *must*.

Dolly glanced sideways, noting the happy distraction on his face, his unusual silence, and she knew he was thinking the same thing; that he was busy even now, working out the very best way to ask her. She felt elated; she wanted to skip and twirl and dance.

It wasn't the first time he'd said he wanted to marry her; they'd teased around the topic before, whispered conversations of 'Imagine if . . .' at the back of dim cafes in the parts of town her parents never went to. She always found the subject deeply exciting; unspoken, but implicit in their playful descriptions of the farmhouse they'd live in and the life they'd have together, was the suggestion of closed doors, and a shared bed, and a promise of freedom – both physical and moral – that was irresistible to a schoolgirl like Dolly, whose mother still ironed and starched her uniform shirts.

Picturing the two of them like that made her giddy, and she reached for his arm as they left the sunlit fields and wound their way through the shaded alleyway. When she did, he stopped walking, and pulled her with him to stand against the stone wall of a nearby building.

He smiled in the shadows, nervously it seemed to her, and said, 'Dolly.'

'Yes.' It was going to happen. Dolly could hardly breathe.

'There's something I've been meaning to talk to you about, something important.'

She smiled then, and her face was so glorious in its openness and expectation that Jimmy's chest burned. He couldn't believe he'd finally done it, kissed her like he wanted to, and it had been every bit as sweet as he'd imagined. Best of all was the way she'd kissed him back; there was a future in that kiss. They might come from opposite sides of town, but they weren't so different, not where it counted; not in the way they felt about each other. Her hands were soft within his own as he said what he'd been turning over in his mind all day. 'I had a phone call the other day from London, a fellow called Lorant.'

Dolly nodded encouragingly.

'He's starting a magazine called *Picture Post* – a journal dedicated to printing images that tell stories. He saw my photographs in the *Telegraph*, Doll, and he's asked me to come and work for him.'

He waited for her to squeal, to jump, to clutch at his arms with excitement. It was everything he'd dreamed of doing, ever since he'd first found his father's old camera and tripod in the attic, the box with the sepia photographs inside. But Dolly didn't move. Her smile was lopsided now, frozen in place. 'In London?' she said.

'Yes.'

'You're going to London?'

'Yes. You know, big palace, big clock, big smoke.'

He was trying to be funny, but Dolly didn't laugh; she blinked a couple of times and said on an exhalation, 'When?'

'September.'

'To live?'

'And work.' Jimmy faltered; something was wrong. 'A photographic journal,' he said vaguely, before frowning. 'Doll?'

Her bottom lip had begun to tremble and he thought she might be going to cry.

Jimmy was alarmed. 'Doll? What is it?'

She didn't cry, though. She flung her arms out to the sides and then brought them back to rest on her cheeks. 'We were going to be married.'

'What?'

'You said – and I thought – but then – '

She was cross with him, and Jimmy had no idea why. She was gesticulating with both hands now, her cheeks were pink, and she was speaking very quickly, her words a blur so that all he could make out was 'farmhouse' and 'Father' and then, oddly, 'bicycle factory'.

Jimmy tried to keep up, didn't succeed, and was feeling pretty bloody helpless when finally she gave an enormous sigh, planted her hands on her hips, and looked so spent, so indignant, that he couldn't think what to do except take her in his arms and smooth her hair as he might have done with a cranky child. It could have gone either way, so he smiled to himself as he felt her calming down. Jimmy walked a pretty steady emotional line and Dolly's passions caught him off guard sometimes. They were intoxicating, though: she was never pleased if she could be delighted, never annoyed if she could be furious.

'I thought you wanted to marry me,' she said, lifting her face to look at him, 'but you're going to London instead.'

Jimmy couldn't help laughing. 'Not *instead*, Doll. Mr Lorant is going to pay me, and I'm going to save everything I can. I want to marry you more than anything – are you kidding? I just want to be sure and do it right.'

'But it *is* right, Jimmy. We love each other; we want to be together. The farmhouse – the fat hens and a hammock and the two of us dancing together in bare feet . . .'

Jimmy smiled. He'd told Dolly all about his father's childhood on the farm, the same adventure stories that had used to thrill him as a boy, but she'd embroidered them and made them her very own. He loved the way she could take a simple truth and turn it into something wonderful with the gleaming threads of her incredible imagination. Jimmy reached out to cup her cheek. 'I can't afford the farmhouse yet, Doll.'

'A gypsy caravan, then. With daisies on the curtains. And one hen . . . maybe two so they don't get lonely.'

He couldn't help it: he kissed her. She was young, she was romantic, and she was his. 'Not long, Doll, and we're going to have all the things we've dreamed about. I'm going to work so hard – you just wait and see.'

A pair of squawking gulls cut through the alley overhead, and he reached for her, running his fingers down her sun-warmed arms. She let him take her by the hand and he squeezed it firmly, leading her back towards the sea. He loved Dolly's dreams, her infectious spirit; Jimmy had never felt so alive as he had since he met her. But it was up to him to be sensible about their future, to be wise enough for the two of them. They couldn't both fall prey to fancies and dreams; no good would come of that. Jimmy was smart, all his teachers had told him so, back when he was still in school, before his dad took a turn for the worse. He was a quick learner, too; he borrowed books from the Boots lending library and had almost read his way through it. All he'd been lacking was an opportunity, and now, finally, one had come his way.

They walked the rest of the alleyway in silence until the prom came into view, brimming with afternoon sea-goers, their shrimp-paste sandwiches all finished now, and returning to the sand. He stopped and took Dolly's other hand, too, slotting his fingers between hers. 'So,' he said softly.

'So.'

'I'll see you in ten days.'

'Not if I see you first.'

Jimmy smiled, and leaned to kiss her goodbye, but a child ran by just then, shouting and chasing a ball that had rolled into the alley, and the moment was spoiled. He pulled back, oddly embarrassed by the boy's intrusion.

Dolly gestured with her body towards the promenade. 'I guess I should be getting back.'

'Try to stay out of trouble, won't you?'

She laughed, and then planted a kiss square on his lips. With a smile that made him ache, she ran back towards the light, the hem of her dress flicking against her bare legs.

'Doll,' he called after her, just before she disappeared. She turned, and the sun behind made her hair seem like a dark halo. 'You don't need fancy clothes, Doll. You're a thousand times more beautiful than that girl today.'

She smiled at him – at least he thought she did; it was difficult to tell with her face in shadow – and then she lifted a hand and waved and she was gone.

What with the sun and the strawberries and the fact that he'd had to run to make his train, Jimmy slept for most of the return journey. He dreamed of his mother, the same old chestnut he'd been having for years now. They were at the fair, the two of them, watching the magic show. The magician had just closed his pretty assistant inside the box (which always bore a rather striking resemblance to the coffins his father made downstairs at W. H. Metcalfe & Sons, Undertaker and Toymaker) when his mother bent down and said, 'He'll try to get you to look away, Jim. It's all about distracting the audience. Don't you look away.' Jimmy, eight years old or so, nodded earnestly, widening his eyes and refusing to let them blink, even when they began to water so badly that it hurt. But he must've done something wrong, for the door to the box swung open and – poof! – the woman had gone, vanished, and Jimmy had somehow missed the whole thing. His mother laughed, and it made him feel queer, all cold and juddery in his limbs, but when he looked for her she was no longer beside him. She was inside the box now, telling him that he must've been day-dreaming, and her perfume was so strong that—

'Tickets, please.'

Jimmy woke with a start and his hand went straight to his haversack on the seat beside him. It was still there. Thank God. Foolish of him to fall asleep like that, especially when his camera was inside. He couldn't afford to lose it; Jimmy's camera was his key to the future.

'I said tickets, sir.' The inspector's eyes narrowed to slits.

'Yes, sorry. Just a minute.' He dug it out of his pocket and handed it over for punching.

'Continuing on to Coventry?'

'Yes, sir.'

With a whiff of regret that he hadn't, after all, uncovered a fare cheat, the inspector handed back Jimmy's ticket and rapped his hat before moving along the carriage.

Jimmy took his library book from his haversack, but he didn't read it. He was too het up with memories of Dolly and the day, thoughts of London and the future, to concentrate on *Of Mice and Men*. He was still a little confused as to what had happened between them. He'd meant to impress her with his news, not make her upset – there was something almost sacrilegious in disappointing a person as spirited and glowing as Doll was – but Jimmy knew he'd done the right thing.

She didn't want to marry a man with nothing, not really. Doll loved 'things': trinkets and pretties and keepsakes to collect. He'd watched her today, and he'd seen her looking at the people in the bathing hut, the girl in the silver dress; he knew that whatever her fantasies about the farmhouse, she longed for excitement and glamour and all the things money could buy. Of course she did. She was beautiful and funny and charming; she was seventeen years old. Dolly didn't know what it was to go without, and neither should she. She deserved a man who could offer her the very best of everything, not a lifetime of butcher's leftovers got on the cheap and a drop of condensed milk in her tea when they couldn't stretch to sugar. Jimmy was working hard to become that man, and as soon as he did, by God, he was going to marry her and never let her go.

But not until then.

Jimmy knew first-hand what happened to people with nothing who married for love. His mother had disobeyed her wealthy father to marry Jimmy's dad, and for a time the two of them had been blissfully happy. But it hadn't lasted.

Jimmy could still remember his confusion when he woke up to find his mother gone. 'Just up and disappeared,' he'd heard people whispering in the street; and Jimmy had thought of that magic show they'd seen together only the other week. He'd marvelled, picturing his mother disappearing, the warm flesh of her body disintegrating into particles of air before his eyes. If anyone was capable of such magic, Jimmy decided, it was his mother.

As with so many of the great matters of childhood, it was his peers who showed him the light, long before a kindly adult thought to do the same. *Little Jimmy Metcalfe got a bolter for a mum; ran off with a rich man, left poor Jim without a crumb.* Jimmy brought the rhyme home from the school playground, but his dad had very little to say on the matter; he'd grown thin and tired-looking, and had started spending a lot of time by the window, pretending he was waiting on the postman with an important business letter. He just kept patting Jimmy's hand and saying they'd be all right, that the two of them would muddle through, that they still had each other. It had made Jimmy nervous the way his father kept saying that, as if he were trying to convince himself, and not his son at all.

Jimmy leaned his forehead against the train window and watched the tracks whizz by beneath him. His father. The old man was the only sticking point in his plans for London. He couldn't be left alone in Coventry, not these days, but he was sentimental about the house where Jimmy had grown up. Lately, with his dad's mind wandering the way it did, Jimmy sometimes found the old boy setting the table for Jimmy's mother, or worse, sitting at the window as he'd used to, waiting for her to come home.

The train pulled into Waterloo station and Jimmy slung his haversack over his shoulder. He'd find a way. He knew he would. The future stretched ahead, and Jimmy was determined to be equal to it. Holding tightly to his camera, he leapt from the carriage and headed for the underground to catch the train back to Coventry.

Dolly, meanwhile, was standing in front of the wardrobe mirror in her room at Bellevue, draped in a magnificent piece of silver satin. She was going to return it later, of course, but it would've been a crime not to try it on first. She straightened, and stood for a moment watching herself. The rise and fall of her breasts as she breathed, the contours of her décolletage, the way the dress rippled with life across her skin. It was like nothing she'd worn before, like nothing in her mother's stodgy wardrobe. Not even Caitlin's mother had a dress like this. Dolly was transformed.

She wished Jimmy could see her now, like this. Dolly touched her lips and her breath hitched at the memory of his kiss, the weight of his eyes upon her, the way he'd looked when he took her photograph. It had been her first proper kiss. She was a different person now from the one she'd been this morning. She wondered if her parents would notice, whether it was apparent to everyone that a man like Jimmy, a grown man with rough edges and work-hardened hands and a job in London taking photographs, had looked at her with hunger and kissed her like he meant it.

Dolly smoothed the dress over her hips. Smiled a slight greeting to an invisible acquaintance. Laughed at a silent joke. And then, with a swirl, she let herself fall back across the narrow bed, arms wide. 'London' – she said it out loud

to the paint that was peeling in curls off the ceiling. Dolly
had made a decision and the excitement was almost enough
to kill her. She was going to go to London; she'd tell her
parents as soon as the holiday was over and they all went
back to Coventry. Mother and Father would hate the idea,
but it was Dolly's life and she refused to bow to convention;
she didn't belong in a bicycle factory; she was going to do
exactly what she wanted. There was adventure waiting for
her out there in the big wide world: Dolly just had to go
and find it.

Nine

London, 2011

It was grey out, and gloomy, and Laurel was glad she'd brought her heavier coat. The documentary producers had offered to send a car, but she'd said no, the hotel wasn't far and she preferred to walk. She did, too. She enjoyed walking, always had, and it came these days with the added bonus that it kept the doctors happy. Today, though, she was particularly pleased to go by foot; with any luck the fresh air would help to clear her head. She felt unusually nervous about the afternoon's interview. Just thinking about the glaring lights, the unblinking eye of the camera, the amiable young journalist's questions, drove Laurel's fingers into her bag for a cigarette. So much for keeping the doctors happy.

She stopped on the corner of Kensington Church Street to strike a match, glancing at her watch as she shook the flame away. They'd finished the film's rehearsal ahead of schedule and the interview wasn't until three. She drew thoughtfully on her cigarette; if she hurried, there was still time to make a little detour along the way. Laurel glanced towards Notting Hill. It wasn't far, it wouldn't take long; nonetheless she vacillated. She sensed herself at a crossroads of sorts, a raft of shadowy implications lurking behind the seemingly simple decision. But no, she was overthinking it – of course she should go and take a look. It would be silly not to, having found herself so near. Hugging her handbag close, she started briskly away from the High Street. ('Clip along, loves,' their mother used to say, 'don't dilly-dally.' Just because the words amused her.)

Laurel had caught herself staring at her mother's face during the birthday party, as if she might find answers to the riddle written there. (How did you know Henry Jenkins, Ma? I take it you weren't good friends.) They'd held the party on Thursday morning in the hospital garden – the weather had been fine and, as Iris pointed out, after the sorry excuse for a summer they'd had it would've been a crime not to take advantage of the sunshine.

Such a wonderful face, their mother's. As a younger woman she'd been beautiful, far more beautiful than Laurel, more so than any of her daughters, with the possible exception of Daphne. She certainly wouldn't have had directors pushing *her* towards character roles. But one thing you could bank on was that, beauty – the sort that came with youth – didn't last, and their mother had grown old. Her skin had sagged, spots had appeared, along with mysterious puckers and discolorations; her bones had seemed to subside as the rest of her shrank and her hair frayed to nothing. But still that face remained, every aspect bright with mischief, even now. Her eyes, though tired, had the glint of one who never stopped expecting to be amused, and her mouth turned up at the corners as if she'd just remembered a joke. It was the sort of face that drew strangers, that enchanted them and made them want to know her better. The way she had of making you feel, with a slight twitch of the jaw, that she too had suffered as you did, that everything would be better now simply for having come within her orbit: that was her real beauty – her presence, her joy, her magnetism. That, and her splendid appetite for make-believe.

'My nose is far too big for my face,' she'd said once when Laurel was small and watching her dress for something or other. 'My God-given talents were wasted. I'd have made a fine *parfumier*.' She'd turned from the mirror then and given the sort of playful smile that always made Laurel's heart beat a little faster in anticipation. 'Can you keep a secret?'

Laurel, sitting on the end of her parents' bed, had nodded, and her mother had leaned forward so that the tip of her nose touched Laurel's own little button. 'That's because I used to be a crocodile. A long time ago, before I became a mummy.'

'Did you really?' Laurel said with a gasp.

'Yes, but it became rather tiresome. All that snapping and swimming. And tails can be very heavy, you know, especially when they're wet.'

'Is that why you changed to become a lady?'

'No, not at all. Heavy tails aren't pleasant, but they're no reason to shirk one's duties. One day I was lying on the banks of a river—'

'In Africa?'

'Of course. You didn't think we had crocodiles here in England, did you?'

Laurel shook her head.

'There I was, sunning myself, when a little girl wandered by with her mummy. They were holding hands and I realized that I should very much like to do the same thing.

So I did. I became a person. And then I had you. It all worked out rather well, I have to say, except for this nose.'

'But how?' Laurel blinked wondrously. 'How did you turn into a person?'

'Well now.' Dorothy returned to the mirror and straightened her shoulder straps. 'I can't tell you all my secrets, can I? Not all at once. Ask me again some day. When you're older.'

Ma always did have an imagination. 'Well, she had to, hadn't she,' said Iris with a snort as she drove them home from the birthday party. 'All of us to put up with. A lesser woman would've gone stark raving mad.' Which, Laurel had to concede, was true. She knew she would have. Five children squawking and squabbling, a farmhouse that dripped somewhere new each time it rained, birds nesting in the chimneys. It was like some kind of nightmare.

Except that it hadn't been. It had been perfect. The sort of home life that was written about by sentimental novelists in the type of books branded nostalgic by critics. (Until that whole business with the knife. *That's more like it*, the critics would've puffed.) Laurel could vaguely remember rolling her eyes from the depths of her teenage glooms, and wondering how anyone could be content with such a dull domestic lot. The word bucolic hadn't been invented then, not for Laurel, who was far too busy in 1958 with Kingsley Amis to bother with *The Darling Buds of May*. But she hadn't wanted her parents to change. Youth is an arrogant place, and to believe simply that they were less adventurous than she was had suited Laurel just fine. Not for a moment had she considered that there might be anything beyond

Ma's appearance as a happy wife and mother; that she might have been young once herself, and determined not to turn into her own mother; that she might even be hiding from something in her past.

Now, though, the past was everywhere. It had seized Laurel in the hospital when she saw the photo of Vivien, and it hadn't let go since. It waited for her around every corner; it muttered in her ear by dead of night. It was cumulative, gathering weight each day, bringing with it bad dreams and knives that glistened, and little boys with tin rockets and the promise of going back, of fixing things. She couldn't concentrate properly on anything else, not the film that was due to start production next week, nor the documentary interview series she was recording. Nothing seemed to matter except learning the truth about her mother's secret past.

And there *was* a secret past. If Laurel hadn't been sure enough already, Ma had all but confirmed it. At her ninetieth birthday party, as her three great-granddaughters wove necklaces from daisies, and her grandson tied a hanky round his own son's bleeding knee, and her daughters made sure everyone had cake and tea enough, and someone shouted, 'Speech! Speech!', Dorothy Nicolson had smiled beatifically. The late-flowering roses blushed on the bushes behind her and she clasped her hands together, idly rolling the rings that fell now loosely around her knuckles. And then she sighed. 'I'm so fortunate,' she said, in a slow rickety voice. 'Look at all of you, look at my children. I'm so thankful, so lucky to have . . .' Her old lips had trembled then, and her eyelids fluttered shut, and the others had rushed around her with kisses and cries of 'Dearest, darling

Mummy!' so they'd missed it when she said, '. . . a second chance.'

But Laurel had heard it. And she'd stared harder at Ma's lovely, tired, familiar, secretive face. Scouring it for answers. Answers she knew were there to be found. Because people who'd led dull and blameless lives did not give thanks for second chances.

Laurel turned into Campden Grove and met a large drift of leaves. The street-sweeper hadn't been around yet and she was glad. She crunched through the thickest clump and time looped back upon itself so she was both here and now, and eight years old again, playing in the woods behind Greenacres. 'Fill the bag right to the top, girls. We want our flames to reach the moon.' That was Ma, and it was Bonfire Night. Laurel and Rose in wellington boots and scarves, Iris a bundled baby blinking from the pushchair. Gerry, who would come to love the woods best of all, was but a whisper, a distant firefly in the rosy sky. Daphne, also unborn, was making her presence felt, swimming and swirling and leaping in their mother's belly: *I'm here! I'm here! I'm here!* ('That happened when you were dead,' they used to tell her when conversation turned to something from before she was born. The suggestion of death hadn't bothered her, but the idea that the whole noisy show had been rolling along without her scorched.)

Halfway along the street, just past Gordon Place, Laurel stopped. There it was, number 25. Wedged between 24 and 26, just as it should be. The house itself was much like the others, white Victorian with black iron railings on the first-floor balcony and a dormer window in the shallow slate roof. A baby's pram, the sort that looked as if it might well double as a lunar module, was sitting on the tessellated-tile front path, and a garland of Halloween pumpkin heads, drawn by a child, had been strung across the ground-floor window. There was no blue plaque on the front, only the street number. Evidently no one had seen fit to suggest to English Heritage that Henry Ronald Jenkins's tenure at 25 Campden Grove should be marked for posterity. Laurel wondered if the current residents knew that their house had once belonged to a famous writer. Probably not, and why should they? Lots of people in London lived in a house that could lay claim to having once been lived in by a Somebody, and Henry Jenkins's fame had been fleeting.

Laurel had found him on the Internet, though. Opposite problem there – one couldn't disentangle oneself from that net for all the love and money in England. Henry Jenkins was one of millions of ghosts who lived inside it, milling wraithlike until the right combination of letters was entered and they were briefly resurrected. At Greenacres, Laurel had made a tentative attempt to surf the Web on her new phone, but just as she'd worked out where she was supposed to enter the search terms, the battery had died. Borrowing Iris's laptop for such clandestine purposes was out of the question, so she'd spent her final hours in Suffolk in silent excruciation, helping Rose scrub mould from the bathroom grout.

When Mark, the driver, came as arranged on Friday, they'd made affable small talk about the traffic, the coming theatre season, the likelihood of the roadworks being finished in time for the Olympics, all the way back down the M11. Safely arrived in London, Laurel had forced herself to stand in the dusk with her suitcase, waving goodbye until the car disappeared from sight, and then she'd gone calmly up the stairs, unlocked the flat without a hint of key fumbling, and let herself in. She'd closed the door quietly behind her and then, only then, in the safety of her very own sitting room, had she let the suitcase and the facade drop. Without even pausing to switch on the lights, she'd fired up her laptop and typed his name into Google. In the fraction of time it took for results to appear, Laurel became a nail-biter again.

The Henry Jenkins Wikipedia page wasn't detailed, but it provided a bibliography and a brief biography (born Yorkshire, 1901; married in Oxford, 1938; lived at 25 Campden Grove, London, died Suffolk, 1961); his novels were listed on a few second-hand bookstore sites (Laurel ordered two); and he was mentioned on pages as varied as the 'Nordstrom School Alumni List' and 'Stranger than Fiction: Mysterious Literary Deaths'. Laurel was able to glean some information about his writing – fiction that was semi-autobiographical; a focus on bleak settings and working-class anti-heroes, until his breakthrough love story in 1939 – and that he'd worked for the Ministry of Information during the war, but there was far more material about his unmasking as the Suffolk Summer Picnic Stalker. She pored over it, page by page, teetering on the rim of panic as she waited for a familiar name or address to leap out and bite her.

It didn't happen. No mention anywhere of Dorothy Nicolson, mother of Oscar-winning actress and the Nation's (second) Favourite Face, Laurel Nicolson; no more specific geographical reference than 'a meadow outside Lavenham,

Suffolk'; no salacious gossip as to birthday knives or crying babies or family parties by the stream. Of course. Of course there wasn't. The gentlemanly deceit of 1961 had been shored up nicely by the online history-makers: Henry Jenkins was an author who'd enjoyed success preceding the Second World War but found his star on the wane afterwards. He lost money, influence, friends, and eventually his sense of decency; what he managed to find, in turn, was infamy, and even that had now largely faded. Laurel read the same sorry story over and over again, and each time the pencil-drawn picture became more permanent. She almost started to believe the fiction herself.

But then she went one click too far. A seemingly innocuous link to a website titled 'The Imaginarium of Rupert Holdstock'. The photograph appeared onscreen like a face at the window: Henry Jenkins, unmistakable, though younger than when she'd watched him coming up the driveway. Laurel's skin flushed hot and cold. Neither of the newspaper articles she'd found when it happened had included a photograph and this was the first time she'd seen his face since that afternoon from the tree house.

She couldn't help it; she ran an image search. Within 0.27 seconds Google had assembled a screen tiled with identical photographs of marginally different proportions. Seeing them en masse made him look macabre. (Or was it her own associations doing that? The creak of the gate hinge; Barnaby's growl; the white sheet turned russet-red.) Row upon row of black and white portraits: formal attire, dark moustache, heavy brows framing an alarmingly direct gaze. 'Hello, Dorothy.' The multiple sets of thin lips seemed to move on the screen. 'It's been a long time.'

   Laurel slammed the laptop lid shut and cast the room
into darkness.

She'd refused to look at Henry Jenkins any longer, but she'd
thought about him, and she'd thought about this house, just
around the corner from her own, and when the first book
arrived by overnight mail and she sat up reading it from
cover to cover, she'd thought about her mother, too. *The
Sometime Maid* was the eighth novel by Henry Jenkins,
published in 1940 and detailing the love affair between a
respected author and his wife's maid-companion. The girl –
Sally, she was called – was something of a minx, and the
male protagonist a tortured fellow whose wife was beautiful
but cold. It wasn't a bad read, once one made allowance for
the stuffy prose: the characters were richly drawn and the
narrator's dilemma was timeless, particularly as Sally and
the wife became friends. The ending saw the narrator on the
verge of breaking off his affair, but agonizing over what the
repercussions might be. Poor girl had become hopelessly
obsessed with him, you see, and who could blame her? As
Henry Jenkins wrote himself, he – that is, the protagonist –
was quite a catch.

   Laurel looked again at the attic window of 25
Campden Grove. Henry Jenkins was known to have written
largely from life; Ma had worked for a time as a maid (that
was how she came to Grandma Nicolson's boarding house);
Ma and Vivien had been close; Ma and Henry Jenkins, in
the end, decidedly not. Was it drawing too long a bow to
think that Sally's story might be her mother's? That Dorothy
had at one time lived inside that little room up there
beneath the slate, that she'd fallen in love with her employer

and that she'd been let down? Would it explain what Laurel had witnessed at Greenacres, a scorned woman's fury and all that?

Perhaps.

As Laurel wondered how she was going to find out whether a young woman named Dorothy had worked for Henry Jenkins, the front door of number 25 – which was red; there was a lot to like about a person with a red front door – opened, and a noisy tangle of plump stockinged legs and knitted pom-pom beanies spilled out onto the pavement. Householders generally didn't appreciate strangers scoping out their homes, so she ducked her head and riffled through her bag, trying to look like a perfectly normal woman on an errand and not one who'd been chasing ghosts all afternoon. Like any nosy parker worth her salt, she still managed to keep an eye on the action, watching as a woman emerged, with a baby in a pram, three small people at her legs, and – good grief – another childish voice singing at her from somewhere back inside the house.

The woman was crab-stepping the pram towards the top of the stairs and Laurel hesitated. She was about to offer help when the fifth child, a boy, taller than the others but still no more than five or six years old, emerged from the house and took up the front. Together he and his mother carried the pram downstairs. The family set off towards Kensington Church Street, the little girls skipping ahead, but the boy lingered behind. Laurel watched him. She liked the way his lips moved slightly as if he might be singing to himself, and the way he was using his hands, flattening them out and then tilting his head to watch them undulate towards one another like floating leaves. He was utterly unaware of his surroundings and his focus made him be-witching. He reminded her of Gerry as a boy.

Darling Gerry. He'd never been ordinary, their brother. He hadn't spoken a word for the first six years of his life and people who didn't know him had often presumed he was backward. (People who *did* know the noisy Nicolson girls saw his silence as nothing other than inevitable.) Those strangers had been wrong, too. Gerry wasn't backward, he was smart – fiercely smart. Science smart. He collected facts and proofs, truths and theorems, and answers to questions Laurel hadn't even thought to ask, about time and space and the matter in between. When he did finally decide to communicate in words, out loud, it was to ask whether any of them had an opinion as to how engineers planned to help keep the Leaning Tower of Pisa from toppling over (it had been on the news some nights before).

'Julian!'

Laurel's memory dissolved and she looked up to see the little boy's mother calling to him, as if from another planet, 'Juju-bean.'

The boy guided his left hand into safe landing before looking up. His eyes met Laurel's and widened. Surprise at first, but then something else. Recognition, she knew; it happened a lot, if not always accompanied by realization. ('Do I know you? Have we met? Do you work at the bank?')

She nodded and started to leave, until, 'You're Daddy's lady,' the boy dead-panned.

'*Ju*-li-an.'

Laurel turned back to face the odd little man. 'What's that?'

'You're Daddy's lady.'

But before she could ask him what he meant, the lad was gone, tripping over his feet on his way to meet his mother, both hands sailing the invisible currents of Campden Grove.

Ten

Laurel hailed a taxi on Kensington High Street. 'Where to, love?' said the driver as she scrambled into the back and out of the sudden rain.

'Soho – Charlotte Street Hotel, thank you kindly.'

A pause ensued, accompanied by scrutiny in the rear-view mirror, and then, as the car lurched into traffic, 'You look familiar. What do you do, then?'

You're Daddy's lady – now what on earth did that mean? 'I work in a bank.'

As the driver launched an invective against bankers and the global credit crunch, Laurel pretended great focus on the screen of her mobile phone. She scrolled randomly through the names in her address book, stopping when she reached Gerry's.

He'd arrived late to Ma's party, scratching his head and trying to remember where he'd left her present. No one expected anything different from Gerry, and they were all as thrilled as ever to see him. Fifty-two now, but somehow still an adorable scatty boy wearing ill-fitting trousers and the brown slub jumper Rose had knitted him thirty Christmases before. A great fuss was made, the other sisters falling over one another as they fetched him tea and cake. And even Ma had woken from her doze, her tired old face briefly transformed by the dazzling smile of pure joy she'd been saving for her only son.

Of all her children, she missed him specially. Laurel knew this because the kinder nurse had told her so. She'd stopped Laurel in the hallway when they were setting up for the party and said, 'I was hoping to catch you.'

Laurel, always quick to raise her guard: 'What is it?'

'No need to panic, nothing awful. It's just your mum's been asking after someone. A fellow, I think. Jimmy? Would that be it? She wanted to know where he was, why he wasn't visiting.'

Laurel had considered the name and then shaken her head and told the nurse the truth. She couldn't think that Ma knew any Jimmies. She hadn't added that she was the wrong daughter to ask, that there were far more dutiful among the sisters. (Though not Daphne. Thank God for Daphne. In a family of daughters it was a happy thing not to be the worst.)

'Not to worry.' The nurse had smiled reassurance. 'She's been going in and out a bit lately. It's not unusual for them to get confused at the end.'

Laurel had flinched at the generic 'them', the ghastly bluntness of 'end', but Iris had appeared then with a faulty kettle and a frown for England, and so she'd let the matter go. It was only later, when she was sneaking a cigarette in the hospital portico, that Laurel had realized the mix-up, that of course *Gerry* was the name Ma was saying, and not Jimmy at all.

The driver swerved off the Brompton Road and Laurel clutched her seat. 'Building site,' he explained, skirting round the back of Harvey Nichols. 'Luxury apartments. Twelve months it's been, and still that bloody crane.'

'Irritating.'

'Sold most of 'em already, y'know. Four million quid a pop.' He whistled through his teeth. 'Four million quid – I'd buy m'self an island for that.'

Laurel smiled with what she hoped was not encouragement – she loathed being drawn into conversation about other people's money – and held her phone closer to her face.

She knew why she had Gerry on her mind, why she was spotting his likeness in the faces of strange little boys. They'd been close once, the pair of them, but things had changed when he was seventeen. He'd come to stay with Laurel in London on his way up to Cambridge (a full scholarship, as Laurel told everyone she knew, sometimes those she didn't) and they'd had fun – they always did. A daytime session of *Monty Python and the Holy Grail*, and then dinner from the curry house down the road. Later, riding a delectable tikka masala high, the two of them had climbed out through the bathroom window, dragging pillows and a blanket after them, and shared a joint on Laurel's roof.

The night was especially clear – stars, more stars than usual, surely? – and down on the street, the distant easy warmth of other people's revelry. Smoking made Gerry unusually garrulous, which was fine with Laurel because it made her wondrous. He'd been trying to explain the origins of everything, pointing to star clusters and galaxies and making explosion gestures with his delicate febrile hands, and Laurel had been squinting and making the stars blur and bend, letting his words run together like water. She'd been lost in a current of nebulas and penumbras and supernovas and hadn't realized his monologue was ended until she heard him say, '*Lol*' in that pointed way people have when they've already said the word more than once.

'Eh?' Closing one eye and then the other so the stars jumped across the sky.

'I've been meaning to ask you something.'

'Eh?'

'God.' He laughed. 'I've said this in my head so many times and now I can't get the bloody words out.' He pushed his fingers through his hair, frustrated, and made an airy animal noise. 'Humph. OK, here goes: I've been meaning to ask you if something happened, Lol, back when we were kids? Something . . .' He dropped his voice to a whisper. 'Something *violent*?'

She'd known then. Some sixth sense had made her pulse start rippling beneath her skin and she'd been hot all over. He remembered. They'd always presumed he was far too young, but he remembered.

'Violent?' She sat up but didn't turn to face him. She didn't think she could look into his eyes and lie. 'You mean aside from Iris and Daphne in a bid for the bathroom?'

He didn't laugh. 'I know it's stupid, only sometimes I get this feeling.'

'You get a *feeling*?'

'Lol—'

'Because if it's spooky feelings you want to talk about, it really should be Rose—'

'Jesus.'

'I could put a call through to the ashram if you like—'

He tossed a cushion at her. 'I'm bloody serious, Lol. It's doing my head in. I'm asking you because I know you'll tell me the truth.'

He smiled a little then, because seriousness wasn't something they did often or well, and Laurel thought for the millionth time how deeply she loved him. She knew for a fact that she couldn't have loved her own child more.

'It's like I'm remembering something, only I can't remember what it is. As if the event has gone but the feelings, the ugliness and the fear, shadows of them anyway, are still there. Do you know what I mean?'

Laurel nodded. She knew exactly what he meant.

'Well?' He lifted one shoulder uncertainly and then dropped it again, almost in defeat, although she hadn't disappointed him yet. 'Is there anything? Anything at all?'

What could she have said? The truth? Hardly. There were certain things one didn't tell one's baby brother no matter how tempting. Not on the eve of his going up to university, not on the roof of a four-storey building. Not even when it was suddenly the thing she wanted more than anything in the world to share with him. 'Nothing I can think of, G.'

He didn't ask again and he made no sign that he didn't believe her. After a time he went back to explaining stars and black holes and the beginning of everything, and Laurel's chest ached with love and something like regret. She made sure not to look too closely because there was something about his eyes, right then, that made her see the bonny little baby who'd cried when Ma put him down on the gravel beneath the wisteria, and she didn't think she could bear that.

The next day Gerry left for Cambridge, and there he remained, an award-winning, game-changing, universe-expanding honours student. They'd seen each other some-times, and written when they could – hastily scribbled accounts of backstage antics (her) and increasingly cryptic notes sketched on the back of cafeteria napkins (him) – but in some ungraspable way it was never the same again. A door she hadn't realized was open had closed. Laurel wasn't sure if it was just her, or whether he, too, discerned that a fault line had fractured silently across the surface of their friendship that night on the roof. She'd regretted it, the decision not to tell him, but not until much later. She'd thought she was doing the right thing, protecting him, but now she wasn't so sure.

'Right then, love. Charlotte Street Hotel. That'll be twelve quid.'

'Thank you.' Laurel put her phone into her handbag and gave the driver a ten and a five-pound note. It occurred to her now that Gerry might be the one person aside from their mother whom she might talk to about it; he'd been there, too, that day; they were tied, the two of them, to each other and to what they'd witnessed.

Laurel opened the door, almost hitting her agent, Claire, who was hovering on the pavement with an umbrella. 'Lord, Claire, you scared me,' she said as the taxi pulled away.

'All part of the service. How are you? All right?'

'Fine.'

They kissed cheeks and hurried into the dry and the

warmth of the hotel. 'The crew's still setting up,' said Claire, shaking out the umbrella. 'Lights and all that jazz. Would you like something in the restaurant while we wait? Tea or coffee?'

'A stiff gin?'

Claire raised a thin brow. 'You're not going to need it. You've done this a hundred times before and I'm going to sit in. If the journalist even looks like deviating from the brief I'll be all over him like a rash.'

'A pleasant thought indeed.'

'I'd make a rather good rash.'

'I don't doubt it.'

They'd just been served a pot of tea when a young girl with a ponytail and a shirt that said *Whatever* approached the table and announced that the crew was ready when they were. Claire waved over a waitress, who said she'd bring the tea things after them, and they took the lift up to the room.

'OK?' said Claire as the doors closed on reception.

'OK,' Laurel agreed, and she tried very hard to believe it.

The documentary team had booked the same room as before: it wasn't ideal to film a single conversation over the course of a week, and there was the small matter of continuity to think of (in whose service Laurel had brought with her, as instructed, the blouse she'd been wearing last time).

The producer met them at the door and the wardrobe manager directed Laurel to the ensuite, where an iron had been set up. The knot in her stomach tightened and perhaps it showed on her face, for Claire offered, 'Come with you, shall I?'

'Certainly not,' Laurel tossed back, forcing aside all

thoughts of Ma and Gerry and the dark secrets of the past. 'I should think I'm perfectly capable of dressing myself.'

The interviewer – 'Call me Mitch' – beamed when he saw her and gestured to the armchair by a vintage seamstress's mannequin. 'I'm so glad we could do this again,' he said, enclosing her hand inside both of his and pumping it keenly. 'We're all really excited by how it's coming together. I watched some of last week's footage – it's very good. Your episode's going to be one of the highlights in the series.'

'I'm pleased to hear it.'

'We don't need a lot today – there are just a few bits and pieces I'd like to cover, if that's OK with you? Just so we don't have any black spots when we cut the story together.'

'Of course.' There was nothing she'd rather do than explore her black spots, except perhaps root canal surgery.

Minutes later, made-up and miked up, Laurel arranged herself in the armchair and waited. Finally, the lights came on and an assistant compared the set-up with polaroids from the previous week; silence was called and someone held a clapperboard in front of Laurel's face. Snap went the crocodile.

Mitch leaned forwards in his seat.

'And we're rolling,' said the cameraman.

'Ms Nicolson,' Mitch began, 'we've spoken a lot about the highs and lows of your theatrical career, but what our viewers want to know is how their heroes were made. Can you tell me about your childhood?'

The script was straightforward enough; Laurel had written it herself. Once upon a time, in a farmhouse in the country, there lived a girl with a perfect family: lots of sisters, a baby brother, and a mother and father who loved each other almost as much as they loved their children. The girl's childhood was smooth and even, filled with long sunlit spaces and makeshift play, and when the nineteen fifties yawned to an end and the sixties began to swing, she took herself towards the bright lights of London and arrived on the wave of a cultural revolution. She'd been smiled upon by luck (gratitude played well in interviews), she'd refused to give up (only the glib ascribe all good fortune to chance), she hadn't been out of work since finishing drama school.

'Your childhood sounds idyllic.'

'I suppose it was.'

'Perfect, even.'

'No one's family is perfect.' Laurel's mouth felt dry.

'Do you think your childhood formed you as an actress?'

'I expect so. We are all shaped by that which came before. Isn't that what they say? They, who seem to know everything.'

Mitch smiled and scribbled something in the notebook on his knee. His pen scratched across the surface of the paper and as it did, Laurel experienced a jolt of memory. She was sixteen, and sitting in the Greenacres sitting room while a policeman wrote down every word she said—

'You were one of five siblings: was there a battle for attention? Did it force you to develop ways of being noticed?'

Laurel needed some water. She looked about for Claire, who seemed to have vanished. 'Not at all. Having so many sisters and a baby brother taught me how to disappear into

the background.' So adroitly, she could slip away from a
family picnic in the middle of a game of hide-and-seek.

'As an actor you could hardly be accused of disappearing into the background.'

'But acting isn't about being noticed or showing off, it's
about observation.' A man had said that to her once at the
stage door. She'd been leaving after a theatre session,
buzzing still with the high of performance, and he'd stopped
her to say how much he'd enjoyed it. 'You've a great talent
for observation,' he'd said. 'Ears, eyes and heart, all at once.'
The words had been familiar, a quote from some play or
other, but Laurel couldn't remember which one.

Mitch cocked his head. 'Are you a good observer?'

Such a strange thing to remember now, that man at
the stage door. The quote she couldn't place, so familiar, so
elusive. It had driven her mad for a time. It was doing a
good job of it now too. Her thoughts were jumbled. She
was thirsty. There was Claire, watching from the shadows
by the door.

'Ms Nicolson?'

'Yes?'

'Are you a good observer?'

'Oh yes. Yes, indeed.' Hidden in a tree house, quiet as
can be. Laurel's heart was racing. The warmth of the room,
all those people staring at her, the lights—

'You've said before, Ms Nicolson, that your mother was
a strong woman. She lived through the war, she lost her
family in the Blitz, she started again. Did you inherit her
strength, do you think? Is that what's enabled you to
survive, indeed to thrive, in a notoriously tough business?'

The next line was easy to deliver; Laurel had done so

many times before. Now, though, the words wouldn't come. She sat like a stunned mullet as they dried to sawdust in her mouth. Her thoughts were swimming – the house on Campden Grove, the smiling photograph of Dorothy and Vivien, her tired old mother in a hospital bed – and time thickened so that seconds passed like years. The cameraman straightened, the assistants began to whisper to one another, but Laurel sat trapped beneath the furious bright lights, unable to see past the glare, seeing instead her mother, the young woman in the photo who'd left London in 1941, running from something, looking for a second chance.

A touch on her knee. The young man, Mitch, with a concerned expression: did she need a break, would she like a drink, fresh air, was there anything at all he could do?

Laurel managed to nod. 'Water,' she said. 'A glass of water, please.'

And then Claire was by her side. 'What is it?'

'Nothing, just a little warm in here.'

'Laurel Nicolson, I'm your agent and, more to the point, one of your oldest friends. Let's try that again, shall we?'

'My mother,' said Laurel, tightening her lip as it threatened to quiver, 'she isn't well.'

'Oh, darling.' The other woman took up Laurel's hand.

'She's dying, Claire.'

'Tell me what you need.'

Laurel let her eyes close. She needed answers, the truth, to know for certain that her happy family, her entire childhood wasn't a lie. 'Time,' she said eventually. 'I need time. There isn't much left.'

Claire squeezed her hand. 'Then you shall have some.'

'But the film—'

'Don't give it another thought. I'll take care of that.'

Mitch arrived with a fresh glass of water. He hovered nervously while Laurel drank it.

Claire said, 'All right?' to Laurel and, when she nodded, turned to Mitch. 'Just one more question and then, regrettably, we'll have to call it a day. Ms Nicolson has another engagement to get to.'

'Of course.' Mitch swallowed. 'I hope I didn't . . . I certainly didn't mean any offence—'

'Don't be silly, none taken.' Claire smiled with all the warmth of an Arctic winter. 'Let's get on, shall we?'

Laurel set down the glass and readied herself. A great weight had lifted from her shoulders, replaced by the clarity of firm resolve: during the Second World War, as bombs rained down on London, and plucky residents mended and made do and spent their nights huddled together in leaky shelters, as they craved oranges and cursed Hitler and longed for an end to the devastation, as some found courage they'd never known before and others experienced fear they hadn't imagined, Laurel's mother had been one of them. She'd had neighbours, and probably friends, she'd traded coupons for eggs and been thrilled when she came by an occasional pair of stockings, and in the midst of it all her path had crossed that of Vivien and Henry Jenkins. A friend she would lose and a man she would one day kill.

Something terrible had happened between the three of them – it was the only explanation for the seemingly inexplicable – something horrific enough to justify what Ma had done. In what little time remained, Laurel intended to find out what that something was. It was possible she wouldn't like what she found, but that was a chance she was willing to take. It was one she *had* to take.

'Last question, Ms Nicolson,' said Mitch. 'We were speaking last week about your mother, Dorothy. You've said that she was a strong woman. She lived through the war, she lost her family in the Coventry Blitz, she married your father and started again. Did you inherit her strength, do you think? Is that what's enabled you to survive, indeed to thrive, in a notoriously tough business?'

This time Laurel was ready. She delivered the line perfectly, no need at all for the prompt. 'My mother was a survivor; she's a survivor still. If I've inherited half her courage, I can count myself a very lucky woman.'

Part Two

DOLLY

Eleven

'Too hard, silly girl. Too, damn, hard!' The old woman brought down the handle of her cane with a *thwump* beside her. 'Need I remind you I am a *lady* and not a plough horse in need of shodding?'

Dolly smiled sweetly and shifted back a little further on the bed, out of harm's way. There were a number of things in her job she didn't particularly enjoy, but it wouldn't have taken much thought, if asked, for her to answer that the very worst part of being employed as Lady Gwendolyn Caldicott's companion was keeping the old girl's toenails tidy. The weekly task seemed to bring out the worst in both of them, but it was a necessary evil and thus Dolly performed it without complaint. (At the time, that is; later, in the sitting room with Kitty and the others, she complained in such lavish detail that they had to beg through tears of laughter for her to stop.)

'There you are then,' she said, sliding the file into its sheath and rubbing her dusty fingers together. 'Perfect.'

'Harrumph.' Lady Gwendolyn straightened her turban with the heel of one hand, managing to knock ash from the wilting cigarette she'd forgotten she was holding. She peered down her nose and across the vast purple ocean of her chiffon-draped body as Dolly lifted the pair of tiny polished feet for inspection. 'I expect they'll have to do,' she said, and then grumbled about it not being like the good old days when one had a proper lady's maid at one's beck and call.

Dolly pasted a fresh smile on her face and went to fetch the papers. It was a little over two years since she'd left Coventry, and the second year was shaping up to be a great improvement on the first. She'd been so green when she arrived – Jimmy had helped her find a small room of her own (in a better part of town than his, he'd said with a grin) and a job selling dresses, and then the war had started and he'd disappeared. 'People want stories from the front line,' he'd told her just before he left for France, when they were sitting together by the Serpentine, he sailing paper boats, she smoking moodily. 'Somebody has to tell them.' The closest Dolly had come to glamour or excitement that first year was the occasional glimpse of a finely dressed woman on her way past John Lewis to Bond Street, and the wide-eyed focus of the other tenants at Mrs White's boarding house when they gathered in the sitting room after dinner and pleaded with Dolly to tell them again how her father had shouted at her when she left home, and told her she was never to darken his doorstep again. It made her feel interesting and intrepid when she described how the gate had closed behind her, the way she'd flicked her scarf over her shoulder and marched to the station with not so much as a glance back at her family home. But later, alone in the narrow bed in her tiny dark room, the memory had made her shiver a bit with the cold.

Everything had changed, though, after the shop-girl job

at John Lewis fell through. (A silly misunderstanding, really, it was hardly Dolly's fault if some people didn't appreciate honesty, and the inalienable fact was that shorter skirts *didn't* suit everyone.) It was Dr Rufus, Caitlin's father, who'd come to her rescue. On hearing about the incident, he'd mentioned that one of his acquaintances was seeking a companion for his aunt. 'A tremendous old lady,' he'd said over lunch at the Savoy. He took Dolly out for a 'treat' each month when he came to London, usually when his wife was busy shopping with Caitlin. 'Rather eccentric, I believe, lonely. Never recovered after her sister left to get married. Do you get on with the elderly?'

'Yes,' said Dolly, concentrating on her champagne cocktail. It was the first time she'd had one and it made her a bit dizzy, though in a lovely unexpected way. 'I expect so. Why not?' Which had been good enough for the beaming Dr Rufus. He wrote her a reference and put in a word with his friend; he even offered to drive her to the interview. The nephew would have preferred to close up the ancestral house for the duration, Dr Rufus explained as they wound their way through Kensington, but his aunt had put the stopper on that. The stubborn old thing (you really did have to admire her spirit, he said) had refused to go with her nephew's family to the safety of their country estate, digging in her heels and threatening to call her lawyer if she wasn't left in peace.

Since then, in the ten months she'd been working for Lady Gwendolyn, Dolly had heard the story again, many times. The old woman, who drew special pleasure from revisiting the slights inflicted on her by others, said that her 'weasel' nephew had attempted to make her leave – 'against my will' – but she'd insisted on staying 'in the one place I've ever been happy. It's where we grew up, Henny Penny and I. They'll have to carry me out in a coffin if they want to move me. I dare say I'll find a way to haunt Peregrine, even then, if he dares to take it on.' Dolly, for her part, was thrilled by Lady Gwendolyn's stand, for it was the old girl's insistence on staying put that had brought her to live inside the wonderful house on Campden Grove.

And it *was* wonderful. The outside of number 7 was classic: three storeys up and one down, white stucco render with black accents, set back from the pavement behind a small garden; the inside, however, was sublime. William Morris paper on every wall, splendid furniture that wore the divine grime of generations, shelves groaning beneath the exquisite weight of rare crystal, silver and china. It existed in stark contrast to Mrs White's boarding house over in Rillington Place, where Dolly had handed over half her weekly shop-girl wages for the privilege of sleeping in a one-time closet that seemed always to smell of corned-beef hash. From the moment she'd first stepped through Lady Gwendolyn's front door, Dolly had known that no matter what it took, no matter how many pounds of flesh she had to give, she must somehow come to live within its walls.

And so she had. Lady Gwendolyn had been the one fly in the ointment: Dr Rufus had been right when he said she was eccentric; he'd failed though to mention she'd been marinating in the bitter juices of abandonment for the better part of three decades. The results were somewhat frightening, and Dolly had been convinced for the first six months that her employer was on the verge of sending her off to B. Cannon & Co. to be turned into glue. She knew better now:

Lady Gwendolyn could be brusque at times, but that was just her way. Dolly had also discovered recently, much to her gratification, that where the old woman's companion was concerned, curtness masked a real affection.

'Shall we run through the headlines, then?' said Dolly brightly, returning to perch on the end of the bed.

'Suit yourself.' Lady Gwendolyn gave a rubbery shrug, flapping one small moist paw over the other on her paunch. 'I'm sure I don't mind either way.'

Dolly opened the latest edition of *The Lady* and flicked through to the Society pages; she cleared her throat, adopted a voice of fitting reverence, and began to read out the goings-on of people whose lives sounded like fantasy. It was a world Dolly had never known existed; oh, she'd seen the grand houses on the outskirts of Coventry and occasionally heard Father speak in important tones about a special order for one of the *better* families, but the stories Lady Gwendolyn told (when the mood took her) about the adventures she'd had with her sister, Penelope – lounging at the Café Royal, living together for a time in Bloomsbury, posing for a sculptor who was in love with them both – well, they were beyond Dolly's wildest imaginings, and that really was saying something.

As Dolly read now about today's best and brightest, Lady Gwendolyn, propped fulsomely against her satin pillows, feigned disinterest while listening intently to every word. It was always the same; her curiosity was such that she never could hold out for long.

'Oh dear. It seems things aren't at all well for Lord and Lady Horsquith.'

'Divorce, is it?' The old woman sniffed.

'Reading between the lines. She's out with that other fellow again, the painter.'

'No surprises there. No discretion at all, that woman, ruled only by her ghastly – ' Lady Gwendolyn's top lip curled as she spat out the culprit – '*passions*.' (Only she said *pessions*, a lovely, posh pronunciation Dolly liked to practise when she knew herself alone.) 'Just like her mother before her.'

'Which one was she again?'

Lady Gwendolyn raised her eyes to the Bordeaux ceiling medallion. 'Really, I'm quite sure Lionel Rufus never said that you were slow. I might not approve entirely of smart women, but I certainly won't abide a fool. Are you a fool, Miss Smitham?'

'I do hope not, Lady Gwendolyn.'

'Harrumph,' she said, in a tone that suggested she had yet to make her final ruling. 'Lady Horsquith's mother, Lady Prudence Dyer, was an outspoken bore who used to tire us all silly with her agitations for the female vote. Henny Penny used to do the most amusing imitation of the woman – she could be terribly entertaining when the mood took her. As tends to happen, Lady Prudence wore people down to the brink of their patience until no one in Society could tolerate a minute more of her company. Be selfish, be churlish, be bold or wicked, but never, Dorothy, *never* be tedious. After a time, she upped and disappeared.'

'Disappeared?'

Lady Gwendolyn gave a lazy flourish of the wrist, dropping ash like magic dust. 'Boarded a boat for India, Tanganyika, New Zealand . . . God only knows.' Her mouth collapsed into a trout-like pout and she appeared to be chewing something over, whether a small piece of lunch she'd found between her teeth, or a juicy morsel of secret intelligence, it was hard to guess. Until, finally, with a sly smile, she added, 'God, that is, and the little birdie who told me she was holed up with a native fellow in a horror of a place called Zanzibar.'

'*Really.*'

'Quite.' Lady Gwendolyn drew so emphatically on her cigarette that her eyes became two penny-sized slots. For a woman who hadn't ventured from her boudoir in the thirty years since her sister left, she really was exceedingly well informed. There were very few people in the pages of *The Lady* that she didn't know, and she was remarkably adept at getting them to do precisely as she wished. Why, even Caitlin Rufus had married her husband at the decree of Lady Gwendolyn – an elderly chap, dull it had to be said, but stupendously wealthy. Caitlin in turn had become the worst sort of bore, spending hours complaining about how beastly it was finally to marry ('Oh, *so* very well, Doll') and acquire her own home just as all the best wallpapers were being withdrawn from shops. Dolly had met The Husband once or twice and swiftly come to the conclusion that there had to be a better way of acquiring the finer things than by marrying a man who thought a game of whist and a grope with the maid behind the dining-room curtains was jolly good sport.

Lady Gwendolyn flapped her hand impatiently for Dolly to continue, and Dolly promptly obliged. 'Oh, now look – here's a cheerier one. Lord Dumphee has become engaged to the Honourable Eva Hastings.'

'Nothing cheery about an engagement.'

'Of course not, Lady Gwendolyn.' It was always a subject round which to tread lightly.

'All very well for a dull sort of girl to hitch her wheel to a man's wagon, but consider yourself warned, Dorothy – men enjoy a bit of sport, and they all like to catch the brightest prize, but once they do? That's when the fun and games end. His games, her fun.' She rolled her wrist. 'Go on then, read the rest. What does it say?'

'There's a party to celebrate the engagement this Saturday evening.'

That news brought a mildly interested grumble. 'Dumphee House? Tremendous place – Henny Penny and I went there for a grand ball once. By the end people had taken off their shoes and were dancing in the fountain . . . It *is* being held at Dumphee House, I suppose?'

'No.' Dolly scanned the announcement. 'It would appear not. They're having guests to an invitation-only party at the 400 Club.'

As Lady Gwendolyn launched into a blustering tirade against the low tone of such places – '*Night*clubs!' – Dolly drifted. She'd only been to the 400 once, with Kitty and some of her soldier friends. Deep down in the cellars next door to where the Alhambra Theatre used to stand in Leicester Square, dark and intimate and deepest red as far as the eye could see: the silk on the walls, the plush banquettes with their single flickering candles, the velvet curtains that spilled like wine to meet the scarlet carpets.

There'd been music and laughter and servicemen everywhere, and couples swaying dreamily on the small shadowy dance floor. And when a soldier with too much whisky under his belt, and a rather uncomfortable swelling in his trousers, leaned against her and slurred wetly of all the things he'd like to do when he got her alone, Dolly had spied over his shoulder a stream of bright young things – better-dressed, more beautiful, just *more*, than the rest of the club-goers – slipping behind a red cord and being greeted by a small man with a long black moustache. ('Luigi Rossi,' Kitty had said with an authoritative nod when they were drinking a nightcap of gin and lemon under the kitchen table back at Campden Grove. 'Didn't you know? He runs the whole shebang.')

'I've had enough of that now,' said Lady Gwendolyn, extinguishing her cigarette with such force she knocked the tub of corn ointment from the table beside her. 'I'm tired and I'm not feeling well – I need one of my sweets. Oh, but I fear I'm not long for this world. I barely slept a wink last night, what with the noise, the terrible noise.'

'Poor Lady Gwendolyn,' said Dolly, putting *The Lady* aside and digging out the grande dame's bag of boiled sweets. 'We have that nasty Mr Hitler to thank for that, his bombers really are—'

'I don't mean the bombers, silly girl. I'm talking about *them*. The others, with their infernal – ' she shuddered theatrically and the timbre of her voice lowered – 'giggling.'

'Oh,' said Dolly. '*Them*.'

'A ghastly lot of girls,' declared Lady Gwendolyn, who was yet to meet any of them. '*Office* girls, at that, typing for the ministries – they're bound to be fast. What on earth was the War Office thinking? I realize of course that they must be accommodated, but *here*? In my beautiful house? Peregrine is beside himself – the letters I've had! Can't bear to think of such creatures living amongst the heirlooms.'

Her nephew's displeasure threatened to bring a smile, but the profound bitterness at Lady Gwendolyn's core quickly smothered it. She reached to grip Dolly's wrist. 'They're not entertaining *men* in my home, are they, Dorothy?'

'Oh no, Lady Gwendolyn. They know your feelings on the matter, I made sure of that.'

'Because I won't have it. I won't have fornication under my roof.'

Dolly nodded soberly. This, she knew, was the Great Matter at the heart of her mistress's asperity. Dr Rufus had explained all about Lady Gwendolyn's sister, Penelope. They'd been inseparable when they were young, he said, similar enough in looks and manner that most people took them for twins, even though there were eighteen months between them. They'd gone to dances, country house weekends, always the two of them together – but then Penelope committed the crime for which her sister would never forgive her. 'She fell in love and got married,' Dr Rufus had said, drawing on his cigar with the storyteller's satisfaction at having reached his punch line. 'And, in the process, broke her sister's heart.'

'There, there,' said Dolly soothingly now. 'It won't come to that, Lady Gwendolyn. Before you know it the war will be over and they'll all go back to wherever it is they came from.' Dolly had no idea if that was true – for her part, she hoped it wasn't: the big house was very quiet at night, and Kitty and the others were a bit of fun – but it was the only thing to say, especially when the old lady was so worked up. Poor thing, it must be terrible to lose one's soulmate. Dolly couldn't imagine life without hers.

Lady Gwendolyn fell back against her pillow. The

diatribe against nightclubs and their ills, her rich imaginings of the Babylonian behaviour within, memories of her sister and the threat of fornication beneath her roof – all had taken their toll. She was weary and drawn, as crumpled as the barrage balloon that had come down over Notting Hill the other day.

'Here now, Lady Gwendolyn,' said Dolly. 'Look at this lovely butterscotch I've found. Let's just pop it in and put you down for a rest, shall we?'

'Well, all right then,' the old woman grumbled. 'Just an hour or so, though, Dorothy. Don't let me sleep past three – I don't want to miss our game of cards.'

'Perish the thought,' Dolly said, posting the boiled sweet through her mistress's pursed lips.

With the old girl sucking away furiously, Dolly went to the window to pull the blackout curtains shut. As she unlatched the curtains from their ties, her attention fell to the house opposite, and what she saw made her heart leap.

Vivien was there again. Sitting at her desk behind the tape-crossed window, still as a statue but for the fingers of one hand, twisting the end of her long strand of pearls. Dolly waved eagerly, willing the other woman to see her and wave back, but she didn't, she was lost in her own thoughts.

'Dorothy?'

Dolly blinked. Vivien (spelled the same way as Vivien Leigh, lucky thing) was quite possibly the most beautiful woman she'd ever seen. She had a heart-shaped face, deep brown hair that gleamed in its Victory roll, and full curled lips painted scarlet. Her eyes were wide set and framed by dramatic arched brows, just like Rita Hayworth's or Gene Tierney's, but it was more than that which made her beautiful. It wasn't the fine skirts and blouses she wore, it was the *way* she wore them, easily, casually; it was the strings of pearls strung airily around her neck, the brown Bentley she'd used to drive before it was handed over like a spare pair of boots to the Ambulance Service. It was the tragic history Dolly had learned in dribs and drabs – orphaned as a child, raised by an uncle, married to a handsome wealthy author named Henry Jenkins, who held an important position with the Ministry of Information.

'Dorothy? Come and put my sheets to rights and fetch my sleep mask.'

Ordinarily, Dolly might've been a bit envious to have a woman of that description living at such close quarters, but with Vivien it was different. All her life, Dolly had longed for a friend like her. Someone who *really* understood her (not like dull old Caitlin or silly frivolous Kitty), someone with whom she could stroll arm in arm down Bond Street, elegant and buoyant, as people turned to look at them, gossiping behind their hands about the dark leggy beauties, their careless charm. And now, finally, she'd found Vivien. From the very first time they'd passed each other walking up the Grove, when their eyes had met and they'd exchanged that smile – secretive, knowing, complicit – it had been clear to both of them that they were two of a kind and destined to be the very best of friends.

'Dorothy!'

Dolly jumped and turned from the window. Lady Gwendolyn had managed to get herself into a frightful mess of purple chiffon and duck-down pillows, and was scowling, red-cheeked, from its centre. 'I can't find my sleep mask anywhere.'

'Come on then,' said Dolly, glancing once more at Vivien before tugging the blackouts together. 'Let's see if we can't find it together.'

After a brief but successful search the mask was discovered, pressed flat and warm beneath Lady Gwendolyn's significant left thigh. Dolly removed the vermillion turban and propped it atop the marble bust on the chest of drawers, and then rolled the satin mask onto her mistress's head.

'Careful,' Lady Gwendolyn snapped. 'You'll stop me breathing if you hold it over my nose like that.'

'Oh dear,' Dolly said. 'We wouldn't want that now, would we?'

'Harrumph.' The old woman let her head sink back so far into the pillows that her face seemed to float above the rest of her, an island in a sea of skin folds. 'Seventy-five years, all of them long, and what have I got to show for it? Deserted by my nearest and dearest, my closest companion a girl who takes my money for her trouble.'

'Now, now,' Dolly said, as if to a fractious child, 'what's all this about trouble? You mustn't even joke about such a thing, Lady Gwendolyn. You know I'd care for you if I wasn't paid a penny.'

'Yes, yes,' the old lady grumbled. 'Well. That's enough of that.'

Dolly pulled Lady Gwendolyn's blankets up nice and high. The old woman adjusted her chins over the satin ribbon edging and said, 'You know what I ought to do?'

'What's that, Lady Gwendolyn?'

'I ought to leave it all to you. That would teach my scheming nephew a lesson. Just like his father, that boy –

out to steal everything I hold dear. I've a good mind to call
in my solicitor and make it official.'

Really, there was nothing to say in the face of such comments; naturally it was thrilling to know Lady Gwendolyn
held her in such high esteem, but to seem pleased would
have been terribly coarse. Brimming with pride, Dolly
turned away and busied herself with straightening the old
woman's turban.

It was Dr Rufus who'd first made Dolly aware of what Lady
Gwendolyn was thinking. They'd been having one of their
lunches a few weeks ago, and after a good long chat about
Dolly's social life ('What about boyfriends, Dorothy? Surely
a girl like you must have dozens of young men chasing her
round the block? My advice? Look for an older, *professional* fellow – someone who can give you everything you
deserve'), he'd asked about life at Campden Grove. When
she told him she thought it was all going well, he'd swirled
his whisky so that the ice cubes tinkled and given her a
wink. 'Better than well, from what I hear. I had a letter from
old Peregrine Wolsey just last week. He wrote that his aunt
was so fond of "my girl", as he put it – ' at this Dr Rufus
seemed to drift into his own reverie, before remembering
himself and continuing – 'that he was worried for his inheritance. He was awfully upset with me for putting you in his
aunt's path.' He'd laughed then, but Dolly had managed
only a thoughtful smile. She'd continued to think about
what he'd said for the rest of that day and all through the
following week.

The fact of the matter was that what Dolly had told Dr
Rufus was true. After a rather shaky start, Lady Gwendolyn,

widely reputed (not least by her own account) to disdain all other human beings, had taken quite a shine to her young companion. Which was all to the good. It was just a terrible shame Dolly had been forced to pay such a high price for the old woman's affection.

The telephone call had come in November; Cook had answered and called out to Dorothy that it was for her. It stung to remember now, but Dolly had been so excited to be wanted on the telephone in such a grand house that she'd hurried down the stairs, snatched up the receiver and put on her most important voice: 'Hello? Dorothy Smitham speaking'. And then she'd heard Mrs Potter, her mother's friend from next door in Coventry, shouting down the line that her family was, 'All dead, the lot of 'em. Incendiary bomb – no time to get out to the Andy.'

A gulf had opened up inside Dolly in that moment: it felt as if her stomach had dropped, leaving a great swirling sphere of shock, loss and fear in its place. She'd let go of the phone, and stood there in the enormous entrance hall of number 7 Campden Grove, and she'd felt infinitesimally small and alone and at the whim of the next wind that might blow. All the parts of Dolly, the memories she had of different instances in her life, fell like a deck of cards, landing out of order, the images on them fading already. Cook's help arrived right then, and said, 'Good morning', and Dolly wanted to scream at her that it wasn't a good morning at all, that everything had changed, couldn't the stupid girl see that? But she didn't. She'd smiled in return and said, 'Good morning,' and taken herself back upstairs to where Lady Gwendolyn was ringing her silver bell furiously and flapping about in search of the eyeglasses she'd carelessly lost.

Dolly didn't speak to anyone about her family at first, not even Jimmy, who'd heard, of course, and was desperate to console her. When she told him she was all right, that there was a war on and everyone must suffer their losses, he thought she was being brave, but it wasn't courage that kept Dolly quiet. Her feelings were so complicated, the memories of the way she'd left home so raw, it just seemed better not to start talking for fear of what she might say and how she might feel. She hadn't seen either of her parents since she'd gone to London: her father had forbidden her from making contact unless to say she was going to 'start behaving properly', but her mother had written secret letters, regularly if not warmly, her most recent hinting at a trip to London to see for herself 'the fancy house and the grand lady you write about so often'. But it was too late for all that now. Her mother would never meet Lady Gwendolyn or step inside number 7 Campden Grove or see the great success Dolly had made of her life.

As for poor Cuthbert – Dolly could hardly bear to think of him. She remembered his last letter, too, every word of it: the way he'd described in minute detail the Anderson shelter they were building in the back garden, the pictures of Spitfires and Hurricanes he'd collected to decorate inside, what he was planning to do with the German pilots he captured. He'd been so proud and deluded, so excited about the part he was going to play in the war, so plump and ungainly, such a happy little baby, and now he was gone. And the sadness Dolly felt, the loneliness at knowing herself to be an orphan now, was so immense she saw nothing for it but to dedicate herself to the work she was doing for Lady Gwendolyn and say no more about it.

Until one day the old woman was reminiscing about the lovely voice she'd had when she was a girl, and Dolly had thought of her mother, and the blue box she'd kept hidden in the garage, filled with dreams and memories that were now nothing more than rubble, and she'd burst into tears, right there on the end of the old lady's bed, nail file in hand.

'Whatever's the matter?' Lady Gwendolyn had said, her small mouth falling open to register the same amount of shock she might have felt if Dolly had taken off her clothes and started dancing round the room.

Caught in a rare unguarded moment, Dolly had told Lady Gwendolyn everything. Her mother and father and Cuthbert, what they were like, the sorts of things they'd said, the times they'd driven her mad, the way her mother used to try to brush her hair smooth and Dolly had resisted, the trips to the seaside, the cricket and the donkey. Finally, Dolly had recounted the way she'd flounced out of home when she left, barely stopping when her mother called to her – Janice Smitham, who'd sooner have gone without food than raise her voice in earshot of the neighbours – and ran out wielding the book she'd bought for Dolly as a going-away present.

'Harrumph,' Lady Gwendolyn had said when Dolly finished speaking. 'It hurts, of course, but you're not the first to lose your family.'

'I know.' Dolly drew in a deep breath. The room seemed to echo with the sound of her own voice of moments before, and she wondered if she was about to be let go. Lady Gwendolyn did not like outbursts (unless they were her own).

'When Henny Penny was taken from me I thought
I'd die.'

Dolly nodded, still waiting for the axe to fall.

'You're young, though; you'll make a go of it. Just look
at her across the road.'

It was true, Vivien's life had come up roses in the end,
but there were a few marked differences between them. 'She
had a wealthy uncle who took her in,' said Dolly quietly.
'She's an heiress, married to a famous writer. And I'm . . .'
She bit her bottom lip, anxious not to start crying again.
'I'm . . .'

'Well, you're not entirely alone, are you, silly girl?'

Lady Gwendolyn had held out her bag of sweets then
and for the first time ever offered one to Dolly. It had taken
a moment to realize what the old woman was suggesting,
but when she did, Dolly had reached tentatively inside the
bag to withdraw a red and green gobstopper. She'd held it
in her hand, fingers closed around it, aware that it was melting against her warm palm. Dolly had answered solemnly: 'I
have you.'

Lady Gwendolyn had sniffed and looked away. 'We
have each other, I suppose,' she'd said, in a voice made fluty
by unexpected emotion.

Dolly reached her bedroom and added the newest copy of
The Lady to the pile of others. Later, she'd take a closer
look and pull out the best pictures to glue inside her Book
of Ideas, but right now she had more important things to
take care of.

She hopped down on all fours and dug about beneath
her bed for the banana she'd been hoarding since Mr

Hopton the greengrocer 'found' it for her under the counter on Tuesday. Humming a little melody to herself, she crept back out of the door and along the corridor. Strictly, there was no reason to be creeping at all – Kitty and the others were busy stabbing at their typewriters in the War Office, Cook was standing in line at the butcher's armed with a handful of ration cards and a foul temper, and Lady Gwendolyn was snoring peacefully in her bed – but it was so much more fun to creep than to walk. Especially when one had a whole glorious hour of freedom ahead.

She ran up the stairs, pulled out the little key she'd had cut, and let herself into Lady Gwendolyn's dressing room. Not the poky little closet from which Dolly selected a flowing coverall each morning to clad the great lady's bod; no, no, not this. The *dressing* room was a grand arrangement in which were housed countless gowns and shoes and coats and hats, the likes of which Dolly had rarely glimpsed outside the Society pages. Silks and furs hung side by side in huge open wardrobes, and bespoke pairs of little satin shoes sat prettily upon the mighty shelves. The circular hat boxes, stamped proudly with the names of their Mayfair milliners – Schiaparelli, Coco Chanel, Rose Valois – towered towards the ceiling in columns so high a dainty white stepladder had been furnished to enable their retrieval.

In the bow of the window, with its rich velvet curtains that brushed the carpet (drawn always now against the German planes), a cabriole-leg table held an oval mirror, a set of sterling-silver brushes, and a host of photographs in fancy frames. Each depicted a pair of young women, Penelope and Gwendolyn Caldicott, most of them official portraits with the studio's name in cursive in the bottom corner, but a few taken candidly while they were attending this or that Society party. There was one photograph in particular that drew Dolly's eye every time. The two Caldicott sisters were older here – thirty-five at least – and had been photographed by Cecil Beaton on a grand spiral staircase. Lady Gwendolyn was standing with one hand low on her hip, eyeballing the camera, while her sister was glancing at something (or someone) out of shot. The photograph had been taken at the party where Penelope fell in love, the night her sister's world came tumbling down.

Poor Lady Gwendolyn; she wasn't to know her life was set to change that night. She looked so pretty, too: it was impossible to believe that the old woman upstairs had ever been that young or striking. (Dolly, like all the young perhaps, didn't for a second imagine the same fate lay in store for her.) It showed, she thought sadly, how heavily loss and betrayal could weigh on a person, poisoning them within, but also without. The satin evening dress Lady Gwendolyn was wearing in the photograph was dark in colour and luminous, bias-cut so that it clung lightly to her curves. Dolly had searched high and low in the wardrobes until she finally found it, draped over a hanger among a host of others – imagine her pleasure to discover it was deepest red, surely the most magnificent of all colours.

It was the first of Lady Gwendolyn's dresses she ever tried on, but certainly not the last. No, before Kitty and the others had come, when nights at Campden Grove had been her own to do with as she wished, Dolly had spent a lot of time up here, a chair jammed beneath the doorknob as she stripped down to her underwear and played at dressing up. She'd sat at the table sometimes, too, scattering clouds of powder across her bare décolletage, sorting through the drawers of diamond clasps and tending her hair with the boar-bristle brush – what she'd have given to own a brush like that, with her own name curled along its spine . . .

There wasn't time for all that today, though. Dolly sat cross-legged on the velvet settee below the chandelier and set about peeling her banana. She closed her eyes as she took a first bite, letting out a sigh of supreme satisfaction – it was true, forbidden (or at least severely rationed) fruits really were the sweetest. She ate her way right down to the bottom, relishing every mouthful, and then draped the skin delicately along the seat beside her. Pleasantly sated, Dolly dusted off her hands and got to work. She'd made a promise to Vivien and she intended to keep it.

Down on her knees by the racks of swaying dresses, she slid the hat box from where she'd stashed it. She'd made a start the previous day, slotting the embellished cloche hat in with another and using the empty box to house the small pile of clothing she'd since assembled. It was the sort of thing Dolly could imagine she might have done for her own mother if things had turned out differently. The Women's Voluntary Service, whose ranks she'd recently joined, was collecting unwanted items to be mended, moulded and made to make do, and Dolly was anxious to do her bit. Indeed, she wanted to *thrill* them with her contribution and, while she was at it, help Vivien, who was organizing the drive.

At the last meeting, there'd been heated discussion about all the bits and bobs that were needed now the raids had increased – bandages, toys for homeless children, hospital pyjamas for soldiers – and Dolly had volunteered a load of unwanted clothing to be cut up and converted as necessary. Indeed, while the old dears bickered over who was the better seamstress, and whose pattern they ought to use for the rag dolls, Dolly and Vivien (it sometimes seemed they were the only members under the age of a hundred!) had exchanged a conspiratorial glance and quietly got on with the rest of the business, murmuring to one another when they needed more thread or another piece of material, and trying to ignore the heated squawking all around them.

It had been lovely, spending time together like that; it was one of the main reasons Dolly had joined the WVS in the first place (that, and in hope the Labour Exchange would be less likely to conscript her into something ghastly like munitions). With Lady Gwendolyn's recent clinginess – she refused to spare Dolly for more than one Sunday each month – and Vivien's brisk schedule as the perfect wife and volunteer, it was virtually impossible to see one another otherwise.

Dolly worked swiftly and was inspecting a rather insipid blouse, trying to decide whether the Dior signature inside the seam should earn it a reprieve from reincarnation as a strip of bandages, when a thump from downstairs made her start. The door slammed shut, promptly followed by Cook bellowing for the girl who came in of an afternoon to help with the cleaning. Dolly glanced at the wall clock. It was almost three, and time therefore to wake the sleeping bear. She sealed the hat box and tucked it out of sight, smoothed her skirt, and prepared herself for yet another afternoon spent playing Old Maid.

*

'Another letter from your Jimmy,' said Kitty, waving it at Dolly when she came into the drawing room that night. She was sitting cross-legged on the chaise longue while Betty and Susan flicked through an old copy of *Vogue* beside her. They'd moved the grand piano out of the way months ago, much to Cook's horror, and the fourth girl, Louisa, dressed only in her underwear, was striking a series of rather perplexing callisthenics attitudes on the Bessarabian rug.

Dolly lit a cigarette and curled her legs beneath her in the old leather wingback chair. The others always saved the wingback chair for Dolly. No one ever said as much, but her position as Lady Gwendolyn's companion conferred on her a certain status within their little household. Never mind that she'd only lived at 7 Campden Grove a month or two longer than they had, the girls were forever turning to Dolly, asking all manner of questions about how things worked and whether they might be permitted to explore the house. The whole thing had amused her at first, but now she couldn't think why: it seemed absolutely the right way for the girls to act.

Cigarette on her lip, she tore open the envelope. The letter was brief, written, it said, while he was standing like a pilchard in a packed troop train, and she picked through the scrawl to find the important bits: he'd been taking photographs of war damage somewhere up north, he was back in London for a few days and he was desperate to see her – was she free on Saturday night? Dolly could have squealed.

'There's the cat that got the cream,' said Kitty. 'Come on then, tell us what he says.'

Dolly kept her eyes averted. The letter wasn't remotely juicy but it didn't hurt to let the others think it was, especially Kitty, who was always telling them lurid details about her latest conquest. 'It's personal,' she said finally, adding a secretive smile for good measure.

'Spoilsport.' Kitty pouted. 'Keeping a handsome RAF pilot all to yourself! When are we going to meet him, anyway?'

'Yes,' Louisa chimed in, hands on her hips as she bent forwards from the waist. 'Bring him round one evening so we can see for ourselves that he's the right sort of fellow for our Doll.'

Dolly eyed Louisa's heaving bust as she bounced her hips from side to side. She couldn't exactly remember how they'd got the impression Jimmy was with the RAF; an assumption made many months ago and, at the time, Dolly had been struck by the idea. She hadn't set them straight and now it seemed rather too late. 'Sorry, girls,' she said, folding the letter in half. 'He's far too busy at the moment – flying secret missions, war business, I'm really not at liberty to speak about the details – and even if he weren't, you know the rules.'

'Oh, come on,' Kitty said. 'The old battle axe'll never know. She hasn't been downstairs since horse-drawn carriages went out of fashion, and it's not like any of us is going to tell.'

'She knows more than you think,' Dolly said. 'Besides, she relies on me. I'm the closest thing she has to family. She'd let me go if she even suspected I was seeing a fellow.'

'Would that be so bad?' Kitty said. 'You could come and work with us. One smile and my supervisor would take you in a jiffy. Bit of a lech, but jolly good fun once you know how to handle him.'

'Oh yes!' said Betty and Susan, who had a curious knack for speaking in unison. They looked up from their magazine. 'Come and work with us.'

'And give up my daily flaying? I hardly think so.'

Kitty laughed. 'You're mad, Doll. Mad or brave, I'm not sure which.'

Dolly shrugged; she certainly wasn't going to discuss her reasons for staying with a busybody like Kitty.

She took up her book instead. It was lying on the side table where she'd left it the night before. The book was new, the first she'd ever owned (except for the unread copy of *Mrs Beeton's Book of Household Management* her mother had thrust so hopefully into her hands). She'd gone to Charing Cross Road especially on one of her Sundays off and bought it from a bookseller there.

'*The Reluctant Muse.*' Kitty leaned forwards to read the cover. 'Haven't you already read that one?'

'Twice, actually.'

'That good?'

''Tis, rather.'

Kitty wrinkled her pretty little nose. 'Not much of a reader myself.'

'No?' Dolly wasn't either, not usually, but Kitty didn't need to know that.

'Henry Jenkins? That name's familiar . . . oh now, isn't he the fellow across the street?'

Dolly gave a vague wave of her cigarette. 'I believe he lives around here somewhere.' Of course, it was the very reason she'd chosen the book. Once Lady Gwendolyn had let slip that Henry Jenkins was well known in literary circles for including rather too much fact in his fiction ('A fellow I could mention was furious to find his dirty laundry aired. Threatened to bring a lawsuit but died before he had the chance – accident prone, just like his father. Lucky for Jenkins . . .'), Dolly's curiosity had worked at her like a file. After careful discussion with the bookseller, she'd divined that *The Reluctant Muse* was a love story about a handsome author and his much younger wife, and had eagerly handed over her treasured savings. Dolly had spent a delicious week thereafter, eye pressed up close to the window of the Jenkins's marriage, learning all sorts of details she'd never have dared to ask Vivien outright.

'Terrifically good-looking chap,' Louisa said, lying prone now on the rug, arching her spine cobra-style to blink at Dolly. 'Married to that woman with the dark hair, the one who walks around like she's got a broomstick up her—'

'Oh!' cried Betty and Susan, wide-eyed. '*Her.*'

'Lucky girl,' Kitty said. 'I'd kill for a husband like him. Have you seen the way he looks at her? Like she's a piece of perfection and he can't quite believe his luck.'

'I wouldn't mind if he glanced *my* way,' said Louisa. 'How do you think a girl meets a man like him?'

Dolly knew the answer to that – how Vivien met Henry – it was right there in the book, but she didn't volunteer it. Vivien was her friend. To discuss her like this, to know that the others had noticed her too, that they'd speculated and wondered and drawn their own conclusions, made Dolly's ears burn with indignation. It was as if something that belonged to her, something precious and private that she cared about deeply, was being riffled through like – well, like a hat box of salvaged clothes.

'I heard she's not entirely well,' Louisa said. 'That's why he never takes his eyes off her.'

Kitty scoffed. 'She doesn't look one bit ill to me. Quite the contrary. I've seen her reporting to the WVS canteen round on Church Street when I'm coming home of an evening.' She lowered her voice and the other girls leaned close to hear her. 'I heard it was because *she* had a wandering eye.'

'Ooh,' Betty and Susan cooed together. 'A lover!'

'Haven't you noticed how careful she is?' Kitty continued, to the rapt attention of the others. 'Always greeting him at the door when he gets home, dressed to the nines and placing a glass of whisky in his waiting hand. Please! That's not love, it's a guilty conscience. You mark my words – that woman's hiding something, and I think we all know what that something is.'

Dolly had heard as much as she could stand; in fact, she found herself in rather emphatic agreement with Lady Gwendolyn that the sooner the girls left number 7 Campden Grove, the better. They really were an unsophisticated lot. 'Is that the time?' she said, clapping her book closed. 'I'm going to go and have my bath.'

Dolly waited until the water had reached the five-inch line and turned the tap off with her foot. She poked her big toe inside the spout to stop it dripping. She knew she ought to call someone about fixing it, but who was there left nowadays? Plumbers were too busy putting out fires and turning off exploded water mains to care about a little drip, and it always seemed to settle down eventually. She rested her neck on the tub's cool rim and adjusted herself to keep her curlers and kirby grips from digging into her head. She'd tied the whole lot up with a scarf so the steam wouldn't make her hair lank; wishful thinking, of course; Dolly couldn't remember the last time her bath had been steaming.

She blinked at the ceiling as dance music drifted up from the wireless downstairs. It really was a lovely room, black and white tiles and lots of shiny metallic rails and taps. Lady Gwendolyn's ghastly nephew, Peregrine, would have a pink fit if he saw the lines strung across it with knickers and brassieres and stockings hung out to dry. The thought rather pleased Dolly.

She reached over the side of the tub and took up her cigarette in one hand, *The Reluctant Muse* in the other. Keeping both clear of the water (it wasn't hard – five inches didn't go far), she flicked through until she found the scene she was looking for. Humphrey, the clever but unhappy writer, has been invited by his old headmaster to return to his school and talk to the boys about literature, followed by dinner in his master's private quarters. He's just excused himself from the table and left the residence to stroll back through the darkling garden to the spot where he's parked his car, and is thinking about the direction his life has taken, the regrets he's acquired and the 'cruel passing of time', when he reaches the estate's old lake and something catches his eye:

Humphrey dimmed his flashlight and stayed where he was, quiet and still in the shadows of the bathing house. In the nearby clearing on the bank of the lake, glass lanterns had been strung from the branches and candles flickered in the

warm night air. A girl on the threshold of adulthood was
standing amongst them, feet bare and only the simplest of
summer dresses grazing her knees. Her dark hair fell loose
in waves over her shoulders and moonlight dripped over the
scene to cast a lustre along her profile. Humphrey could see
that her lips were moving, as if she spoke the lines of a
poem beneath her breath.

Her face was exquisite, yet it was her hands that
entranced him. While the rest of her body was perfectly still,
her fingers were moving together in front of her chest, the
small but graceful motions of a person weaving together
invisible threads.

He had known women before, beautiful women who
flattered and seduced, but this girl was different. There was
beauty in her focus, a purity of purpose that reminded him
of a child's, though she was most certainly a woman. To find
her in these natural surrounds, to observe the free flow of
her body, the wild romance of her face, enchanted him.

Humphrey stepped out of the shadows. The girl saw
him but she didn't start. She smiled as if she'd been expect-
ing him and gestured towards the rippling lake. 'There's
something magical about swimming in the moonlight, don't
you think?'

It was the end of a chapter and the end of her cigarette,
and Dolly disposed of both. The water was growing tepid
and she wanted to wash herself before it turned any colder.
She lathered her arms thoughtfully, wondering as she rinsed
off the soap if that was the way Jimmy felt about her.

Dolly climbed out of the tub and slipped a towel from
the rack. She caught sight of herself unexpectedly in the

mirror and stopped very still, trying to imagine what a stranger might see when he looked at her. Brown hair, brown eyes – not too close together, thank goodness – a rather pert little retroussé nose. She knew she was pretty, she'd known that since she was eleven years old and the postman began to behave strangely when he saw her in the street, but was her beauty of a different kind from Vivien's? Would a man like Henry Jenkins have stopped, spellbound, to watch her whisper in the moonlight?

Because, of course, Viola – the girl in the book – was Vivien. Aside from the biographical similarities, there was the depiction of the girl standing in moonlight by the lake, her curled lips, feline eyes, the way she was staring so intently at something no one else could see. Why, it might have been describing Dolly's view of Vivien from Lady Gwendolyn's window.

She moved closer to the mirror. She could hear her own breathing in the still of the bathroom. What must it have been like, she wondered, for Vivien to know that she had made a man like Henry Jenkins, older, more experienced, and with an entrée to literature and Society's finest circles, so enchanted? How like a real princess must she have felt when he proposed marriage, when he swept her away from the humdrum of her normal existence and took her back to London, to a life in which she blossomed from a wild young girl into a pearl-wearing, Chanel No. 5-scented beauty, stunning on her husband's arm as the pair of them held court in the most glamorous clubs and restaurants. That was the Vivien Dolly knew; and, she suspected, the one she more resembled.

Knock, knock. 'Anyone alive in there?' Kitty's voice on

the other side of the bathroom door caught Dolly by surprise.

'Just a minute,' she called back.

'Oh, good, you *are* there. I was beginning to think you might've drowned.'

'No.'

'Going to be much longer?'

'No.'

'Only it's almost gone half nine, Doll, and I'm meeting a rather splendid airman at the Caribbean Club. Up from Biggin Hill for the night. I don't suppose you fancy a dance? He said he's going to bring some friends. One of them asked after you specially.'

'Not tonight.'

'Did you hear me say *airmen*, Doll? Brave and dashing heroes?'

'I already have one of those, remember? Besides, I've a shift at the WVS canteen.'

'Surely the widows, virgins and spinsters can do without you for a night?'

Dolly didn't answer, and after a few moments Kitty said, 'Well, if you're sure. Louisa's keen as mustard to take your place.'

As if she ever could, thought Dolly. 'Have fun,' she called, and then she waited as Kitty's footsteps retreated.

Only when she heard the other girl descending the stairs did she untie the knot of her scarf and slip it from her head. She knew she'd have to re-do them later, but it didn't matter. She began to unwind her curlers, dropping them into the empty sink. When they were all out, she combed her hair

with her fingers, pulling it down in soft waves around her
shoulders.

There now. She turned her head from side to side; she
began to whisper beneath her breath (Dolly didn't know
any poems, but she figured the lyrics to 'Chattanooga Choo
Choo' would do just as well); she lifted her hands and
moved her fingers before her as if she were weaving invisible
threads. Dolly smiled a little at what she saw. She looked
just like Viola in the book.

Twelve

Saturday night at last, and Jimmy was combing his dark hair back, trying to convince the longer bit at the front to stay put. It was a losing battle without Brylcreem, but he hadn't been able to stretch to a new tin this month. He'd been doing his best with water and a bit of sweet-talking but the results were not encouraging. The light bulb flickered above him and Jimmy glanced upwards, willing it not to die yet; he'd already robbed the sitting-room lamps, and the bathroom was next. He didn't fancy bathing in the dark. The bulb dimmed and Jimmy stood in the half-light, strains of music drifting through the floor from the wireless in the flat downstairs. When it brightened again his spirits lifted with it and he started whistling along to Glenn Miller's 'In the Mood'.

The dinner suit belonged to his dad, from back in the days of W. H. Metcalfe & Sons, and it was a whole lot more formal than anything Jimmy owned. He felt a bit of a chump, to be honest – there was a war on and it was bad enough, he always thought, not to be in uniform, let alone all done up like a playboy. But Dolly had said to dress well – *Like a gentleman, Jimmy!* she'd written in her letter, *a real gentleman* – and there wasn't much in his wardrobe that met that brief. The suit had come with them when they moved down from Coventry, just before the war started;

it was one of the few vestiges of the past Jimmy had
been unable to part with. Just as well, as things turned
out – Jimmy knew better than to disappoint Dolly when she
got an idea in her head, especially lately. There'd been a distance between them the past few weeks, ever since her
family was hit; she'd been avoiding his sympathy, putting on
a brave face, stiffening if he tried to embrace her. She
wouldn't even talk about their deaths, turning the conversation instead to her employer, speaking about the old woman
in a far more affectionate way than she'd used to. Jimmy
was glad she'd found someone to help her with her grief –
of course he was – he just wished it could have been him.

He shook his head. What a conceited bugger he was,
feeling sorry for himself when Doll was trying to deal with
such enormous loss. It was just so unlike her, clamming up
like that; it scared Jimmy: it felt as if the sun had gone
behind thick clouds and he glimpsed how cold it would be
if he no longer had her in his life. That's why tonight was so
important. The letter she'd sent him, her insistence that he
dress like a toff – it was the first time since the Coventry
Blitz that he'd seen her old spirit returned, and he wasn't
about to risk losing it again. Jimmy turned his attention
back to the suit. He couldn't quite believe it fitted so closely:
his father in his suit had always seemed to Jimmy a giant.
Now it seemed possible he had merely been a man.

Jimmy sat down on the worn patchwork quilt of his
narrow bed and took up his socks. There was a hole in one
that he'd been putting off darning for weeks, but he twisted
the top to the side so he could trap it underneath and
decided it would do. He wriggled his toes and eyed his
shoes, polished on the floor beside him, then glanced at his

watch. Still an hour before they were due to meet. He'd gone and got himself ready far too early. No surprises there; Jimmy was as jumpy as a cat.

He lit a cigarette and lay back on his bed, one arm folded behind his head. There was something hard beneath him and he reached under his pillow, pulling out *Of Mice and Men*. It was a library copy, the very same he'd borrowed back in the summer of '38, but Jimmy had paid the lost-book fee rather than return it. He'd enjoyed the novel well enough, but that wasn't why he'd kept it. Jimmy was superstitious: he'd had it with him that day at the seaside, and even to look at the book's cover was to bring back the sweetest memories. It was also the perfect repository for his most prized possession. Tucked inside, where no one else would think to look, was the photograph he'd taken of Dolly in that field by the sea. Jimmy retrieved it and smoothed back a dog-eared corner. He drew on his cigarette and exhaled, running his thumb along the outline of her hair, over her shoulder, round the curve of her breast—

'Jimmy?' His father was rummaging in the cutlery drawer on the other side of the wall. Jimmy knew he ought to go and help him find whatever it was he thought he needed. He hesitated though. Searching gave the old man something to do, and in Jimmy's experience a man was always better off when he was busy.

He turned his attention back to the photograph, as he had done a million times since it was taken. He knew every detail by heart, the way she was winding her hair around one finger, the set of her chin, the challenge in her eyes that was so Dolly, always acting bolder than she was ('Something to remember me by?' She'd certainly given him that);

he could almost smell the salt and feel the sun on his skin, the press of her body arching beneath him when he'd laid her back and kissed her—

'Jimmy? I can't find the whatsit, Jim-boy.'

Jimmy sighed and counselled patience to himself. 'All right, Dad,' he called. 'There in a minute.' He gave the photograph a rueful smile – it wasn't altogether comfortable staring at his girl's naked breast while his father was having a spot of bother on the other side of the plaster. Jimmy slid the picture back between the book's pages and sat up.

He pulled on his shoes and tied the laces, took his cigarette from his lip and glanced around the walls of his small bedroom; since the war began he hadn't stopped working, and the faded green wallpaper was covered with prints of his best photographs, his favourites at any rate. There were the ones he'd taken at Dunkirk, a group of men so tired they could barely stand, one with his arm slung over the others' shoulders, another with a stained bandage tied across his eye, all of them trudging wordlessly as they watched the ground before them and thought only of the next step; a soldier asleep on the beach, missing both boots and hugging his filthy water canister for dear life; a horrifying helter-skelter of boats, and planes firing from above, and men who'd walked so far already only to be shot at in the water as they tried to escape from hell.

Then there were the photographs he'd taken in London since the Blitz started. Jimmy eyed a series of portraits on the far wall. He stood and went to have a closer look. The East End family pulling the remains of their possessions on the back of a handcart; the woman in her apron hanging laundry on a kitchen clothes line with the fourth wall of the room missing, the private space suddenly made public; the mother reading bedtime stories to her six children in the Anderson shelter; the stuffed panda with half its leg blown off; the woman sitting on a chair with a blanket around her shoulders and a blaze behind her where her house used to stand; the old man searching for his dog in the rubble.

They haunted him. He sometimes felt he was stealing a piece of their souls, snatching a private moment for himself when he took his shot; but Jimmy didn't take the transaction lightly, they were joined, he and his subjects. They watched him from his walls and he felt a debt to them, not only in having borne witness to a fixed instant in their human experience, but also to the ongoing responsibility of keeping their stories alive. Jimmy would often hear the grim announcements on the BBC '*Three firemen, five policemen, and one hundred and fifty-three civilians are known to have lost their lives*' (such clean, measured words to describe the horror he'd inhabited the night before), and he'd see the same few lines printed in the newspaper, but then that would be it. There was no time for any more these days, no point in leaving flowers or writing epitaphs, because it would all take place again the following night, and the one after that. The war left no space for individual grief and memorial, the sort he'd seen in his father's funeral home as a boy, but Jimmy liked to think his photographs went some way to keeping a record. That one day, when it was all ended, the images might survive and people of the future would say, 'That's how it was.'

By the time Jimmy made it to the kitchen, his father had forgotten his search for the mysterious whatsit and was sitting at the table, dressed in pyjama bottoms and a singlet.

He was feeding his golden canary crumbs of broken biscuits Jimmy had got for him on the cheap. 'Here, Finchie,' he was saying, sticking his finger through the bars of the cage. 'Here you are, Finchie love. There's a good lad now.' He turned his head when he heard Jimmy behind him. 'Hello there! You're dressed up, boy-o.'

'Not really, Dad.'

His father was looking him up and down and Jimmy made a silent prayer he wouldn't realize the provenance of the suit. Not that his father would've minded the loan – the old man was generous to a fault – rather the whole thing was likely to bring back confusing memories that would upset him.

In the end his father merely nodded approval. 'You look very nice, Jimmy,' he said, bottom lip trembling with paternal feeling. 'Very nice indeed. You make a fellow proud, you do.'

'All right, Dad, easy does it,' said Jimmy gently. 'I'll get big-headed if you're not careful. I'll be a right horror to live with then.'

His father, still nodding, smiled faintly.

'Where's your shirt, Dad? In your bedroom? I'll just go and fetch it – can't have you catching cold now, can we?'

His father shuffled after him but stopped in the middle of the corridor. He was still there when Jimmy came back from the bedroom, a bewildered expression on his face, as if he were trying to remember why he'd left his seat in the first place. Jimmy took him by the elbow and walked him carefully back to the kitchen. He helped him into his shirt and sat him in his usual seat; Dad got confused if he had to use any of the others.

The kettle was still half full and Jimmy put it back on the stove to boil. It was a relief to have the gas back on; the mains had been hit by an incendiary bomb a few nights back and Jimmy's father had had an awful time trying to settle of a night without his milky cuppa. Jimmy spooned a careful portion of leaves into the pot but held off putting in more. Stocks were low at Hopwood's and he couldn't risk running short.

'Will you be home for supper, Jimmy?'

'No, Dad. I'm going to be out till late tonight, remember? I've left you some sausages on the stove.'

'Right-o.'

'Rabbit sausages, worse luck, but I've found you something special for after. You'll never guess – an orange!'

'An orange?' The old man's face flickered with the light of a passing memory. 'I got an orange once for Christmas, Jimmy.'

'Did you, Dad?'

'Back when I was a nipper on the farm. Such a beautiful big orange. My brother Archie ate it when I wasn't looking.'

The kettle started to whistle and Jimmy topped up the pot. His father was crying softly as he always did when Archie's name came up – his older brother was killed in the trenches twenty-five years or so earlier – but Jimmy ignored the fact. He'd learned over time that his father's tears for past grief would dry as quickly as they'd come, that the best thing to do was to push on cheerfully. 'Well, not this time, Dad,' he said. 'Nobody's going to eat this one but you.' He poured a good slug of milk into his father's cup. His dad liked a milky tea and it was one of the few things they didn't run short of thanks to Mr Evans and the pair of cows he kept in the barn at the side of his shop. Sugar was another story, and Jimmy scraped a small portion of condensed milk into the tea in lieu. He gave it a stir and carried the cup and saucer to the table. 'Now listen, Dad, the sausages'll stay warm in the saucepan till you're ready, so there's no need for you to turn on the burner, all right?' His father was brushing Finchie's crumbs along the tablecloth. 'Right, Dad?'

'What's that?'

'Your sausages are cooked, so don't go turning on the stove.'

'Right-o.' His father took a sip of tea.

'No need to turn on the taps either, Dad.'

'What's that, Jim?'

'I'll help you get cleaned up when I get in.'

His father looked up at Jimmy, perplexed for a second, and then he said, 'You look nice, boy-o. Off somewhere tonight, are you?'

Jimmy sighed. 'Yes, Dad.'

'Somewhere fancy, is it?'

'I'm just catching up with someone.'

'A lady friend?'

Jimmy couldn't help smiling at his father's coy term. 'Yes, Dad. A lady friend.'

'Someone special?'

'Very.'

'You'll have to bring her home one of these days.' His father's eyes held a hint of their old cleverness and mischief and Jimmy ached suddenly for how things used to be, back when he was the child and his dad did the looking after. He was immediately ashamed: he was twenty-two now, for Christ's sake, far too old to be longing for childish things. His shame was only increased when his father smiled, eager but uncertain, and said, 'Bring your young lady home one evening, Jimmy? Let your mother and me see she's good enough for our boy.'

Jimmy leaned to kiss his father on the head. He didn't bother explaining about his mother any more, that she was gone, that she'd left the pair of them over a decade ago to be with a new fellow with a smart car and a big house. To what end would he tell him? It made the old man happy to think she'd just popped out to stand in line for rationed groceries, and who was Jimmy to remind him how things really were? Life could be cruel enough these days without the truth making it worse. 'You take care now, Dad,' he said. 'I'm going to lock the door after me, but Mrs Hamblin next door has the key and she'll help you down to the shelter when the raids start.'

'Never know, Jimmy. Six o'clock already and still no sign of Jerry. He might've given himself a night off.'

'I wouldn't bet on it. There's a moon out there like a robber's lantern. Mrs Hamblin will come for you all right, soon as the alert sounds.'

His father was playing with the edge of Finchie's cage.

'All right, Dad?'

'Yes, yes. All right, Jimmy. You have a good time now and stop worrying so much. Your old man's not going any-where. Didn't get me in the last lot, ain't going to get me in this.'

Jimmy smiled, and swallowed the lump that was always in his throat these days, of love balled together with a sadness he couldn't articulate, a sadness that was about so much more than just his ailing father. 'That's the way, Dad. Now, you enjoy your tea and have a good listen to the wireless. I'll be back before you know it.'

Dolly was hurrying through a moonlit street in Bayswater. There'd been a bomb two nights ago, an art gallery with an attic full of paints and varnishes and an absentee landlord who'd made no provisions, and the place was still in disarray: bricks and charred pieces of wood, dislodged doors and windows, mountains of broken glass everywhere. Dolly had seen the fire burning from where she liked to sit sometimes on the roof of number 7, a great blaze in the distance, fierce and spectacular flames sending plumes of smoke into the lit-up sky.

She pointed her shaded torch at the ground, skirted around a sandbag, almost lost her heel in a blast hole, and had to hide from an overzealous warden when he blew his whistle and told her she ought to be a sensible girl and get herself inside – couldn't she see there was a bomber's moon on the rise?

In the beginning, Dolly had been afraid of the bombs like everybody else, but lately she found she rather liked being out in the Blitz. Jimmy, when she mentioned it to him, had been worried that after what happened to her family she was looking to be hit herself, but it wasn't that at all. There was just something utterly invigorating about it, and Dolly experienced a curious lightness of heart, a feeling very like elation, as she scurried along the night-time streets. She wouldn't have been anywhere but London; this was life, this Blitz, nothing like it had ever happened before, and likely it never would again. No, Dolly wasn't one bit frightened any more, not of being hit by the bombers – it was difficult to explain, but somehow she just knew it wasn't her fate.

To be faced with danger and find oneself fearless was thrilling. Dolly was aglow, and she wasn't alone either; a special atmosphere had gripped the city and it sometimes felt that everybody in London was in love. Tonight, though, it was something above and beyond the usual excitement that had her hurrying through the rubble. Strictly speaking, she needn't have been racing at all – she'd left in good time, having administered to Lady Gwendolyn her nightly three drams of sherry, just enough to send her into the arms of blissful slumber and keep her there through even the loudest of raids (the old dear was both too grand and sad to use the shelter) – but Dolly was so excited by what she'd done that merely to walk was a physical impossibility; propelled by the force of her own daring, she could've run a hundred miles and still not been out of breath.

She didn't, though. She had her stockings to think of, didn't she? They were her last pair without ladders and there really was nothing like a sharp piece of Blitz debris for ruining one's nylons, Dolly knew that from experience. Damage these, and she'd be forced to draw lines up the back of her leg with an eyebrow pencil, just like common Kitty. No, thank you very much. Taking no chances, when a bus pulled in near Marble Arch, Dolly jumped aboard.

There was a pocket of standing room at the back and she filled it, trying not to inhale the salty breath of a pompous man delivering a treatise on meat rationing and how best to sauté liver. Dolly resisted the urge to tell him that the recipe sounded bloody offal (ha!), and as soon as they'd rounded Piccadilly Circus, she leapt off again.

'Have a good night, darling,' called an elderly man in ARP uniform, as the bus drove into the distance.

Dolly answered with a wave. A pair of soldiers, home on leave and singing 'Nellie Dean' in drunken voices, linked arms with her as they passed, one on either side, and led her in a little spin. Dolly laughed as they each kissed one of her cheeks, and then called goodbye as they continued on their merry way.

Jimmy was waiting for her on the corner of Charing Cross Road and Long Acre; Dolly could see him in the moonlit square, right where he'd said he'd be, and she stopped short. There was no doubt about it, Jimmy Metcalfe was one fine-looking man. Taller than she remembered, a bit leaner, but the same dark hair swept back, and those cheekbones that made him seem as if he were always on the verge of saying something amusing or clever. He wasn't the only handsome man she'd met, certainly not (at times like this it was all but a civic duty to bat one's eyelashes at a soldier home on leave), but there was just something about him, some dark animal quality perhaps – a strength both physical and of character – that made Dolly's heart pound against her ribs like nobody's business.

He was such a *good* person, so honest and straightforward, that being with him made Dolly feel as if she'd won a race of sorts. Seeing him tonight, dressed in a black dinner suit just as she'd told him to, made her want to squeal with glee. It really did look tremendous on him – if she hadn't known better, Dolly would've presumed him a real gentleman. She took her lipstick and compact mirror from her handbag, angled herself to catch some moonlight, and accentuated her cupid's bow. She made a kissing motion to the mirror and then snapped it shut.

She glanced down at the brown coat she'd finally chosen, wondering vaguely about the fur trim on the collar and cuffs; mink, she supposed, though very possibly fox. It wasn't exactly the latest design – out of date by at least two decades – but the war made that sort of thing less important. Besides, clothing that cost a lot to buy never really went out of fashion; that's what Lady Gwendolyn said, and she knew an awful lot about such things. Dolly gave the sleeve a sniff. The mothball smell had been terribly strong when she first liberated the coat from the dressing room, but she'd suspended it from the bathroom window while she was bathing, and then sprayed it with as much atomized perfume as she could bear to part with, and it really was much better now. Hardly noticeable, what with the general smell of burning on the London air these days. She straightened the belt, careful to conceal the moth hole at the waist, and gave herself a little shake. She was so excited her nerves were tingling; she couldn't wait for Jimmy to see her. Dolly straightened the diamond brooch she'd pinned to the soft fur collar, tossed her shoulders back, and primped the curls pinned at the nape of her neck. With a deep breath she thrust forwards from the shadows – a princess, an heiress, a girl with the whole world at her feet.

It was cold out, and Jimmy had just lit a cigarette when he saw her. He had to look twice to make sure it was Dolly coming towards him – the fancy coat, dark curls that gleamed in the moonlight, the long-legged stride as her heels clipped confidence on the pavement. She was a vision – so beautiful, so fresh and polished, that it made Jimmy's heart constrict. She'd grown up since last he'd seen her. More than that, he knew suddenly, as he took in her new poise and glamour, as he shifted uncomfortably in his father's old suit, she'd grown away – away from him. He felt the distance with a jolt.

She arrived, wordless, in a cloud of perfume. Jimmy wanted to be witty, he wanted to be suave, he wanted to tell her she was perfection, the only woman in the world he could ever love. He wanted to say the very thing that would bridge this horrid new distance between them once and for all; to tell her about the progress he was making with his work, his editor's excited talk on evenings when they'd made their print deadline, about the opportunities that lay ahead for Jimmy when 'all this war business' was over, the name he could make for himself with his photographs, the money he stood to earn. But her beauty, and its contrast with the war and its cruelty, the hundreds of nights he'd gone to sleep picturing their future, and their past in Coventry and that long-ago picnic by the sea – all combined to blindside him, and the words wouldn't come. He managed half a smile and then, without giving it another thought, grabbed a handful of Dolly's hair and kissed her.

The kiss was like a starter's gun. She felt at once a welcome settling of her nerves, and a great rush of excitement at what was yet to come. Her plans, since she'd formed them, had been eating away at her all week and now, finally, it was time. Dolly was anxious to impress him, to show him how grown up she was now, a woman of the world, not the schoolgirl she'd been when he first met her. She allowed herself a moment to relax, to imagine herself into character, before pulling back to gaze up at his face. 'Hello there,' she said, in the same breathy tone Scarlett O'Hara might have used.

'Hello yourself.'

'Fancy meeting you here.' She ran her fingers lightly down his suit lapels. 'And dressed very smartly, I see.'

He shrugged a shoulder. 'What, this old thing?'

Dolly smiled, but tried not to laugh (he always made her laugh). 'Well then,' she said, glancing at him from beneath her lashes, 'I expect we should get started. We've a lot to do tonight, Mr Metcalfe.'

She hooked her arm through his and tried not to drag him as they walked quickly down Charing Cross Road to join the snaking queue for the 400 Club. They shuffled forwards as guns fired in the east and searchlights swept the sky like so many Jacob's ladders. A plane flew overhead when they were almost at the door, but Dolly ignored it; even a full-blown air raid wouldn't have induced her to give up her spot in the line now. They reached the top of the stairs and music drifted up towards them, chatter and laughter and a furious sleepless energy that made Dolly so giddy she had to hold on tightly to Jimmy's arm to keep from falling.

'You're going to love it inside,' she said. 'Ted Heath and his band really are divine, and Mr Rossi who runs the place is such a darling.'

'You've been here before?'

'Oh, sure, loads of times.' A teensy exaggeration – she'd been once – but he was older than she was, and had an important job where he travelled and met all sorts of

people, and she was still, well, *her*, and she desperately
wanted him to think her more sophisticated than the last
time he'd seen her, more desirable. Dolly laughed and
squeezed his arm. 'Oh now, don't look like that, Jimmy.
Kitty would never let up if I didn't keep her company sometimes; you know you're the only one I love.'

At the bottom of the stairs they passed through a cloakroom and Dolly stopped to leave her coat. Her heart was
beating like a hammer; she'd been longing for this moment,
practising and planning, and now it was finally here. She
thought back to all Lady Gwendolyn's stories, the things she
and Penelope had done together, the dances, the adventures,
the handsome men who'd chased them round London, and
she turned her back on Jimmy and let the coat fall free. As
he caught it, she made a slow pirouette, just the way she
had in all her imaginings, and then she struck a pose, revealing (drum roll, ladies and gentlemen) The Dress.

It was red, sleek, candescent, the sort of thing designed to
show off every curve on a woman's body, and Jimmy almost
dropped the coat when he saw it. His gaze ran all the way
down her figure and then all the way back up again; the
coat left his hand, a ticket replaced it, and he couldn't have
told you how.

'You—' he started. 'Doll, you look – that dress is incredible.'

'What?' She lifted a shoulder, just as he'd done outside.
'This old thing?' And then she grinned at him and was
Dolly again, and when she said, 'Come on. Let's get in
there,' he couldn't think of anywhere else he'd rather be.

*

Dolly scanned the area beyond the red cord, the small, packed dance floor, the table Kitty had called the 'Royal Table', right up close to the band; she'd thought she might see Vivien here tonight – Henry Jenkins was friendly with Lord Dumphee, the pair of them frequently photographed together in *The Lady* – but first inspections revealed no one she knew. Never mind, the night was still young; the Jenkinses might show up later. She steered Jimmy towards the back of the room, between the close-set round tables, past the people dining and drinking and dancing, until their progress brought them finally to Mr Rossi and the start of the cordoned-off area.

'Good evening,' he said when he saw them, pressing his hands together and making a little bow. 'You're here for the Dumphee engagement, of course?'

'What a wonderful club,' purred Dolly, not exactly answering the question. 'It's been such a long time, too long – Lord Sandbrook and I were just saying we ought to make it into London more often.' She glanced at Jimmy, smiling encouragement. 'Weren't we, darling?'

The hint of a frown pulled at Rossi's brow as he tried desperately to place them, but it didn't last long. Years at the helm of his nightclub had left him adept at keeping Society's ship on course and her passengers well flattered. 'Dear Lady Sandbrook,' he said, taking Dolly's hand and brushing a light kiss on its top, 'the place has been dark for the want of you, but you're here now and light returns.' He shifted his attention to Jimmy. 'And you, Lord Sandbrook. I trust you've been well?'

Jimmy said nothing and Dolly held her breath; she

knew how he felt about her 'games', as he called them, and she'd felt his hand stiffen against her back the second she started talking. If she were honest, the uncertainty of how he'd react only added to the adventure. Until he responded, everything else was magnified: Dolly could hear the beating of her own heart as she waited for his answer, a happy squeal in the crowd, the shattering of a glass breaking somewhere, the band beginning another song . . .

The little Italian fellow who'd called him by another man's name was watching keenly for an answer, and Jimmy had a sudden vision of his father at home in his striped pyjamas, the walls of their flat with the sad-looking green paper, Finchie in his cage with the broken biscuits. He could feel Dolly's stare, urging him to play his part; he knew she was watching, he knew what she wanted him to say, but it seemed to Jimmy there was something somehow crushing in answering to a name like that one. Something deeply disloyal to his poor old dad, whose mind was so mixed up, who waited for a wife who wouldn't come and cried for a brother dead these past twenty-five years, and who'd said of the crummy flat when they arrived in London, 'This is real nice, Jimmy. You've done a good job, boy – you make your mum and dad as proud as punch.'

He glanced sideways at Dolly's face and saw what he'd known he would – hope, writ large on every feature. These games of hers, they drove him mad, not least because more and more, lately, they seemed to highlight the distance between what she wanted from life and what he could afford to give her. They were harmless enough though, weren't they? No one was going to be hurt tonight because

Jimmy Metcalfe and Dorothy Smitham stood on the other side of a red cord. And she wanted it so badly, she'd gone to so much trouble with the dress and all, getting him to wear a suit – her eyes, for all the mascara she was wearing, were as wide and expectant as a child's, and he loved her so well, he couldn't stand to be the one to spoil things for her, not for the sake of his own foolish pride. Not for some vague notion that his lack of standing was something to hold firm to, and certainly not when it was the first time since her family died that Dolly had seemed like her old self.

'Mr Rossi,' he said with a broad smile, holding his hand out to shake the other man's firmly. 'Terribly good to see you, old man.' It was the poshest voice he could muster at short notice; he hoped to God it would do.

Being on the other side was every bit as wonderful as Dolly had dreamed it would be. Every bit as glorious as she'd gleaned from Lady Gwendolyn's stories. It wasn't that anything was *obviously* different – the red carpets and silk-covered walls were just the same, couples danced cheek to cheek on both sides of the rope, waiters carried meals and drinks and glasses back and forth – indeed, a less intelligent observer might not even have perceived that there were two sides at all, but Dolly knew. And she rejoiced to be on this one.

Of course, having achieved the Holy Grail, she was at something of a loss as to what to do next. For want of a better idea, Dolly helped herself to a glass of champagne, took Jimmy by the hand and slid into a plush banquette against the wall. Really, if she were honest, to watch was enough: the ever-shifting carousel of colourful dresses and smiling faces kept her enthralled. A waiter came by and asked what they'd like to eat and Dolly said eggs and bacon and they arrived, her champagne flute never seemed to empty, the music didn't stop.

'It's like a dream, isn't it?' she said glowingly. 'Aren't they all *wonderful*?'

At which Jimmy paused in striking his match to offer a noncommittal, 'Sure.' He dropped the flaming match into a brass ashtray and drew on his cigarette. 'What about you though, Doll? How's old Lady Gwendolyn? Still commanding all nine circles of hell?'

'Jimmy, you shouldn't say that sort of thing. I know I probably complained a bit at first, but she's really quite a darling once you get to know her. Calling on me a lot lately – we've become very close in our way.' Dolly leaned close so that Jimmy could light her cigarette. 'Her nephew's worried she's going to leave me the house in her will.'

'Who told you that?'

'Dr Rufus.'

Jimmy gave an ambiguous grunt. He didn't like it when she mentioned Dr Rufus; it didn't matter how many times Dolly reassured him that the doctor was her friend's father and far too ancient, really, to be interested in her in *that* way, Jimmy just frowned and changed the subject. Now he took her hand across the table. 'And Kitty? How's she.'

'Oh, well, Kitty . . .' Dolly hesitated, remembering the unfounded talk of Vivien and love affairs the other night. 'She's fighting fit, of course, her type always is.'

'Her type?' Jimmy repeated quizzically.

'I just mean she'd do well to pay more attention to her work and less to what's happening in the street and at the nightclubs. I expect some people simply can't help themselves.' She glanced at Jimmy. 'You wouldn't like her, I think.'

'No?'

Dolly shook her head and drew on her cigarette. 'She's a gossip and, I have to say, inclined to wantonness.'

'Wantonness?' He was amused now, a smile playing around his lips. 'Dear, dear me.'

She was serious – Kitty made quite a habit of sneaking her male friends in after dark; she thought Dolly didn't know, but really, the noise sometimes, one would've had to be deaf not to realize. 'Oh yes, quite,' said Dolly. There was a single candle flickering in its glass on the table and she swivelled it idly this way and that.

She hadn't told Jimmy about Vivien yet. She didn't know why exactly; it wasn't that she thought he wouldn't approve of Vivien, certainly not, rather that she'd felt an instinct to keep the blossoming friendship a secret, something all her own. Tonight, though, seeing him in person, fizzing a bit with the sweet champagne she was sipping, Dolly had the urge to tell him everything. 'Actually,' she said, nervous suddenly, 'I don't know that I've mentioned in my letters, but I've made a new friend.'

'Oh?'

'Yes, Vivien.' Just saying her name made Dolly thrill a little with happiness. 'Married to Henry Jenkins – you know, the author. They live across the street at number 25 and we've become rather firm friends.'

'Is that right?' He laughed. 'It's the oddest coincidence, but I just recently read one of his books.'

Dolly might have asked which one, but she didn't

because she wasn't really listening; her mind was swirling with all the things she'd been wanting to say about Vivien and had been holding in. 'She's really something else, Jimmy. Beautiful, of course, but not in an ordinary *showy* sort of way; and very kind, always helping at the WVS – I told you about the canteen we're running for service folk, didn't I? I thought so. She understands, too, about what happened – my family, in Coventry. She's an orphan herself, you see, raised by her uncle after her parents died, a great old school near Oxford, built on the family estate. Did I mention she's an heiress; she actually owns the house on Campden Grove, not her husband, it's hers.' Dolly drew breath, but only because she wasn't sure of the details. 'Not that she goes on about it; she's not like that at all.'

'She sounds tremendous.'

'She is.'

'I'd like to meet her.'

'W-well,' Dolly stammered, 'of course – one of these days.' She drew hard on her cigarette, wondering why the suggestion made her feel a sort of dread. Vivien and Jimmy meeting was not among the many future scenarios she'd envisaged; for one thing, Vivien was extremely private; for another, well, Jimmy was Jimmy. Very sweet, of course, kind and clever – but not exactly the sort of person Vivien would approve of, not as a boyfriend for Dolly. It wasn't that Vivien was unkind; she was just of a different class – from both of them, really, but Dolly, having been taken under Lady Gwendolyn's wing, had learned enough to be accepted by someone like Vivien. Dolly hated lying to Jimmy, she loved him; but she certainly wasn't about to hurt his feelings by putting it to him straight. She reached out and rested her hand on his arm, picking a piece of lint from the fraying cuff of his suit jacket. 'Everyone's just so busy with the war at the moment, aren't they? There's simply no time for being social.'

'I could always—'

'Jimmy, listen – they're playing our song! Shall we dance? Come on, do let's dance.'

Her hair smelled of perfume, that intoxicating scent he'd noticed when she first arrived, almost shocking in its intensity and promise, and Jimmy could have stayed that way forever, his hand in the small of her back, her cheek pressed against his, their bodies moving slowly together. He was tempted to forget the way she'd come over all evasive when he mentioned meeting her friend; the flash he'd had that the distance between them lately wasn't all about what happened to her family, that this Vivien, the rich lady across the road, might have something to do with it. In all probability there was nothing to it – Dolly liked to have secrets, she always had. And what did it matter anyway, right here and now, so long as the music kept playing?

It didn't, of course; nothing lasts forever and the faithless song ended. Jimmy and Dolly pulled apart to clap, and that's when he noticed the man with a thin moustache watching them from the edge of the dance floor. This in itself would have been no cause for alarm, but the man was also in conversation with Rossi, who was scratching his head with one hand, making extravagant hand gestures with the other, and consulting some sort of list.

A guest list, Jimmy realized with a jolt. What else would it be?

It was time to make a discreet exit, stage right. Jimmy took Dolly's hand and made to lead her away, casual as you please. There was every chance, he figured, if they went quickly and quietly, they'd be able to duck beneath the red cord, meld into the crowd and make a silent escape, no harm done.

Dolly, unfortunately, had other ideas; having made it to the dance floor, she was now rather reluctant to leave it. 'Jimmy, no,' she was saying, 'no, listen, it's "Moonlight Serenade".'

Jimmy started to explain, glancing back towards the man with the thin moustache, only to find that he was almost upon them, cigar clenched between his teeth, hand outstretched. 'Lord Sandbrook,' the man was saying to Jimmy, with the wide, confident smile of a man with pots of money hidden under his bed, 'so glad you could make it, old chap.'

'Lord Dumphee.' Jimmy took a stab. 'Congratulations to you and . . . your fiancée. Great party.'

'Yes, well, I'd have rather kept it small, but you know Eva.'

'I do indeed.' Jimmy laughed nervously.

Lord Dumphee puffed his cigar so it smoked like a train engine; his eyes narrowed ever so slightly, and Jimmy realized his host was also flying blind, doing his best to call to mind the provenance of his mysterious guests. 'You're friends of my fiancée's,' he said.

'Yes, that's right.'

Lord Dumphee was nodding. 'Of course, of course.' And then there came more puffing, more smoke, and just as Jimmy thought they might be safe— 'Only, it must be my memory – quite appalling it is, old chap, I blame the war and these blasted nights without sleep – but I can't think Eva mentioned a Sandbrook. Old friends, are you?'

'Oh, yes. Ava and I go way back.'

'Eva.'

'Precisely.' Jimmy tugged Dolly forwards. 'Have you met my wife, Lord Dumphee, have you met—'

'Viola,' Dolly said, smiling as though butter wouldn't melt in her mouth. 'Viola Sandbrook.' She lifted a hand and Lord Dumphee took out his cigar to kiss it. He pulled back but didn't let go, holding Dolly's hand aloft and letting his eyes roam greedily over her dress and every curve beneath it.

'Darling!' The trilling call came from across the floor. 'Darling Jonathan.'

Lord Dumphee dropped Dolly's hand at once. 'Ah,' he said, like a schoolboy caught by Nanny looking at nudie pictures, 'here comes Eva now.'

'Is that the time?' Jimmy said. He clasped Dolly's hand and squeezed it to signal his intent. She squeezed right back. 'Excuse me, Lord Dumphee,' he said. 'Many congratulations, but Viola and I have a train to catch.'

And with that, they were flying. Dolly could hardly keep from laughing as they dashed and weaved through the crowded nightclub, paused at the cloakroom for Jimmy to thrust forward the ticket and seize Lady Gwendolyn's coat, before hurrying up the stairs, two at a time, and into the dark cool of night-time London.

There'd been someone behind them in the 400 as they ran – Dolly had glanced back to see a red-faced man puffing like an overfed hound – and they didn't stop until they'd crossed Litchfield Street, blended with the theatre crowd coming out of St Martin's, and ducked into tiny Tower Lane. Only then did they collapse against the bricks, both of them breathless and laughing.

'His face—' Dolly said, gasping for air, 'Oh, Jimmy, I don't think I'll ever forget it as long as I live. When you said about the train, he was so . . . so *flummoxed*.'

Jimmy laughed too, a warm sound in the dark. It was pitch black where they were standing; even the full moon hadn't managed to spill over the eaves to flood the narrow laneway with its silvery light. Dolly was giddy, infused with life and happiness and the peculiar energy that came from having slipped inside another skin. There was nothing that made her spin quite like it, the invisible moment of transition when she stopped being Dolly Smitham and became instead Someone Else. The details of that Someone Else weren't particularly important; it was the frisson of performance she adored, the sublime pleasure of masquerade. It was like stepping into another person's life. Stealing it for a time.

Dolly looked up at the starlit sky. There were so many more stars in the blackout; it was one of the most beautiful things about the war. There were great rumpling eruptions in the distance, anti-aircraft guns giving it back as best they could; but up there the stars just kept on twinkling for all they were worth. They were like Jimmy, she realized, faithful, steadfast, something you could count on in your life.

'You really would do anything for me, wouldn't you?' she said with a contented sigh.

'You know I would.'

He wasn't laughing any more and, swift as the wind, the mood in the lane changed. *You know I would*. She did know it too, and in that instant the fact both thrilled and frightened her. Rather, her reaction did. To hear him say it, Dolly felt a string pluck deep down low within her belly. She trembled. Without thinking, she reached for his hand in the dark.

It was warm, smooth, large, and Dolly lifted it to brush a kiss along his knuckles. She could hear him breathing and she matched her own breaths to his.

She felt brave and grown-up and powerful. She felt beautiful and alive. Heart racing, she took his hand and placed it on her breast.

A soft sound in his throat, a sigh. 'Doll—'

She silenced him with a delicate kiss. She couldn't have him talking, not now; she might not find the nerve again. Calling to mind everything she'd ever heard Kitty and Louisa laughing about in the kitchen at number 7, Dolly reached her hand down to rest it on his belt. She let it slide further.

Jimmy groaned, leaned to kiss her, but she shifted her lips to whisper in his ear, 'You said you'd do anything I asked?'

He nodded against her neck and answered, 'Yes.'

'How about you walk a girl home and put her safely to bed?'

Jimmy sat up long after Dolly had fallen asleep. The night had been exhilarating and he didn't want it to be over yet. He didn't want anything to break the spell. A heavy bomb crashed somewhere nearby and the framed pictures rattled on the wall. Dolly stirred in her sleep, and Jimmy laid a hand gently on her head.

They'd hardly spoken on the walk back to Campden Grove, each of them too aware of the weighted meaning in her words, of the fact that a line had been crossed and they were now on a course that couldn't be reversed. He'd never been to the place she lived and worked, Dolly was funny about it – the old woman had rather definite ideas on the matter, she'd said, and Jimmy had always respected the fact.

When they arrived at number 7, she'd led him past the sandbags and through the front door, closing it softly behind them. It was dark inside the house, even blacker than out due to the curtains, and Jimmy had almost stumbled before Dolly switched on a small table lamp at the bottom of the staircase. The bulb threw a fluttery circle of light across the carpet and up the wall, and Jimmy glimpsed for the first time how grand this house of Dolly's really was. They didn't linger, and he was glad – the grandeur was unsettling. It was evidence of everything he wanted to give her but couldn't, and to see her so comfortable in it made him anxious.

She'd unbuckled the straps of her high-heeled shoes, hooked them over one finger, and taken him by the hand. With a finger to her lips, and a tilt of her head, she'd started up the stairs.

'I'll take care of you, Doll,' Jimmy had whispered when they made it to her bedroom. They'd run out of things to say to one another and were standing together by the bed, each waiting for the other to do something. She'd laughed when he said it, but there'd been a nervous edge to her voice and

he'd loved her all the more for the hint of youthful uncertainty that the laugh betrayed. He'd felt a bit on the back
foot ever since she'd propositioned him in the alley, but
now, hearing her laugh like that, sensing her apprehension,
Jimmy was back in charge and the world was suddenly set
to rights.

There was a part of him that wanted to tear the dress
from her body, but instead he reached out to slip his finger
beneath one of her fine straps. Her skin was warm, despite
the cold night, and he felt her tremble at his touch. The
slight, sudden movement made his breath catch in his
throat. 'I'll take care of you,' he said again. 'I always will.'
She didn't laugh this time, and he leaned to kiss her. God, it
was sweet. He unbuttoned the red dress, slid the straps from
her shoulders and let it fall lightly to the ground. She stood,
staring at him, her breasts rising and falling with each short
breath, and then she smiled, one of those half-smiles of
Dolly's that teased him and made him ache, and before he
knew what was happening she'd pulled his shirt loose from
his trousers . . .

Another bomb exploded, and plaster dust sifted down
from the mouldings high above the door. Jimmy lit a cigarette as the anti-aircraft guns fired their replies. Still Dolly
slept, her eyelashes black against her dewy cheeks. He
stroked her arm lightly. What a fool he'd been, what an
absolute fool – refusing to marry her when she'd all but
pleaded with him. Here he'd been fretting about the distance he sensed between them without stopping for a
minute to consider his part in creating it. The old ideas he'd
been clinging to about marriage and money. Seeing her
tonight, though, seeing as he hadn't before, just how easily

he could have lost Dolly to this new world of hers, had made everything clear. He was just lucky she'd waited for him, that she still felt the same way. Jimmy smiled, smoothing her dark, glossy hair; that he was lying here beside her was proof of that.

They'd have to live in his flat at first – not what he'd dreamed of for Dolly, but his dad was settled and there wasn't much point in moving while the war was still going on. When it was all over they could look at leasing something in a better area, maybe even talk to the bank about borrowing for their own place. Jimmy had some money set aside – he'd been saving for years, every spare penny in a jar – and his editor was very encouraging about his photographs.

He drew on his cigarette.

For now, though, they'd have a war wedding, and there was nothing shameful in that. It was romantic, he thought – love in a time of strife. Dolly would look gorgeous no matter what, she could have her friends as bridesmaids – Kitty, and the new one, Vivien, whose mention gave him an uneasy feeling – and Lady Gwendolyn Caldicott, perhaps, in place of her mother and father; and Jimmy already had the perfect ring to give her. It had been his own mother's and was stored now in a black velvet box at the back of his bedroom drawer. She'd left it when she went, with a note explaining why, on the pillow where his father slept. Jimmy had been looking after it ever since; at first so he could give it back when she returned; later, to remember her by; but increasingly, as he grew older, so he could someday make a new start with the woman he loved. A woman who wouldn't leave him.

Jimmy had adored his mother when he was a boy. She'd been his enchantment, his first love, the great gleaming moon whose wax and wane held his own small human spirit in its thrall. She used to tell him a story, he remembered now, whenever he couldn't sleep. It was about the *Nightingale Star*, a boat, she said, a magical boat – a great old galleon with wide sails and a strong, trusty mast, that sailed through the seas of sleep, night after night, in pursuit of adventure. She used to sit right by him on the side of the bed, stroking his hair and weaving tales of the mighty ship, and her voice as it spoke of the wondrous journeys would soothe him as nothing else could. Not until he was floating on the edge of sleep, the ship pulling him towards the great star in the east, would she lean down to whisper in his ear, 'Off you go now, my darling. I'll see you tonight on the *Nightingale Star*. Wait for me, won't you? We'll have ourselves a great adventure.'

He'd believed it for such a long time. After she left with the other fellow, that rich man with his silver tongue and his big expensive motorcar, he'd told himself the story each night, certain he would see her in his sleep, take hold of her and make her come back home.

He'd thought there'd never be another woman he could love that much. And then he'd met Dolly.

Jimmy finished his cigarette and checked his watch; it was almost five. He'd better leave now if he was going to be home in time to put an egg on for his dad's breakfast.

He stood up as quietly as he could, pulled on his trousers and did up his belt. He lingered for a moment, watching Dolly, and then he leaned to plant the lightest of kisses on her cheek. 'I'll see you on the *Nightingale Star*,' he said softly. She stirred, but didn't wake, and Jimmy smiled.

He slipped down the stairs and out into the freezing grey of wintry pre-dawn London. There was snow on the air, he could smell it, and he blew out great puffs of mist as he walked, but Jimmy wasn't cold. Not this morning. Dolly Smitham loved him, they were going to be married, and nothing would ever be wrong again.

Thirteen

Greenacres, 2011

It struck Laurel, as she sat down to a dinner of baked beans on toast, that this was very likely the first time she'd ever been alone at Greenacres. No mother or father going about their business in another room, no excitable sisters making the floorboards creak upstairs, no baby brother, no pets. Not so much as a hen roosting in the boxes outside. Laurel lived by herself in London, she'd done so on and off for the better part of forty years; to be frank, she was rather fond of her own company. Tonight, though, surrounded by the sights and sounds of childhood, she felt a loneliness the depths of which surprised her.

'Are you sure you'll be all right?' Rose had asked that afternoon before she left. She'd lingered in the entrance room, twisting the end of her long strand of African beads and inclining her head towards the kitchen. 'Because I could stay, you know. I wouldn't mind a bit. Perhaps I *should* stay? I'll just call Sadie and tell her I won't be able to make it.'

It was a strange turn-up for the books, Rose to be worried about Laurel, and Laurel had been taken aback. 'Nonsense,' she'd said, perhaps a little sternly, 'you'll do no such thing. I'll be perfectly fine by myself.'

Rose remained unconvinced. 'I don't know, Lol, it's just – it's not like you to phone like that, out of the blue. You're usually so busy, and now . . .' The beads threatened to snap their bonds. 'I'll tell you what, why don't I just ring Sadie and tell her we'll catch up tomorrow? It's really no bother.'

'Rose, please – ' Laurel did a lovely line in exasperation – 'for the love of God, go and see your daughter. I told you, I'm just here to have a little down time before I start filming *Macbeth*. To be honest, I'm rather looking forward to the peace and quiet.'

She had been, too. Laurel was grateful that Rose had been able to meet her with the keys, but her head was buzzing with the list of what she knew and what she still needed to find out about her mother's past, and she'd been eager to get inside and put her thoughts in order. Watching Rose's car disappear down the driveway had filled her with a sense of enormous anticipation. It had seemed to mark the beginning of something. She was here at last; she'd done it, left her life in London in order to get to the bottom of her family's great secret.

Now, though, alone in the sitting room with an empty dinner plate for company and a long night stretching ahead, she found her certainty waning. She wished she'd given Rose's offer a little more thought; her sister's gentle patter was just the thing to keep one's mind from drifting someplace dark, and Laurel could've used the help right now. The problem was the ghosts, for of course she wasn't really alone at all, they were everywhere: hiding behind corners, drifting up and down the stairs, echoing against the bathroom tiles. Little girls in bare feet and smocks and various lanky states of growing up; the tall lean figure of Daddy whistling in the shadows; but most of all Ma, who was everywhere at once, who was this house, Greenacres, whose passion and energy infused each plank of wood, each pane of glass, each stone.

She was in the corner of the room right now – Laurel could see her there, wrapping a birthday present for Iris. It was a book about ancient history, a children's encyclopedia, and Laurel could remember being stirred at the time by the beautiful illustrations inside, black and white and somehow mysterious in their depictions of long-ago places. The book, as an object, had seemed distinctly important to Laurel, and she'd felt jealous when Iris unwrapped it on their parents' bed next morning, when she started turning the pages with proprietorial care and readjusting the ribbon bookmark. There was something about a book that inspired dedication and a swelling desire to possess it, especially in Laurel, who hadn't many of her own.

They hadn't been a particularly bookish family – it always surprised people to hear that – but they'd never gone without stories. Daddy had been full of dinner-table anecdotes, and Dorothy Nicolson was the sort of mother to invent her own fairy tales rather than read them out of books. 'Did I ever tell you,' she'd said once when Laurel was small, and resistant to sleep, 'about the *Nightingale Star*?'

Laurel had shaken her head eagerly. She liked Mummy's stories.

'Have I not? Well, that explains it then. I did wonder why I never saw you there.'

'Where, Mummy? What's the nightingale star?'

'Why, it's the way home, of course, little wing. And it's the way there, too.'

Laurel was confused. 'The way where?'

'Everywhere – anywhere . . .' She smiled then, in that way she had that always made Laurel feel glad to be near her, and leaned closer, as if to tell a secret, her dark hair falling forwards over one shoulder. Laurel loved to hear secrets; she was very good at keeping them too, so she listened closely when Mummy said, 'The *Nightingale Star* is a great ship that leaves each night from the rim of sleep. Have you ever seen a picture of a pirate ship, one with billowing white sails and rope ladders that swing and sway in the wind?'

Laurel nodded hopefully.

'Then you'll know her when you see her, for she looks just like that. The straightest mast you can imagine, and a flag at the very top, silver cloth with a white star and a pair of wings at its centre.'

'How do I get aboard, Mummy? Will I have to swim?' Laurel wasn't a very good swimmer.

Dorothy laughed. 'That's the best part of all. The only thing you have to do is wish, and when you fall asleep tonight, you'll find yourself on her warm decks, about to set sail on a grand adventure.'

'Will you be there, too, Mummy?'

Dorothy had a faraway look on her face; a mysterious expression she wore sometimes, as if remembering something that made her feel a little bit sad. But then she smiled, and ruffled Laurel's hair. 'Of course I will, poppet. You didn't think I'd let you go alone, did you?'

In the distance, a late train whistled into the station and Laurel let out a sigh. It seemed to echo from one wall to

another and she considered switching on the television, just
to have some noise. Ma had steadfastly refused to upgrade
to a set with a remote control though, so she tuned the old
wireless to BBC Radio 3 and picked up her book instead.

It was her second Henry Jenkins novel, *The Reluctant
Muse*, and truth be told Laurel was finding it rather hard
going. In fact, she was beginning to suspect the man was
something of a male chauvinist. Certainly his main character, Humphrey (just as irresistible as the male lead in his
other book), had some questionable ideas about women.
Adoration was one thing, but he seemed to look upon his
wife, Viola, as a precious possession; not so much a flesh-
and-blood woman as a blithe spirit whom he had captured
and thereby saved. Viola was an 'element of the wild'
brought to London in order to be civilized – by Humphrey,
of course – but whom the city must never be permitted to
'corrupt'. Laurel rolled her eyes in impatience. She found
herself wishing Viola would just pick up her pretty skirts
and run in the opposite direction as fast and as far as
she could.

She didn't, of course; she agreed to marry her hero –
this was Humphrey's story, after all. Laurel had liked the
girl at first, she'd seemed a spirited and worthy heroine,
unpredictable and fresh, but the more she read, the less of
that girl she saw. Laurel realized that she was being unfair:
poor Viola was barely an adult and could therefore hardly
be blamed for having questionable judgement. And really,
what would Laurel know? She'd never succeeded in sustain-
ing a relationship for longer than two years. Nonetheless,
Viola's marriage to Humphrey was not Laurel's idea of a
fine romance. She persisted through two further chapters

that took the pair to London and established the creation of
Viola's gilded cage, before it all became too much and she
slapped the book down in frustration.

It had only just gone nine, but Laurel decided that was
late enough. She was tired after the day's travel and she
wanted to be up early next morning so she could get to the
hospital in good time and hopefully find her mother at her
best. Rose's husband, Phil, had brought over a spare car
from his garage – a 1960s Mini, green as a grasshopper –
and she was going to drive herself into town as soon as she
was ready. Tucking *The Reluctant Muse* beneath her arm,
she washed her plate and took herself up to bed, leaving the
dark ground floor of Greenacres to the ghosts.

'You're in luck,' the sour nurse told Laurel when she arrived
the next morning, managing to make it sound a regrettable
state of affairs. 'She's up and in fine fettle. Last week's party
tired her, you know, but visits from family seem to do them
the world of good. Just try not to excite her too much.' And
then she smiled with a remarkable deficit of warmth and
returned her attention to the plastic clipboard she was clearing.

Laurel abandoned plans for a rousing session of Irish
dancing and started down the beige hallway. She arrived at
her mother's door and knocked lightly. When there was no
answer, she gently opened it. Dorothy was reclined in the
armchair, her body curved away from the door, and Laurel's
first thought was that she was sleeping. It wasn't until she
crept closer that she realized her mother was awake and
paying close attention to something in her hands.

'Hello there, Ma,' said Laurel.

The old woman startled and turned her head. There was a foggy look about her eyes, but she smiled when she registered her daughter. 'Laurel,' she said softly. 'I thought you were in London.'

'I was. I've come back for a bit.'

Her mother didn't ask why, and Laurel wondered whether perhaps a person reached an age when so much was kept from them, so many details of life discussed and decided elsewhere, misheard or misunderstood, that to be surprised was no longer disconcerting. She wondered whether she, too, would find one day that absolute clarity was neither possible nor desirable. What a ghastly prospect. She wheeled the tray table aside and sat down on the spare vinyl-covered chair. 'What's that you've got there?' She nodded at the object in her mother's lap. 'Is it a photograph?'

Dorothy's hand trembled as she held out the small silver frame she'd been cradling. It was old and dented, but freshly polished. Laurel couldn't think that she'd ever seen it before. 'From Gerry,' her mother said. 'A gift for my birthday.'

It was the perfect gift for Dorothy Nicolson, patron saint of all discarded things, and that was typical of Gerry. Just when he seemed completely disconnected from the world and all who dwelt in her, he managed a stroke of astonishing insight. Laurel felt a pang when she thought of her brother: she'd left a message for him on his university voicemail – three messages, in fact, since she'd decided to leave London. The last she'd recorded late at night after a half bottle of red, and she feared it had been rather more plain spoken than those previous. She'd told him she was home at Greenacres, determined to find out what happened 'back when we were kids', that the other sisters didn't yet know the details and she needed him to help. It had seemed a good idea at the time, but she hadn't heard back.

Laurel put on her reading glasses to look closely at the sepia photograph. 'A wedding party,' she said, taking in the arrangement of formally attired strangers pressed behind the spotted glass. 'No one we know, though, is it?'

Her mother didn't answer, not exactly. 'Such a precious thing,' she said, shaking her head with slow sadness. 'A charity shop – that's where he found it. Those people . . . they should be hanging on someone's wall, not lying in a box of unwanted things . . . It's terrible, isn't it, Laurel, the way we throw people away?'

Laurel agreed that it was. 'The photo's lovely, isn't it?' she said, running a thumb over the glass. 'Wartime by the look of the clothing, though he's not in uniform.'

'Not everyone wore one.'

'Shirkers, you mean.'

'There were other reasons.' Dorothy took back the picture. She studied it again and then reached, shakily, to set it down beside the framed picture of her own austerity wedding.

At mention of the war, Laurel had felt opportunity spread before her, the vertigo of anticipation. Surely there could be no better moment to raise the matter of her mother's past. 'What did you do in the war, Ma?' she asked with careful nonchalance.

'I was with the Women's Voluntary Service.'

Just like that. No hesitation, no reluctance, nothing to suggest this was the first time mother and daughter had ever broached the topic. Laurel grasped keenly at the thread of conversation. 'You mean knitting socks and feeding soldiers?'

Her mother nodded. 'We had a canteen in a local crypt. We served soup . . . Sometimes we ran a mobile canteen.'

'What, out in the streets, dodging the bombs?'

Another slight nod.

'Ma – ' Laurel was lost for words. The answer itself, the fact of having received one at all – 'You were brave.'

'No,' Dorothy said, with surprising sharpness. Her lips quivered. 'There were far braver people than I.'

'You've never mentioned it before.'

'No.'

Why not? Laurel wanted to plead. *Tell me.* Why was it all such a big secret? Henry Jenkins and Vivien, her mother's childhood in Coventry, the war years before she met Daddy . . . What had happened to make Ma seize her second chance so firmly, to turn her into the kind of person who could kill the man who threatened to bring her past back home to haunt her? Instead, Laurel said, 'I wish I'd known you back then.'

Dorothy smiled faintly. 'That would have been difficult.'

'You know what I mean.'

Her mother shifted in her chair, an ill expression pulling at the lines of her papery brow. 'I don't think you'd have liked me very much.'

'What do you mean? Why ever not?'

Dorothy's mouth twitched, as if the thing she wanted to say would not come out.

'Why not, Ma?'

Dorothy forced a smile, but a shadow in her voice and in her eyes belied it. 'People change as they get older . . .

grow wiser, make better decisions . . . I am *very* old, Laurel. Anyone who lives as long as I have can't help but collect regrets along the way . . . things they did in the past . . . things they wish they'd done differently.'

The past, regrets, people changing – Laurel felt the thrill of having arrived at last. She tried to sound light, a loving daughter asking her elderly mother about her life. 'What sort of things, Ma? What would you have done differently?'

But Dorothy wasn't listening. Her gaze had a distant look about it; her fingers were busy working the edges of the blanket on her lap. 'My father used to tell me I'd get myself into trouble if I wasn't careful . . .'

'All parents say that sort of thing,' Laurel said with gentle caution. 'I'm sure you never did anything worse than the rest of us.'

'He tried to warn me, but I never listened. I thought I knew best. I was punished for my bad decisions, Laurel – I lost everything . . . everything I loved.'

'How? What happened?'

But the previous speech, whatever memories it brought with it, had tired Dorothy – the wind lost from her sails – and she was slumped now against her cushions. Her lips moved a little but no sound came out, and after a moment she gave up, turning her head back towards the misted window.

Laurel studied her mother's profile, wishing she had been a different sort of daughter, wishing there was more time, that she could go back and do it all again, not leave everything to the last and find herself sitting at her mother's hospital bed with so many blanks to fill. 'Oh, now,' she said brightly, trying a different tack, 'Rose showed me something rather special.' She fetched the family album from its shelf and slipped the picture of her mother and Vivien from inside. For all her attempts at composure, she noticed that her fingers were trembling. 'It was inside a trunk, I believe, somewhere at Greenacres.'

Dorothy took the proffered photograph and looked at it.

Doors opened and closed in the hallway, a buzzer sounded in the distance, cars stopped and started on the turning circle outside.

'You were friends,' Laurel prompted.

Her mother nodded, haltingly.

'In the war.'

Another nod.

'Her name was Vivien.'

This time Dorothy looked up. Surprise flitted across her lined face, followed by something else. Laurel was on the verge of explaining about the book and its inscription when her mother said, 'She died,' so quietly that Laurel almost didn't hear. 'Vivien died in the war.'

Laurel remembered reading about it in Henry Jenkins's obituary. 'A bombing raid,' she said.

Her mother gave no sign of having heard. She was staring again at the photo. Her eyes had glazed, and her cheeks were suddenly moist. 'I hardly recognize myself,' she said in a thin and ancient voice.

'It was a long time ago.'

'Another lifetime.' Dorothy drew a crumpled handkerchief from somewhere and pressed it to her cheeks.

Her mother was still speaking softly behind her hanky, but Laurel couldn't make out all the words: something about bombs, and noise, and being frightened to start again.

She leaned closer, skin tingling with a strong sense that answers were at hand. 'What's that, Ma?'

Dorothy turned to Laurel and the look on her face was as fearful as if she'd just seen a ghost. She reached out and gripped Laurel's sleeve; when she spoke, her voice was frayed. 'I did something, Laurel,' she whispered, 'during the war ... I wasn't thinking straight, everything had gone horribly wrong ... I didn't know what else to do and it seemed like the perfect plan, a way to put things right, but he found out – he was angry.'

Laurel's heart lurched. *He.* 'Is that why the man came, Ma? Is that why he came that day, on Gerry's birthday?' Her chest felt tight. She was sixteen again.

Her mother was still clenching Laurel's sleeve, her face ashen and her voice as thin as a reed. 'He found me, Laurel ... he never stopped looking.'

'Because of what you did in the war?'

'Yes.' Barely audible.

'What was it, Ma? What did you do?'

The door opened and Nurse Ratched appeared carrying a tray. 'Lunchtime,' she said briskly, wheeling the table into position. She half-filled a plastic cup with lukewarm tea, and checked there was still water in the jug. 'Just ring the bell when you're finished, dear,' she sang in a too-loud voice. 'I'll come back and help you to the toot.' She glanced about the table to check everything was as it should be. 'Anything else you need before I go?'

Dorothy was dazed, spent, her eyes searching the other woman's face.

The nurse smiled brightly, bending from the waist so she was nice and close. 'Anything else you need, dear?'

'Oh.' Dorothy blinked and gave a small bewildered smile that broke Laurel's heart. 'Yes, yes please. I need to speak to Dr Rufus—'

'Dr Rufus? You mean Dr *Cotter*, dear.'

A cloud of confusion cast its brief shadow on her pale face, and then, 'Yes,' she said with an even fainter smile. 'Of course, Dr Cotter.'

The nurse said she'd send him in when she could, and then turned towards Laurel, tapping a finger to her temple and delivering a Significant Look. Laurel resisted the urge to garrotte the woman with her handbag strap as she squeaked around the room in her soft-soled shoes.

The wait for the nurse to leave them was interminable: she collected old cups, marked things on the medical chart, paused to comment idly on the driving rain. Laurel was almost burning with suspense when the door finally closed behind her.

'Ma?' she prompted, more sharply than she'd have liked.

Dorothy Nicolson looked at her daughter. Her face was pleasantly blank and Laurel realized with a jolt that whatever it was that had pressed so urgently before the interruption was no longer there. It had receded, back to the place where old secrets go. The frustration was breathtaking. She could ask again, say, 'What did you do that brought that man after you? Was it something to do with Vivien? Tell me, please, so I can let the whole thing go,' but the beloved face, that weary old-lady's face, was staring at her now in a state of mild perplexity, a slight, worried smile forming as she said, 'Yes, Laurel?'

Mustering every bit of patience she could – there was

always tomorrow, she would try again then – Laurel smiled back and said, 'Would you like some help with your lunch, Ma?'

Dorothy didn't eat much; she'd wilted in the past half hour, and Laurel was struck anew by just how frail she'd become. The green armchair was a rather humble affair, one they'd brought from home, and Laurel had seen her mother sitting in it countless times over the decades. Somehow, though, the chair had changed proportions in the past few months and was now a great hulking thing that devoured Ma's frame like a surly bear.

'Why don't I give your hair a brush?' said Laurel. 'Would you like that?'

The ghost of a smile skimmed Dorothy's lips and she nodded slightly. 'My mother used to brush my hair.'

'Did she?'

'I pretended not to like it – I wanted to be independent – but it was lovely.'

Laurel smiled as she collected the antique hairbrush from the shelf behind the bed; she passed it gently over her mother's dandelion fluff and tried to picture what she must have been like as a little girl. Full of adventure, no doubt, naughty at times, but with the sort of spirit that made people fond rather than cross. Laurel supposed she'd never know, not unless her mother told her.

Dorothy's eyelids, paper-thin, had closed and the fine wiry nerves inside them twitched occasionally at whatever mysterious pictures were forming on the black beneath. Her breathing slowed as Laurel stroked her hair, and when it took on the rhythm of slumber, Laurel set down the brush as quietly as she could. She pulled the crocheted rug a little higher on her mother's lap and kissed her lightly on the cheek.

'Goodbye, Ma,' she whispered. 'I'll come again to-morrow.'

She was tiptoeing from the room, careful not to jiggle her bag or make too much noise with her shoes, when a drowsy voice said, 'That boy.'

Laurel turned, surprised. Her mother's eyes were still closed.

'That boy, Laurel,' she mumbled.

'Which boy?'

'The one you've been going around with – Billy.' Her misty eyes opened and she turned her head towards Laurel. She lifted a feeble finger and her voice when she spoke was soft, sad. 'You think I don't notice? You think I wasn't young once myself? That I don't know how it feels to fancy a handsome boy?'

Laurel realized then that her mother was no longer in the hospital room; that she was back at Greenacres, talking to her teenage daughter. The fact was unnerving.

'Are you listening to me, Laurel?'

She swallowed, found her voice. 'I'm listening, Mummy.' It had been a long time since she'd called her mother that.

'If he asks you to marry him and you love him, then you must say yes . . . Do you understand me?'

Laurel nodded. She felt strange, dizzy and rather hot. The nurses had said her mother's mind was drifting these days, in and out of the present like a radio tuner slipping its station, but what had brought her here? Why would her focus settle on a boy she'd barely known, a fleeting crush of Laurel's from so very long ago?

Dorothy's lips moved against one another softly, and then she said, 'I made so many mistakes ... so many mistakes.' Her cheeks were moist with seeping tears. 'Love, Laurel, that's the only reason to get married. For love.'

Laurel made it as far as the toilets in the hospital corridor. She turned on the tap, cupped her hands and collected some water to toss on her face; she leaned her palms on the basin. There were hairline fractures near the plughole and they merged together as her vision glazed. Laurel closed her eyes. Her pulse was beating like a jackhammer in her ears. God, she was shaken.

It wasn't merely the fact of being spoken to like a teenager, the instant erasure of fifty years, the conjuring of a long-ago boy, the faraway feeling of first love fluttering at her edges. It was the words themselves, the urgency in Ma's voice as she spoke, the sincerity that suggested she was offering her teenage daughter the wealth of her own experience. That she was pressing Laurel to make choices that she, Dorothy, had not – to avoid making the mistakes she had.

But it didn't make sense. Her mother had loved her father; Laurel knew it just as certainly as she knew her own name. They'd been married for five and a half decades before Daddy's death, without so much as a sniff of marital disharmony. If Dorothy had married for some other reason, if she'd regretted that decision all this time, she'd done a terrific job of pretending otherwise. No one could keep up a performance like that, surely? Of course they couldn't. Besides, Laurel had heard the story of how her parents met and fell in love a hundred times before; she'd seen her mother gazing at her father's face as he recounted the way he'd known at once that they were meant to be together.

Laurel looked up. Grandma Nicolson had had her doubts though, hadn't she? Laurel had always been aware of something uncomfortable between her mother and grandmother – a formality in the way they spoke to one another, the stern set of the older woman's mouth when she was looking at her daughter-in-law and thought no one else was watching. And then, when Laurel was fifteen or so and they were visiting Grandma Nicolson's boarding house by the sea, she'd overheard something she shouldn't have. She'd spent too long in the sun one morning and come in early with a raging headache and a bad case of sunburned shoulders. She was lying in her darkened bedroom, nursing a wet flannel on her forehead and a feeling of great hardship in her breast, when Grandma Nicolson and her elderly boarder, Miss Perry, happened along the corridor.

'He's a real credit to you, Gertrude,' Miss Perry was saying. 'Of course, he always was a good lad.'

'Yes, worth his weight in gold, my Stephen. More help around here than his father ever was.' Grandma had paused, waiting for the knowing grunt of agreement that was forthcoming from her consort, and then continued, 'Kind-hearted, too. Never could resist a stray.'

That's when Laurel had grown interested. The words were weighted with the echoes of previous conversations and certainly Miss Perry seemed to know precisely what Grandma was referring to. 'No,' she'd said. 'The lad didn't stand a chance, did he? Not with one as beautiful as her.'

'Beautiful? Well, I suppose, if you like that sort of thing.

A bit too – ' Grandma paused, and Laurel craned to hear which word she'd pluck – 'a bit too *ripe* for my tastes.'

'Oh yes,' Miss Perry backpedalled fast, 'terribly ripe. Knew a good wicket when she saw it though, didn't she?'

'She did.'

'Knew a soft touch when she met it.'

'Indeed.'

'And to think he might've married a nice *local* girl like that Pauline Simmonds down the street. I always thought she might have been sweet on him.'

'Of course she was,' Grandma snapped, 'and who could blame her? Hadn't counted on Dorothy, though, had we? Poor Pauline didn't stand a chance, not against one like her, not when she had her mind set.'

'Such a shame.' Miss Perry knew her cue and her line. 'Such a terrible shame.'

'Bewitched him, she did. My dear boy didn't know what had hit him. He believed she was an innocent, of course, and who could blame him – back from France just a few short months when they married. She had his head in a spin – she's one of those people, isn't she, who gets whatever she sets her mind to.'

'And she wanted him.'

'She wanted an escape, and my son gave it to her. No sooner were they wed and she dragged him away from everything and everyone he knew to start again in that tumbledown farmhouse. I blame myself, of course.'

'But you mustn't!'

'I was the one who brought her into this house.'

'There was a war on, it was near impossible to get good staff – you weren't to know.'

'But that's just it. I should have known; I should have made it my business to know. I was far too trusting. At least, I was at the start. I made enquiries about her but not until after, and by then it was too late.'

'What do you mean? Too late for what? What did you find out?'

But whatever it was Grandma Nicolson had found remained a mystery to Laurel, for the two of them moved out of earshot before her grandmother could expand. To be honest it hadn't concerned Laurel too much at the time. Grandma Nicolson was a prude and an attention-seeker who liked to make her eldest granddaughter's life a misery by reporting to her parents if she so much as looked at a boy on the beach. Whatever it was Grandma thought she'd discovered about their mother, Laurel had decided as she lay there cursing her throbbing head, it was bound to be an exaggeration, if not an all-out fiction.

Now, though – Laurel dried her face and hands – now she wasn't so sure. Grandma's suspicions – that Dorothy had been seeking an escape, that she wasn't as innocent as she appeared, that her hasty marriage had been one of con-venience – seemed to tally, in some ways, with the things her mother had just told her.

Had Dorothy Smitham been running from a broken engagement when she turned up at Mrs Nicolson's boarding house? Was that what Grandma had found out? It was pos-sible, but there had to be more to it than that. A previous relationship might have been enough to sour her grand-mother's milk – Lord knows it hadn't taken much – but surely it wasn't the sort of thing her mother might still be crying over sixty years later (guiltily, it seemed to Laurel: all that talk of mistakes, of not thinking straight) – unless she'd run away from her fiancé without telling him? But why, if she'd loved him so much, would Ma have done such a thing? Why hadn't she just married him? And what did any of it have to do with Vivien and Henry Jenkins?

There was something Laurel wasn't seeing – lots of things, probably. She let out a hot sigh of exasperation that echoed around the small tiled bathroom. She felt thoroughly thwarted. So many disparate clues that meant nothing on their own. Laurel tore off a piece of toilet tissue and dabbed the mascara that had smeared beneath her eyes. The whole mystery was like the beginning of a child's dot-to-dot, or a constellation in the night sky. Their father had once taken them sky-watching when Laurel was small. They'd set up camp on the rise above Blindman's Wood and, as they waited for the dusk to deepen and the stars to appear, he'd told them about the time he'd been lost as a boy and followed the stars home. 'You just have to look for the pictures,' he'd said, lining up his telescope on its stand. 'If you ever find yourself alone in the dark, they'll show you the way back.'

'But I can't see any pictures,' Laurel had protested, rubbing her mittens together and squinting at the twinkling stars above.

Daddy had smiled at her then, fondly. 'That's because you're looking at the stars themselves,' he'd said, 'instead of the spaces in between. You have to draw lines in your mind, that's when you'll begin to see the whole picture.'

Laurel stared at herself in the hospital mirror. She blinked and the memory of her lovely father dissolved. A sudden pressing ache of mortal grief took its place – she missed him, she was getting older, her mother was fading.

What a bloody mess she looked. Laurel took out her comb and did what she could with her hair. It was a start. Finding pictures in the constellations had never been her strong suit. Gerry was the one who'd been able to wow them all by making sense of the night-time sky; even as a small boy he'd pointed out patterns and pictures where Laurel saw only scattered stars.

Thoughts of her brother tugged at Laurel. They ought to be together on this search, damn it. It belonged to both of them. She took out her phone and checked for missed calls.

Nothing. Still nothing.

She scrolled through the address book until she found his office number and pressed call. She waited, biting her thumbnail, ruing (not for the first time) her brother's contrary refusal to get a mobile, as a distant telephone on a cluttered Cambridge desk rang and rang and rang. Finally, a click and then: 'Hello, you've reached Gerry Nicolson. I'm shooting stars at the minute. You're welcome to leave your details.'

No promise that he'd do anything with them though, Laurel noted wryly. She didn't leave a message. She'd just have to go on alone for now.

Fourteen

London, January 1941

Dolly handed over her umpteenth cup of soup and smiled at whatever it was the young fireman had just said. The laughter, the chatter, the piano music were all too loud to know for sure, but judging by the look on his face it was something flirtatious. It never hurt to smile, so Dolly did, and when he took his soup and went in search of somewhere to sit she was rewarded, finally, with a break in the flow of hungry mouths to feed and an opportunity to sit down and rest her weary feet.

They were *killing* her. She'd been held up leaving Campden Grove when Lady Gwendolyn's bag of sweets went 'missing' and the old woman had descended into a colossal misery. The sweets turned up eventually, pressed into the mattress beneath the grande dame's grande derrière; but by then Dolly was so strapped for time she'd had to run all the way to Church Street in a pair of satin shoes made for no greater duty than being admired. She'd arrived out of breath and sore of foot, only to have her hopes of sneaking in beneath the veil of carousing soldiers dashed. She was spied mid-flight by the team leader, Mrs Waddingham, a snout-faced woman with a terrible case of eczema that kept her in gloves and a filthy mood, no matter the weather.

'Late again, Dorothy,' she said, through lips as tight as a dachshund's arse. 'I need you in the kitchen serving soup; we've been run off our feet all evening.'

Dolly knew the feeling. Worse luck, a quick glance confirmed her haste had been in vain – Vivien wasn't even there. Which made no sense, because Dolly had checked carefully that they'd be working the evening shift together; what was more, she'd waved at Vivien from Lady Gwendolyn's window not one hour before, when she saw her leaving number 25 in her WVS uniform.

'Get on then, girl,' said Mrs Waddingham, making a scoot-scoot motion with her gloved hands. 'Into the kitchen you go. The war's not going to wait for a girl like you, now, is it?'

Dolly battled an urge to fell the other woman with a sharp jab to the shins, but decided it wouldn't be proper. She bit back a smile – sometimes imagining really was as good as doing – and gave Mrs Waddingham an obsequious nod instead.

The canteen had been set up in the crypt of St Mary's Church and the 'kitchen' was a small draughty alcove across which a trestle table had been dressed with a skirt and a string of Union Jacks to form a counter. There was a small sink in the corner, and a paraffin stove to keep the soup hot; best of all as far as Dolly was concerned right now, a spare pew leaned against the wall.

She took a last glance around to make sure her absence wouldn't be noticed: the room was full of satisfied servicemen, a couple of ambulance drivers were playing table tennis, and the rest of the WVS ladies were busy clicking their knitting needles and tongues in the far corner. Mrs Waddingham was among them, her back turned to the kitchen, and Dolly decided to risk the dragon's wrath. Two hours was an awfully long time to be on one's feet. She sat down and slipped off her shoes; with a sigh of sweet relief, she arched her stocking-clad toes slowly back and forth.

WVS members weren't supposed to smoke in the canteen (fire regulations), but Dolly dug into her bag and pulled out one of the crisp new packets she'd got from Mr Hopton the grocer. The soldiers always smoked – no one had the heart to stop them – and a permanent grey tobacco cloud hugged the ceiling; Dolly decided no one would notice if a little more drifted its way. She eased herself onto the tiled floor and struck the match, giving herself over finally to thoughts of the rather momentous thing that had happened that afternoon.

It had all got off to rather an ordinary start: Dolly had been dispatched to the grocer's after lunch and, embarrassing as it was to remember now, the task had put her in a foul mood. It wasn't easy to find sweets these days, sugar being rationed and all, but Lady Gwendolyn was never one to take no for an answer and Dolly had been forced to trawl the back streets of Notting Hill in search of the friend of someone's uncle's landlord, who – it was rumoured – still had such contraband to sell. She'd only just got back to number 7 two hours later, and was still removing her scarf and gloves when the doorbell rang.

The type of day she'd been having, Dolly had fully expected to see a rabble of pesky kids collecting scrap metal for Spitfires; instead, she'd found a tidy little man with a thin moustache, and a strawberry birthmark covering one cheek. He was carrying an enormous black alligator brief-case, bulging at the seams, the weight of which appeared to be causing him some discomfort. One glance at his neat comb-over was enough to recognize, however, that he wasn't the sort to admit vexation.

'Pemberly,' he said briskly. 'Reginald Pemberly, solicitor at law, here to see Lady Gwendolyn Caldicott.' He leaned closer to add, with a secretive lowering of the voice, 'It's a matter of some urgency.'

Dolly had heard mention of Mr Pemberly ('A mouse of a man, not a patch on his father. Knows how to keep a clean ledger, though, so I permit him to do my business . . .'), but she'd never come face to face with him before. She let him in, out of the freezing cold, and ran upstairs to check that Lady Gwendolyn was happy to see him. She was never happy, not really, but where matters of money were concerned she was ever vigilant, and so – despite sucking in her cheeks with sullen disdain – she waved a porcine hand to signal that the fellow might be admitted to her bower.

'Good afternoon, Lady Gwendolyn,' he puffed (there were three flights of stairs, after all). 'So sorry to call sud-denly like this, but it's the bombing, you see. I was hit rather hard back in December, and I've lost all my papers and files. Dreadful nuisance, as you can imagine, but I'm putting it all back together now – I'm going to carry the lot on my person henceforth.' He tapped his bulging bag.

Dolly was dismissed and spent the next half hour in her bedroom, glue and scissors in hand, updating her Book of Ideas, and glancing at her wristwatch with increasing anxiety as the minutes ticked ever closer to her WVS shift.

Finally, the silver bell tinkled upstairs and she was summoned again to her lady's chamber.

'Show Mr Pemberly out,' Lady Gwendolyn said, pausing
to concede a bloated hiccup, 'then come back and tuck me in
for the night.' Dolly smiled and nodded, and was waiting for
the solicitor to heave up his bag when the old girl added,
with customary insouciance, 'This is Dorothy, Mr Pemberly,
Dorothy Smitham. The one I was telling you about.'

There'd been an immediate shift in the solicitor's bearing after that. 'A pleasure to make your acquaintance,' he'd
said with great deference, and then he'd stood back for
Dolly and held open the door. They'd exchanged polite conversation all the way down the stairs, and when they
reached the front, and were conducting their farewells, he'd
turned to her and said, with a hint of awe, 'You've done a
remarkable thing, young lady. I can't think that I've ever
seen dear Lady Gwendolyn so *cheerful*, not since the terrible
business with her sister. Why, she didn't so much as raise a
hand at me, let alone her cane, the whole time I was with
her. Splendid stuff. Little wonder she's so tremendously partial to you.' And then he'd stunned Dolly by surrendering a
little wink.

*A remarkable thing . . . not since the terrible business
with her sister . . . so tremendously partial to you.* Sitting on
the flagstones in the crypt canteen, Dolly smiled softly as she
turned over the memory. It was such a lot to take in. Dr
Rufus had hinted at Lady Gwendolyn changing her will to
include Dolly, and the old woman sometimes made teasing
comments along those lines, but it wasn't the same thing,
was it, as actually talking to her solicitor, telling him how

fond she was of her young companion, that they'd become like fam—

'Hello there.' A familiar voice cut through Dolly's thoughts. 'What's a fellow got to do to get some service around here?'

Dolly glanced up, startled, and saw Jimmy leaning to peer over the counter at her. He laughed, and that lock of dark hair fell across his eyes. 'Playing hookey, are we, Miss Smitham?'

Dolly felt the blood drain from her face. 'What are you doing here?' she said, scrambling to her feet.

'I was in the area. Working.' He indicated the camera slung over his shoulder. 'I thought I'd swing by and collect my girl.'

She lifted a finger to her lips and shushed him, extinguishing her cigarette on the wall. 'We said we'd meet at Lyons Corner House,' she whispered, hurrying to the counter and straightening her skirt. 'I'm not finished my shift yet, Jimmy.'

'And I can see how terribly busy you are.' He smiled, but Dolly didn't.

She glanced beyond him at the busy room. Mrs Waddingham was still nattering about knitting and there was no sign of Vivien – all the same, it was risky. 'You go on without me,' she said in a low voice. 'I'll come as soon as I can.'

'I don't mind waiting; it gives me a chance to watch my girl in action.' He leaned across the counter to kiss her but Dolly pulled away.

'I'm working,' she said, by way of explanation. 'I'm wearing my uniform. It wouldn't be proper.' He didn't look entirely convinced by her sudden dedication to protocol and Dolly tried a different tack. 'Listen,' she said, as lightly as she could. 'You go and sit down – here, take some soup. I'll finish up, get my coat, and we can leave. All right?'

'All right.'

She watched him go, and she didn't exhale until he'd found a seat, way over on the other side of the room. Dolly's fingers were tingling with nerves. What on earth was he thinking, coming here when she'd been so explicit about meeting him at the restaurant? If Vivien had been working as she was scheduled to, there'd have been nothing for Dolly to do but introduce the two of them, and that would've been disastrous for Jimmy. It was one thing at the 400, with him so dashing and handsome in the guise of Lord Sandbrook, but here, tonight, dressed in his usual clothing, all tattered and dirty from a night out working in the Blitz . . . Dolly shuddered to think what Vivien would say if she realized Dolly had a boyfriend like him. Worse, what would happen if Lady Gwendolyn were to find out?

So far – and it hadn't been easy – Dolly had managed to keep Jimmy a secret from both of them, just as she'd been careful not to overwhelm him with chatter about her life at Campden Grove. But how was she supposed to keep her two worlds separate if he made a habit of doing the very opposite of what she asked? She fed her feet back inside the painful, pretty shoes and chewed her bottom lip. It was complicated, and she'd never be able to explain it to him, not so that he'd understand, but it was Jimmy's feelings she was trying to spare. He didn't belong here at the canteen, just as he didn't belong at number 7 Campden Grove or behind the red cord at the 400. Not like she did.

Dolly glanced over at him, eating his soup. They'd had such fun together, the two of them – the other night at the 400 and afterwards in her room; but the people in this part of her life couldn't know they'd been together like that, not Vivien and *certainly* not Lady Gwendolyn. Dolly's whole body burned with anxiety imagining what would happen if her old companion found out about Jimmy. The way her heart would break all over again if she feared herself at risk of losing Dolly, just as she'd lost her sister . . .

With a troubled sigh, Dolly left the counter and went to fetch her coat. She was going to have to talk to him, find a delicate way to make him understand that it was best for both of them if they played things a little cooler. He wouldn't be happy, she knew: he hated playing pretend; he was one of those frightfully principled people with a habit of seeing things too rigidly. But he'd come around; she knew he would.

Dolly was almost starting to feel cheery when she reached the storeroom and slipped her coat from its hook, but then Mrs Waddingham brought her spirits right back down. 'Taking an early mark are we, Dorothy?' Before she could answer, the other woman sniffed suspiciously and said, 'Is that tobacco smoke I smell back here?'

Jimmy sneaked his hand into his trouser pocket. It was still there, the black velvet box, just as it had been the last twenty times he'd checked. The whole thing was becoming a bit of a compulsion, really, which was why the sooner he put the ring on Dolly's finger, the better. He'd been over it countless times in his head, but he was still nervous as hell. The problem was he wanted it to be perfect, and Jimmy didn't believe in perfect, not generally speaking, not after everything he'd seen, the broken world and all its death and grief. Dolly did, though, so he was going to do his best.

He'd tried to make a reservation at one of the fancy restaurants she mooned over these days, the Ritz or Claridge's, but it turned out they were fully booked and no amount of explanation or appeal could convince them to give him a table. Jimmy had been disappointed at first, and the familiar old feelings of wanting to be better established, richer than he was, came to the surface. He'd pushed them aside, though, and decided it was for the best: he didn't go in for all that fancy stuff anyway, and on a night as important as this one Jimmy didn't want to feel he was pretending to be something he wasn't. In any case, as his boss had joked, with rationing as it was you could expect to be offered the same Woolton Pie at Claridge's as you'd get at Lyons Corner House, only dearer.

Jimmy looked back at the counter, but Dolly wasn't there any more. He supposed she was fetching her coat and fixing her lipstick, or one of the other things girls thought they had to do to be beautiful. He wished she wouldn't; she didn't need make-up and fancy clothing. They were like veneers, Jimmy sometimes thought, concealing the essence of a person, the very things that made her vulnerable and real and therefore most beautiful to him. Dolly's complexities and imperfections were part of what he loved about her.

Idly, he scratched his upper arm and wondered what had been going on before, why she'd acted so strangely when she saw him. He'd surprised her, he knew, turning up at the counter like that, calling out to her when she thought she was alone, hidden away with a cigarette and that distracted dreamy smile on her face. Dolly was usually thrilled at being taken unawares – she was the bravest, most daring person he knew, and nothing made her jumpy – but she'd definitely been skittish when she saw him. She'd seemed a different girl from the one who'd danced beside him through the streets of London the other night, and then led him back to her room.

Unless she had something behind the counter she didn't want him to see – Jimmy took out his cigarette packet and fed one out onto his lip – a surprise for him, perhaps, something she was planning on showing him later at the restaurant. Or maybe he'd caught her remembering their night together, that might explain why she'd seemed so startled, almost embarrassed, when she looked up and saw him standing there. Jimmy struck a match and dragged hard, considering. It was impossible to guess, and as long as the odd behaviour wasn't one of her games of pretend (not tonight, please God, he had to stay in control of tonight), he supposed it didn't matter.

He slipped his hand in his pocket and then shook his head, because of course the ring box was right where it had been two minutes ago. The compulsion was getting ridiculous; he needed to find a way to distract himself until he could put the damn thing on Dolly's finger. Jimmy hadn't brought a book, so he took up the black folder in which he kept his printed photographs. He didn't usually carry it with him when he was out on the job, but he'd come straight from a meeting with his editor and hadn't had time to take it home.

He turned to his most recent photograph, one he'd taken in Cheapside on Saturday night. It was of a little girl, four or five years old he guessed, standing in front of the kitchen of her local church hall. Her own clothes had been destroyed in the same raid that killed her family, and the Salvation Army hadn't had any children's clothes to give her. She was wearing an enormous pair of bloomers, an adult-size cardigan and a pair of tap shoes. They were red and she'd adored them. The St John's ladies were fussing about in the background, finding biscuits for her, and she'd been tapping her feet like Shirley Temple when Jimmy saw her, as the woman minding her kept an eye on the door in hopes that one of her family would miraculously appear, whole and intact and ready to take her home.

Jimmy had taken so many war pictures, his walls and his memories were clogged with various strangers who'd stood defiant in the face of devastation and loss; just this week he'd been to Bristol and Portsmouth and Gosport; but there was something about that little girl – he didn't even know her name – that Jimmy couldn't forget. He didn't want to forget. Her little face made happy by so little after suffering what was surely a child's greatest loss; an absence that would ripple across the years to change her whole life. Jimmy ought to know – he still found himself scanning the faces of bomb-blast victims, searching for his mother.

Small individual tragedies like this little girl's were nothing to the larger scale of the war; she and her tap shoes could be swept as easily as dust beneath history's carpet. That photograph was real, though; it captured its moment and preserved it for the future like an insect in amber. It reminded Jimmy why what he did, recording the truth of the war, was important. He needed to be reminded sometimes, on nights like this one, when he looked around the room and felt his lack of a uniform so keenly.

Jimmy killed his cigarette in the soup bowl that someone before him had helpfully set out for the purpose. He glanced at his watch – fifteen minutes had passed since he'd sat down – and wondered what was keeping Dolly. Just as he was debating whether to gather his things and go looking for her he sensed a presence behind him. He turned, expecting to see Doll, but it wasn't her. It was someone else, someone he'd never seen before.

At last Dolly had managed to extricate herself from Mrs Waddingham, and was coming back through the kitchen, wondering how shoes that looked such a dream could possibly hurt one's feet so badly, when she glanced up and the world just about stopped turning. Vivien had arrived.

She was standing by one of the trestle tables.

Deep in conversation.

With Jimmy.

Dolly's heart started to thump in her chest and she hid herself behind the pillar at the edge of the kitchen counter. She tried not to be seen while making perfectly sure to see everything. Eyes wide, she peered around the bricks and realized with horror that it was worse than she'd thought. Not only were the two of them talking together, but by the way they were gesturing back towards the table – Dolly stood on tippy-toes and winced – at Jimmy's folder, open on its surface, she could only deduce that they were discussing his photographs.

He'd shown them to Dolly once, and she'd been appalled. They were awful, nothing at all like those he'd used to take back in Coventry, of sunsets and trees and lovely houses in rippling meadows; neither were they like any of the war newsreels she and Kitty had been to watch at the cinema, the smiling images of returned servicemen, tired and dirty but triumphant; children lined up waving at railway stations; stalwart women handing oranges to cheerful Tommies. Jimmy's photos were of men with broken bodies and dark hollowed cheeks, and eyes that had seen things they ought not to have seen. Dolly hadn't known what to say; she'd wished he hadn't shown them to her in the first place.

What could he be thinking, showing them to Vivien now? She who was so pretty and perfect, the very last person on earth who ought to be troubled by that sort of ugliness. Dolly felt protective of her friend; there was a part of her that wanted to fly over there, slam the folder shut and end the whole thing, but she couldn't. Jimmy was just as likely to kiss her again, or worse, refer to her as his fiancée and make Vivien think they were engaged. Which they weren't, not officially – they'd talked about it, of course, back when they were kids, but that was a long time ago. They were older now, and the war changed things, it changed people. Dolly swallowed hard; this moment was everything she'd feared most, and now that it had happened she had no choice but to wait in excruciating limbo for it all to be over.

It felt like hours passed before Jimmy finally closed his folder and Vivien turned away. Dolly breathed a huge sigh of relief, and then she panicked. Her friend was coming straight up the aisle between the tables, frowning slightly as she headed for the kitchen. Dolly had been so looking forward to seeing her, but not like this, not before she knew exactly what Jimmy had said. As Vivien neared the kitchen, Dolly made a split-second decision. She ducked down and hid behind the counter, pretending to fossick beneath the red and green Christmas valance with the demeanour of someone engaged in terribly important war business. As soon as she'd felt Vivien brush past, Dolly grabbed her bag and hurried to where Jimmy was waiting. All she could think of was getting him out of the canteen before Vivien saw them together.

They didn't go to the Lyons Corner House in the end. There was a restaurant by the railway station, a plain building with boarded-up windows and a blast hole patched by a sign that said *More Open than Usual*. When they reached it, Dolly declared that she couldn't possibly walk another step. 'I've blisters, Jimmy,' she said, feeling like she might be going to cry. 'Let's just duck in here, shall we? It's freezing out – I'm sure it's going to snow tonight.'

It was warmer inside, thank goodness, and the waiter found them a nice enough booth in the back with a radiator burning nearby. Jimmy took Dolly's coat to hang by the door and she unpinned her WVS hat, setting it down by the salt and pepper. One of her grips had been digging into her head all night and she rubbed the spot briskly as she eased off her wretched shoes. Jimmy stopped on his way back and spoke quietly to the waiter who'd seated them, but Dolly was far too preoccupied with what he might have said to Vivien to wonder why. She shook a cigarette out of her packet and struck the match so hard it snapped. She was certain Jimmy was hiding something: he'd been acting oddly ever since they left the canteen, and now, coming back to the table, he could hardly meet her eyes without quickly looking away.

No sooner had he sat down than the waiter brought them a bottle of wine and began pouring two glasses full. The gurgling noise seemed very loud, embarrassing somehow, and Dolly looked beyond Jimmy to take in the rest of the room. Three bored waiters stood muttering to one another in the corner while the bartender polished his clean bar. There was only one other couple dining, the two of them whispering over their table as Al Jolson crooned from a gramophone on the bar. The woman had an over-eager look about her, rather like Kitty with her new beau – RAF, or so she said – running a hand down the fellow's shirt and giggling at his jokes.

The waiter set down the bottle and adopted a posh voice, telling them there'd be no à la carte menu tonight due to the shortages, but that the chef could prepare them a set menu du jour.

'Good,' said Jimmy, hardly looking at the fellow. 'Yes, thank you.'

The waiter left and Jimmy lit himself a cigarette, smiling at Dolly briefly before shifting his attention to something just above her head.

Dolly could stand it no longer. Her stomach was churning and she had to know what he'd been saying to Vivien, whether he'd mentioned her name. 'So,' she said.

'So.'

'I was wondering—'

'There's something—'

They both stopped, they both dragged on their cigarettes. Each considered the other through a haze of smoke.

'You first,' said Jimmy with a smile, opening his hands and looking directly into her eyes in a way she might've found exciting if she weren't so anxious.

Dolly chose her words carefully. 'I saw you,' she said, flicking ash into the ashtray, 'in the canteen. You were talking.' His face was hard to read; he was watching her closely. 'You and Vivien,' she added.

'That was Vivien?' said Jimmy, eyes widening. 'Your new friend? I didn't realize – she didn't say her name. Oh, Doll, if you'd only come sooner you could have introduced us.'

He seemed genuinely disappointed, and Dolly breathed a sigh of tentative relief. He hadn't known Vivien's name. Maybe that meant she didn't know his either, nor how he came to be visiting the canteen tonight. She tried to sound nonchalant. 'What were you talking about then, the two of you?'

'The war.' He shrugged a shoulder and dragged nervously on his cigarette. 'You know. The usual.'

He was lying to her, Dolly could tell – Jimmy wasn't a good liar. Neither was he enjoying the conversation; he'd answered quickly, too quickly, and now he was avoiding her gaze. What could they possibly have discussed that was making him so cagey? Had they talked about her? Oh God – what had he said? 'The war,' she repeated, pausing to give him an opportunity to expand. He didn't. She offered him a brittle smile. 'That's a rather general topic.'

The waiter arrived at their table, sliding a steaming plate before each of them. 'Mock fish scallops,' he said grandly.

'*Mock* fish scallops?' Jimmy sputtered.

The waiter's mouth twitched and his facade slipped a little. 'Artichokes, I believe, sir,' he said in a low voice. 'Chef grows 'em on his allotment.'

Jimmy watched Dolly across the white tablecloth. This was not the way he'd planned it, to propose to her in an empty dive, after buying her crumbed artichoke and sour wine, and making her burn with anger. Silence set up camp between them and the ring box weighed heavily in Jimmy's trouser pocket. He didn't want to be arguing, he wanted to be sliding the ring onto her finger, not simply because it bound her to him – though of course he longed for that – but because it honoured something good and true. He poked at his food.

He couldn't have messed it up more if he'd tried. Worse, there was nothing he could think of doing that would fix it. Dolly was angry because she knew he wasn't telling her everything, but the woman, Vivien, had asked him not to repeat what she'd said. More than that, she'd pleaded with him, and there'd been something about the way she looked when she did so that made him close his mouth and nod. He dragged his artichoke through some miserable white sauce.

Maybe she hadn't meant Dolly, though. Now there was a thought – they were friends. Dolly would probably laugh if he told her, and wave her hand and say that of course she already knew. Jimmy took a sip of wine, thinking it through, wondering what his father would have done in the same situation. He had a feeling his dad would've observed the promise to Vivien, but then again, look what happened to him – he'd lost the woman he loved. Jimmy wasn't about to let the same thing happen to him.

'Your friend,' he said casually, as if there'd been no awkwardness between them, 'Vivien – she saw one of my photographs.'

Dolly's attention came to rest on him but she said nothing.

Jimmy swallowed, shutting out all thoughts of his father, those talks he'd given Jimmy as he was growing up, about valour and respect. He had no choice tonight, he had to tell Dolly the truth, and really, what harm could possibly come? 'It was of a little girl whose family was killed the other night in a raid over Cheapside way. It was sad, Doll, terribly sad, she was smiling, you see, and wearing—' He stopped himself and waved his hand; he could tell by Dolly's expression she was losing patience. 'That's not important – the thing is, your friend knew her. Vivien recognized her from the picture.'

'How?'

It was the first word she'd spoken since their meals arrived, and although it wasn't exactly unreserved forgiveness, Jimmy lightened. 'She told me she has a friend, a doctor, who runs a small private hospital over in Fulham. He turned over part of it to care for war orphans and she helps him sometimes. That's where she met Nella, the little girl in the photograph. She'd been taken there, you see, when no one came forward to claim her.'

Dolly was watching him, waiting for him to continue, but there wasn't anything more he could think to say.

'That's it?' said Dolly. 'You didn't tell her anything about yourself?'

'Not even my name. There wasn't time.' In the distance, from somewhere in the dark cold London night, there came a series of explosions. Jimmy wondered suddenly who was being hit, who was screaming right now in pain and grief and horror.

'And she didn't say anything else?'

He shook his head. 'Not about the hospital. I was about to ask her if I could go with her one day, take something for Nella—'

'You didn't though?'

'I didn't get a chance.'

'And that's the only reason you were being so evasive – because Vivien told you she helps her doctor friend in his hospital?'

He felt foolish in the face of Dolly's incredulity. He smiled and shrank a bit and cursed himself for always taking things so seriously, for not realizing that of course Vivien had been overstating things, and of course Dolly already knew – that he'd been agonizing over nothing. He said, a bit limply, 'She begged me not to tell anyone.'

'Oh, Jimmy,' Dolly said, laughing as she reached across the table to brush his arm gently. 'Vivien didn't mean *me*. She meant for you not to tell other people – strangers.'

'I know.' Jimmy stilled her hand in his, felt her smooth fingers beneath his own. 'It was stupid of me not to realize. I'm not myself tonight.' He was aware suddenly that he was standing at the edge of something; that the rest of his life, their life together, began on the other side. 'In fact,' he said, his voice cracking just a little, 'there's something I've been wanting to ask you, Doll.'

Dolly had been smiling distractedly as Jimmy stroked her hand. A doctor friend, a *male* friend – Kitty had been right:

Vivien had a lover, and suddenly everything made sense. The secrecy, Vivien's frequent absences from the WVS canteen, the distant expression on her face as she sat in the window at number 25 Campden Grove, dreaming. She said, 'I wonder how they met,' just as Jimmy was saying, 'There's something I've been wanting to ask you, Doll.'

It was the second time that night they'd spoken at once, and Dolly laughed. 'We have to stop doing that,' she said. She felt unexpectedly lucent and giggly, as if she could laugh all night. Perhaps it was the wine. She'd had more to drink than she realized. Then again, the relief at knowing Jimmy hadn't revealed himself made her feel rather euphoric. 'I was just saying—'

'No.' He reached to press a fingertip to her lips. 'Let me finish, Doll. I have to finish.'

His expression took her by surprise. It was one she didn't see often, determined, almost urgent, and although she was desperate to know more about Vivien and her doctor friend, Dolly closed her mouth.

Jimmy let his hand slip sideways to caress her cheek. 'Dorothy Smitham,' he said, and something inside her caught at the way he said her name. She melted. 'I fell in love with you the first time I saw you. Do you remember, that cafe in Coventry?'

'You were carrying a bag of flour.'

He laughed. 'A true hero. That's me.'

She smiled and pushed her empty plate aside. She lit a cigarette. It was cold, she realized, the radiator had stopped ticking. 'Well, it was a very big bag.'

'I've told you before there's nothing I wouldn't do for you.'

She nodded. He had, many times. It was sweet, and she didn't want to interrupt him when he was saying it again, but Dolly didn't know how much longer she could keep her questions and thoughts about Vivien from bubbling to the surface.

'I meant it, Doll. I'd do anything you asked.'

'Do you think you could get the waiter to check the heating?'

'I'm serious.'

'So am I. It's freezing in here all of a sudden.' She wrapped her arms across her middle. 'Can you feel it?' Jimmy didn't answer, he was too busy digging in his trouser pocket for something. Dolly glimpsed their waiter and tried to get his attention. He appeared to see her, but then turned and headed back towards the kitchen. She noticed then that the other couple had gone and they were the only ones left in the restaurant. 'I think we should leave,' she said to Jimmy. 'It's late.'

'Just a minute.'

'But it's cold.'

'Forget the cold.'

'But Jimmy—'

'I'm trying to ask you to marry me, Doll.' He'd surprised himself, she could tell by his face, and he laughed. 'I'm making a bit of a mess of it, apparently – I've never done it before. I don't intend to do it again.' He eased out of his seat and went to kneel before her, taking a deep breath. 'Dorothy Smitham,' he said, 'will you do me the honour of becoming my wife?'

Dolly waited to understand, for him to break character and laugh. She knew he was joking; he was the one who'd insisted back in Bournemouth that they wait until he'd saved enough money. Any minute now he'd laugh and ask her if she'd like to order some dessert. But he didn't. He stayed where he was, staring up at her. 'Jimmy?' she said. 'You'll get chilblains down there. Hop up, quickly.'

He didn't. Without looking away, he raised his left hand and revealed a ring between his fingertips. It was a band of yellow gold with a small stone in a claw setting – old enough not to be new, too modern to be a real antique. He'd brought a prop, she realized, blinking at it. She had to admire him, he really was doing a splendid job playing his part. She wished she could say the same for herself, only he'd caught her off guard. Dolly wasn't used to Jimmy initiating games of pretend – that was her job – and she wasn't sure she liked it. 'Let me wash my hair and think about it,' she quipped.

His own hair had fallen across one eye and he tossed his head to shift it. There was no hint of a smile on his face as he stared at her for a moment, as if he were collecting his thoughts. 'I'm asking you to marry me, Doll,' he said, and something in the honest woody quality of his voice, the complete absence of subterfuge and double meaning, made Dolly feel the first inkling of suspicion that he might in fact be in earnest.

She thought he was joking. Jimmy almost laughed when he realized that. He didn't, though; he swiped his hair out of his eyes and thought about the way she'd taken him upstairs the other night, the way she'd looked at him as her red dress dropped to the ground, as she lifted her chin and met his gaze, and he'd felt young and strong and so very glad to be alive right then, right there, with her. He thought about the way he'd sat up afterwards, unable to sleep for the blessed knowledge that a girl like her could possibly be in love with him, the way he'd known as he watched her dream that he would love her all his life and hers, until they were old together, sitting on comfortable armchairs in their farmhouse, their children all grown up and flown away, taking it in turns to make each other cups of tea.

He wanted to tell it all to her, to remind her, to make her see the picture as clearly as he did, but Jimmy knew that Dolly was different, that she liked surprises and didn't need to see the ending when they were still right at the start. Instead, when all his thoughts had been gathered like leaves, he said as plainly as he could, 'I'm asking you to marry me, Doll. I'm still not a rich man, but I love you, and I don't want to waste another day without you.' And then he watched as her face changed, and he saw in the corners of her mouth and the minute shift of her brows that at last she understood.

As Jimmy waited, Dolly sighed, long and slowly. She reached for her hat, frowning a little as she turned it round and round by the brim. She'd always favoured the dramatic pause, so he wasn't really worried as he followed the perfect line of her profile, just as he had on that hill by the sea; as she said, 'Oh, Jimmy,' in a voice not quite her own; as she turned to him and he saw a fresh tear sliding down her cheek. 'What a thing to ask; what a damnable thing to ask me right now.'

Before Jimmy could ask her what she meant, she hurried past him, bumping her hip against another table in her hurry to get away, disappearing into the cold and the dark of wartime London without so much as hinting at a backwards glance. It was only after minutes had passed and she still hadn't returned that Jimmy finally grasped what had happened. And he saw himself suddenly, as if from above, as if the subject of his very own photograph, a man who'd somehow lost everything, kneeling alone on the dirty floor of a dingy restaurant that had become very cold.

Fifteen

Suffolk, 2011

Laurel did wonder afterwards how it was possible she'd come this far without thinking to google her mother's name. Then again, nothing she knew about Dorothy Nicolson led her to suspect for a second that she might have an online presence.

She didn't wait to get home to Greenacres. She sat in the parked car outside the hospital, took out her phone and typed 'Dorothy Smitham' into the search window. She went too quickly, of course, spelled it incorrectly and had to do it all over again. She steeled herself against whatever the results might show, and then pressed the search button. There were 127 hits. A genealogy site in America, a Thelma Dorothy Smitham looking for friends on Facebook, a White Pages listing in Australia, and then, halfway down the page, an entry on the BBC People's War archive, subtitled 'A London telephonist remembers World War Two'. Laurel's finger was shaking as she selected that option.

The page contained the wartime memories of a woman called Katherine Frances Barker who'd worked as a telephonist for the War Office in Westminster during the Blitz. It had been submitted, said the note at the top, by Susanna Barker on behalf of her mother. There was a photograph at the top of a spritely old woman posing somewhat coquettishly against a raspberry velour sofa with crocheted headrests. The annotation read:

Katherine 'Kitty' Barker relaxing at home. When WW2 broke out, Kitty moved to London, where she worked as a telephonist for the duration. Kitty would have liked to join the WRNS, but communications was considered an essential service and she wasn't able to leave.

The article itself was rather long and Laurel skimmed it, waiting for her mother's name to jump out from the text. A few paragraphs down she found it.

I had grown up in the Midlands and had no family in London, but during the war there were services set up to find accommodation for war workers. I was fortunate compared to some, being sent to board in the home of a rather grand woman. The house was at number 7 Campden Grove, Kensington, and although you might not think so, my time spent there during the war was very happy. There were three other office girls staying, too, and a couple of Lady Gwendolyn Caldicott's staff members who had remained when war broke out, a cook and a girl called Dorothy Smitham who was a companion of sorts to the mistress of the house. We became friendly, Dorothy and I, but lost touch when I married my husband, Tom, in 1941. Friendships were forged very quickly during the war – I suppose that should come as no shock – and I have often wondered what became of my friends from that time. I hope they survived.

Laurel was buzzing. It was incredible, the effect of seeing her mother's name, her name from before, in print. Especially in a document like this one, recounting the very time and place that Laurel was curious about.

She read the paragraph again and her excitement didn't wane. Dorothy Smitham had been real. She'd worked for a woman named Lady Gwendolyn Caldicott and lived at number 7 Campden Grove (the same street as Vivien and Henry Jenkins, Laurel noted with a thrill), and she'd had a friend called Kitty. Laurel searched for the date of the entry's submission: 25 October 2008 – a friend who was quite possibly still alive and willing to talk to Laurel. Each discovery was another shining star in the great black sky, forming the picture that would lead Laurel home.

Susanna Barker invited Laurel to call for tea that afternoon. Finding her had proved so simple that Laurel, who'd never believed in an easy ride, had felt a surge of constitutional suspicion. She'd done no more than punch the names Katherine Barker and Susanna Barker into the Numberway online directory page, and then set about dialling each of the resulting numbers. She struck pay dirt on the third. 'Mother plays golf on Thursdays and talks to students at the local grammar on Fridays,' Susanna said. 'There's a space in her diary today at four, though?' Laurel had taken the slot gladly, and was now following Susanna's careful directions along a meandering lane through drenched green fields on the outskirts of Cambridge.

A plump, jolly sort of woman with a fuzz of coppery rain-frizzed hair was waiting for her by the front gate. She was wearing a cheery sun-yellow cardigan over a brown dress, and clutching an umbrella with both hands in an attitude of polite anxiety. Sometimes, thought the actress inside Laurel ('ears, eyes and heart, all at once'), you could tell everything there was to know about a person by a single gesture. The woman with the umbrella was nervous, dependable and grateful.

'Why, hello there,' she trilled as Laurel crossed the street towards her. Her smile exposed a magnificent amount of glossy gum. 'I'm Susanna Barker and it's just such an enormous pleasure to meet you.'

'Laurel. Laurel Nicolson.'

'But of course I know who you are! Come in, come in, please. Terrible weather, isn't it? Mother says it's because I killed a spider inside. Silly me, I ought to know better by now. It always brings the rain, though, doesn't it?'

Kitty Barker was bright as a button and sharp as a pirate's sword. 'Dolly Smitham's daughter,' she said, bringing her tiny fist down on the table with a thump. 'What a bloody marvellous surprise.' When Laurel attempted to introduce herself and explain how she'd found Kitty's name on the Internet, the frail hand waved impatiently and its mistress barked, 'Yes, yes, my daughter told me already – you said so on the phone.'

Laurel, who'd been accused of brusqueness more than once herself, decided to find the woman's efficiency refreshing. Presumably, at the age of ninety-two, one neither minced a word nor wasted a moment. She smiled and said, 'Mrs Barker, my mother never spoke much about the war when I was growing up – I gather she wanted to put it all

behind her – but she's unwell now and it's become important to me to know everything I can about her past. I
thought perhaps you might tell me a bit about London
during the war, in particular about my mother's life back
then.'

Kitty Barker was only too happy to comply. That is, she
leapt with alacrity to fulfil the first part of Laurel's request,
launching into a lecture on the Blitz while her daughter
brought the tea and scones.

Laurel paid full attention for a time, but her concentra-
tion began to waver when it became clear that Dorothy
Smitham was only going to be a bit player in this story. She
studied the wartime memorabilia on the sitting-room wall,
posters entreating people not to take the squander bug with
them when they went shopping, rather to remember their
vegetables.

Kitty was still describing the ways in which a person
might come to accidental harm in the blackout, and as
Laurel watched the clock tick past the half hour her focus
drifted to Susanna Barker, gazing at her mother with rapt
attention and mouthing along to each and every line. Kitty's
daughter had heard these anecdotes many times before,
Laurel realized, and suddenly she understood the dynamic
perfectly – Susanna's nerviness, her eagerness to please, the
reverence with which she spoke of her mother. Kitty was
Ma's opposite; she'd created of her war years a mythology
from which her own daughter could never escape.

Perhaps all children were held captive, in some part, by
their parents' pasts. What, after all, could poor Susanna ever
hope to achieve compared to her mother's tales of heroism
and sacrifice? For the first time, Laurel felt some small

gratitude to her parents for having spared their children such a heavy burden. (On the contrary, it was her mother's *lack* of history that kept Laurel imprisoned. One couldn't help but appreciate the irony.)

A glad thing happened then: just as Laurel was losing hope of learning anything of importance, Kitty paused midway through her account to scold Susanna for having taken too long pouring the tea. Laurel seized her chance, wresting the conversation back to Dorothy Smitham. 'What a tremendous story, Mrs Barker,' she said, using her most Dame-ish, actressy tone. 'Fascinating – tremendous bravery all round. But what of my mother? Can you tell me a little bit about her?'

Interruption was clearly not customary, and a stunned silence befell proceedings. Kitty canted her head as if trying to divine an explanation for such effrontery, while Susanna took assiduous care to avoid Laurel's eyes as she made a wobbly job of pouring the tea.

Laurel refused to be abashed. A small childish part of her enjoyed having shut down Kitty's monologue. She'd taken a liking to Susanna, and the woman's mother was a bully; Laurel had been taught to stand up to those. She continued cheerfully, 'Did Ma help out with the efforts at home?'

'Dolly did her bit,' said Kitty grudgingly. 'All of us at the house were part of a roster, taking it in turns to sit on the roof with a bucket of sand and a stirrup pump.'

'And what about socially?'

'She enjoyed a good time, as did we all. There was a war on. One had to take pleasure where one found it.'

Susanna offered the milk and sugar tray but Laurel

waved it away. 'I expect a pair of pretty young girls like you must have had a lot of boyfriends, too.'

'Of course.'

'Was there anyone special for my mother, do you know?'

'There *was* a fellow,' said Kitty, taking a sip of black tea. 'But I can't for the life of me think what his name was now.'

But Laurel had an idea – it had come to her suddenly. Last Thursday at the birthday party, the nurse had said Ma was asking after someone, wondering why he hadn't been to visit. At the time, Laurel had presumed she'd misheard, that it was Gerry she was asking after; now, though, having seen the way her mother's thoughts were drifting between the present and the past, Laurel knew that she'd been wrong. 'Jimmy,' she said. 'Was the man's name Jimmy?'

'Yes!' said Kitty. 'Yes, that's it. I remember now, I used to tease her and say he was her very own Jimmy Stewart. Not that I ever met him, mind. I was only guessing at his looks from what she'd told me.'

'You never met him?' That was odd. Ma and Kitty had been friends, they'd lived together, they were young – meeting one another's boyfriends would have been de rigueur, surely?

'Not even once. She was very particular about that. He was RAF and far too busy to pay visits.' Kitty's mouth pursed in a rather sly manner. 'So she said, anyway.'

'What do you mean?'

'Only that my Tom was RAF and he was most certainly not too busy to come calling, if you know what I mean.' She grinned fiendishly, and Laurel smiled to show that yes, she understood perfectly well.

'You think my mother might have lied?' she pressed.

'Not lied, exactly, so much as embroidered the truth. It was always hard to tell with Dolly. She had quite an imagination.'

Laurel knew that well enough. All the same, it seemed strange that she'd have kept the man she loved a secret from her friends. People in love usually wanted to trumpet it from the rooftops and Ma had never been one to keep her emotions concealed.

Unless there'd been something about Jimmy that meant his identity *needed* to be kept secret. There was a war on – perhaps he'd really been a spy. That would certainly explain Dorothy's secrecy, her inability to marry the man she loved, her own need to escape. Tying Henry and Vivien Jenkins to the scenario was going to be a little more problematic, unless Henry had somehow found out about Jimmy and it posed a threat to national security.

'Dolly never brought Jimmy home because the old woman whose house it was didn't approve of male visitors,' Kitty said, casually poking a needle into the balloon of Laurel's grand theory. 'Old Lady Gwendolyn had a sister once – thick as thieves they were when they were young; lived together in the house at Campden Grove, and never one went that the other didn't follow. It all broke apart, though, when the younger one fell in love and got married. She moved away with her husband, and her sister never forgave her. Locked herself in her bedroom for decades and refused to see anyone. Hated people, she did, though evidently not your mother. Close, they were; Dolly was loyal to the old woman and a stickler for that rule. She had no difficulty breaking just about any other, mind you – no one

like her for getting nylons and lipsticks on the black market
– but she stuck to that one like her life depended on it.'

Something in the way Kitty put that last comment gave
Laurel pause.

'You know, looking back, I think that was the beginning.' Kitty frowned with the effort of staring down the
tunnel of old memories.

'The beginning of what?' Laurel said, presentiment tingling in her fingertips.

'Your mother changed. Dolly had been such a lot of fun
when the rest of us first arrived at Campden Grove, but then
she got all funny about keeping the old lady happy.'

'Well, Lady Gwendolyn was her employer. I expect
she—'

'There was more to it than that. She started going on
and on about the old lady looking upon her as family. She
began acting more posh, too, treating us as if we weren't
good enough for her any more – she made *new* friends
instead.'

'Vivien,' said Laurel, suddenly. 'You mean Vivien
Jenkins.'

'I see your mother told you about *her*,' said Kitty, with
a caustic twist to her lips. 'Forgot about the rest of us, sure
enough, but not Vivien Jenkins. No surprise in that, of
course, no surprise at all. An author's wife, she was, lived
across the street. Terribly snooty – beautiful, of course, you
couldn't deny that, but cold with it. She wouldn't lower herself to stop and talk to you in the street. Dreadful influence
on Dolly – she thought Vivien was the bee's knees.'

'They saw a lot of one another?'

Kitty took up a scone and spooned a glob of glistening

jam on top. 'I'm sure I wouldn't know the details,' she said tartly, spreading the red preserve flat. 'I was never invited to join them and Dolly had stopped telling me her secrets by then. I expect that's why I didn't know anything was wrong until it was too late.'

'Too late for what? What was wrong?'

Kitty landed a dollop of cream on her scone and eyed Laurel over the top. 'Something happened between them, your mother and Vivien, something nasty. Early 1941; I remember because I'd just met my Tom – that's probably why it didn't bother me as much as it might've otherwise. Dolly got herself into a terrible dark mood afterwards, snapping all the time, refusing to come out with us, avoiding Jimmy. Like a different person, she was – wouldn't even go to the canteen.'

'The WVS canteen?'

Kitty nodded, poised to take a delicate mouthful of scone. 'She loved working there, was always skipping out on the old lady, ducking down to fill a shift – very brave, your mother, never frightened of the bombs – but all of a sudden she stopped. Wouldn't go back for all the tea in China.'

'Why not?'

'She didn't say, but I know it was something to do with *her*, the other one across the street. I saw them together the day they fought, you know; I was on my way back from work, a little earlier than usual due to an unexploded bomb that had turned up near my office, and I saw your mother coming out of the Jenkins's house. Well! The look on her face.' Kitty was shaking her head. 'Forget about the bombs

– the way Dolly looked I thought *she* might've been about to explode.'

Laurel took a sip of tea. She could think of one scenario that might stop a woman from seeing both her friend and her boyfriend at the same time. Had Jimmy and Vivien become involved in an affair? Was that why her mother had broken off her engagement and run away to start a new life? Certainly it would explain Henry Jenkins being angry – though not with Dorothy, surely; and nor did it account for Ma's recent expressions of regret about the past. There was nothing regrettable about picking oneself up and starting again: it was a brave thing to do. 'What do you think happened?' she probed gently, setting down her cup.

Kitty lifted her bony shoulders, but there was something devious about the gesture. 'Dolly really never told you anything about it, did she?' Her expression was one of surprise disguising deeper pleasure. She sighed theatrically. 'Well, I suppose she always was a one for keeping secrets. Some mothers and daughters just aren't as close as others, are they?'

Susanna beamed; her mother took a bite of scone.

Laurel had a strong feeling Kitty was holding something back. Being one of four sisters she also had a pretty good idea how to winkle it out. There weren't many confidences indifference couldn't shake lose. 'I've taken up enough of your time, Mrs Barker,' she said, folding her napkin and realigning her teaspoon. 'Thank you for talking to me. It's been most helpful. Let me know, won't you, if you think of anything else that might explain what happened between Vivien and my mother.' Laurel stood up and pushed in her chair. Started towards the door.

'You know,' said Kitty, following her, 'there is something else, now I think of it.'

It wasn't easy, but Laurel managed not to smile. 'Oh?' she said. 'What's that?'

Kitty sucked in her lips as if she were about to speak against her will and she wasn't quite sure how it had come to this. She barked at Susanna to top up the pot and, when her daughter was gone, ushered Laurel back to the table. 'I told you about Dolly's foul mood,' she began. 'Awful, it was. Terribly dark. And it lasted all the rest of our time together at Campden Grove. Then one night, a few weeks after my wedding, my husband had gone back on duty and I arranged to go out dancing with a few of the girls from work. I almost didn't ask Doll – she'd been such a bore of late – but I did, and quite unexpectedly she agreed to come.

'She arrived at the dance club, dressed to the nines and laughing like she'd given herself a head start with the whisky. Brought a friend with her, too, a girl she'd grown up with in Coventry – Caitlin something-or-other, very hoity-toity at first but she soon warmed up – no choice with Doll around. She was one of those people – spirited – made you want to have a good time just because she was.'

Laurel smiled faintly, recognizing her mother in the description.

'She was certainly having a good time that night, let me tell you. She had a wild look in her eyes, laughing and danc-ing and saying the oddest things. When it was time to go, she grabbed me by the arms and told me she had a plan.'

'A plan?' Laurel felt each hair on the back of her neck stand up straight.

'She said Vivien Jenkins had done something spiteful to

her, but she had a plan that was going to set everything to rights. She and Jimmy were going to live happily ever after; everyone was going to get what they deserved.'

It was just as her mother had told Laurel in the hospital. But things hadn't gone to plan, and she hadn't married Jimmy. Instead, Henry Jenkins had been made angry. Laurel's heart was racing but she did her best to seem unmoved. 'Did she tell you what her plan was?'

'She didn't and, to be honest, I didn't put much stock in it at the time. Things were different in the war. People were always saying and doing things they wouldn't have otherwise. You never knew what the next day might bring, whether you'd even wake up to see it – that sort of uncertainty has a way of loosening a person's scruples. And your mother always did have a flair for the dramatic. I figured all her talk of revenge was just that – talk. It wasn't until afterwards that I wondered if she'd not been more serious than I realized.'

Laurel edged a little closer. 'Afterwards?'

'She disappeared into thin air. That night in the dance club was the last I saw of her. Never heard from her again, not so much as a word, and she didn't return any of my letters. I thought she might've been got by a bomb, until I had a visit from an older woman, just after the war ended. Very secretive it was – she was asking after Doll, wanting to know if there was anything "unmentionable" she might have done in her past.'

Laurel had a flashback to the dark cool of Grandma Nicolson's spare bedroom. 'A tall woman with a handsome face and an expression like she'd been sucking lemons?'

Kitty cocked a single brow. 'Friend of yours?'

'My grandmother. Paternal.'

'Ah,' Kitty smiled toothily, 'the mother-in-law. She didn't mention that, only told me she was your mother's employer and was performing a little background check. So they still got married, your mum and dad – he must've been terribly keen on her.'

'Why? What did you tell my grandmother?'

Kitty blinked, all innocence. 'I was hurt. I'd worried about her when I didn't hear, and then to learn she'd just up and left and never bothered to say a word.' She waved her hand vaguely. 'I might've embellished just a little, given Dolly a few more boyfriends than she'd really had, a taste for liquor . . . nothing too serious.'

But quite sufficient to explain Grandma Nicolson's sour grapes: boyfriends were bad enough, but a taste for liquor? That was akin to sacrilege.

Laurel was anxious suddenly to be outside the cluttered cottage, alone with her thoughts. She thanked Kitty Barker and started to gather her things.

'Remember me to your mother, won't you?' Kitty said, accompanying Laurel to the door.

Laurel assured her that she would and pulled on her coat.

'I never did get to say a proper goodbye. I thought about her, over the years, especially when I knew she'd survived the war. There wasn't much I could've done, though – Dolly was very determined, one of those girls who always got exactly what she wanted. If she wanted to disappear, there's no one who'd have been able to stop or find her.'

Except Henry Jenkins, thought Laurel, as Kitty Barker's door closed behind her. He'd been able to find her, and

Dorothy had made sure that whatever reason he had for seeking her out had died with him that day at Greenacres.

Laurel sat in the green Mini at the front of Kitty Barker's cottage, engine running. The air vents were on full and she willed the heating to hurry up and make things warm. It was past five o'clock and darkness had begun to hover outside the window. The spires of Cambridge University glinted against the dusky sky, but Laurel didn't see them. She was far too busy imagining her mother – the young woman in that photograph she'd found – standing in a dance club, grabbing Kitty Barker by the wrists and telling her in a wild voice that she had a plan, that she was going to set things right. 'What was it, Dorothy?' Laurel mumbled to herself, reaching now for her cigarettes. 'What on earth did you do?'

Her mobile phone rang while she was still digging in her handbag and she fished it out, hope crystallizing in an instant that it would be Gerry, returning her calls at last.

'Laurel? It's Rose. Phil has his Toastmasters' meeting tonight, and I was thinking you might like some company. I could bring over dinner, perhaps a DVD?'

Laurel, deflated, stalled while she tried to invent an excuse. She felt bad about lying, especially to Rose, but this quest of hers wasn't something she was yet able to share, not with her sisters anyway; to sit through a rom-com making light chit-chat while her mind raced ahead trying to unknot her mother's past would have been agony. A pity – there was a part of her that would have loved to hand the whole tangled mess over to someone else and say, 'See what you can make of this'; but the burden was hers, and although she had every intention of telling her sisters eventually, she refused to do so – indeed, she *couldn't* do so – until she damn well knew the whole of what there was to tell.

She tousled her hair, still racking her brain for a reason to turn down dinner (Lord but she was hungry now she thought about it) and as she did, she noticed the proud towers of the university, majestic in the gloomy distance.

'Lol? Are you there?'

'Yes. Yes, I am.'

'The line's not very good. I said, would you like me to make you dinner?'

'No,' Laurel said quickly, glimpsing suddenly the hazy outline of a rather good idea. 'Thanks, Rosie, but no. How about I give you a call tomorrow?'

'Everything all right? Where are you?'

The line was becoming cracklier and Laurel had to shout. 'Everything's fine. It's just—' She grinned as her plan became clear and sharp. 'I'm not going to be home tonight, not until rather late.'

'Oh?'

'Afraid not. I've just remembered, Rose, there's someone else I've got to go and see.'

Sixteen

London, January 1941

The last fortnight had been awful and Dolly couldn't help blaming Jimmy. If only he hadn't spoiled things by *pushing* like that. She'd been all set to talk with him about the two of them keeping a lower profile, and then he'd gone and asked her to marry him and a rift had opened up inside her that refused now to close. On one side was Dolly Smitham, the naive young girl from Coventry who thought marrying her sweetheart and living forever in a farmhouse by a stream was the sum of her life's desires; on the other was Dorothy Smitham, friend to the glamorous, wealthy Vivien Jenkins, heir and companion to Lady Gwendolyn Caldicott – a grown woman who didn't need to invent elaborate fantasy futures for herself because she knew exactly the tremendous adventures that lay ahead.

Which wasn't to say Dolly hadn't felt sick walking out of the restaurant like that, the waiters watching and wondering; she'd had a pressing sense, though, that if she stayed any longer she might have said yes, just to get him up off the floor. And where would that have left her? Sharing a little flat with Jimmy and Mr Metcalfe, and worrying all the time about where their next jug of milk would come from? Where would it have left her with Lady Gwendolyn?

The old woman had shown Dolly such enormous kindness, she'd come to think of her practically as family; how would she have coped with being deserted a second time? No, Dolly had done the right thing. Dr Rufus had agreed when she'd started crying about it over lunch: she was young, he'd said, she had her whole life ahead of her, there was no sense in tying herself down now.

Kitty (of course) had noticed something was askew and responded by parading her own RAF catch across the threshold of number 7 at every opportunity, flashing her mean little engagement ring and asking pointed questions about Jimmy's whereabouts. Canteen duty was almost a relief by comparison. At least it would've been if Vivien ever showed up to lift her spirits. They'd glimpsed one another only once since the night Jimmy came in unannounced. Vivien had been delivering a box of donated clothing and Dolly had started making her way over to say hello when Mrs Waddingham ordered her back to the kitchen on pain of death. Witch. It was almost worth signing up at the Labour Exchange never to have to see the woman again. Fat chance of that, though. Dolly had received a letter from the Ministry of Labour, but when Lady Gwendolyn caught wind of it she promptly ensured that officials at the highest level understood Dolly was indispensable in her current position and couldn't possibly be spared to make smoke bombs.

Now, a pair of firemen with black soot all over their faces arrived at the counter and Dolly dialled up a smile, putting a dimple in each cheek as she ladled soup into two bowls. 'Busy night, boys?' she asked.

'Bloody ice in the hoses,' the shorter man replied. 'You should see it out there. We're fighting flames in one house, and there's icicles hanging from the one next door where the water's struck it.'

'How dreadful,' Dolly said, and the men agreed, before dragging themselves over to collapse at a trestle table, leaving her alone once more in the kitchen.

She leaned her elbow on the countertop and rested her chin in her hand. No doubt Vivien was busy these days with that doctor of hers. Dolly had felt a little disillusioned when Jimmy first told her – she'd have preferred to hear about the liaison directly from Vivien – but she understood the need for secrecy. Henry Jenkins wasn't the type to appreciate his wife playing the field: you could tell that just by looking at him. If someone were to overhear Vivien's confidence, or see something suspicious and report back to her husband, all hell would break loose. Little wonder she'd been so insistent that Jimmy not repeat to a soul what she'd told him.

'Mrs Jenkins? Yoo-hoo, Mrs Jenkins.'

Dolly looked up smartly. Had Vivien arrived when she wasn't watching?

'Oh, Miss Smitham – ' the voice lost some of its sunniness – 'it's only you.'

Neat-as-a-pin Maud Hoskins was standing at the counter, a cameo cinching her blouse together at the neck, tight as a rector's collar. Vivien was nowhere to be seen and Dolly's heart sank. 'Only me, Mrs Hoskins.'

'Yes – ' the old woman sniffed – 'so it is.' She glanced about her like a flustered hen, clacking her beak and saying, 'Dear, dear me, I don't suppose you've seen her – Mrs Jenkins, that is?'

'Let me think.' Dolly tapped her lips thoughtfully as she forced her feet back into her shoes beneath the counter. 'No, no, I don't think I have.'

'What a shame. I've something for her, you see. She must have lost it last time she was here and I've been holding onto it ever since, hoping to run into her. She's not been in for days, though.'

'Hasn't she? I hadn't noticed.'

'Not all week. I do hope nothing's wrong.'

Dolly considered telling Mrs Hoskins that she saw Vivien daily, alive and well, from Lady Gwendolyn's bedroom window, but decided it would raise more questions than it answered. 'I'm sure she's fine.'

'I expect you're right. As fine as any of us can hope to be in such testing times as these.'

'Yes.'

'Only, it is a bother. I'm going down to Cornwall to stay with my sister for a while and I had hoped to return the item to her before I left.' Mrs Hoskins looked about uncertainly. 'I suppose I shall have to—'

'Leave it here with me? Of course you shall.' Dolly fixed her most winning smile in place. 'And I'll be certain to make sure she receives it.'

'Oh.' Mrs Hoskins peered from behind her tidy spectacles. 'I hadn't thought to ... I don't know that I should just leave it.'

'Mrs Hoskins, please. I'm only too happy to help. I'm bound to be seeing Vivien soon.'

The older woman drew a short, tidy breath, registering Dolly's use of Vivien's first name. 'Well,' she said, a new note of admiration creeping into her voice. 'If you're sure—'

'I'm sure.'

'Thank you, Miss Smitham. Thank you, kindly. It certainly will lay my mind to rest. It's quite a valuable little piece, I think.' Mrs Hoskins opened her handbag and pulled out a small parcel of tissue paper. She passed it across the counter into Dolly's waiting hand. 'I've wrapped it up for safekeeping. Do be careful, dear – we wouldn't want it falling into the wrong hands, now, would we?'

Dolly didn't unwrap the tissue until she was home. It took every bit of restraint she could summon not to tear it open the moment Mrs Hoskins's back was turned, but she didn't. She tucked the parcel into her handbag and there it remained through the rest of her canteen shift and the scurried journey home to Campden Grove.

By the time she closed her bedroom door behind her, Dolly's curiosity was a physical ache. She leapt onto her bed, shoes and all, and dug the tissue paper from her bag. As she was unwrapping it, something fell onto her lap. Dolly picked it up and turned it over in her fingers, a delicate oval locket on a fine rose-gold chain. One of the links, she noticed, had opened slightly, allowing its partner to slip free. She threaded the end of the open circle back through the next link and then used her thumbnail ever so carefully to close it.

There – fixed. And very well, too; a person would be hard pressed to see where the opening had been. Dolly smiled with satisfaction as she turned her attention back to the locket itself. It was the sort used to hold photographs, she realized, rubbing her thumb over the fine swirling pattern engraved on its pretty front. When Dolly finally managed to open it, she found a photograph of four children, two girls and two boys, sitting on a set of wooden stairs and squinting into bright sunshine. The image had been cut in half to fit the double-sided frame.

Dolly spotted Vivien instantly, the smaller of the girls, standing with one arm leaned on the stair rail, her other hand resting on the shoulder of one of the boys, a small lad with a simple look about him. These were her siblings, Dolly realized, at home in Australia, the portrait obviously taken sometime before Vivien was sent to live in England. Before she met her long-lost uncle and grew to adulthood in a tower on her family's grand estate, the very place where she would one day meet and marry handsome Henry Jenkins. Dolly shivered with pleasure. It was just like a fairy tale – just like Henry Jenkins's book, in fact.

She smiled to see Vivien as a girl. 'I wish I'd known you then,' Dolly said softly, which was silly, because of course it was far better to know her now, to have the chance to be one half of Dolly and Viv of Campden Grove. She took in the little girl's face, identifying the childish version of features she admired so much in the adult woman, and thought how strange it was that you could love someone so well when you'd only known them for a short time.

She closed the locket and noticed that something had been engraved in an elaborate script on the back. 'Isabel,' she read aloud. Vivien's mother, perhaps? Dolly couldn't think that she knew Vivien's mother's name, but it made sense. It seemed the sort of photograph a mother would keep close to her heart: her whole brood bundled up together, smiling for the travelling photographer. Dolly was far too young yet to think about children of her own, but she knew that when she did have them she'd carry a picture just like this one.

One thing was certain, this locket must be terribly important to Vivien if it had once belonged to her mother. Dolly was going to have to guard it with her life. She thought for a moment, and then a smile broke across her face – why, she would keep it in the safest place she knew. Dolly unhooked the clasp and threaded the chain beneath her hair, fastening it round her own neck. She sighed with satisfaction, with gladness, too, as the locket slipped below the line of her blouse and its cold metal met her warm skin.

Dolly pulled off her shoes and tossed her hat onto the window seat, collapsing back against her pillows with her feet crossed at the ankles. She lit a cigarette and blew smoke rings at the ceiling, imagining how thrilled Vivien was going to be when she delivered the locket back to her. She'd probably take Dolly into her arms, hug her and call her 'dearest', and her lovely dark eyes would well with tears. She'd invite Dolly in to sit down beside her on the sofa and they'd talk about all sorts of things. Dolly had a feeling Vivien might even tell her about the fellow, her doctor friend, once they finally had some time together.

She drew the locket from between her breasts and looked down at its pretty swirly surface. Poor Vivien must be devastated, thinking that she'd lost it forever. Dolly wondered whether she ought to let her know immediately that the necklace was safe – perhaps a letter dropped through the front door slot? – but quickly decided against it. She hadn't any writing paper of her own, not without Lady Gwendolyn's monogram on it, and that hardly seemed proper. Better to go in person, anyway. The real question was what she ought to wear.

Dolly flopped over onto her stomach and pulled her Book of Ideas from where she kept it hidden beneath the bed. *Mrs Beeton's Book of Household Management* had been of no interest to Dolly when her mother gave it to her, but paper was worth its weight in gold these days and the book's pages had proven themselves the ideal repository for all her favourite pictures from *The Lady*. Dolly had been cutting them out and gluing them over the top of Mrs Beeton's rules and recipes for well over a year. She flicked through them now, taking careful note of what all the very best women were wearing, comparing the pictures with items she'd noticed in the dressing room upstairs. She stopped when she came to a recent one. It was Vivien, photographed at a fundraising afternoon at the Ritz, glorious in a delicate dress of fine silk. Dolly traced her finger thoughtfully along the outline of the bodice and skirt – there was one just like it upstairs; with a few modifications, it would be perfect. She smiled to herself as she imagined how well she'd look, dashing across the street, at her earliest convenience, to take tea with Vivien Jenkins.

Three days later, in an uncharacteristically obliging turn, Lady Gwendolyn tossed down her bag of boiled sweets and demanded Dolly draw the blackouts and leave her alone to nap. It was almost three in the afternoon and Dolly didn't wait to be told twice. She saw the old woman safely into slumber, then changed into the yellow dress she'd had hanging in her room in readiness, and skipped across the road.

As she stood on the tiled top step, preparing to ring the bell, Dolly pictured Vivien's face when she opened the door and saw her standing there; the grateful smile of relief when they sat down to tea together and the locket was produced. She could have danced with anticipation.

Pausing a second to give her hair a final primp, savouring the moment as her heart quickened, Dolly rang the doorbell.

She waited, listening for the telltale rustling on the other side, and then the door swung inwards and a voice said, 'Hello there, darl—'

Dolly couldn't help but take a step backwards. Henry Jenkins was standing in front of her, taller up close than he'd seemed from a distance, dashing in the way of all powerful men. There was something almost brutal in his bearing, but it dissipated quickly and she decided it was probably just her own surprise colouring things. Certainly, in all her many imaginings, she'd never envisaged this. Henry Jenkins had an important job with the Ministry of Information and was rarely home during the day. She opened her mouth and closed it again; she felt intimidated by his presence, by his size and the darkness of his expression.

'Yes?' he said. There was a flush to his complexion and it crossed Dolly's mind that he'd been drinking. 'Is it scrap fabrics you're after? Because we've already given all we have to spare.'

Dolly found her voice. 'No. No, I'm sorry,' she said. 'I'm not here about fabrics. I've come to see Vivien – Mrs Jenkins.' There now, her poise was returning. She smiled at him. 'I'm a friend to your wife.'

'I see.' His surprise was obvious. 'A friend to my wife. And what might my wife's friend's name be?'

'Dolly – I mean, Dorothy. Dorothy Smitham.'

'Well then, Dorothy Smitham, I expect you'd better come inside, hadn't you?' He stepped back and gestured with his hand.

It occurred to Dolly, as she stepped through the doorway into Vivien's home, that in all the time she'd lived on Campden Grove, it was the first time she'd set foot inside number 25. From what she could tell, it was laid out much the same as number 7, an entrance hall with a flight of stairs leading up to the first floor and a doorway on the left-hand side. As she followed Henry Jenkins into the sitting room, however, she saw that the similarities ended there. The decorating of number 25 had evidently been done this century, and in contrast to Lady Gwendolyn's heavy, curved mahogany furniture and cluttered walls, this place was all light and sharp angles.

It was magnificent: the floor was parquet and a set of tubular chandeliers in frosted glass hung from the ceiling. Dramatic photographs featuring contemporary architecture were arranged along each wall, and the lime-green sofa had a zebra skin draped across one arm. So elegant, so modern – Dolly had to take care to keep her mouth from catching flies as she took it all in.

'Sit. Please,' said Henry Jenkins, indicating a shell-shaped armchair by the window. Dolly sat, straightening the hem of her dress before crossing her legs. She felt embarrassed, suddenly, by what she was wearing. It was becoming enough, for its time, but sitting here, in this splendid room, it felt like a museum piece. She'd thought herself so elegant

in Lady Gwendolyn's dressing room, turning this way and
that before the mirror; now, all she could see were the old-
fashioned trims and flounces – so different really (why
hadn't she noticed before?) from the clean lines of Vivien's
dress.

'I'd offer you tea,' said Henry Jenkins, dabbing the ends
of his moustache in an awkward way that was also rather
charming, 'but we lost our maid this week. Quite a disappointment – the girl was caught stealing.'

He was looking, Dolly realized with a rush of excitement, at her own crossed legs. She smiled, a little uncomfortable – he was Vivien's husband, after all – but flattered,
too. 'I'm sorry,' she said, and then she remembered something she'd heard Lady Gwendolyn say. 'It's terribly difficult
to find good staff these days, isn't it?'

'It is indeed.' Henry Jenkins was standing by the rather
marvellous fireplace, tiled like a chessboard in black and
white. He regarded Dolly quizzically and said, 'Tell me, how
is it you know my wife?'

'We met through the Women's Voluntary Service, and it
turns out we've a lot in common.'

'Such hours you ladies keep.' He smiled, but not easily,
and his pause, the way he was looking at her, gave Dolly the
distinct feeling there was something he wanted to know,
something more he wanted her to say. She couldn't think
what it might be, so she returned his smile and said nothing.
Henry Jenkins glanced at his wristwatch. 'Take today, for
instance. At breakfast, my wife told me she'd be finished her
meeting at two. I came home early to surprise her, but now
it's a quarter past three and there's still no sign. I can only
imagine she's been caught up, but a fellow worries.'

Irritation edged his words and Dolly could understand why – he was an important man who'd taken time away from essential war work only to be left cooling his heels while his wife flitted about town.

'Had you an arrangement to meet my wife?' he asked suddenly, as if the thought had just occurred to him that Dolly, too, was being inconvenienced by Vivien's tardiness.

'Oh, no,' she said quickly. He seemed affronted by the idea and she wanted to reassure him. 'Vivien didn't know that I was coming. I've brought her something, something she lost.'

'Oh?'

Dolly took the necklace out of her handbag and draped it delicately over her fingers. She'd varnished her nails especially with the last of Kitty's Coty Crimson.

'Her locket,' he said softly, reaching to take it. 'She was wearing this when we first met.'

'It's a very nice necklace.'

'She's worn it since she was a girl. It doesn't matter what I buy for her, how beautiful or grand it is, she won't wear any necklace in place of this one. She even wears it with her strings of pearls. I don't think I've ever known her to take it off, and yet – ' he was inspecting the chain – 'it's intact, so she must have done so.' He glanced sideways at Dolly and she shrank slightly beneath the intensity of his regard. Was that the way he looked at Vivien, she wondered, when he was lifting her dress, moving her locket aside to kiss her. 'You said it was found?' he continued. 'I wonder where?'

'I—' Dolly's thoughts made her blush. 'I'm afraid I don't know that – I wasn't the one to find it, you see, it was just

given to me to return to Vivien. On account of our closeness.'

He nodded slowly. 'I wonder, Mrs Smitham—'

'*Miss* Smitham.'

'Miss Smitham.' His lips twitched, the hint of a smile
that only deepened her blush. 'At the risk of sounding
impertinent, I wonder why it is that you didn't return this to
my wife at the WVS canteen? Surely it would have been
more convenient for a busy lady like yourself?'

A busy lady. Dolly liked the way that sounded. 'Not
impertinent at all, Mr Jenkins. Only, I knew how important
it was to Vivien, and I wanted her to have it back as soon as
possible. Our shifts don't always align, you see.'

'How strange.' His fist closed thoughtfully around the
locket. 'My wife reports for duty every day.'

Before Dolly could tell him that no one went to the canteen every day, that there was a shift book and a Mrs
Waddingham who ran a very tight ship, a key turned in the
front lock.

Vivien was home.

Both Dolly and Henry glanced keenly at the closed
sitting-room door, listening to her footsteps on the entrance
hall parquet. Dolly's heart began to chirrup as she imagined
how happy Vivien was going to be when Henry produced
the necklace, when he explained that Dolly was responsible
for bringing it back; the way Vivien would be overcome
with gratitude and, yes, love, and a radiant smile would
spread across her face and she'd say, 'Henry, darling. I'm so
glad you've finally met Dorothy. I've been meaning to invite
you over for tea for such a long time, dearest, but things
have been impossibly busy, haven't they?' And then she'd

make a joke about the hard taskmaster at the canteen, and the two of them would dissolve with laughter, and Henry would suggest they all have dinner together, perhaps at his club . . .

The sitting-room door opened and Dolly sat forward on her seat. Henry moved quickly to take his wife in his arms. The embrace was lingering, romantic, as if he were drawing in her scent, and Dolly realized, with a twinge of envy, how passionately Henry Jenkins loved his wife. She knew already, of course, having read *The Reluctant Muse*, but being in the room, observing them, drove it home. What was Vivien thinking, involving herself with that doctor when she was so well loved by a man like Henry?

The doctor. Dolly looked at Henry's face, his eyes closed as he pressed Vivien's head firmly to his chest; as he held her in the sort of clinch one might expect if months had passed and he'd feared the worst; and she realized, suddenly, that he knew. His agitation that Vivien was late, the pointed questions he'd asked Dolly, the frustrated way he'd spoken of his beloved wife . . . He *knew*. That was, he suspected. And he'd been hoping Dolly might confirm his suspicions either way. *Oh Vivien*, she thought, knotting her fingers as she stared at the other woman's back, *be careful*.

Henry pulled away at last, lifting his wife's chin to stare closely at her face. 'How was your day, my love?'

Vivien waited until his grip loosened and then she took off her WVS hat. 'Busy,' she said, patting the back of her hair flat. She set the hat down on a small table beside her, next to a framed photograph of their wedding day. 'We're boxing scarves and the demand is enormous. It's taking much longer than it should.' She paused, paying judicious care to the rim of her hat. 'I didn't realize you'd be home so early; I'd have made sure I left in good time to meet you.'

He smiled, unhappily, it seemed to Dolly, and said, 'I'd hoped to surprise you.'

'I didn't know.'

'No reason you should. That's the whole nature of surprise, isn't it? To catch a person unawares?' He took her by the elbow and steered her body slightly so she was looking into the room. 'Speaking of surprises, darling, you have a guest. Miss Smitham has come to call.'

Dolly stood, her heart pounding. Finally, her moment had arrived.

'Your friend has come to see you,' Henry continued. 'We've been having a lovely chat about all the good work you do for the WVS.'

Vivien blinked at Dolly, her face completely blank, and then she said, 'I don't know who this woman is.'

Dolly's breath caught. The room began to spin.

'But darling,' said Henry, 'of course you do. She brought this back for you.' He took the necklace from his pocket and put it in his wife's hands. 'You must have taken it off and forgotten it.'

Vivien turned it over, opened the locket and looked at the photographs inside. 'How did you get my necklace?' she said, her voice so cold it made Dolly flinch.

'I . . .' Dolly's head was swimming. She didn't understand what was happening, why Vivien was behaving like this; after all the glances they'd exchanged, brief, certainly, but loaded with fellow feeling; after all the times they'd observed one another through their respective windows; after everything Dolly had imagined for their future. Was it possible Vivien hadn't understood, that she hadn't realized what they meant to one another, that she hadn't also been dreaming of Dolly and Viv? 'It was left at the canteen. Mrs Hoskins found it and asked me to return it, seeing as . . .' *Seeing as we're kindred spirits, best friends, two of a kind.* 'Seeing as we're neighbours.'

Vivien's perfect brows shot up and she stared at Dolly. There was a moment of consideration and then her expression lightened ever so slightly. 'Yes. I know now. This woman is Lady Gwendolyn Caldicott's servant.'

The last word she said with a meaningful glance at Henry and the change in his demeanour was instant. Dolly remembered the way he'd referred to their own maid, the girl dismissed recently for thieving. He looked at the precious piece of jewellery, and said, 'Not a friend, then?'

'Certainly not,' said Vivien, as if the very idea was anathema to her. 'There isn't a friend of mine you haven't met, Henry darling. You know that.'

He stared perplexedly at his wife and then nodded stiffly. 'I did think it odd, only she was so insistent.' And then he turned to Dolly, every doubt and vexation crystallizing in a dark frown that pulled at his brow. He was disappointed in her, she realized; worse than that, his expression was laced with distaste. 'Miss Smitham,' he said, 'I thank you for returning my wife's necklace, but it's time you left.'

Dolly could think of nothing to say. She was dreaming, surely – this wasn't what she'd imagined, what she deserved, the way her life was meant to be. Any minute she would wake up and find herself laughing instead with Vivien and Henry as they all had a glass of whisky and sat down to talk over the trials of life, and she and Vivien, together on the sofa, would turn to one another and giggle about Mrs Waddingham at the canteen, and Henry would smile fondly at the two of them, and say what a pair they were, what an incorrigible darling pair.

'Miss Smitham?'

She managed to nod, picking up her handbag and scurrying past them both on her way back to the entrance hall.

Henry Jenkins followed her, hesitating briefly before swinging the front door wide open. His arm barred the way and Dolly had no choice but to stay where she was and wait for him to let her go. He appeared to be deciding what to say.

'Miss Smitham?' He spoke as one might to a foolish child; worse, a menial servant who'd forgotten her place, given herself over to elaborate fancies and dreams of a life far above her station. Dolly couldn't meet his eyes; she felt faint. 'Run along now, there's a good girl,' he said. 'Look after Lady Gwendolyn, and do try not to get yourself into any more trouble.'

Dusk was beginning to fall, and across the street Dolly saw Kitty and Louisa arriving home from work. Kitty looked up and her mouth formed an o when she saw what was happening, but Dolly didn't have a chance to smile or wave or put a bright face on it. How could she when everything was lost? When everything she'd wished for, all her hopes, had been met with such careless cruelty?

Seventeen

University of Cambridge, 2011

The rain had cleared and a ripe moon broke silver through streaky clouds. Having already paid a visit to the Cambridge University Library, Laurel was now sitting outside Clare College Chapel, waiting to be knocked over by someone on a bicycle. Not just any someone; she had a particular cyclist in mind. Evensong was almost over; she'd been listening from the bench beneath the cherry tree for the past half hour, letting the great organ and the voices of the choir transport her. Any minute, though, it would all stop and a cluster of people would burst from the doors, claim their bikes from the thirty-odd jumble stacked in metal racks by the door, and whizz past her in different directions. One of them, Laurel hoped, would be Gerry; it was something they'd always shared, the two of them, their love of music – the sort of music that made one glimpse answers to questions they hadn't known they were asking – and as soon as she'd arrived in Cambridge and seen signs outside the college advertising Evensong, she'd known it was her best chance of finding her brother.

Sure enough, a few minutes after Britten's *Rejoice in the Lamb* came to its breathtaking conclusion, as people started to emerge in pairs and small groups through the chapel doors, one of them walked out alone. A tall lanky figure whose appearance at the top of the stairs made Laurel smile, because it was surely one of life's most simple blessings to know someone so well you could pick them out immediately from the other side of a dark courtyard. The figure climbed onto a bicycle and pushed off with one foot, wobbling a bit until he picked up pace.

Laurel stepped out onto the road as he came close, waving and calling his name. He almost knocked her over, before stopping and blinking at her through the moonlit dark. The most disarming smile broke across his face and Laurel wondered why she didn't come to visit more often.

'Lol,' he said. 'What are you doing here?'

'I wanted to see you. I tried to call; I left messages.'

Gerry was shaking his head. 'The machine kept beeping, that little red light on the front wouldn't stop bloody blinking at me. It was defective, I think – I had to pull it out of the wall.'

The explanation made such perfect Gerry sense that no matter how infuriating it had been not being able to contact him, no matter that she'd worried he was annoyed with her, Laurel couldn't help but smile. 'Well,' she said, 'it gave me an excuse to come and visit anyway. Have you eaten?'

'Eaten?'

'Food. Annoying habit, I know, but I try to do it a few times a day.'

He mussed his tangle of dark hair as if trying to remember.

'Come on,' said Laurel. 'My shout.'

Gerry walked his bicycle beside her and they talked about music as they made their way to a small pizza restau-

rant built into a hole in the wall overlooking the Arts
Theatre. The very place, Laurel noted, that she'd taken herself off to as a teenager to see Pinter's *Birthday Party*.

It was dimly lit inside, tea lights flickering within glass
jars on red and white checked tablecloths. The place was
crowded with diners, but Gerry and Laurel were pointed to
a free table at the back, right near the pizza oven. Laurel
took off her coat, and a young man with long blond hair
falling in an elaborate sweep across his eyes took their order
for pizzas and wine. He was back in a matter of minutes
with a carafe of Chianti and two tumblers.

'So,' said Laurel, pouring for each of them, 'dare I ask
what you've been working on?'

'Just today I finished an article on the feeding habits of
teenage galaxies.'

'Hungry, are they?'

'Very, it seems.'

'And older than thirteen years, I'm guessing.'

'A little. Around three to five billion years after the
Big Bang.'

Laurel watched as her brother went on, talking eagerly
about the ESO Very Large Telescope in Chile ('It does what
a microscope does for a biologist') and explaining that faint
blobs in the sky were actually distant galaxies, and that
some ('It's incredible, Lol') appeared to have no rotation of
their gas – ('None of the current theories predicts them') –
and she nodded and reacted, though somewhat guiltily
because she wasn't really listening to him at all. She was
thinking about the way, when Gerry was excited, his words
tumbled into one another, as if his mouth was having trouble keeping up with his beautiful mind; the way he took

breaths only when he absolutely had to; the way his hands opened expressively and his long fingers strained, but with precision, as if they balanced stars on their very tips. They were Daddy's hands, Laurel realized as she watched him; Daddy's cheekbones and gentle eyes behind his glasses. In fact, there was a lot of Stephen Nicolson in his only son. Gerry had inherited his laugh from their mother, though.

He'd stopped talking and was gulping now from his wine glass. For all the nervousness Laurel felt about this quest she was on, in particular the conversation she knew was still ahead of her, there was an uncomplicatedness about being with Gerry that made her yearn for something she couldn't quite articulate. There was an echo of a memory of how things used to be between them, and she wanted to draw out the feeling a little longer before she spoiled it with her confession. She said, 'And what's next? What can possibly compete with the eating habits of teenage galaxies?'

'I'm creating the Latest Map of Everything.'

'Still setting yourself small achievable goals, I see?'

He grinned. 'Should be a breeze – it's not like I'm including all of space, just the sky. Only five hundred and sixty million stars, galaxies and other objects, and I'm done.'

Laurel was contemplating that number when their pizzas arrived, and the whiff of garlic and basil reminded her she hadn't eaten since breakfast. She ate with the voracity of a teenage galaxy, quite sure no food anywhere had ever tasted so good as that pizza right then. Gerry asked about her work and, between mouthfuls, Laurel told him about the documentary and the new version of *Macbeth* she was filming. 'At least, I will be. I've taken a little time off.'

Gerry held up a large hand. 'Wait – time off?'

'Yes.'

He tilted his head. 'What's wrong?'

'Why does everyone keep asking me that?'

'Because you don't take time off.'

'Nonsense.'

Gerry lifted his eyebrows. 'Are you making a joke? I've been told I miss them sometimes.'

'No, I'm not making a joke.'

'Then I have to inform you that all empirical evidence goes against your assertion.'

'Empirical evidence?' Laurel scoffed. 'Please. You can hardly talk. When's the last time you took time off?'

'June 1985, Max Seerjay's wedding in Bath.'

'Well then.'

'I didn't say I was any different. You and I are two of a kind, both wedded to our work: that's how I know something's wrong.' He swiped his paper napkin across his lips and leaned back against the charcoal-coloured brick wall. 'Anomalous time off, anomalous visit to see me – I can only deduce the two are related.'

Laurel sighed.

'Stalling exhalation. All the proof I need. Want to tell me what's going on, Lol?'

She folded her napkin in half and half again. It was now or never; all this time she'd been wishing Gerry was along with her for the ride – now was the time to buckle him in. She said, 'Do you remember that time you came to stay with me in London? Right before you started here?'

Gerry answered in the affirmative by quoting from *Monty Python and the Holy Grail*. '"Please! This is supposed to be a happy occasion".'

Laurel smiled. '"Let's not bicker and argue over who killed who". Love that film.' She shifted a piece of olive from one side of her plate to the other, hedging, trying to decide which were the right words. Impossible, because there were none, not really, best just to leap in. 'You asked me something, that night on the roof; you asked me whether anything happened back when we were kids. Something violent.'

'I remember.'

'Do you?'

Gerry gave a single, efficient nod.

'Do you remember what I said?'

'You told me there was nothing you could think of.'

'Yes. I did. I did say that,' she agreed softly. 'But I lied to you, Gerry.' She didn't add that it had been for his own good or that she'd thought she was doing the right thing. Both were true, but what did it matter now? She didn't want to excuse herself, certainly not; she'd lied and she deserved whatever recriminations came her way – not only for withholding the truth from Gerry, but for what she'd told those policemen. 'I lied.'

'I know you did,' he said, finishing off his crust.

Laurel blinked. 'You do? How?'

'You wouldn't look at me when I asked, and you called me "G". You never do that unless you're obfuscating.' He gave a nonchalant shrug. 'Nation's greatest actress, maybe; still no match for my powers of deduction.'

'And people say you don't pay attention.'

'They do? I had no idea. I'm crushed.' They smiled at one another, but carefully, and then Gerry said, 'Do you want to tell me now, Lol?'

'I do. Very much. Do you still want to know?'

'I do. Very much.'

She nodded. 'All right, then. All right.' And so she started at the beginning: a girl in a tree house on a summer's day in 1961, a stranger on the driveway, a tiny boy in his mother's arms. She took special care to describe how well the mother loved that boy, the way she paused on the doorstep just to smile at him and breathe in his milky smell and tickle his fat, waxy feet; but then the man in the hat stepped on stage and the spotlight swung towards him. His furtive tread as he passed through the gate at the side of the house, the way the dog knew before anyone else that darkness this way came, his bark alerting their mother, who turned and saw the man and, as the girl in the tree house watched, became suddenly frightened.

When she reached the part of the story involving knives and blood and a little boy crying in the gravel, Laurel thought, as she listened to her own voice as if it were coming from outside her body and watched her grown brother's face across the table, how odd it was to be having this very private conversation in public, and yet how necessary the noise and hum of this place was to her ability to tell it. Here, in a pizza restaurant in Cambridge, with students laughing and joking all around them, young and clever scholars with their whole lives still ahead of them, Laurel felt enclosed and safe, more comfortable somehow, and able to utter words she didn't think she'd have managed in the silence of his college lodging, words like: 'She killed him,

Gerry. The man – Henry Jenkins was his name – he died there that day on our front path.'

Gerry had been listening closely, staring at a patch of tablecloth, his face revealing nothing. Now a muscle twitched in his shadowed jaw and he gave a small nod, more to acknowledge the end of her story than to respond to its content. Laurel waited, finished her glass of wine and poured some more for each of them. 'So,' she said. 'That's it. That's what I saw.'

At length, Gerry looked up at her. He said, 'I guess that explains it then.'

'Explains what?'

His fingers trembled with nervous energy as he spoke. 'I used to see this thing sometimes as a kid, out of the corner of my eye, this dark shadow that made me frightened for no reason. Hard to describe. I'd turn and there'd be nothing there, just this awful feeling that I'd glanced around too late. My heart used to race and I'd have no idea why. I told Ma once; she took me to have my eyes tested.'

'That's why you got glasses?'

'No, turns out I was short-sighted. The glasses didn't help with the shadow, but they sure made people's faces less fuzzy.'

Laurel smiled.

Gerry didn't. The scientist in him was relieved, Laurel knew, to have an explanation for something previously inexplicable, but the part of him that was son to a much-loved parent was not so easily assuaged. 'Good people do bad things,' he said, and then he clawed at his shock of hair. 'Christ. What a bloody clichéd thing to say.'

'It's true though,' said Laurel, wanting to comfort him. 'They do. Sometimes with good reason.'

'What reason?' He looked at her and he was a child again, desperate for Laurel to explain it all away. She felt for him – one minute he was happily contemplating the wonders of the universe, the next his sister was telling him his mother had killed a man. 'Who was this guy, Lol? Why did she do it?'

In the most straightforward fashion she could manage – it was best with Gerry to appeal to his sense of logic – Laurel told him what she knew about Henry Jenkins, that he was an author, married to their mother's friend, Vivien, during the war. She also told him what Kitty Barker had said, that there'd been a terrible falling-out between Dorothy and Vivien in early 1941.

'You think their argument is related to what happened at Greenacres in 1961,' he said. 'You wouldn't mention it otherwise.'

'I do.' Laurel remembered Kitty's account of the night out with her mother, the way she'd behaved, the things she'd been saying. 'I think Ma became upset by whatever happened between them and she did something to punish her friend. I think her plan – whatever it was – turned out badly, far worse than she'd expected, but by then it was too late to put things right. Ma fled London, and Henry Jenkins was angered enough by whatever happened to come looking for her twenty years later.' Laurel wondered at the way a person could outline such dreadful theories in such a frank, no-nonsense way. To an observer, Laurel knew, she would seem cool and calm and keen to get to the bottom of things; she betrayed no hint of the deep distress that was gnawing away at her insides. She lowered her voice, though, to say, 'I even wonder if she wasn't responsible in some way for Vivien's death.'

'God, Lol.'

'Whether she's had to live with her guilt all this time and the woman we know was formed as a result; whether she's spent the rest of her life atoning.'

'By being the perfect mother to us.'

'Yes.'

'Which was working out fine until Henry Jenkins came looking to even the score.'

'Yes.'

Gerry had fallen silent; a faint frown creased the skin between his eyes; he was thinking.

'Well?' Laurel pressed, leaning closer to him. 'You're the scientist – does the theory have legs?'

'It's plausible,' said Gerry, nodding slowly. 'Not difficult to believe remorse might act as a motivator for change. Nor that a husband might seek to avenge a slight against his wife. And if what she did to Vivien was bad enough, I can see she'd have thought her only choice was to silence Henry Jenkins once and for all.'

Laurel's heart sank. There was a very small part of her, she realized, that had been clinging to the hope he might laugh, poke holes in her theory with the sharp point of his stupendous brain, and tell her she ought to take a good long lie-down and leave off reading Shakespeare for a while.

He didn't. The logician in him had taken the reins and he said, 'I wonder what she could have done to Vivien that she came to regret so much.'

'I don't know.'

'Whatever it was, I think you're right,' he continued. 'It must have turned out worse than she'd intended. Ma never would've harmed her friend on purpose.'

Laurel offered a noncommittal response, recalling the way her mother had brought the knife down on Henry Jenkins's chest without a moment's hesitation.

'She wouldn't have, Lol.'

'No, I wouldn't have thought so either – not at first. Have you considered, though, that perhaps we're just making excuses because she's our mother and we know and love her?'

'We probably are,' Gerry agreed, 'but that's all right. We *do* know her.'

'We think we do.' Something Kitty Barker said had been playing on Laurel's mind, about wartime and the way it heightened passions; the threat of invasion, the fear and the dark, night after night of broken sleep. 'What if she was a different person back then? What if the pressure of the Blitz got to her? What if she changed after she married Daddy and had us?' After she was given her second chance.

'No one changes that much.'

From nowhere, the crocodile story leapt into Laurel's mind. *Is that why you changed to become a lady, Mummy?* she'd asked, and Dorothy had answered that she'd given up her crocodile ways at the same time she'd become a mother. Was it drawing too long a bow to think the story might have been a metaphor, that even then her mother might have been confessing to some other sort of change? Or was Laurel reading far too much into a tale that was meant merely to please a child? She pictured Dorothy that afternoon, turning back towards her mirror, straightening the shoulder straps of her lovely dress, as eight-year-old Laurel asked, wide-eyed, how such a wondrous transformation had taken place. *Well now,* her mother had said, *I can't tell you all my secrets, can I? Not all at once. Ask me again some day. When you're older.*

And Laurel intended to do just that. She was hot, all of a sudden, the other diners were laughing and crowding the room, and the pizza oven let out great tidal waves of warm toasty air. Laurel opened her wallet and pulled out two twenties and a five, tucking the notes beneath the bill and waving away Gerry's attempts to contribute. 'I told you, my shout,' she said. She didn't add that it was the very least she could do, having brought her dark obsession into his starlit world. 'Come on,' she said, drawing on her coat. 'Let's walk.'

Chatter from the restaurants faded behind them as they crossed King's College quad on their way to meet the Cam. It was quiet by the river and Laurel could hear the punts rocking gently on the moon-silvered surface. A bell sounded in the distance, stark and stoic, and in a college room somewhere someone was practising the violin. The beautiful sad music plucked at Laurel's heart and she knew, suddenly, that she'd made a mistake in coming here.

Gerry hadn't said much since they'd left the restaurant. He was walking silently beside her now, pushing his bike with one hand. His head was bowed, his gaze trained on the ground before him. She'd let the burden of the past trick her into sharing it; she'd convinced herself that Gerry ought to know, that he too was bound to the monstrous thing she'd witnessed. But he'd been little more than a baby back then, a tiny person, and now he was a sweet man, his mother's favourite, incapable of considering that she might have once done something dreadful. Laurel was about to say as much, to apologize and somehow make light of her own obsessive interest, when Gerry said, 'What's next, then? Have we got any leads?'

Laurel glanced at him.

He'd stopped beneath the yellow glow of a streetlamp and was prodding his glasses further up the bridge of his nose. 'What? You weren't going to let it go, were you? Obviously we need to find out what happened. It's part of our story, Lol.'

Laurel couldn't think that she'd ever loved him quite so much as that moment. 'There is something,' she said, her breath catching. 'Now you mention it. I went to visit Ma this morning and she came over all hazy and asked the nurse to send in Dr Rufus when she saw him.'

'Not so strange in a hospital, is it?'

'Not in itself, except her doctor's name is Cotter, not Rufus.'

'A slip of the tongue?'

'I don't think so. There was a certainty in the way she said it. Besides . . .' The shadowy image of a young man named Jimmy, loved once by her mother, lamented now, came to Laurel's mind. 'It's not the first time she's spoken of someone she used to know. I think the past is going round and round in her head; I think she almost *wants* us to know the answers.'

'Did you ask her about it?'

'Not about Dr Rufus, but I did about a few other things. She answered openly enough, but the conversation upset her. I'll talk to her again, of course, but if there's another way, I'm eager to try that too.'

'Agreed.'

'I went to the library earlier to see if there was any way of finding out details of a doctor who was operating in Coventry and maybe London, too, in the nineteen thirties and forties. I only had his surname and had no idea what sort of doctor he was, so the librarian suggested we start by checking the database for the *Lancet*.'

'And?'

'I found a Dr Lionel Rufus. Gerry, I'm almost certain it's him: he lived in Coventry at the right time and published papers in the field of personality psychology.'

'You think she was his patient? That Ma might've suffered from some sort of condition back then?'

'I've no idea, but I intend to find out.'

'I'll do it,' said Gerry suddenly. 'There are people I could ask.'

'Really?'

He was nodding, and his words tumbled together excitedly as he said, 'You go back to Suffolk. I'll let you know as soon as I find anything.'

It was more than Laurel had dared hope for – no it wasn't, it was *exactly* what she'd hoped for. Gerry was going to help her; together they were going to find out what really happened. 'You realize you might find something terrible.' She didn't want to scare him off, but she had to warn him. 'Something that makes a lie of everything we thought we knew about her.'

Gerry smiled. 'Aren't you the actress? Isn't this the bit where you're supposed to tell me that people aren't a science – that characters are multi-faceted, and one new variable doesn't disprove the whole theorem?'

'I'm just saying. Be prepared, little brother.'

'I'm always prepared,' he said with a grin, 'and I'm still backing our mum.'

Laurel raised her eyebrows, wishing she had his faith. But she had seen what happened that day at Greenacres, she knew what their mother was capable of. 'Not very scientific of you,' she said sternly, 'not when everything points towards the one conclusion.'

Gerry took her hand. 'Did the hungry teenage galaxies teach you nothing, Lol?' he said softly, and Laurel felt a surge of worry and protective love, because she saw in his eyes how much he needed to believe things would all work out, and she knew in her own heart how unlikely it was. 'Never discount the possibility of turning up an answer none of the current theories predicts.'

Eighteen

Dolly was quite sure she'd never been so humiliated in all her life. If she lived to be a hundred years old, she knew she wouldn't forget the way Henry and Vivien Jenkins had stared at her as she left, those bemused mocking expressions distorting their horrid lovely faces. They'd almost succeeded in making Dolly feel as if she *were* nothing more than a neighbour's maid, come calling in an old dress borrowed from her mistress's wardrobe. Almost. Dolly was made of sterner stuff than that, though. As Dr Rufus was always telling her: 'You're one in a million, Dorothy, you really are.'

At their most recent lunch, two days after what had happened, he'd leaned back in his seat at the Savoy and eyed her over his cigar. 'Tell me, Dorothy,' he'd said, 'why do you think this woman, this Vivien Jenkins, was so dismissive of you?' Dolly had shaken her head thoughtfully, before telling him what she now believed. 'I think when she came across the two of us, Mr Jenkins and I, together like that in the sitting room . . .' Dolly glanced away, slightly embarrassed as she remembered the way Henry Jenkins had looked at her. 'Well, I'd taken rather special care with my appearance that day, you see, and I suspect it was just more than Vivien could stand.' He'd nodded appreciatively and then his eyes had narrowed as he stroked his chin. 'And how did *you* feel, Dorothy, when she slighted you that way?' Dolly had thought she might cry when Dr Rufus asked that. She didn't, though; she smiled bravely, driving her finger-nails into her palms and priding herself on her self-control as she said, 'I felt mortified, Dr Rufus, and very, very hurt. I don't think I've ever been treated so shabbily, and by some-one I used to call a friend. I really felt—'

'Stop it – stop it now!' In the bright sunlit room at 7 Campden Grove, Dolly started as Lady Gwendolyn kicked a small foot free and shouted, 'You'll take my toe off if you're not careful, silly girl.'

Dolly noted with contrition the tiny white triangle where the old woman's pinky toenail had been. It was thoughts of Vivien that had done it. Dolly had gone much harder and faster with the file than she ought to have. 'I'm so sorry, Lady Gwendolyn,' she said. 'I'll be more gentle—'

'I've had enough of that. Fetch me my sweets, Dorothy. I passed a bilious night. Wretched ration recipes – veal knuckle with stewed red cabbage for dinner! Little wonder I tossed and turned and dreamed of ghastly things.'

Dolly did what she was told, waiting patiently as the old woman sorted through the bag to find the largest bull's eye.

Mortification had passed quickly through indignity and shame to arrive at full-blown anger. Why, Vivien and Henry Jenkins had all but called her a thief and a liar, when all she'd wanted was to return Vivien's precious necklace. The irony was almost too great to bear, that Vivien – she who was sneaking about behind her husband's back, telling lies to everyone who cared about her, entreating those who didn't not to give away her secrets – should be the one to cast her cold, dark-eyed judgement on Dolly, the very person who'd leapt to her defence time and again when others spoke ill of her.

Well – Dolly frowned determinedly as she sheathed the nail file and tidied up the dressing table – not any more. Dolly had made a plan. She hadn't spoken to Lady Gwendolyn, not yet, but when the old woman learned what had happened – that her young friend had been betrayed, just as she had – Dolly was sure she'd give her blessing. They were going to throw a huge party when the war ended, a stupendous affair, a grand masquerade with costumes and lanterns and fire-eaters. All the most fabulous people would come, and there'd be photographs in *The Lady*, and it would be talked about for years to come. Dolly could just picture the guests arriving in Campden Grove, dressed to the nines and parading right past number 25, where Vivien Jenkins sat watching from the window, uninvited.

In the meantime, she was doing her best to shun the pair of them. There were some people, Dolly was learning, whom it was better *not* to know. Henry Jenkins wasn't difficult to avoid – Dolly didn't see much of him at the best of times – and she'd managed to keep clear of Vivien by withdrawing from the WVS. It had been a relief, actually: in one fell swoop she'd freed herself from Mrs Waddingham's jurisdiction and gained the time to devote herself more fully to keeping Lady Gwendolyn happy. Just as well, too, as things turned out. The other morning, at an hour when ordinarily she'd have been off working at the canteen, Dolly had been massaging Lady Gwendolyn's cramping legs when the door-bell rang downstairs. The old woman had rolled her wrist towards the window and told Dolly to take a peek and see who'd come to bother them this time.

Dolly had been worried at first it would be Jimmy – he'd called a few times now, during the day thank God when no one else was home and she'd been able to avoid a scene – but it hadn't been him. As Dolly peered through Lady Gwendolyn's window, the glass pane criss-crossed with tape against bomb blasts, she'd seen Vivien Jenkins below, glancing over her shoulder as though it was beneath her to be calling at number 7 and she was embarrassed even to be seen on the doorstep. Dolly's skin had flushed hot because she knew, instantly, why Vivien had come. It was just the sort of petty unkindness Dolly was coming to expect from her: she planned to report to Lady Gwendolyn the thieving habits of her 'servant'. Dolly could just picture Vivien, posed sleekly on the dusty chintz armchair by the old woman's bedside, crossing her long slender legs and leaning forward in a conspiratorial way to deplore the quality of servants these days. 'It's so difficult to find somebody *trustworthy*, isn't it, Lady Gwendolyn? Why, we've had our own spot of bother lately . . .'

As Dolly had watched Vivien on the doorstep, still checking the street behind her, the grande dame had barked from her bed, 'Well, Dorothy – I'm not going to live forever. Who is it?' Dolly had suppressed her trepidation and reported, as blithely as she could, that it was just a mean-looking woman collecting clothes for charity. When Lady Gwendolyn gave a snort and said, 'Don't let her in! She's not getting her grubby fingers on *my* dressing room,' Dolly had been only too happy to comply.

*

Thwump. Dolly jumped. Quite without realizing it, she'd gravitated to the window and had been gazing down blankly at number 25. *Thwump, thwump*. She turned to see Lady Gwendolyn staring at her. The old woman's cheeks were puffed out full to accommodate the enormous bull's eye and she was smacking her cane on the mattress to gain attention.

'Yes, Lady Gwendolyn?'

The old lady wrapped her arms across her body and mimed freezing.

'You're a little cold?'

Nod, nod.

Dolly disguised her sigh with an acquiescent smile – she'd only just removed the covers after complaints of overheating – and went to the bedside. 'Let's see if we can't fix you up then, shall we?'

Lady Gwendolyn closed her eyes and Dolly started drawing up the blankets, but the task was easier said than done. The old woman's twisting and turning with the cane had made a mess of the bedclothes and the blanket was caught, pinned beneath her other leg. Dolly scooted round to the far side of the bed and tugged as hard as she could to bring it loose.

Later, she would look back and blame the dust for what happened next. At the time, though, she was far too busy heaving and hauling to notice. Finally, the blanket came free and Dolly shook it, dragging it as high as she could to tuck the top beneath the old woman's chin. It was while she was folding over the hemmed edge that Dolly sneezed with unusually dramatic force. *Ahh-choooooo!*

The shock gave Lady Gwendolyn a jolt and her eyes flew wide open.

Dolly excused herself, rubbing her tickling nose. She blinked to clear her eyes and through the glaze noticed that the grande dame had started flailing her arms; her hands were flapping like a pair of frightened birds.

'Lady Gwendolyn?' she said, leaning closer. The old woman's face had turned beetroot-red. 'Dear Lady Gwendolyn, what is it?'

A rasping sound came from Lady Gwendolyn's throat and her skin darkened to aubergine. She was gesturing wildly now towards her throat. Something was stopping her from speaking—

The bull's eye, Dolly realized with a gasp; it was stuck like a plug in the old woman's throat. Dolly didn't know what to do. She was frantic. Without thinking, she thrust her fingers into Lady Gwendolyn's mouth, trying to fish out the sweet.

She couldn't reach.

Dolly panicked. Perhaps if she pounded the old lady's back, or squeezed her round the middle?

She attempted both, her heart racing, her pulse hammering in her ears. She tried to lift Lady Gwendolyn, but she was so heavy, her silk coverall so slippery – 'It's all right,' Dolly heard herself saying as she fought to keep her grip. 'It's going to be all right.'

Over and over she said it, heaving with all her might as Lady Gwendolyn struggled and flailed in her arms: 'It's all right, it's going to be all right, everything's all right.'

Until finally Dolly ran out of breath and stopped speaking and when she did, realized that her companion had grown heavier, that she was no longer writhing or gasping for air, that everything was unnaturally still.

Then all was quiet in the stately bedroom but for Dolly's breathing, and the eerie creaking of the bed as she eased herself out from beneath her dead mistress and let the still-warm body sink back into its familiar position.

The doctor, when he arrived, stood at the end of the bed and decreed it 'a clear case of natural extinguishment'. He looked to Dolly, who was holding Lady Gwendolyn's cold hand, wiping her eyes with a handkerchief, and added, 'She'd always had a weakness of the heart. Scarlet fever as a girl.'

Dolly contemplated Lady Gwendolyn's face, especially stern in death, and nodded. She hadn't mentioned either the bull's eye or the sneeze; there hadn't seemed any point. It didn't change things, not now, and she would've sounded a fool blathering on about sweets and dust. The bull's eye had dissolved, anyway, in the time it took the doctor to make his way through streets ripped up by last night's raids.

'There, there, dear girl,' the doctor said, patting Dolly's hand. 'I know you were fond of her. And she of you, too, might I add.' And then he returned his hat to his head, collected his bag, and said he'd leave the name of the Caldicott family's preferred funeral people on the table downstairs.

Lady Gwendolyn's last will and testament was read in the library at number 7 Campden Grove on the twenty-ninth day of January 1941. Strictly speaking, it needn't have been read at all, not publicly; a discreet letter to each person named therein was Mr Pemberly's preference (the solicitor suffered terribly with stage fright) but Lady Gwendolyn, with an instinct for drama, had insisted. It didn't surprise Dolly, who, as one of the beneficiaries, was invited to attend the reading. The old woman's hatred for her only nephew was no secret, and what better way to punish him from beyond the grave than to withhold his expected inheritance *and* have him sit through the public shame of seeing the whole lot pass to someone else.

Dolly dressed carefully, just as Lady Gwendolyn would have wanted her to, eager to look the part of the worthy heiress, without seeming to be trying too hard.

She was nervous as she waited for Mr Pemberly to get on with it. The poor man was stuttering and stammering his way through the preliminary articles, his birthmark reddening as he reminded those assembled (Dolly and Lord Wolsey) that his client's wishes, having been ratified by himself, an impartial and qualified solicitor at law, were final and binding. Lady Gwendolyn's nephew was a great bulldog of a man, and Dolly hoped he was listening carefully to the stilted disclaimers. She couldn't imagine he was going to be too happy when he realized what his aunt had done.

Dolly was right. Lord Peregrine Wolsey was incensed to the point of apoplexy when the will was finally read. He was an impatient gentleman at the best of times and had started steaming from the ears long before Mr Pemberly even finished his preamble. Dolly could hear him huffing and puffing at each new sentence that didn't begin, 'I give and bequeath to my nephew, Peregrine Wolsey . . .' At length though, the solicitor drew breath, took out a handkerchief to mop his damp brow, and moved on to the business of dispensing his client's largesse. 'I, Gwendolyn Caldicott, revoking all other wills and testaments by me heretofore made, give and bequeath to the wife of my nephew, Peregrine Wolsey, the bulk of my wardrobe, and to my nephew himself, the contents of my late father's dressing room.'

'*What*?' the fellow roared so suddenly he spat out his cigar stub. 'What the bloody hell is the meaning of this?'

'Please, Lord Wolsey,' Mr Pemberly jabbered, his birthmark darkening further to an angry shade of purple, 'I'd ask you to p-p-*please* sit quietly a m-m-moment longer while I f-f-f-finish.'

'Why, I'll *sue* you, you grubby worm. I know it was you, getting in my aunt's ear—'

'Lord Wolsey, p-p-*please*, I beg you.'

Mr Pemberly continued his reading, encouraged by a kindly head bob from Dolly. 'I give and bequeath the residue and remainder of my property and estate, real, personal and mixed, including my dwelling at number 7 Campden Grove, London, with the exception of the few items named hereafter, to the Kensington Animal Shelter,' he looked up. 'A representative of which was unable to attend today . . .' Which was about the point when Dolly stopped hearing anything but the deafening ring of betrayal's bells in her ears.

Lady Gwendolyn had, of course, left a provision for 'my young companion, Dorothy Smitham', but Dolly was in too much shocked distress to listen when it was read. Only later that night in the privacy of her own bedroom, as she pored over the letter Mr Pemberly had put into her shaking hands while he dodged threats from Lord Wolsey, did she realize her inheritance comprised a small selection of coats from the dressing room upstairs. Dolly recognized the listed items at once. With the exception of a rather tatty white fur, she'd given all of them away already, in the hat-box loads she'd donated so joyously to the WVS clothes drive organized by Vivien Jenkins.

Dolly was livid. She seethed and burned and spat. After all she'd done for the old woman, the numerous indignities she'd had to bear – those toenails and the ear-cleaning sessions, the regular sprays of venom she'd endured. She hadn't suffered them gladly – Dolly never would have tried to argue that – but she'd suffered them nonetheless, and not for nothing. She'd given up everything for Lady Gwendolyn; she'd thought they were like family; she'd been led to believe a great inheritance awaited her, by Mr Pemberly most recently, but also by Lady Gwendolyn herself. Dolly couldn't understand what could possibly have happened to make her change her mind.

Unless . . . The answer came like the fall of an axe, swift and absolute. Dolly's hands began to tremble and the solicitor's letter dropped to the floor. But of course, it all made perfect sense. Vivien Jenkins, that spiteful woman, had come to visit Lady Gwendolyn after all; it was the only explanation. She must have sat by her window, biding her time and watching for an opportunity, one of the rare instances over the past fortnight when Dolly had been left no choice but to leave the house on an errand. Vivien had waited, and then she'd pounced; sat with Lady Gwendolyn, filling the old woman's head with wicked lies about Dolly, she who'd never had anything but the grande dame's best interests at heart.

The Kensington Animal Shelter's first act as owner of 7 Campden Grove was to contact the War Office and insist that alternative arrangements be made for the office girls who were currently being lodged in the house. The dwelling was to be converted immediately for use as an animal hospital and rescue centre. The decree didn't worry Kitty and Louisa, both of whom were married to respective RAF pilots within days of one another in early February; the other two girls remained as indistinguishable in death as they had been in life, hit by a bomb as they skipped together arm in arm on their way to a dance in Lambeth on 30 January.

Which just left Dolly. It wasn't easy to find a room in London, not for someone who'd become accustomed to the finer things in life, and Dolly looked at three squalid arrangements before returning to the Notting Hill boarding house she'd lived in two years ago, back in her shop-girl days when Campden Grove was just a name on a map, and not the repository for her life's great dreams and disappointments. Mrs White, the widowed owner of 24 Rillington Place, was delighted to see Dolly again (though 'see' was rather too optimistic a description: the old biddy was blind as a bat without her glasses), and further delighted to report that Dolly's old room was still available – just as soon as she handed over her bond and ration book, of course.

Little wonder the room was still free. There were few people, Dolly was sure, even in wartime London, who were desperate enough for somewhere to live that they'd hand over good money to sleep within its walls. It was more an afterthought, really, rather than a room: what was left when a bedroom in the original house had been subdivided into two unequal halves. The window had gone with the other portion, leaving a very small, very dark closet-like area on Dolly's side of the plaster wall. There was space for a narrow bed, a side table, a tiny sink, and not much besides. Still, lack of light and ventilation kept the price low and Dolly didn't have a lot to accommodate – everything she owned was in the suitcase she'd carried with her when she danced out of her parents' house three years earlier.

One of the first things she'd done upon arriving was to arrange her two books, *The Reluctant Muse* and Dorothy Smitham's Book of Ideas, on the single shelf above the sink. There was a part of her that never wanted to see the Jenkins book again, but she'd so few possessions left, and Dolly so loved special things, that she couldn't bear to be rid of it. Not yet. She turned the book around instead so the spine was against the wall. The display was still rather sad, so Dolly added the Leica camera Jimmy had given her one birthday. Photography hadn't been her caper – it required too much stillness and waiting for Dolly – but the room was so stark and empty she'd have proudly flaunted a commode if she'd owned one. At last, she took the fur coat she'd inherited, put it on a hanger and slipped it over the hook on the back of the door: all the better to see it no matter where she happened to be standing in the tiny room. That old white coat had become an emblem of sorts for every one of Dolly's dreams that had been reduced to tatters. She stared at it, and she stewed, and she directed all the fury she felt towards Vivien Jenkins deep into the coat's matted fur.

Dolly took a job in a nearby munitions factory because Mrs White wouldn't have hesitated to throw her out if she didn't make her weekly payments, and because it was the sort of work that could be done without devoting more than a single per cent of one's attention to it. Which left the rest of Dolly's mind free to dwell on the ills done to her. She would come home at night, force down some of Mrs White's corned-beef hash, and then leave the other girls to laugh together about their boyfriends and shout at Lord Haw-Haw on the wireless, while she took to her narrow bed, smoking her way through her last packets of cigarettes and thinking about everything she'd lost: her family and Lady Gwendolyn and Jimmy . . . She thought, too, about the way Vivien had said, 'I don't know this woman' – her mind kept coming back to that – and she saw Henry Jenkins pointing her to the door, and she felt again the hot and cold waves of shame and anger coursing through her body.

So it went, day after day the same, until one night in the middle of February, things happened differently. Most of the day had been like any other: Dolly had worked a double shift at the factory and then stopped to buy dinner at the nearby British Restaurant because she simply couldn't stomach another night of Mrs White's foul cooking. She sat there at her seat in the corner until the place closed, watching all the other diners from behind her cigarette, especially the couples as they stole kisses across the tabletops and laughed together as if the world were a good place. Dolly could vaguely remember feeling that way herself, being full of laughter and happiness and hope.

On the way home, taking a short cut down a narrow lane as bombers sounded in the distance, Dolly tripped in the blackout – she'd left her torch at Campden Grove when she'd had to leave (Vivien's fault) – and she fell down deep inside a bomb crater. Dolly's ankle was twisted and her knee bled through the new ladder in her best stockings, but it was her pride that took the greatest battering. She had to limp the whole way back to Mrs White's boarding house (Dolly refused to call it 'home' – it wasn't her home, that had been stolen from her – Vivien's fault) in the cold and the dark, and by the time she arrived the door had already been locked and bolted. Curfew was something Mrs White took very seriously; not to keep Hitler out (though she held grave fears that 24 Rillington Place was top of his invasion force's list), but rather to make an example of the dirty stop-outs among her tenants. Dolly clenched her fists and limped down the side alley. Her knee was stinging badly now, and she winced as she scaled the wall, using the old iron bolt as a foothold. The blackout made it darker than normal and there was no moon to speak of, but somehow she managed to clamber through the jumble of the back garden to reach the storeroom window with the weak latch. As quietly as she could, Dolly jimmied it with her shoulder until the lock budged and she could tap it upwards and scramble through.

The hallway smelled of stale grease and old cheap meats, and Dolly held her breath as she climbed the grubby stairs. When she reached the first floor, she noticed a thin strip of light beneath the door to Mrs White's rooms. No one was quite sure what went on behind that door, only that it was a rare night that Mrs White's light was out

before the last of the girls turned in. She could be com-
muning with the dead or sending covert radio messages to
the Germans for all Dolly knew, and frankly she didn't care.
So long as it kept the landlady occupied while her truant
tenants sneaked home to roost, everyone got along fine.
Dolly continued along the corridor, taking extra care to
avoid the squeaky floorboards, opened her bedroom door
and sealed herself safely inside.

Only then, with her back pressed hard against the door,
did Dolly finally surrender herself to the throbbing pain that
had built inside her chest all night. Without even dropping
her handbag to the floor, she began to cry as freely as a
child; hot spurting tears of shame and pain and anger. She
looked down at her filthy clothing, her messed-up knee, the
blood that had mixed with dirt and spread across everything; she blinked through her scalding tears to take in the
ghastly, bare little room, the bedspread with holes in it, the
sink stained brown around the plughole; and she realized
with crashing certainty the absence of anything in her life
that was good or precious or true. She knew, too, that it was
all Vivien Jenkins's fault – *all* of it: the loss of Jimmy, Dolly's
destitution, her tedious job in the factory. Even the mishap
tonight – her torn-up knee and damaged stockings, being
locked out of the boarding house, having to suffer the insult
of breaking into a place where she paid good money to stay
– would never have happened if Dolly hadn't laid eyes on
Vivien, if she hadn't volunteered to take that necklace back,
if she hadn't tried to be such a good friend to so unworthy
a woman.

Dolly's tearful gaze alit then on the shelf containing her
Book of Ideas. She saw the book's spine turned inward and

grief swelled inside her to the point of exploding. Dolly pounced on the book. She sat cross-legged on the floor with it, fingers stumbling through the pages to arrive at the segment, a third of the way in, where she'd so lovingly collected and glued the Society photographs of Vivien Jenkins. They were pictures she'd once pored over, memorizing and aspiring to every detail. She couldn't believe how stupid she'd been, how badly misled.

With all her might, Dolly tore those pages from the book. Ripping like a wildcat, she turned that woman's image into the smallest shreds possible; every drop of rage was funnelled into the task. That stiff secretive way Vivien Jenkins regarded the camera – *rip* – never smiling as broadly as she might – *rip* – see how she felt being treated like a piece of rubbish – *rip*.

Dolly was poised to shred further – she'd have gladly gone on all night – when something caught her eye. She froze, peering closer at the scrap in her hands, breathing heavily – yes, there it was.

In one of the photographs, the locket had slipped from beneath Vivien's blouse and was clearly visible, sitting crookedly atop her silk ruffle. Dolly touched the spot with her fingertip and gasped as she felt the scorch of the day she'd returned the locket.

Dropping the fragment on the ground beside her, Dolly leaned her head back against the mattress and closed her eyes.

Her head was spinning. Her knee ached. She was spent.

Eyes still closed, she dug out her packet of cigarettes and lit one, smoking dejectedly.

It was still so fresh. Dolly saw the whole thing in her mind – the unexpectedness of being admitted by Henry Jenkins, the questions he'd asked her, his obvious suspicions about his wife's whereabouts.

What might have happened, she wondered, if they'd been given a little longer together? It had been on the tip of her tongue to correct him that day, to explain about the shifts at the canteen. What if she had? What if she'd been allowed the chance to say, 'Why, no, Mr Jenkins, I'm afraid that's not possible. I'm not sure what she tells you, but Vivien doesn't report for duty at the canteen more than, oh, once a week.'

But Dolly hadn't said it, had she, none of it. She'd wasted the one opportunity she'd had to let Henry Jenkins know he wasn't imagining things; that his wife was indeed rather more engaged in other affairs than he'd have liked. She'd thrown away her only chance to put Vivien Jenkins right in the middle of a splendid mess of her own making. For she couldn't very well tell him now, could she? Henry Jenkins wasn't likely to give Dolly the time of day, not now that – thanks to Vivien – he thought her a thieving servant, not now that her circumstances were so reduced, and certainly not without any proof.

It was hopeless – Dolly let out a long deflating stream of smoke. Unless she happened to glimpse Vivien in a clinch with a man who wasn't her husband, unless she then happened to procure a photograph of the pair of them together, an image that confirmed all of Henry's fears, it was useless. And Dolly didn't have time to hide in dark alleyways, talk her way into strange hospitals, and somehow be watching at the very right moment in the very right place. Perhaps if she knew where and when Vivien would be with her doctor, but what were the chances of—

Dolly gasped and sat bolt upright. It was so simple she could have laughed. She *did* laugh. All this time she'd been stewing over how unfair it all was, wishing there were some way to put things right, and the perfect opportunity had been staring her in the face.

Nineteen

'She says she wants to come home.'

Laurel rubbed her eyes with one hand and felt about on the bedside table with the other. Finally she found her glasses. 'She wants what?'

Rose's voice came down the line again, slower this time and overly patient, as if she were speaking to someone for whom English was a second language. 'She told me this morning. She wants to come home. To Greenacres.' Another pause. 'Instead of the hospital.'

'Ah.' Laurel looped her frames on beneath the phone and squinted out of the bedroom window. Lord, but it was bright. 'She wants to come home. And what about the doctor? What did he say?'

'I'm going to speak with him when he's finished his rounds, but – oh, Lol,' her voice hushed, 'the nurse told me she thought it was time.'

Alone in her girlhood bedroom, watching as the morning sunlight crept along the faded wallpaper, Laurel sighed. It was time. There was no need to ask what the nurse meant by that. 'Well then.'

'Yes.'

'Home she must come.'

'Yes.'

'And we'll look after her here.' There came no reply and Laurel said, 'Rose?'

'I'm here. Do you mean it, Lol? You're going to stay, you're going to be there, too?'

Laurel spoke around the cigarette she was trying to light. 'Of course I mean it.'

'You sound funny. Are you . . . *crying*, Lol?'

She shook out the match and freed her mouth. 'No, I'm not crying.' Another pause and Laurel could almost hear her sister twisting her worry beads into knots. She said, more gently this time, 'Rose, I'm all right. We're both going to be all right. We'll do this together, you'll see.'

Rose made a small choked noise, possibly of assent, maybe of doubt, and then changed the subject. 'You got in OK last night then?'

'I did. Rather later than expected, though.' In fact, it had been three in the morning when she finally let herself into the farmhouse. She and Gerry had gone back to his rooms after dinner and spent much of the night speculating about their mother and Henry Jenkins. They'd decided that while Gerry was chasing down Dr Rufus, it made sense for Laurel to see what she could learn about the elusive Vivien. She was the lynchpin between their mother and Henry Jenkins, after all, and the probable reason he came looking for Dorothy Nicolson in 1961.

The task had seemed perfectly achievable at the time; now though, in the clear light of day, Laurel didn't feel so sure. The whole plan had the flimsy quality of a dream. She glanced at her bare wrist, wondering vaguely where she'd left her watch. 'What time is it, Rosie? It seems rudely bright.'

'It's just gone ten.'

Ten? Oh God. She'd slept in. 'Rosie, I'm going to hang up now, but I'm coming straight to the hospital. Will you still be there?'

'Until midday, when I pick up Sadie's youngest from nursery.'

'Right. I'll see you soon, then – we'll talk to the doctor together.'

Rose was with the doctor when Laurel arrived. The nurse on the desk told Laurel she was expected and pointed her in the direction of the cafeteria adjoining reception. Rose must've been looking out for her, because she'd started waving before Laurel even set foot inside. Laurel wove her way between the tables and as she got closer saw that Rose had been crying, not lightly. There were balled tissues scattered across the tabletop and smeary black smudges beneath her wet eyes. Laurel sat down next to her and said hello to the doctor.

'I was just telling your sister,' he said, in precisely the sort of professional caring tone Laurel would have used to play a health worker delivering bad but inevitable news, 'that in my opinion we've exhausted every avenue of treatment. It won't come as a surprise to you, I think, when I tell you that it's now just a matter of managing the pain and keeping her as comfortable as we can.'

Laurel nodded. 'My sister tells me our mother wants to come home, Dr Cotter. Is that possible?'

'We wouldn't have a problem with that.' He smiled.

'Naturally, if she wanted to remain in the hospital we'd be able to accommodate that wish, too – in fact, most of our patients stay with us until the end—'

The end. Rose's hand reached for Laurel's beneath the table.

'But if you're willing to care for her at home . . .'

'We are,' Rose said quickly. 'Of course we are.'

'. . . then I think now is probably the right time for us to talk about you taking her home.'

Laurel's fingers itched for their lack of a cigarette. She said, 'Our mother doesn't have long.' It was a statement rather than a question, a function of Laurel's own processing of the fact, but the doctor answered nonetheless.

'I've been surprised before,' he said, 'but in response to your question, no, she doesn't have long.'

'London,' said Rose, as they walked together down the flecked-linoleum hospital corridor towards their mother's room. Fifteen minutes had passed since they'd bade farewell to the doctor but Rose was still clutching a soggy tissue in her fist. 'A meeting for work then, is it?'

'Work? What work? I told you, Rose, I'm on a break.'

'I wish you wouldn't say that, Lol. You make me nervous when you say things like that.' Rose lifted a hand to acknowledge a passing nurse.

'Things like what?'

'You, having a break.' Rose stopped and shuddered; her wild and woolly hair shook with her. She was wearing denim overalls with a novelty brooch on the bib in the shape of a fried egg. 'It isn't natural; it isn't normal. You know I don't like change – it makes me worry.'

Laurel couldn't help laughing. 'There's nothing to worry about, Rosie. I'm simply popping up to Euston to look at a book.'

'A book?'

'Some research I'm doing.'

'Ha!' Rose started walking again. 'Research! I knew you weren't really taking a break from work. Oh, Lol, what a relief,' she said, fanning her tear-stained face with her hand. 'I have to say I feel so much better.'

'Well then,' said Laurel, smiling, 'I'm glad to have been of service.'

It had been Gerry's idea to start the search for Vivien at the British Library. A late-night Google session had led them only to Welsh rugby sites and other dead ends in curious far-flung undulations of the Web, but the library, Gerry insisted, wouldn't disappoint. 'Three million new items every year, Lol,' he'd said as he filled in the registration details. 'That's six miles of shelf space; they're bound to have something.' He'd grown excited when he described the online service – 'They'll mail copies of whatever you find directly to your house' – but Laurel had decided (perversely, said Gerry with a smile) that it was easier simply to make the trip in person. Perversity be damned – Laurel had played in detective series before, she knew sometimes there was nothing for it but to pound the pavement in a search for clues. What if the information she found led to more? Far better to be in situ than to have to make another electronic order and wait; far better to be doing than waiting.

They reached Dorothy's door and Rose pushed it open. Their mother was asleep on her bed, seemingly thinner and weaker than she had been even the morning before, and it struck Laurel abruptly that her decline was becoming more rapid. The sisters sat together for a time, watching as Dorothy's chest gently rose, gently fell, and then Rose took a dusting cloth from her handbag and started wiping around the display of framed photographs. 'I suppose we ought to pack these up,' she said softly. 'Ready to take home.'

Laurel nodded.

'They're so important to her, her photos. They always have been, haven't they?'

Laurel nodded again, but she didn't speak. Mention of photos had got her thinking about the one of Dorothy and Vivien together in wartime London. It had been dated May 1941, the same month their mother started work at Grandma Nicolson's boarding house and Vivien Jenkins was killed in an air raid. Where had the photograph been taken? she wondered. And by whom? Was the photographer someone the girls had known – Henry Jenkins, perhaps? Or Ma's boyfriend, Jimmy? Laurel frowned. So much of the puzzle still seemed out of reach.

The door opened then and sounds of the outside world drifted through in the wake of their mother's nurse – people laughing, buzzers sounding, phones ringing. Laurel watched as the nurse moved efficiently about the room, checking Dorothy's pulse, her temperature, marking things down on that chart at the end of the bed. She offered Laurel and Rose a kind smile when she had finished and told them she'd hold onto their mother's lunch in case she woke later and was hungry. Laurel thanked her and she left, closing the door behind her and casting the room back into a still, silent terminus in which to wait. Wait for what, though? No wonder Dorothy wanted to go home.

'Rose?' said Laurel suddenly, watching as her sister straightened the clean photo frames.

'Mm?'

'When she asked you to get that book for her, the one with the photograph inside, was it strange to see inside her trunk?' More to the point, was there anything else in there that might help solve Laurel's mystery? She wondered whether there was any way to ask without tipping Rose off to her search.

'Not really. I didn't think much about it, to be honest. I went as quickly as I could for fear she'd follow me up the stairs if she thought I was taking too long. Thankfully she was sensible and stayed in bed where I'd put her—' Rose gasped.

'What? What is it?'

Rose sighed with relief, brushing her hair from her forehead. 'No, it's all right,' she said, shaking her hand. 'I just couldn't for the life of me remember what I'd done with the key. She was being difficult, you see; she came over all agitated when she saw I'd found the book. She was pleased, I think – I mean, she must have been, it was she who'd wanted it in the first place – but she was snippy, too, quite irascible; you know how she can get.'

'You've remembered now though?'

'Oh yes, of course – it's back in her bedside table.' She shook her head at Laurel and smiled guilelessly. 'Really, I wonder about my brain sometimes.'

Laurel smiled back. Dear, innocent Rose.

'Sorry, Lol – you were asking me something . . . about the trunk?'

'Oh no, it was nothing. Just making conversation.'

Rose glanced at her watch then and announced that she'd have to leave to collect her granddaughter from nursery. 'I'll pop in later tonight, though, and I think Iris is in tomorrow morning. Between us we ought to be able to get everything packed for the move on Saturday . . . You know, I almost feel excited.' But then her face clouded. 'I expect that's a terrible thing to feel, under the circumstances.'

'I don't think there are any rules about such things, Rosie.'

'No, perhaps you're right.' Rose leaned down to kiss Laurel's cheek, and then she was gone, leaving behind a trail of her lavender fragrance.

It had been different with Rose in the room, another moving, bustling, breathing body. Without her, Laurel was even more conscious than before of just how faded and still her mother had become. Her phone beeped with an incoming message and she leapt to check it, clutching gratefully at the lifeline to the outside world. It was a form email from the British Library, confirming that the book she'd ordered would be available the following morning and reminding her to bring identification to complete her registration for a reader's pass. Laurel read it through twice and then slid the phone reluctantly back into her bag. The message had offered a moment of welcome distraction; now she was back where she'd started, in the stultifying stasis of the hospital room.

She could stand it no longer. The doctor had said her

mother would most likely sleep all afternoon due to her pain medication, but Laurel took up the photo album anyway. She sat close to the bedside and started at the beginning, the photograph taken when Dorothy was a young woman, working for Grandma Nicolson at her seaside boarding house. She made her way through the years, recounting her family's story, hearing the reassuring sound of her own voice, feeling vaguely that by continuing to speak in such a normal way she might somehow keep life in the room.

Finally, she reached a photograph of Gerry on his second birthday. It had been taken early, as they gathered the picnic together in the kitchen, just before they set off for the stream. Teenage Laurel – look at that fringe! – had Gerry on her hip, and Rose was tickling his tummy, making him gurgle and laugh; Iris's pointed finger had made it into the shot (angry about something, no doubt), and Ma was in the background, hand to her head as she regarded the contents of the hamper. On the table – Laurel's heart almost stopped; she'd never noticed it there before – was the knife. Right by the vase of dahlias. *Remember it, Ma*, Laurel found herself thinking. *Pack the knife and you'll never need to come back to the house. None of it will happen. I'll climb down from the tree house before the man walks up the driveway and no one will be any the wiser that he came that day*.

But it was childish logic. Who was to say Henry Jenkins wouldn't have come back again if he'd found the house empty? And perhaps his next visit would have been even worse. The wrong person might have been killed.

Laurel closed the album. She'd lost the spirit for narrating the past. Instead she smoothed her mother's sheet across her chest and said, 'I went to see Gerry last night, Ma.'

From nowhere, as if a sound upon the wind: 'Gerry . . .'

Laurel glanced at her mother's lips. They were still, but slightly parted. Her eyes were closed. 'That's right,' she said, more eagerly, 'Gerry. I went to see him in Cambridge. He was so well, such a clever boy. He's mapping the sky, did you know? Did you ever think that little boy of ours would do such incredible things? He says they're talking about sending him to research for a time in the States, a tremendous opportunity.'

'Opportunity . . .' Ma breathed the word. Her lips were dry and Laurel reached for the cup of water, feeding the bendy straw gently into her mouth.

Her mother drank stiltedly, not a lot. Her eyes opened slightly. 'Laurel,' she said softly.

'I'm here, no need to fret.'

Dorothy's delicate eyelids quivered with the effort of staying open. 'It seemed . . .' She was breathing shallowly. 'It seemed harmless.'

'What did?'

Tears had begun – not so much to fall as to seep from her eyes. The deep lines of her pale face glistened. Laurel took a tissue from the box and patted her mother's cheeks, as tenderly as she would a small frightened child. 'What seemed harmless, Ma? Tell me.'

'It was an opportunity, Laurel. I took . . . I took . . .'

'Took what?' A jewel, a photograph; *Henry Jenkins's life*?

Dorothy clutched Laurel's hand tighter and opened her watery eyes as wide as she could manage. There was a new

note of desperation in her voice when she continued, determination too – as if she'd been waiting a long time to say
these things and, despite the fierce effort it took, she was
going to finish. 'It was an opportunity, Laurel. I didn't think
it would hurt anybody, not really. I just wanted – I thought
I deserved – that it was fair.' Dorothy drew a raspy breath
that sent jitters down Laurel's spine. Her next words
spooled out like a spider's thread. 'Do you believe in fairness, that if we're robbed we should be able to take
something back for ourselves?'

'I don't know, Ma.' Every ounce of Laurel ached to see
her mother, the ancient ailing woman who'd chased away
monsters and kissed away tears, racked now by guilt and
contrition. She wanted desperately to offer comfort; she
wanted equally to know what her mother had done. She
said gently, 'I suppose it depends on what it is that's stolen
from us, and what it is we propose to take for ourselves in
return.'

The intensity of her mother's expression dissolved and
her eyes watered now at the brightness of the window.
'Everything,' she said. 'I felt that I'd lost everything.'

Later that afternoon, Laurel sat smoking in the middle of
the Greenacres attic floor. The bleached boards were smooth
beneath her, solid, and the last of the late afternoon sun fell
through the tiny four-paned window in the roof's peak,
landing like a spotlight on her mother's locked trunk. Laurel
drew slowly on her cigarette. She'd been sitting there for
half an hour now, with only her ashtray, the trunk's key and
her conscience for company. The key had been easy enough
to find, tucked where Rose had said it would be, right at the

back of their mother's bedside-table drawer. All Laurel had to do now was slip it into the padlock, twist, and she'd know.

But know what? More about the opportunity Dorothy had glimpsed? What it was she'd taken or done?

It wasn't that she expected to find a full written confession inside; nothing like that. Only that it seemed an important, rather obvious place to look for clues to her mother's mystery. Surely if she and Gerry were going to tear around the country troubling other people for information that might help fill in the blanks, it was a somewhat glaring oversight not to have done what they could at home first. And really, it was no more invasive of her mother's privacy than the digging they'd started to do elsewhere, was it? Opening the trunk was no worse than talking to Kitty Barker, or chasing Dr Rufus's notes, or going to the library tomorrow in search of Vivien Jenkins. It just *felt* worse.

Laurel eyed the padlock. With her mother out of the house, she was just about able to convince herself it was no big deal – Ma had let Rose retrieve the book for her, after all, and she didn't play favourites (except where Gerry was concerned, and they were all guilty of that); ergo, Ma wouldn't mind Laurel seeing inside the trunk either. A tenuous logic, perhaps, but it was all she had. And once Dorothy came home to Greenacres it all turned to dust. There was no way, Laurel knew, she'd be able to go through with the search with her mother just downstairs. It was now or never.

'Sorry, Ma,' said Laurel, ridding herself of her cigarette with a decisive squish, 'but I have to know.'

She stood up carefully, feeling like a giantess as she

went to the sloping edge of the attic. She knelt to insert the key and crack the padlock open. That was the moment; she felt it in her heart; even if she never opened the lid the crime was already committed.

Better then, surely, to be in for a pound as for a penny? Laurel stood and started to lift the old trunk's lid; she didn't look, though. The stiff leather hinges creaked with paucity of use, and Laurel held her breath. She was a child again, breaking a rule set in stone. Her head felt light. And now the lid was open, as far as it could go. Laurel took her hand away and the hinges strained beneath its weight. Drawing in a deep breath of resolution, she crossed the Rubicon and looked inside.

There was something on top, an envelope, old and a bit yellowed, that had been addressed to Dorothy Nicolson at Greenacres Farm. The stamp was olive-green and featured a young Queen Elizabeth in her coronation robes; Laurel felt a sudden quiver of memory when she saw that image of the queen, as if it were important, though how she couldn't guess. There was no sender's address, and she bit down on her lip as she opened the envelope and slipped a cream card from inside. There were two words written across it in black ink: *Thank you.* Laurel turned it over and found nothing more. She agitated the card back and forth, wondering.

There were lots of people who might've had reason to thank her mother over the years, but to do so in such an anonymous way – no return address, no name at the bottom of the card – was decidedly odd; the fact that Dorothy had kept it under lock and key, odder still. Evidence, Laurel realized, that her mother must have known precisely from whom it had come; further, that whatever the person was thanking Ma for was something secret.

All of which was exceedingly mysterious – sufficiently so to quicken Laurel's heart – but not necessarily relevant to her search. (Conversely, there was every chance it was *the* vital clue, but Laurel couldn't think there was any way of knowing that for sure, not at this point; not unless she asked her mother outright, and she didn't intend to do that. Yet.) She returned the card to its envelope and slipped it down the inside edge of the trunk, where it lodged beside a little figurine made of wood; Mr Punch, Laurel realized with a half-smile, thinking of the holidays they used to have at Grandma Nicolson's.

There was another item in the trunk, an object so large it almost filled the whole space. It looked like a blanket, but when Laurel reached in, drew it out and shook it to full length, she saw it was a coat, a rather tatty fur that must once have been white. Laurel held it by the shoulders at arm's length, letting it hang, sizing it up the way one might when deciding whether to purchase a jacket in a shop.

The wardrobe at the far end of the attic had a mirrored door. They used to play inside that wardrobe when they were children, at least Laurel had; the others had been too frightened, which had made it the perfect place for her to hide from them when she needed the freedom to disappear inside her made-up stories.

Laurel took the coat to the wardrobe and slipped her arms into its sleeves. She regarded herself, turning slowly from one side to the other. The coat fell just past her knees, with buttons down the front and a belt around the middle. It was a lovely cut, no matter what you thought of fur; the

attention to detail, the line. Laurel was willing to bet someone had paid a lot of money for this coat, back when it was
new. She wondered if that person had been her mother, and
if so, how a young girl working as a maid had afforded such
a fine thing.

As she watched her reflection, a distant memory came.
It wasn't the first time Laurel had worn the coat. It had been
a rainy day, back when she was just a girl. They'd been driving their mother crazy all morning running up and down
the stairs and Dorothy had banished them to the attic for a
game of dressing up. The Nicolson children had an enormous dressing-up box that their mother kept stocked with
old hats and shirts and scarves, funny things she found
along the way that might be turned by childish magic into
something fine.

While her sisters draped themselves in the old
favourites, Laurel had spied a bag in the corner of the attic,
something white and furry poking from its top. She'd taken
out the coat and put it on at once. Then she'd stood before
this very mirror, admiring herself, thinking how grand it
made her look: like a wicked but wonderful Snow Queen.

Laurel was a child and therefore she didn't see the thin-
ning patches of fur, nor the dark stains around the hem; but
she did recognize the sumptuous authority inherent in such a
coat. She spent a marvellous few hours ordering her sisters
into cages, threatening to set her wolves upon them if they
didn't follow her orders, cackling with evil laughter. By the
time their mother called them down for lunch, Laurel had
become so attached to the coat and its curious power that
she didn't consider taking it off.

Dorothy's expression when she saw her eldest daughter

arrive in the kitchen had been hard to read. She hadn't been pleased, but she hadn't shouted either. It had been worse than that. Her face had drained of all colour and her voice when she spoke was trembling. 'Take it off,' she'd said. 'Take it off now.' When Laurel didn't leap directly to action, her mother had come quickly to where she was standing and started pulling the coat from her shoulders, muttering about the day being too hot, the coat too long, the attic ladder too steep for wearing such a thing. Why, she was lucky not to have tripped and fallen and killed herself. She had glanced at Laurel then, the fur coat bundled in her arms, and the look on her face had been almost accusatory, a mixture of distress and betrayal, almost fear. For a single awful moment, Laurel had thought her mother might be going to cry. She didn't, though; she ordered Laurel to sit down at the table, and then she disappeared, taking the coat with her.

Laurel didn't see the fur again. She'd asked about it once, some months later when she needed a costume for a play at school, but Dorothy had only said, without meeting Laurel's eyes, 'That old thing? I threw it out. It was nothing more than food for the rats up there in the attic.'

But here it was now, hidden away in her mother's trunk, kept for decades under lock and key. Laurel exhaled thoughtfully, tucking her hands inside the pockets of the coat. There was a hole in the satin lining of one, and her fingers slipped right through. She touched something; it felt like the corner of a piece of cardboard. Laurel caught hold of whatever it was and drew it out through the hole.

It was a piece of white card, neat, rectangular, with something printed on it. The type had faded and Laurel had to take it to the remaining patch of sunlight to make out the words. It was a train ticket, she realized, stamped with a single fare from London to the station nearest Grandma Nicolson's town. The date on the ticket was 23 May 1941.

Twenty

London, February 1941

Jimmy hurried across London, an unfamiliar spring in his step. It had been weeks since he'd had any contact with Dolly – she'd refused to see him when he tried to visit her at Campden Grove, and she hadn't answered any of his letters – but now, finally, this. He could feel her letter in his pocket, the same one in which he'd carried the ring that awful night – he hoped it wasn't an ill omen. The letter had arrived at the newspaper office earlier in the week, a simple note imploring him to meet her at the park bench in Kensington Gardens, the one nearest the Peter Pan sculpture. There was something she needed to talk to him about, something she hoped might please him.

She'd changed her mind and wanted to marry him. That had to be it. Jimmy was trying to be wary, he hated to jump to conclusions, not when he'd suffered so hard after she turned him down, but he couldn't stop his thoughts – admit it, his hopes – from going there. What else could it be? Something that would please him: there was only one thing he could think of that would do that. God knew, Jimmy could do with some good news.

They'd been bombed out ten days before. The whole thing had come out of nowhere. There'd been a lull lately,

more eerie in its way than the worst of the Blitz – all that
quietude and peace had a way of getting people on edge –
but on 18 January a stray bomb had fallen right on top of
Jimmy's flat. He'd come home from a night out working
and seen the telltale mayhem as he turned the corner. God,
but he'd held his breath as he ran towards the fire and ruins.
He'd stopped hearing anything but his own voice and his
own body working, breathing and pumping blood, as he
combed through the wreckage, shouting his father's name,
cursing himself for not having found a safer place, for not
having been there when the old man needed him most.
When Jimmy turned up Finchie's crushed cage, he'd let out
a startling animal noise of pain and grief, the sort he hadn't
known himself capable of making. And he'd had the God-
awful experience of suddenly inhabiting a scene from one of
his photographs, except the ruined house was *his* house, the
discarded possessions *his* possessions, the lost loved one *his*
dad, and he'd known then that no matter how much praise
his editors heaped upon him, he'd failed gravely in his
attempts to capture the truth inherent in that moment; the
fear and panic and startling *realness* of having suddenly
lost everything.

He'd turned away and dropped, bone-heavy, to his
knees and that was when he'd seen Mrs Hamblin from the
flat next door, waving dazedly at him from across the street.
He'd gone to her, taken her in his arms and let her sob
against his shoulder, and he'd wept too, hot tears of help-
lessness and anger and sorrow. And then she'd lifted her
head and said, 'Have you seen your dad yet?' and Jimmy
had answered, 'I couldn't find him,' and she'd pointed down
the street. 'He went with the Red Cross, I think. A lovely

young medic offered him a cup of tea, and you know what he's like for tea, he'd—'

Jimmy hadn't stuck around to hear more. He'd started running towards the church hall where he knew the Red Cross would be. He'd burst through the front doors and seen his father almost right away. The old boy was sitting at a table with a cup of tea in front of him and Finchie on his forearm. Mrs Hamblin had got him to the shelter in time, and Jimmy didn't think he'd ever been so grateful to a person in his life. He'd have given her the world if he could, so it was a great pity he owned nothing fit for giving. He'd lost all his savings in the blast, along with everything else. He'd been left with the clothes on his back, and the camera he'd been carrying. And thank God for that – what would he have done otherwise?

Jimmy flicked his hair out of his eyes as he walked. He had to put his father out of his mind, their cramped temporary digs. The old man made him vulnerable and he didn't want to be weak today. He couldn't afford to be. Today was about being in control, dignified, maybe even a little stand-offish. It was hatefully proud of him perhaps, but he wanted Dolly to see him and know she'd made a mistake. He hadn't dressed up like a monkey in his father's suit this time – he couldn't – but he'd made an effort.

He turned off the street and into the park, making his way past the lawn that had been given over to Victory vegetable gardens, along the paths that seemed naked without their iron railings, and he prepared himself to see her again. She'd always had a power over him, a way, just by looking, of bending him to her will. Those eyes, bright with laughter, that had watched him over the top of her cup of tea in a

Coventry cafe; the curl of her lips when she smiled, a little bit teasing at times, but, God, so exciting, so full of life. He was warming now just at the thought of her, and he took himself in hand, concentrated on remembering exactly how much she'd hurt him, embarrassed him, too – the look on the waiters' faces when they saw Jimmy alone in the restaurant, still holding the ring; he'd never forget the way they'd looked at him, the way they must have laughed when he left. Jimmy stumbled on the edge of the path. Christ. He had to take control, quell his optimism and longing, safeguard himself against the possibility of further disappointment.

He did his best, he really did, but he'd loved her too long, he supposed (later, when he was back at home, when he thought back over the day's events), and love made fools of men, everyone knew that. Case in point: entirely without meaning to and against his better judgement, when Jimmy Metcalfe got near the meeting place he began to jog.

Dolly was sitting on the bench, exactly where she'd said she'd be. Jimmy saw her first and stopped short, catching his breath and straightening his hair, his cuffs, his posture, while he watched her. His initial excitement turned quickly to wonder. It had only been three weeks (though the circumstances of their separation made it feel more like three years) but she'd changed. She was Dolly, she was beautiful, but there was something wrong with her, he knew it even from a distance. Jimmy felt suddenly dislocated; he'd been ready to be tough, petulant if pushed, but to see her sitting there, arms wrapped around her body, eyes downcast, smaller somehow than he remembered – it was the last thing he'd expected and it caught him off guard.

She saw him then and smiled, a tentative brightening of her face. Jimmy returned it and started towards her, wondering what on earth could possibly have happened; whether someone had hurt her, done something to knock the spirit clean out of her, knowing at once that he'd kill them if they had.

She stood as he drew near, and they embraced, her bones fine and birdlike beneath his hands. She wasn't wearing enough clothing; it had been snowing on and off, and her tatty old fur coat wasn't warm enough. She held onto him for a long time and Jimmy – who'd been so hurt, so furious at the way she'd treated him, at her refusal to explain herself; who'd promised himself to keep the bitterness uppermost in his mind when he saw her today – found that he was stroking her hair the way he would a lost and vulnerable child.

'Jimmy,' she said finally, her face still pressed against his shirt. 'Oh, Jimmy—'

'Shh,' he said. 'There now, don't cry.'

She did though, light soft tears that didn't seem to end, and she gripped the sides of his chest with her hands, making him feel concerned and oddly excited, too. God, what the hell was the matter with him?

'Oh Jimmy,' she said again. 'I'm so sorry. I'm so ashamed.'

'What are you talking about, Doll?' He took her shoulders and reluctantly she met his eyes.

'I made a mistake, Jimmy,' she said. 'I've made so many. I should never have treated you that way. That night in the restaurant, what I did – leaving like that, walking away. I'm so, so sorry.'

He didn't have a handkerchief but he had a lens cloth and he used it to wipe her cheeks gently dry.

'I don't expect you to forgive me,' she said. 'And I know we can't go back in time, I do know that, but I had to tell you. I've felt so guilty and I needed to apologize in person so you could see that I meant it.' She blinked through her tears and said, 'I do mean it, Jimmy. I'm so very sorry.'

He nodded then. He ought to have said something, but he was too surprised and touched to find the right words. It seemed to be enough, because she smiled, more broadly now, in reply. Jimmy saw a flash of her old vibrancy in the smile and it made him want to freeze her in that moment so it couldn't disappear again. She was the sort of person who needed to be kept happy, he realized. Not as a matter of selfish expectation, but as a simple fact of design; like a piano or a harp, she'd been made to function best at a certain tuning.

'There – ' she let out a relieved sigh – 'I did it.'

'You did it,' he said, his voice catching, and he couldn't help himself, he traced the shape of her top lip with his finger.

She pressed her lips to kiss it lightly and then closed her eyes. Her lashes were dark and wet against her cheeks.

She stayed like that for a time, as if she, too, wanted somehow to stop the world from spinning onwards. When she finally pulled away she glanced up at him shyly. 'So,' she said.

'So.' He took out his cigarettes and offered her one. She took it gladly.

'You read my mind. I'm all out.'

'That's not like you.'

'No? Well, I've changed, I suppose.'

She said it casually but it tallied so completely with what he'd seen when he first arrived that Jimmy frowned. He lit both cigarettes and then gestured with his in the direction from which he'd come. 'We should go,' he said, 'we'll be up on spying charges if we stand here whispering any longer.'

They walked back to where the gates used to stand, talking like polite strangers about nothing important. When they reached the road they stopped, each waiting for the other to decide what came next. Dolly took the initiative, turning towards him to say, 'I'm glad you came, Jimmy. I didn't deserve it, but thank you.' There was a note of finality in her voice that at first he didn't understand, but when she smiled bravely and held out a hand, he realized she was leaving. That she'd made her apology, done what she'd thought would please him, and now she was going to walk away.

And in that second, Jimmy saw the truth like a shining light. The only thing that would ever please him was to marry her, to take her with him and look after her and make things right again. 'Doll, wait—'

She'd hooked her handbag over her arm and started to turn away, but she looked back when he said it.

'Come with me,' he continued, 'I'm not working until later. Let's get something to eat.'

Once upon a time Jimmy would've gone about things differently, planned it all out and tried to make things perfect, but not now. Pride, perfection be damned; he was in too much of a rush. He'd seen first-hand that moments in life didn't last – one stray bomb and it was all over. He waited only as long as it took for them to put in an order with the waitress and then he steeled himself and said, 'My offer, Doll, it still stands. I love you, I've always loved you. I want nothing more than to marry you.'

She stared at him, wide-eyed with surprise. And who could blame her: she'd only just finished contemplating the merits of eggs over rabbit, and now this. 'You do? Even after—?'

'Even after.' He reached across the table and she placed her small hands in his. Without her white coat, he could see scratches on her pale thin arms. He looked back to her face, more determined than ever to take care of her. 'I can't offer you a ring, Doll,' he said, interlacing his fingers with hers. 'My flat was bombed and I lost everything; I thought I'd lost Dad for a while.' Dolly nodded slightly, apparently still stunned, and Jimmy went on. He had the vague sense he was veering off course, saying too much, not saying the right things, but he couldn't seem to stop. 'I didn't, thank God. He's a survivor, my dad, he was with the Red Cross by the time I got to him, making himself comfy with a hot cup of tea.' Jimmy smiled briefly at the memory and then shook his head. 'Anyway – my point is that the ring was lost. I'll buy you a new one as soon as I can, though.'

Dolly swallowed, and her voice when she spoke was soft, sad. 'Oh, Jimmy,' she said, 'how little you must think of me to believe that I'd care about a thing like that.'

It was Jimmy's turn for surprise. 'You don't?'

'Of course not. I don't need a ring to bind me to you.' She squeezed his hands and her eyes shone with tears. 'I love you too, Jimmy. I always have. What can I ever do to convince you of that?'

They ate quietly, taking turns to look up from their meal and smile at the other. When they had finished, Jimmy lit a cigarette and said, 'I suppose your old lady will want you to marry out of Campden Grove?'

Her face fell when he said it.

'Doll? What is it?'

She told him everything then, that Lady Gwendolyn had died, and that she, Dolly, was no longer at Campden Grove but living again in the tiny room on Rillington Place. That she'd been left with nothing and was working long shifts in a munitions factory to pay for her board.

'But I thought Lady Gwendolyn had undertaken to leave you something in her will,' said Jimmy. 'Isn't that what you told me, Doll?'

She glanced towards the window, a bitter expression washing away the happiness of moments ago. 'Yes,' she said. 'She promised me, but that was before. Before things changed.'

From the drawn look on her face, Jimmy knew that whatever it was that had happened between Dolly and her employer was responsible for the dispiritedness he'd sensed in her earlier. 'What things, Doll? What changed?'

She didn't want to recount the story, he could tell that much from the way she refused to look at him, but Jimmy needed to know. It was selfish but he loved her, he was going to marry her and he refused to let her off the hook. He sat silently, making it clear he'd wait as long as it took, and she must've realized he wouldn't take no for an answer because finally she sighed. 'A woman interfered, Jimmy, a powerful woman. She took against me and made it her business to make my life a misery.' She glanced back from the window towards him. 'I was all alone. I didn't stand a chance against Vivien.'

'Vivien? From the canteen? But I thought you were friends?'

'So did I,' Dolly said, and she smiled sadly. 'We were, I think, at first.'

'What happened?'

Dolly shivered in her thin white blouse and glanced at the table; there was something measured in her countenance, and Jimmy wondered whether she was embarrassed by what she was about to tell him. 'I was returning something to her, a necklace she'd lost, but when I knocked on her door she wasn't home. Her husband let me in – I told you about him, Jimmy, the author. He asked me to come inside and wait, and I accepted.' She bent her head and her curls shook gently. 'Perhaps I shouldn't have, I don't know, because when Vivien arrived home and saw me, she was furious. I could see it in her face, she suspected us of . . . well, you can imagine. I tried to explain, I was sure I'd be able to make her see sense, but then . . .' She turned her attention back to the window and a strain of weak sunlight caught her high cheekbone. 'Well – let's just say I was wrong.'

Jimmy's heart had started to pound; he felt indignation but also dread. 'What did she do, Doll?'

Her throat moved, a quick up-and-down motion as she swallowed, and Jimmy thought she might be going to cry. She didn't, though, she turned to face him, and her expression – so sad, so hurt – made something inside him break. Her voice was barely a whisper. 'She invented terrible lies about me, Jimmy. She painted me as false in front of her husband, but then, far worse, she told Lady Gwendolyn I was a thief and couldn't be trusted.'

'But that's, that's . . .' He was dumbfounded, outraged on her behalf. 'That's contemptible.'

'The worst of it, Jimmy, is she's a liar herself. She's been having an affair for months now. Remember at the canteen when she told you about that doctor friend of hers?'

'The fellow who runs the children's hospital?'

'It's all a front – I mean, the hospital's real enough, the doctor, too, but he's her lover. She uses it as a cover so no one thinks twice when she goes to visit.'

She was shaking, he noticed, and who could blame her? Who wouldn't be upset to discover that their friend had betrayed them in such a cruel way? 'Doll, I'm sorry.'

'There's no need to pity me,' she said, trying so hard to be brave it made him ache inside. 'It hit pretty hard, but I promised myself I wouldn't let her beat me.'

'That's my girl.'

'It's just—'

The waitress arrived to clear their plates, glancing between them as she fumbled with Jimmy's knife. She thought they were fighting, Jimmy realized; the way they'd fallen silent when she came near, the way Doll had quickly turned her head away while Jimmy struggled to respond to the waitress's practised chit-chat ('Big Ben's not skipped a beat, you know'; 'As long as St Paul's is still standing'). She was stealing glances now at Dolly, who was doing her best to hide her face. Jimmy could see her profile though and her bottom lip had begun to tremble. 'That's all,' he said, trying to hurry the waitress along. 'That's all, thank you.'

'No pudding? I could tell you the—'

'No, no, that's all.'

She sniffed, 'As you like – ' and turned on her rubber heel.

'Doll?' said Jimmy, when they were alone again. 'You were saying something?'

Her fingers were pressed lightly against her mouth to stop herself from crying. 'It's just that I loved Lady Gwendolyn, Jimmy, I loved her like a mother. And to think she went to her grave believing me a liar and a thief – ' She broke off and tears began to slip down her cheeks.

'Shhh. There now, please don't cry.' He moved to sit beside her, kissing away each new tear as it fell. 'Lady Gwendolyn knew how you felt about her. You showed her every day. And you know what?'

'What?'

'You were right. You're *not* going to let Vivien beat you. I'm going to make sure of it.'

'Oh, Jimmy.' She played with the loose button on his shirt, twisting it on its thread. 'It's so kind of you, but how? How will I ever win against someone like her?'

'By leading a long and happy life.'

Dolly blinked at him.

'With me.' He smiled, tucking a strand of her hair behind her ear. 'We're going to beat her together by getting married, and saving our pennies, and then moving away to the seaside or the country, whichever you prefer, just like we always dreamed of; we're going to beat her by living happily ever after.' He kissed the tip of her nose. 'Right?'

A moment passed and then she nodded slowly, a little doubtfully it seemed to Jimmy.

'Right, Doll?'

This time she smiled. It was slight though and slipped as quickly as it had come. She sighed, resting her cheek in her hand. 'I don't mean to be ungrateful, Jimmy. I just wish we could do it sooner, go away right now and make a fresh start. I sometimes think it's the only way I'll get better.'

'It won't be long, Doll. I'm working all the time, taking photographs every day, and my editor's positive about my future. I reckon if I—'

Dolly gasped and gripped his wrist. Jimmy stopped midway. 'Photographs,' she said, her breath catching. 'Oh, Jimmy, you've just given me an idea, a way we *can* have everything, right now – the seaside and all the rest you were talking about – and we can teach Vivien a lesson at the same time.' Her eyes were shining. 'That's what you want, isn't it? To go away together, to start a new life?'

'You know it is, but the money, Doll, I don't have—'

'You're not listening to me. Don't you see, that's exactly what I'm saying, I know a way for us to get the money.'

Her eyes were fixed on his, bright now, almost wild, and although she hadn't told him the rest of her idea, something inside him began to sink. Jimmy refused to let it. He wouldn't let anything ruin this happy day.

'Do you remember,' she said, taking one of his cigarettes from the packet on the table, 'you once said you'd do anything for me?'

Jimmy watched her strike the match. He remembered saying it; he'd meant it too. But something in the way her eyes were gleaming, her fingers fumbling with the matchbox, filled him with foreboding. He didn't know what she was going to say next, only that he had the strongest sense he didn't want to hear it.

Dolly drew hard on the cigarette, breathing out a rich stream of smoke. 'Vivien Jenkins is a very wealthy woman, Jimmy. She's also a liar and a cheat who went out of her way to hurt me, to turn my loved ones against me and steal the inheritance Lady Gwendolyn promised. But I know her, and I know she has a weakness.'

'Oh?'

'A devoted husband who'd be heartbroken to learn she was being unfaithful.'

Jimmy nodded like some sort of machine, programmed to respond.

Dolly continued, 'I know it sounds funny, Jimmy, but hear me out. What if someone were to acquire an incriminating photograph, something showing Vivien and another man together?'

'What about it?' His voice sounded flat, not at all like his own.

She glanced at him, a nervous smile starting on her lips. 'I have a feeling she'd pay rather a lot of money to have that photo for herself. Just enough that two young lovers who deserve a break could run away together.'

It occurred to Jimmy then, as he struggled to wrap his head around what she was saying, that this was all part of one of Dolly's games. That she was going to break character any minute and dissolve into laughter and say, 'Jimmy, I'm joking, of course! What do you take me for?'

But she didn't. Instead she reached across the leather bench seat, took his hand and kissed it gently. 'Money,

Jimmy,' she whispered, holding his hand to her warm cheek. 'Just like you used to talk about. Enough money for us to get married and start again and live happily ever after – isn't that what you've always wanted?'

It was, of course, she knew it was.

'She deserves it, Jimmy. You said it yourself – she deserves to pay after everything she's done.' Dolly drew on her cigarette, speaking quickly through the smoke. 'She was the one who convinced me to break it off with you, you know. She poisoned me against you, Jimmy. Made me think we shouldn't be together. Can't you see, she's caused us both so much pain?'

Jimmy didn't know how to feel. He hated what she was suggesting. He hated himself even more for not telling her so. He heard himself say, 'I suppose you want me to take this photograph, is that it?'

Dolly smiled at him. 'Oh no, Jimmy, that's not it at all. There's too much chance involved, far too much risk in waiting to catch them in the act. My idea's much simpler than that, child's play by comparison.'

'Well then,' he said, staring at the metal strip around the tabletop. 'What is it, Doll? Tell me.'

'*I'm* going to take the photograph.' She gave his button a playful tweak and it fell off in her fingers. 'And you're going to be *in* it.'

Twenty-one

It was a smooth run down the motorway and Laurel was driving along Euston Road by eleven, scanning for car parks. She found one by the mainline station, and eased the little green Mini into a slot. Perfect – the British Library was only a hop, skip and a jump away, and she'd spied the black and blue awning of a Caffè Nero round the corner. All morning with no caffeine and her brain was threatening to melt.

Twenty minutes later, a far more focused Laurel was making her way across the grey and white library foyer towards the Reader Registration Office. The young woman with a nametag that read 'Bonny' didn't appear to recognize her, and having caught a glimpse of herself coming through the glass entry door, Laurel took that as a compliment. After tossing and turning most of the night, her thoughts tying themselves in knots as she wondered what her mother could possibly have taken from Vivien Jenkins, she'd slept late again this morning and given herself only ten minutes at Greenacres to make it from bed to car. Her speed had been commendable, but she couldn't claim to have made the transition in prize peach condition. She tousled a little life into her hair and when Bonny said, 'Can I help you?' Laurel answered, 'My dear, I most certainly hope so.' She took out the piece of paper on which Gerry had written her reader number. 'I believe there might be a book waiting for me in the Humanities Reading Room?'

'Let's have a look, shall we?' Bonny said, typing something on her keyboard. 'I'm just going to need some ID and proof of address to complete your registration.'

Laurel handed over both and Bonny smiled. 'Laurel Nicolson. Just like the actress.'

'Yes,' Laurel agreed. Quite.

Bonny sorted out the reader's pass and pointed Laurel in the direction of the curved staircase. 'You want the second floor. Go straight to the desk; you should find the book waiting for you.'

She did. That is, she found a most helpful gentleman – wearing a red knitted waistcoat and a tangled white beard – waiting for her. Laurel explained what she was looking for, passed him the print-out she'd been given downstairs, and within moments he'd gone to the shelves behind him and was sliding a slim black leather-bound volume across the counter. Laurel read the title under her breath and experienced a frisson of anticipation: *Henry Jenkins: An Author's Life, Loves and Loss.*

She found a seat in the corner and sat down, opening the cover and breathing in the glorious dusty scent of papery possibility. It wasn't a particularly long book, published by an imprint Laurel had never heard of and with a distinctly unprofessional look about it – something in the size and type of font, the lack of margins, and the few poorly reproduced photographs; it also seemed to rely rather heavily for augmentation on extracts from Henry

Jenkins's novels. But it was a starting point, and Laurel was eager to get started. She scanned the table of contents, her heart beginning to trip along swiftly when she found the chapter entitled 'Married Life' that had first sparked her interest when she saw it on the Internet listing.

But Laurel didn't turn straight to page ninety-seven. Every time she closed her eyes lately, the dark shape of the strange man in a black hat was there, burned onto her retina as he walked up the sunlit driveway. She drummed her fingers lightly on the contents page. Here was her chance to find out more about him, to add colour and detail to the silhouette that made her skin shrink, maybe even to discover the reason for what her mother had done that day. Laurel had been frightened before, when she'd searched for Henry Jenkins on the Net, but this, this rather insignificant book, didn't scare her in the same way. The information contained within it had been published for a long time (since 1963, she saw when she checked the copyright page), which meant – allowing for natural attrition – there were likely to be very few copies in existence, most of them lost in dim, less-travelled places. This particular copy had been hidden for decades among miles and miles of other forgotten books; if Laurel found something inside she didn't like she could just close the cover again and send it back. Never speak of it again. She hesitated, but only briefly, before steeling herself. Fingers tingling, she opened quickly to the prologue. With a deep breath of strange and sudden excitement, she began to read about the stranger on the driveway.

When Henry Ronald Jenkins was six years old, he saw a man beaten to within an inch of his life by policemen on the

*High Street of his Yorkshire village. The man, it was whis-
pered amongst the gathering villagers, was a resident of
nearby Denaby – a 'hell upon earth' situated in the valley of
the Crags and considered by many to be the 'worst village
in England'. It was an incident the young Jenkins was never
to forget, and in his debut novel,* Mercy of the Black
Diamonds, *published in 1928, he gave life to one of inter-
war British fiction's most remarkable characters, a man of
alarming truth and dignity, whose plight generated enormous sympathy from readers and critics alike.*

In the opening chapter of Black Diamonds, *police in
steel-capped boots set upon the ill-fated protagonist, Walter
Harrison, an illiterate but hard-working man whose personal heartbreaks have led him to agitate for social change
and which ultimately result in his untimely death. Jenkins
spoke of the real-life event and its profound influence on his
work – 'and on my soul' – in a 1935 radio interview with
the BBC: 'I realized that day, as I watched a man reduced
to nothing by uniformed officers, that there are weak and
there are powerful people in our society, and that goodness
is not a factor in determining into which camp one falls.'
It was a theme that was to find expression in many of
Henry Jenkins's later novels.* Black Diamonds *was declared
a masterpiece and on the strength of its early reviews
became a publishing sensation. His earliest works, in particular, were lauded for their verisimilitude and for the
unflinching portraits they contained of working-class life,
including uncompromising depictions of poverty and physical violence.*

*Jenkins was himself brought up in a working-class
family. His father was a low-level overseer at the*

Fitzwilliams' Collieries; he was a stern man who drank too much – 'but only on Saturdays' – and who ran his family 'as though we were subordinates in the pits'. Jenkins was alone amongst his six brothers in leaving behind the village and the expectations of his birth. Of his parents, Jenkins said: 'My mother was a beautiful woman, but she was vain, too, and disappointed by her lot; she had no real or focused idea as to how her situation might be improved and her frustrations made her bitter. She goaded my father, badgering him constantly about whatever it was that came first to mind; he was a man of great physical strength, but too weak in other ways to be married to a woman like her. Ours was not a happy household.' When asked by the BBC interviewer whether his parents' lives had furnished him with material for his novels, Jenkins laughed and then said: 'More than that, they gave me a firm example of the life I wished more than anything to escape.'

And escape it he did. From such humble beginnings, Jenkins, by virtue of his precocious intelligence and tenacity, managed to pull himself out of the pits and take the literary world by storm. When asked by The Times *about his tremendous rise, Jenkins credited a teacher at his village school, Herbert Taylor, for recognizing his intellectual aptitude as a child and encouraging him to sit scholarship examinations for several of the best public schools. When he was ten years old, Jenkins won a place at the small but prestigious Nordstrom School in Oxfordshire. He left the family home in 1911, boarding the train alone for a journey to the unknown south. Henry Jenkins was never to return to Yorkshire.*

While some former public schoolboys, particularly

those with different social backgrounds to most, speak of a miserable schooling experience, Jenkins would never be drawn on the subject, saying only that: 'Admittance to a school like Nordstrom changed my life in the very best of ways.' His schoolmaster, Jonathan Carlyon, said of Jenkins: 'He was an incredibly hard worker. He passed his final exams with outstanding scores and went up to Oxford University the following year to study at his first preference college.' While conceding Jenkins's intelligence, Oxford friend and fellow author, Allen Hennessy, made light-hearted reference to another pool of talents from which he had to draw: 'I've never met a man with more charisma than Jenkins,' he said. 'If there was a girl you fancied, you learned pretty damn fast not to introduce her to Harry Jenkins. He only had to fix her with one of his famous stares and your chances were out the window.' Which is not to suggest that Jenkins abused his so-called 'powers': 'He was handsome and charming, he enjoyed the attention of women, but he was never a playboy,' said Roy Edwards, Jenkins's publisher at Macmillan.

Whatever effect Jenkins might have had on the fairer sex, his personal life did not enjoy the same smooth path as his publishing career. In 1930, he suffered a broken engagement to Miss Eliza Holdstock, the details of which he declined to discuss publicly, before finally marrying Vivien Longmeyer, the niece of his Nordstrom schoolmaster, in 1938. Despite an age difference of twenty years, Jenkins considered their marriage to be 'the crowning glory of my life', and the couple settled in London, where they enjoyed a happy domestic situation in the final year before the Second World War. In the lead-up to the declaration of war, Jenkins began working for the Ministry of Information; it was a position in which he excelled, a fact that came as no surprise to those who knew him well. As Allen Hennessy said: 'Everything [Jenkins] did, he did to perfection. He was athletic, clever, charming . . . The world is made for men like him.'

Be that as it may, the world is not always kind to men like Jenkins. After the death of his young wife in an air raid during the final weeks of the London Blitz, Jenkins suffered from such immense grief that his life began to unravel. He was never to publish another book; indeed, whether he continued to write at all remains a mystery, along with many other details of the last decade of his life. When he died in 1961, Henry Ronald Jenkins's star had fallen so low that the event barely registered a mention in the very newspapers that had once described him as 'a genius'. Suggestion arose in the early 1960s that Jenkins was responsible for the acts of public indecency that had earned the perpetrator the nickname 'Suffolk Picnic Stalker'; however, the allegations have never been proven. Regardless of whether or not Jenkins was guilty of such obscenity, that this once great man had become the subject of such speculation indicates the depth of his fall from grace. The boy whose headmaster had once referred to him as 'capable of achieving everything to which he set his mind' died with nothing and no one to his name. The enduring question for admirers of Henry Jenkins is how such an ending could come to the man who had once had everything; an ending that bears tragic similarities to that of his character Walter Harrison, whose fate was also to die a quiet, lonely death after a life in which love and loss had become interwoven.

Laurel leaned back in her library chair and let out the breath she'd been holding. There was nothing much there she hadn't already gleaned from Google, and the relief was extraordinary. She felt ten pounds lighter. Better yet, despite the reference to Jenkins's ignominious end, there'd been no mention at all of Dorothy Nicolson or a farmhouse called Greenacres. Thank God. Laurel hadn't realized quite how nervous she'd been about what she might find. Turned out the most disconcerting thing about the prologue was the portrait it painted of a self-made man whose success was the result of nothing more than hard work and considerable talent. Laurel had rather hoped to uncover something that justified the feelings of snarling hatred she'd developed towards the man on the driveway.

She wondered whether there was a chance the biographer had got it all wrong. It was possible; anything was possible. But even as her spirits briefly lifted, Laurel rolled her eyes. Really, her own arrogance knew no limits – a hunch was one thing, presuming to know more on the subject of Henry Jenkins than the fellow who'd researched and written his life story, quite another.

There was a photograph of Jenkins on the frontispiece of the book and she flicked back to it, determined to look beyond the layers of menace her prejudice applied and see the charming, charismatic writer described by the prologue. He was younger in this photograph than in the one she'd seen online, and Laurel had to admit that he was handsome. In fact – it occurred to her as she studied his chiselled features – he reminded her in some way of a fellow actor she'd once been rather in love with. They'd been cast together in a Chekhov play back in the sixties and fallen into a mad tempestuous affair. It hadn't worked out – theatre romances rarely did – but oh, it had been dazzling and intense while it lasted.

Laurel closed the book. Her cheeks were warm and a lovely nostalgic feeling was stirring. Well now. That was unexpected. Rather uncomfortable, too, under the circumstances. Swallowing a small lump of disquiet, Laurel reminded herself of her purpose and made her way to page ninety-seven. With a deep, centring breath she started on the chapter called 'Married Life'.

If Henry Jenkins had been unlucky thus far in his personal relationships, things were about to change for the better. In the spring of 1938, his former headmaster, Mr Jonathan Carlyon, invited Jenkins to return to the Nordstrom School and speak to the final-year students about the travails of literary life. It was there, as he strolled across the estate by evening, that Jenkins met the headmaster's niece and ward, Vivien Longmeyer, seventeen years old at the time and a beauty. Jenkins wrote about their meeting in The Reluctant Muse, *one of his most successful novels and a marked departure from the gritty subject matter of his earlier work.*

How Vivien Jenkins felt about having the details of their courtship and early marriage written about in such a public way remains a mystery, as does the woman herself. The young Mrs Jenkins had barely begun to leave her mark on the world when her life was cut tragically short during the London Blitz. What is known, thanks to her husband's clear adoration of his 'reluctant muse', is that she was a

*woman of remarkable loveliness and allure, about whom
Jenkins's feelings were clear from the first.*

There came then a lengthy extract, taken from *The
Reluctant Muse*, in which Henry Jenkins wrote rapturously
about meeting and courting his young bride. Having
recently suffered through the entire book, Laurel skipped
over it, picking up the thread when the biographer returned
his focus to the facts of Vivien's life:

*Vivien Longmeyer was the daughter of Jonathan
Carlyon's only sister, Isabel, who had eloped from England
with an Australian soldier after the First World War. Neil
and Isabel Longmeyer settled in the small cedar-getting com-
munity of Tamborine Mountain in south-east Queensland,
and Vivien was the second youngest of their four children.
For the first eight years of her life, Vivien Longmeyer lived a
modest colonial existence, until she was sent back to
England to be raised by her maternal uncle at the school he'd
built on her family's grand ancestral estate.*

*The earliest account of Vivien Longmeyer comes from
Miss Katy Ellis, a renowned educator, who was charged
with the duty of chaperoning the child on the crossing from
Australia to England in 1929. Katy Ellis mentioned the girl
in her memoir,* Born to Teach, *suggesting it was this en-
counter with the child that first sparked her lifelong interest
in educating the young survivors of trauma.*

*'The girl's Australian aunt had issued a warning, when she
asked me to act as chaperone, that the child was simple and I
wasn't to be surprised if she chose not to communicate with me
on the voyage. I was young, and therefore not yet equipped to*

castigate the woman for a lack of compassion that bordered on callous, but I was confident enough in my own impressions not to accept her assessment. Vivien Longmeyer was not simple, I could tell that much by looking at her; however, I could also see what it was that made her aunt describe her thus. Vivien had an ability, which verged at times on unsettling, to sit still for very long periods of time, her face – not blank, certainly not that – rather alight with electric thought, but privately and in a manner that made anybody watching her feel excluded.

'I had been an imaginative child myself, often upbraided by my father, a strict Protestant minister, for daydreaming and writing in my journals – a habit I continue to this day – and it seemed quite clear to me that Vivien had a vibrant inner life into which she disappeared. Further, it seemed natural and understandable that a child suffering the simultaneous loss of her family, her home, and the country of her birth might necessarily seek to preserve what small certainties of identity she had left to her by internalizing them.

'Over the course of our long sea voyage, I was able to gain Vivien's trust sufficiently to establish a relationship that continued over many years. We corresponded by letter with warm regularity until her tragic and untimely death during the Second World War, and although I never taught or counselled her in an official capacity I'm pleased to say that we became friends. She didn't have many friends: she was the sort of person others longed to be loved by, yet she did not make connections easily or lightly. Looking back, I consider it a highlight of my career that she opened up to me in detail about the private world she had constructed for herself. It was a "safe" place into which she retreated if ever she was scared or alone, and I was honoured to be permitted a glimpse behind the veil.'

Katy Ellis's description of Vivien's retreat into a 'private world' tallies with accounts of the adult Vivien: 'She was attractive, the sort of person you wanted to look at, but whom afterwards you couldn't really say you knew'; 'She gave you the feeling there was more going on beneath the surface than there seemed'; 'In some way, it was her very self-sufficiency that made her magnetic – she didn't appear to need other people.' Perhaps it was Vivien's 'strange, almost otherworldly air' that caught the eye of Henry Jenkins that evening at the Nordstrom School. Or perhaps it was the fact that she, like him, had survived a childhood marked by tragic violence and been removed soon after to a world peopled by those with vastly different backgrounds from her own. 'We were both outsiders in our way,' Henry Jenkins told the BBC. 'We belonged together, the two of us. I knew it the first time I laid eyes on her. Watching her walk up the aisle towards me, sublime in her white lace, was the completion, in some ways, of a journey that started when I first arrived at Nordstrom School.'

There was a spottily reproduced photograph of the two of them then, taken on their wedding day as they emerged from the school chapel. Vivien was gazing up at Henry, her lace veil rippling in the breeze, as he held her arm and smiled directly at the camera. The people gathered around them tossing rice from the chapel steps were happy, yet the photograph made Laurel sad. Old photographs often did; she was her mother's daughter, and there was something terribly sobering about the smiling faces of people who didn't yet know what fate awaited them. Even more so in a case like this one, where Laurel knew precisely the horrors that lurked around the corner. She had witnessed first-hand the violent death Henry Jenkins would suffer, and she knew, too, that young Vivien Jenkins, so hopeful in her wedding photo, would be dead a mere three years after it was taken.

There is no doubt that Henry Jenkins adored his wife to the point of adulation. He made no secret of what she meant to him, calling her variously his 'grace', and his 'salvation', expressing the sentiment, on more than one occasion, that without her his life would not be worth living. His claims would prove sadly prescient, for after Vivien's death in an air raid on 23 May 1941, Henry Jenkins's world began to crumble. Despite being employed by the Ministry of Information and having detailed knowledge of the Blitz's heavy civilian toll, Jenkins found it impossible to accept that his wife's death could have come by such a mundane cause. In retrospect, Jenkins's rather wild claims – that there was foul play involved in Vivien's death, that she'd been targeted by shady con artists, that she would never have visited the site of the air raid otherwise – were the first indications of a madness that would ultimately claim him. He refused to accept his wife's death as a simple wartime accident, vowing to 'catch the people responsible and bring them to justice'. Jenkins was hospitalized after a breakdown in the mid 1940s, but sadly his mania was to last the rest of his life, leading him back to the fringes of polite society and eventually to his lonely death in 1961, a destitute and broken man.

Laurel slammed the book shut as if to trap its subject between the covers. She didn't want to read any further about Henry Jenkins's certainty that there'd been more to his wife's death than met the eye, nor his vow to find the person accountable. She had a rather pressing and unwelcome feeling that he'd done just that, and that she, Laurel, had witnessed its result. Because Ma, with her 'perfect plan', was the person Henry Jenkins blamed for his wife's death, wasn't she? The 'shady con artist' who'd sought to 'take' something from Vivien, who'd been responsible for drawing Vivien to the site of her death, a place she never would have visited otherwise.

With an involuntary shudder, Laurel glanced behind her. She felt conspicuous all of a sudden, as if unseen eyes were watching her. Her stomach, too, felt as though it had turned to liquid. It was guilt, she realized, guilt by association. She thought about her mother in the hospital, the regret she'd expressed, her talk of 'taking' something, of being grateful for a 'second chance' – they were stars, all of them, appearing in the dark night sky; Laurel might not like the patterns she was beginning to see, but she couldn't deny that they were there.

She looked down at the biography's seemingly innocuous black cover. Her mother knew all the answers, but she hadn't been the only one; Vivien had known them, too. Up to this point, Vivien had seemed a whisper – a smiling face in a photograph, a name in the front of an old book, a figment who'd slipped through the cracks of history and been forgotten.

But she was important.

Laurel had a sudden burning conviction that whatever had gone wrong with Dorothy's plan had everything to do with Vivien. That something intrinsic to the other woman's character made her the very worst person with whom to become entangled.

Katy Ellis's account of the child Vivien was kindly enough, but Kitty Barker had described a 'snooty' woman, a 'dreadful influence', who was superior and cold. Had Vivien's childhood suffering broken something inside her, hardened her and made her into the sort of woman – beautiful and wealthy – whose very power was in her coolness, her interiority, her unattainability? The information in Henry Jenkins's biography, the way he'd been unable to live with her death and had searched over decades for those he held responsible, certainly suggested a woman whose nature proved greatly alluring to others.

With a slight dawning smile, Laurel opened the biography again and flicked quickly through the pages until she'd found the one she was after. There it was. Fumbling the pen a little with excitement, she scribbled down the name 'Katy Ellis' and the title of her memoir, *Born to Teach*. Vivien might not have needed – or indeed had – many friends, but she'd written letters to Katy Ellis, letters in which (was it too much to hope?) she might have confessed her deepest darkest truths. There was every chance those letters still existed somewhere: many people didn't keep their correspondence, but Laurel was willing to bet that Miss Katy Ellis, renowned educator and author of her own memoir, wasn't one of them.

Because the more Laurel turned it over, the clearer it

became: Vivien was the key. Finding out about this elusive figure was the only way to unravel Dorothy's plan; more importantly, where it all went wrong. And now – Laurel smiled – she'd caught her by the edge of her shadow.

PART THREE

VIVIEN

Twenty-two

Vivien was punished in the first place because she had the great misfortune of being caught out the front of Mr McVeigh's Main Street shop. Her father hadn't wanted to do it, anyone could've seen that. He was a soft-hearted man who'd had the last of his iron mined out of him in the Great War, and truth be told he'd always admired the startling spirit of his youngest daughter. But rules were rules, and Mr McVeigh kept blustering about the rod and the child, and spoiling and sparing, and a crowd was gathering, and hell but it was hot ... Still, there was no way any child of his was getting hit, not by his hand, and certainly not for facing up to bullies like that Jones lad. And so he'd done the only thing he could: forbidden her publicly from going on the outing. The punishment had been rashly chosen and was later a source of deep regret and frequent late-night arguments with his wife, but there was no turning back. Too many people had heard him say it. The words left his mouth and as they arrived at Vivien's ears she knew, even at the age of eight, that there was nothing left to do but set her chin and cross her arms and show them all that she didn't give two hoots, she'd never wanted to go anyway.

Which was how she came to be at home, alone, on the

hottest day of the summer in 1929, while her family set off
for the annual Cedar Getters' Picnic in Southport. There'd
been strict instructions from Dad over breakfast, a list of
things to do and a longer list of things not to, a fair bit of
agonized hand-wringing from Mum when she thought she
wasn't being watched, a preventative dose of castor oil for
all the kiddies – double for Vivien because she was bound to
need it twice as much – and then with an excited flurry of
last-minute preparations the rest of them had piled into the
Lizzie Ford and headed off down the goat track.

The house was quiet for the lack of them. And darker
somehow. And the dust motes hung motionless without the
usual moving bodies to orbit around. The kitchen table,
where they'd laughed and argued minutes before, was cleared
now of plates, spread instead with a motley assortment of
jars filled with Mum's cooling jam, and the notepaper Dad
had laid out so that Vivien could write apology notes to Mr
McVeigh and Paulie Jones. So far she'd written 'Dear Mr
McVeigh,' scratched out the 'Dear' and put 'To' above it, and
then she'd sat staring at the blank page beneath, wondering
how many words it would take to fill it. Willing them to
appear before Dad got home.

When it became apparent the notes weren't going
to write themselves, Vivien put down the fountain pen,
stretched her arms above her head, dangled her bare feet
back and forth a bit, and surveyed the rest of the room: the
heavily framed pictures on the wall, the dark mahogany
furniture, the cane daybed with its crocheted rug. This was
Indoors, she thought with distaste, the place of grown-ups
and homework, the cleaning of teeth and bodies, of 'Quiet,'
and 'Don't run,' of combs and lace and Mum having tea

with Aunt Ada, and visits from the reverend and the doctor. It was deathly and dull and a place she did her best to avoid, and yet – Vivien chewed the inside of her cheek, struck by a thought – today Indoors was hers and hers alone, most likely for the only time ever.

Vivien read her sister Ivy's diary first, then combed through Robert's hobby periodicals and examined Pippin's marble collection; finally she turned her attention to her mother's wardrobe. She slipped her feet into the cool lining of shoes that belonged to the long-ago time of before she was born, rubbed the silky fabric of Mum's best blouse against her cheek, layered strings of shiny beads from the walnut box on top of the duchesse around her neck. In the drawer she turned over Dad's Rising Sun service badge, the carefully folded copy of his discharge papers, a parcel of letters tied together with ribbon, and a piece of paper entitled *Certificate of Marriage*, with Mum and Dad's real names printed on it, Mum when she was *Isabel Carlyon* of *Oxford, England,* and not one of them at all.

The lace curtains fluttered and the sweet rich smell of Outdoors pushed through the open sash window – eucalypt and lemon myrtle and overripe mangoes starting to boil on her father's prized tree. Vivien folded the papers back into the drawer and jumped to her feet. The sky was cloudless, blue as the ocean and drum-skin tight. Fig leaves glittered in the bright sunlight, frangipanis sparkled pink and yellow, and birds called to one another in the thick rainforest behind the house. It was going to be a stinker, Vivien realized with satisfaction, and later there'd be a storm. She loved storms: the angry clouds and the first fat drops, the rusty smell of thirsty red dirt, and the lashing rain against the walls as Dad paced back and forth on the veranda with his pipe in his mouth, and a shimmer in his eyes, trying to keep his thrill in check as the palm trees wailed and flexed.

Vivien turned on her heel. She'd done enough exploring; there was no way she was wasting another precious second Indoors. She stopped in the kitchen long enough only to pack the lunch Mum had left her and forage for an extra couple of Anzac biscuits. A line of ants was marching round the sink and up the wall. They knew the rain was coming too. Without another glance at the unwritten letter of apology, Vivien danced out onto the back veranda. She never walked if she could help it.

It was hot outside, and still, and the air was muggy. Her feet burned instantly on the wooden boards. It was a perfect day for the sea. She wondered where the others were now, whether they'd arrived yet at Southport, whether the mums and dads and kids were swimming and laughing and setting up the lunches, or whether her family had boarded one of the pleasure boats instead. There was a new jetty, according to Robert, who'd been eavesdropping on Dad's old army mates, and Vivien had imagined herself dive-bombing off its end, sinking like a macadamia nut, so fast that her skin tingled and cold seawater filled her nose.

She could always go down to Witches Falls for a swim, but on a day like this the rock pool wasn't a patch on the salty ocean; besides, she wasn't supposed to leave the house, and one of the tattletales in town was sure to notice. Worse, if Paulie Jones was there, sunning his fat white belly like a big old whale, she didn't think she'd be able to stop herself. He ought to try calling Pippin simple again and see what happened. Vivien dared him to do it. She *double*-dared him.

Unballing her fists, she eyed the shed. Old Mac the swagger was down there working on repairs and was usually worth a visit, but Dad had forbidden Vivien from bothering him with her questions. He'd enough work to do, and Dad wasn't paying him money he didn't have to drink billy tea and gasbag with a little girl who had her own chores waiting for her. Old Mac knew she was at home today, he'd keep an ear out for trouble, but unless she was sick or bleeding, the shed was out of bounds.

Which left only one place to go.

Vivien scampered down the wide stairs, crossed the grass, rounded the garden beds, where Mum tried stubbornly to grow roses and Dad reminded her affectionately that this wasn't England, and then, turning three expert cartwheels in a row, she headed for the creek.

Vivien had been going there since she learned to walk, weaving between the silver gums, collecting wattle flowers and bottlebrush, careful not to step on jumping ants or spiders as she slipped further and further away from people and buildings and teachers and rules. It was her favourite place in the whole world; it was her own; it belonged to her, and she to it.

Today she was more eager than usual to get to the bottom. Beyond the first rock sheer, where the ground got steep and the ant mounds towered, she clutched her lunch pack and broke into a run, relishing the thump of her heart against her ribcage, the scary thrill of her legs, turning, turning, beneath her, almost tripping, sliding sometimes as she dodged branches, leapt over rocks, skidded down drifts of dried leaves.

Whipbirds cheered overhead, insects burred, the water-fall in Dead Man's Gully chipped and chattered. Fragments of light and colour jittered as she ran, kaleidoscopic. The bush was alive: the trees spoke to one another in parched old voices, thousands of unseen eyes blinked from branches and fallen logs, and Vivien knew if she were to stop and press her ear to the hard ground she'd hear the earth calling to her, singing sounds from ancient times. She didn't stop, though; she was desperate to reach the creek that snaked through the gorge.

Nobody else knew it, but the creek was magic. There was one bend in particular where the banks widened to form a craggy circle; the bed beneath had been formed millions of years ago when the earth sighed and shifted and great rock slabs were brought together jaggedly, so what was shallow at the rims deepened and darkened suddenly at its centre. And that's where Vivien had made her discovery.

She'd been fishing with the glass jars she'd pilfered from Mum's kitchen and kept now in the rotten log behind the ferns. Vivien stored all her treasures inside that log. There was always something to find within the creek's waters: eels and tadpoles, rusted old buckets from the olden days. Once, she'd even found a set of false teeth.

On the day she found the lights, Vivien had been lying on her belly on a rock, arm stretched deep into the pool, trying to catch the biggest tadpole she'd ever seen. She'd swept at it and missed, swept at it and missed, and then she'd reached deeper still so that her face was almost touching the water. And that was when she'd noticed them, several of them, all orange and twinkly, blinking at her from the very bottom of the pool. She'd thought at first it was the sun and squinted up at the distant scraps of sky to check. But it wasn't. The sky was reflected on the water surface all right, but this was different. These lights were deep, beyond the slippery reeds and moss that covered the creek bed. They were something else. Some*where* else.

Vivien had given the lights a lot of thought. She wasn't one for book-learning – that was Robert's thing, and Mum's – but she was good at asking questions. She'd sounded out Old Mac, and then Dad, and finally she'd run into Black Jackie, Dad's tracker mate, who knew more than anyone else about the bush. He'd stopped what he was doing and planted a hand in the small of his back, arching his wiry frame. 'Ya seen them little lights down deep in the pool, did ya?'

She'd nodded, and he'd looked at her hard, without blinking. Eventually, a slight smile had skimmed his lips. 'Ever touched the bottom of that pool?'

'Nah.' She swatted a fly from her nose. 'Too deep.'

'Me neither.' He scratched beneath the rim of his broad hat, and then he made to start again on his digging. Before he drove the shovel into the ground he turned his head. 'What makes ya so sure there is one, if ya haven't seen it fer y'self?'

And that's when Vivien had realized: there was a hole in her creek that ran all the way to the other side of the world. It was the only explanation. She'd heard Dad talking about digging a hole to China, and now she'd gone and found it. A secret tunnel, a way to the earth's core – the place from which all magic and life and time had sprung – and beyond that to the shining stars of a distant sky. The question was, what was she going to do with it?

Explore it, that's what.

Vivien skidded to a halt on the big flat rock slab that formed the bridge between bush and creek. The water was still today, thick and murky in the shallows round the edges. A film of sludge from further upstream had settled across the surface like a greasy skin. The sun was directly overhead and the ground was baking. The limbs of the towering gums creaked in the heat.

Vivien tucked her lunch beneath the thick ferns arching over the rock; something in the cool undergrowth slithered away unseen.

The water was cold at first around her bare ankles. She waded through the shallows, feet gripping to the slimy rocks, suddenly sharp in places. Her plan was to catch a glimpse of the lights to begin with, make sure they were still where they ought to be, and then she was going to swim as far down as she could to get a better look. She'd been practising holding her breath for weeks, and had brought one of Mum's wooden clothes pegs for her nose because Robert reckoned if she could stop the air escaping through her nostrils she'd last for longer.

When she reached the ridge where the rock floor dropped away, Vivien peered into the dark water. It took a few seconds, a bit of squinting and a lot of leaning, but then – there they were!

She grinned and almost lost her footing. Over the ridge a pair of kookaburras chortled.

Vivien hurried back to the edge of the pool, slipping sometimes in her haste. She ran across the flat rock, feet slapping wetly, and dug about in her pack to retrieve the peg.

It was while she was deciding how best to fasten it that she noticed the black thing on her foot. A leech – a big fat whopper of a thing. Vivien bent over, gripped it between her thumb and finger, and pulled as hard as she could. The slippery mongrel wouldn't come off.

She sat down and had another go, but no matter how she squeezed and tugged, it wouldn't budge. The body was slimy in her fingers, wet and squishy. She steeled herself, screwed her eyes shut, and gave it one last wrench.

Vivien cursed with every forbidden word (*Shit! Bloody! Bugger! Bum!*) she'd gleaned in eight years of eavesdropping in Dad's shed. The leech had come free, but a stream of blood flowed in its place.

Her head spun woozily and she was glad she was already sitting. She could watch Old Mac take the heads off chooks, no worries; she'd held her brother Pippin's severed fingertip all the way to Doc Farrell's place after it got chopped off by the axe; she gutted fish faster and cleaner than Robert when they camped down by Nerang River. Faced with her own blood, though, she was worse than useless.

She limped back down to the water's edge and dangled her foot in, swishing it this way and that. Each time she withdrew the limb, blood still streamed. Nothing for it but to wait.

She sat on the rock slab and unpacked her lunch. Sliced silverside from last night's roast, gravy glistening cold on its surface; soft potato and yam that she ate with her fingers; a wedge of bread and butter pudding with Mum's fresh jam smeared on top; three Anzac biscuits and a blood orange, fresh from the tree.

A clutch of crows materialized in the shadows as she ate, staring at her with cold unblinking eyes. When she'd finished, Vivien tossed the last of her crumbs into the bush and a weight of heavy wings beat after them. She dusted off her dress and yawned.

Her foot had stopped bleeding at last. She wanted to explore the hole at the bottom of the pool, but she was suddenly tired; extra tired, like the girl in one of those stories Mum read to them sometimes in a faraway voice that grew less like theirs with every word. It made Vivien feel strange, that voice of their mother's; it was fancy, and while Vivien admired Mum for it, she was jealous too of this part of their mother they didn't own.

Vivien yawned again, so wide that her eyes smarted.

Maybe if she lay down, just for a little while?

She crawled over to the edge of the rock and crept beneath the fern leaves, deep enough that when she rolled onto her back and shimmied a little to the left the last patch of sky disappeared. Leaves lay smooth and cool beneath her, crickets ticked in the undergrowth, and a frog somewhere panted the afternoon away.

The day was warm and she was small and it wasn't surprising that Vivien fell asleep. She dreamed about the lights in the pool, and how long it would take to swim to China, and a long jetty of hot wooden planks, her brothers and sister diving off its end. She dreamed of the storm that was coming and Dad on the veranda, and Mum's English skin, freckled from a day by the sea, and the dinner table that night with all of them around it.

The beating sun arced over the earth's surface, light shifted and sifted through the bush, humidity pulled the drum skin tighter and small beads of sweat appeared at the little girl's hairline. Insects clicked and clacked, the sleeping child stirred when a fern leaf tickled her cheek, and then –

'*Vivien!*'

– her name came suddenly, skimming down the hillside, cutting through the undergrowth to reach her.

She woke with a start.

'Viv-i-*en?*'

It was Aunt Ada, Daddy's elder sister.

Vivien sat up, brushing strands of hair across her damp forehead with the back of her hand. Bush bees hummed nearby. She yawned.

'Young miss, if you're out here, for the love of God, show yourself.'

Most times, Vivien couldn't care less about being obedient, but the voice of her usually unflappable aunt was flapping so hard that curiosity got the better of her and she rolled out from beneath the ferns, snatching up her lunch things. The day had darkened; clouds covered the blue sky and the gorge was now in shadow.

With a wistful glance over her shoulder at the creek, a promise to come back as soon as she could, she started for home.

Aunt Ada was sitting on the back stairs, head in hands, when Vivien emerged from the bush. Some sixth sense must've told her she had company because she glanced sideways, blinking at Vivien with the same perplexed expression she might have worn had a bush sprite appeared on the lawn before her.

'Come here, child,' she said finally, beckoning with one
hand as she pushed herself to standing.

Vivien walked slowly. There was a strange swooping
sensation in her stomach for which she had no name, but
that she would one day come to recognize as dread. Aunt
Ada's cheeks were bright red and there was something
uncontrolled about her; she looked as if she were about to
shout or to clip Vivien across the ears, but she did neither,
bursting into scalding tears instead and saying, 'For God's
sake, get indoors and wash that muck off your face. What
would your poor mother think?'

Vivien was Indoors again. There'd been a lot of Indoors
since it happened. The first black week when the wooden
boxes, or caskets, as Aunt Ada called them, were laid out in
the sitting room; the long nights during which her bedroom
walls retreated into the darkness; the stale muggy days as
grown-ups whispered, and clicked their tongues at the sud-
denness of it all, and sweated into clothes already damp
from the rain that bore down outside the steamy windows.

She'd made a nest against the wall, tucked herself
between the sideboard and the back of Dad's armchair, and
that's where she stayed. Words and phrases buzzed like mos-
quitoes in the fug above – *The Lizzie Ford . . . right over the
edge . . . incinerated . . . hardly recognizable* – but Vivien
blocked her ears and thought instead about the tunnel in the
pond and the great engine room at its centre from which the
world was spun.

For five days she'd refused to leave the spot, and the
adults had humoured her and brought plates of food and
shaken their heads with kindly pity, until finally, with no

obvious sign or warning, the invisible line of leniency was reeled in and she was dragged back into the world.

The wet season had set in well and truly by then, but there'd been one day when the sun had shone and she'd felt the faint stirrings of her old self, sneaking out into the glare of the backyard and finding Old Mac in the shed. He'd said very little, laying a big gnarled hand on her shoulder and squeezing hard, and then he'd handed her a hammer so she could help with the fencing. As the day wore on, she'd thought about visiting the creek, but she hadn't, and then the rain came back and Aunt Ada arrived with boxes, and the house was packed away. Her sister's favourite shoes, the satin ones that had sat all week on the rug, in the same spot she'd kicked them after Mum said they were too good for the picnic, were tossed into a box with Dad's handkerchiefs and his old belt. Next thing Vivien knew there was a For Sale sign on the front lawn and she was sleeping on a strange floor as her cousins blinked curiously at her from their own beds.

Aunt Ada's house was different from her own. The wall paint wasn't flaking, there were no ants wandering the bench tops, cascades of garden flowers did not spill from vases. It was a house where spilling of any kind was not tolerated. A place for everything and everything in its place, Aunt Ada was fond of saying, in a voice that shrilled like a fiddle string wound too tight.

While the rain continued outside, Vivien had taken to lying under the sofa in the good room, pressed against the skirting board. There was a droop of hessian lining, invisible from the door, and to squeeze beyond it was to become invisible herself. It was comforting, that torn sofa base, it reminded her of her own house, her family, their happy tattered clutter. It brought her as close as she ever came to crying. Most times, though, she concentrated only on breathing, taking in the smallest amount of air she could, letting it out so that her chest barely moved. Hours – whole days – could be passed that way, rainwater gurgling down the drainpipe outside, Vivien's eyes closed and her ribcage steady; sometimes, she could almost convince herself she'd managed to stop time.

The room's greatest virtue, though, was its designation as strictly out of bounds. The rule was laid out for Vivien on her first night in the house – the good room was to be used for entertaining, only by the aunt herself, and then only ever when the status of the guest demanded it – and Vivien had nodded solemnly, when prompted, to show that yes, she understood. And she had, perfectly. Nobody used the room, which meant that once the daily dusting was done, she could count on being alone within its walls.

And so she had been, until today.

Reverend Fawley had been sitting on the armchair by the window for the past fifteen minutes as Aunt Ada fussed over tea and cake. Vivien was stuck beneath the sofa, more specifically pinned by the depression of her aunt's backside.

'I don't need to remind you what the Lord would counsel, Mrs Frost,' said the reverend in the cloying voice he saved usually for the little baby Jesus. '"Do not forget to entertain strangers, for by doing so you may be entertaining angels without realizing it."'

'If that girl's an angel, then I'm the Queen of England.'

'Yes, well,' the pious chink of a spoon against porcelain, 'the child has suffered a great loss.'

'More sugar, Reverend?'

'No – thank you, Mrs Frost.'

The sofa base slumped further as her aunt sighed. 'We've all suffered a great loss, Reverend. When I think of my own dear brother, perishing like that . . . falling all that way, the lot of them, the Lizzie Ford going right over the edge of the mountain . . . Harvey Watkins that found them said it was burned so bad he didn't know what he was looking at. It was a tragedy . . .'

'A terrible tragedy.'

'All the same.' Aunt Ada's shoes shifted on the rug, and Vivien could see the toe of one scratching at the bunion trapped within the other. 'I can't keep her here. I've six of my own, and now Mum's moving in with us. You know what she's been like since the doctor had to take her leg. I'm a good Christian woman, Reverend, I'm in church every Sunday, I do my bit for the fete and the Easter fundraiser, but I just can't do it.'

'I see.'

'You know yourself, the girl's not easy.'

There was a pause in conversation as tea was sipped and the particular nature of Vivien's lack of easiness considered.

'If it had been any of the others,' Aunt Ada set her cup on its saucer, 'even poor simple Pippin . . . but I just can't do it. Forgive me, Reverend, I know that it's a sin to say so, but I can't look at the girl without blaming her for all that's happened. She ought to have gone with them. If she hadn't got herself in trouble and been punished . . . They left the picnic early, you know, because my brother didn't like to leave her so long – he was always too soft-hearted – ' She broke off with a great gasping wail and Vivien thought how ugly adults could be, how weak. So used to getting what they wanted that they didn't know the first thing about being brave.

'There, there, Mrs Frost. There, there.'

The sobbing was thick and laboured, like Pippin's when he wanted Mum's attention. The reverend's chair creaked and then his feet came closer. He handed something to Aunt Ada, he must have, for she said, 'Thank you,' through her tears, and then blew her nose wetly.

'No, you keep it,' the reverend said, retreating to his chair. He sat with a heavy sigh. 'One does wonder, though, what's to become of the girl.'

Aunt Ada made some small sniffly noises of recovery and then ventured, 'I thought perhaps the church school out Toowoomba way?'

The reverend crossed his ankles.

'I believe the nuns take good care of the girls,' Aunt Ada went on. 'Firm but fair, and the discipline wouldn't do her any harm – David and Isabel always were too soft.'

'Isabel,' said the reverend suddenly, leaning forward. 'What about Isabel's family? Isn't there anyone who might be contacted?'

'I'm afraid she never said much about them . . . Though, now you mention it, there *is* a brother, I believe.'

'A brother?'

'A schoolteacher, over in England. Near Oxford, I think.'

'Well then.'

'Well then?'

'I suggest we start there.'

'You mean . . . to contact him?' Aunt Ada's voice lightened.

'We can but try, Mrs Frost.'

'Send him a letter?'

'I shall write to him myself.'

'Oh, Reverend—'

'See if the man can't be prevailed upon to act with Christian compassion.'

'To do the right thing.'

'His familial duty.'

'His familial duty.' There was a new giddiness in Aunt Ada's voice. 'And what kind of a man wouldn't? I'd keep her myself, if I could, if it weren't for Mum and my own six and the lack of room.' She stood up and the sofa base sighed with relief. 'Can I get you another slice of cake, Reverend?'

It turned out there was indeed a brother, and he *was* induced by the reverend to behave correctly, and so, like that, Vivien's life was changed again. It all happened remarkably swiftly in the end. Aunt Ada knew a woman who knew a fellow whose sister was travelling across the ocean to a place called London to see a man about a governess position, and she was to take Vivien with her. Decisions were made and details moored neatly together in the stream of grown-up conversation that seemed always to flow above Vivien's head.

A pair of almost-new shoes were found, her hair was forced neatly into plaits, the rest of her into a starchy dress with a ribbon sash. Her uncle drove them down the mountain and on to the railway station to meet the train for

Brisbane. It was raining still, and hot with it, and Vivien
drew with her finger on the steamy window.

The square out front of the Railway Hotel was full
when they arrived, but they found Miss Katy Ellis precisely
where she'd arranged to meet them, beneath the clock at the
ticketing window.

Vivien hadn't guessed even for a second that there were
so many people in the world. They were everywhere, each
one different from the other, scurrying about their business
like bull ants in the damp mess where a rotten log used to
lie. Black umbrellas, and large wooden containers, and
horses with deep brown eyes and flared nostrils.

The woman cleared her throat and Vivien realized she'd
been spoken to. She chased across her memories to recall
what had been said. Horses and umbrellas, bull ants in the
wet, people scurrying – her name. The woman had asked if
she was called Vivien.

She nodded.

'You mind your manners,' scolded Aunt Ada, straightening Vivien's collar. 'It's what your mother and father
would've wanted. You say, "Yes, miss," when you're asked a
question.'

'Unless you disagree, of course, in which case "No,
miss" will do perfectly well.' The woman gave a neat smile
that signalled she was making a joke. Vivien looked between
the pair of expectant faces staring down at her. Aunt Ada's
brows drew together as she waited.

'Yes, miss,' Vivien said.

'And are you well this morning?'

Compliance had never come naturally; once, Vivien
would have spoken her mind and shouted that she wasn't

well at all, she didn't want to go, it wasn't fair and they couldn't make her . . . But not now. It struck Vivien that it was far easier just to say what people wanted to hear. What difference did it make anyway? Words were clumsy things; there were none she could think of to describe the bottom-less black hole that had opened within her, the ache that fed upon her insides each time she thought she heard her father's footsteps coming down the hall, smelled her mother's cologne or, worst of all, saw something she simply had to share with Pippin . . .

'Yes, miss,' she said, to the lively woman with red hair and a long, tidy skirt.

Aunt Ada handed Vivien's suitcase to a porter, patted her niece's head and told her to be good. Miss Katy Ellis checked her tickets carefully and wondered to herself whether the dress she'd packed for her interview in London would do as well as she hoped. And as the train whistled its imminent departure, a small girl wearing neat plaits and someone else's shoes climbed its iron stairs. Smoke filled the platform, people waved and hollered, a stray dog ran barking through the crowds. Nobody noticed as the little girl stepped over the shadowed threshold; not even Aunt Ada, who some might've expected to be shepherding her orphaned niece towards her uncertain future. And so, when the essence of light and life that had been Vivien Longmeyer contracted itself for safekeeping and disappeared deep inside her, the world kept moving and nobody saw it happen.

Twenty-three

London, March 1941

Vivien ran into the man because she wasn't watching where she was going. She was also going very quickly – too quickly, as was her habit. And so they collided, on the corner of Fulham Road and Sydney Street, on a cold grey London day in March. 'Excuse me,' she said, as shock turned to contrition. 'I didn't see you there.' He had a slightly dazed expression on his face and she thought at first that she'd concussed him. She said, by way of further explanation, 'I go too quickly. I always have.' *Speed of light and limb* her father used to say when she was small and whipping through the bush. Vivien shook the memory away.

'My fault,' the man said with a wave of his hand. 'I can be hard to see – practically invisible sometimes. I can't tell you how much of a nuisance it is.'

His comment caught her unawares and Vivien felt the beginnings of a surprised smile. It was a mistake, for he canted his head and regarded her closely, narrowing his dark eyes slightly. 'We've met before.'

'No.' She let her smile drop sharply. 'I don't think so.'

'Yes, I'm sure of it.'

'You're mistaken.' She nodded, signalling, she hoped, an

end to the matter, and then said, 'Good day now,' before continuing on her way.

Moments passed. She was almost at Cale Street when: 'The WVS canteen in Kensington,' he called after her. 'You saw my photograph and told me about your friend's hospital.'

She stopped.

'The hospital for orphaned children, right?'

Vivien's cheeks flushed red-hot and she turned and hurried back to where he stood. 'Stop it,' she hissed, lifting a finger to her lips as she reached him. 'Stop talking now.'

He frowned, evidently confused, and she looked beyond his shoulders, back over her own, before pulling him with her behind a bomb-damaged shopfront, away from the street's prying eyes. 'I'm sure I made it very clear to you that you weren't to repeat what I said—'

'So you *do* remember.'

'Of course I remember. Do I look like a fool?' She glanced towards the street and waited as a woman with a shopping basket idled past. When the woman was gone, she whispered, 'I told you not to mention the hospital to anyone.'

He matched her whisper. 'I didn't think that included you.'

Vivien's next sentence caught before she could say it. He was straight-faced, but something in his tone made her think that he was joking. She didn't let herself acknowledge it, though; it would only encourage him and that was the last thing she wanted to do. 'Well, it did,' she said. 'It did include me.'

'I see. Well. Now I know. Thank you for explaining it to

me.' A small smile played about his lips as he said, 'I certainly hope I haven't ruined everything by telling you your secret.'

Vivien realized she'd been holding his wrist and she let it go as if it burned, taking a step backwards through the rubble, repositioning the neat roll of hair that had slipped forwards on her forehead. The ruby pin Henry had given her on their anniversary was beautiful but it didn't grip like a kirby. 'I need to be getting on now,' she said curtly, and then without another word she walked as quickly as she could back to the street.

She'd remembered him at once, of course. The moment they'd collided and she'd stepped back and seen his face, she'd known him, and she'd felt recognition fire like electricity right through her. She still couldn't explain it, even to herself: the dream she'd had after they met that night in the canteen. Lord, but it had been the sort to make her draw breath when its echoes came to mind the following day. It hadn't been sexual; it had been more intoxicating than that, and far more dangerous. The dream had filled her with a deep and inexplicable yearning for a faraway place and time, a desire that Vivien had thought she'd long outgrown, the absence of which she'd felt like a loved one's passing when she woke up the next morning and realized she'd have to go on without it. She'd tried everything to get it out of her head, that dream, the hungry shadows of it that refused to dissipate; she hadn't been able to meet Henry's eyes across the breakfast table without feeling sure he would see what was hidden there – she who had become so good at hiding things from him.

'Wait a minute.'

Oh God, it was him again; he was following her. Vivien kept walking, faster now, her chin a little higher. She didn't want him to reach her; it was best for all concerned that he didn't. And yet. There was a part of her – the same incautious, curious part that had ruled her as a child and got her into so much trouble, the part Aunt Ada had despaired of and her father had nurtured, the small concealed part that didn't seem to die no matter what was thrown at it – that wanted to know what the man from the dream would say next.

Vivien cursed that part of her. She crossed the street and walked faster along the paving stones, her shoes clipping coldly. Foolish woman. He'd visited her mind that night for no reason other than that her brain had somehow thrown his image into the unconscious jumble that gave rise to dreams.

'Wait,' he said, close behind now. 'God, you weren't joking about your speed. You ought to think about the Olympics. A champion like you – it'd be good for the country's morale, don't you think?'

She felt herself slow marginally as he reached her side, but she didn't look at him, only listened when he said, 'I'm sorry we got off on the wrong foot. I didn't mean to tease back there, I was just so pleased to have run into you like this.'

She glanced at him. 'Oh? Why is that?'

He stopped walking, and there was something in the seriousness of his expression that made her stop too. She looked up and down the street, checking she hadn't been followed by anybody else, as he said, 'No need to be worried, it's just – I've been thinking a lot since we met about the hospital, about Nella – the little girl in the photo.'

'I know who Nella is,' Vivien snapped. 'I saw her just this week.'

'She's still in the hospital, then?'

'She is.'

Her brevity, she saw, made him wince – good – but then he smiled, presumably trying to thaw her. 'Look, I'd like to visit her, that's all. I didn't mean to bother you, and I promise not to get in your way. If you'd take me there sometime, I'd be very grateful.'

Vivien knew she should say no. The last thing she needed – or wanted – was a man like him tagging along when she went to Dr Tomalin's place. The whole affair was dangerous enough as it was; Henry was already growing suspicious. But he was looking at her so keenly, and damn it, his face was full of light and goodness somehow – hope – and that feeling was back, the shimmering craving of the dream.

'Please?' He lifted his hand towards her; in the dream she'd held it.

'You'll need to keep up,' she said sharply. 'And it's only this once.'

'What? You mean now? That's where you're headed?'

'Yes. And I'm running very late.' She didn't add, 'thanks to you,' but she hoped it was implied. 'I have ... an appointment to keep.'

'I won't get in your way. Promise.'

She hadn't meant to encourage him, but she could tell by his grin that she had. 'I'll take you there today,' she said, 'but then you're to disappear.'

'You know I'm not really invisible, right?'

She didn't smile. 'You're to go back to wherever it was you came from and forget all about what I told you that night in the canteen.'

'You have my word.' He held out his hand for her to shake. 'My name's—'

'No.' She said it quickly and saw by his face that she'd taken him by surprise. 'No names. Friends exchange names, and we're not that.'

He blinked and then nodded.

She sounded cold. She was glad; she'd been foolish enough already. 'One more thing,' she said. 'After I've taken you to visit Nella, I trust that you and I will never meet again.'

Jimmy hadn't been joking, not entirely – Vivien Jenkins walked like someone with a target painted on her back. More aptly, like someone trying to stay two paces ahead of the fellow she'd reluctantly agreed to escort to a rendezvous with her lover. He had to jog a little to keep up as she hurried through the rabbit warren of riverside streets, and there was no way he'd have been able to make conversation at the same time. Just as well, too: the less said between them the better. Like she'd said, they weren't friends, nor were they going to be. He was glad she'd spelled it out – it was a timely reminder for Jimmy, who had a habit of getting on with most people, that he didn't want to know Vivien Jenkins any more than she wanted to know him.

He'd agreed to Doll's plan in the end partly because she'd promised him no one would get hurt. 'Can't you see how simple it is?' she'd said, squeezing his hand tightly in the Lyons Corner House by Marble Arch. 'You bump into her accidentally – or so it seems – and while you're to-ing and fro-ing about what a coincidence it is, you tell her you'd like to visit the little girl, the one from the bomb blast, the orphan.'

'Nella,' he'd said, watching the way the sunlight failed to bring a shine to the metal table rim.

'She'll agree – who wouldn't? Especially when you tell her how moved you were by the child's plight – which is true, Jimmy, isn't it? You told me yourself you wanted to go and check how she was getting on.'

He nodded, still not meeting her eyes.

'So you go with her, find a way to arrange one more meeting, and then I turn up and take a photograph of the two of you looking, you know, close. We'll send her a letter – anonymously, of course – letting her know what I have, and then she'll be only too happy to do what's necessary to keep it secret.' Dolly had killed her cigarette by stabbing it violently into the ashtray. 'See? It's so simple it's foolproof.'

Simple, perhaps, foolproof even, but still not right. 'It's extortion, Doll,' he'd said softly, and then, turning his head to look at her, 'It's *stealing*.'

'No – ' Dolly was adamant – 'it's *justice*; it's what she deserves after what she did to me, to *us*, Jimmy – not to mention what she's doing to her husband. Besides, she's got loads of money – she won't even miss the small amount we ask for.'

'But her husband, he'll – '

' – never know. That's the beauty of it, Jimmy – it's all hers. The house they live in on Campden Grove, the private income . . . Vivien's grandmother left it to her with a stipulation that she was to retain control even *after* marriage.

You should have heard Lady Gwendolyn on the matter – she thought it was the most tremendous lark.'

He hadn't answered and Dolly must have sensed his reluctance, because she started to panic. Her already large eyes widened imploringly and she knotted her fingers together, prayer-like. 'Don't you see?' she said. 'She'll hardly feel it, but we'll be able to live together, man and wife. Happily ever after, Jimmy.'

He still hadn't known what to say so he said nothing, toying with a match as the tension between them continued to swell, and his thoughts had drifted, as they always did when he was upset, like a curlicue of smoke, away from the issue at hand. He found himself thinking of his father. The room they were sharing until they found something better, and the way the old man sat at the window watching the street, wondering aloud whether Jimmy's mother would know where to find them now, wondering whether perhaps that's why she didn't come, and asking Jimmy every night if they mightn't please go back to the other flat now. He cried sometimes, and it damn near broke Jimmy's heart to hear the old man sobbing into his pillow and saying over and over to no one in particular that he just wished things could go back to how they'd been. When he had children, Jimmy hoped he'd know just the right words to say to make everything better when they cried as if the world was coming apart, but it was harder somehow when the crying person was your dad. There were so many people weeping into their pillows these days – Jimmy thought of all the lost souls he'd photographed since the war began, the dispossessed and grieving, the hopeless and the brave, and he looked at Doll, lighting another cigarette now and smoking it anxiously, so changed from that girl by the seaside with laughter in her eyes, and he thought there were probably a lot of people who'd join his father in wishing to go back.

Or forwards. The match snapped between his fingers. You couldn't go backwards, could you, that was just wishful thinking, but there was another way out of now and it was forwards. He remembered how he'd felt in the weeks after Dolly said she couldn't marry him, the vast emptiness that had stretched blackly ahead, the loneliness that had kept him awake at night, listening to his father's sobbing and the wretched, endless beating of his own heart, and he wondered finally whether there was really anything so terrible in what Doll suggested.

Ordinarily Jimmy might've answered that yes, there was: he'd once had very clear ideas about right and wrong; but now, with the war, with everything being blown to pieces around them, well – Jimmy shook his head uncertainly – things were just different somehow. There were times, he realized, when a person stuck to their rigid ideas at their own risk.

He brought the pieces of matchstick into perfect alignment and, as he did so, Jimmy heard Doll sigh next to him. He glanced at her as she collapsed back against the leather seat and buried her face in her small hands. He noticed again the scratches on her arms, how thin she'd become. 'I'm sorry, Jimmy,' she said through her fingers. 'I'm so sorry. I shouldn't have asked. It was just an idea. I just – I just wanted . . .' Her voice was hushed now, as if she couldn't bear to hear herself speak the awful, simple truth. 'She made me feel like I was *nothing*, Jimmy.'

Dolly loved to play make-believe, and there was no one

like her for disappearing beneath the skin of an imagined character, but Jimmy knew her well and in that moment her naked honesty cut him to the core. Vivien Jenkins had made his beautiful Doll – who was so clever and sparkly, whose laugh made him feel more alive, who had so damn much to offer the world – feel like she was nothing. Jimmy didn't need to hear any more.

'Hurry up.' Vivien Jenkins had stopped walking and was waiting for him on the doorstep of a brick building indistinguishable from those either side except for a brass plate on the door: *Dr M. Tomalin, MD*. She was checking the fine rose-gold wristwatch she wore like a bracelet and her dark hair caught the sunlight as she glanced down the street behind him. 'I have to move quickly, Mr – ' she drew a sharp breath, remembering their arrangement – 'well, *you* anyway. I'm late enough as it is.'

Jimmy followed her inside, arriving in what once must have been the entrance hall of a grand home but was now being used as a reception area. A woman whose pewter-grey hair was styled patriotically in a determined-looking Victory roll glanced up from where she sat behind a turned-leg desk.

'This gentleman is here to see Nella Brown,' Vivien said.

The other woman's attention shifted to Jimmy and she regarded him for an unblinking instant over the top of her half-spectacles. He smiled; she didn't. He realized that further explanation was necessary, furthermore it was expected. Jimmy took a step closer to the desk. He felt like a character from Dickens all of a sudden, the boy from the forge tugging his forelock in the face of greatness. 'I know Nella,' he said, 'sort of. That is, we met the night her family was killed. I'm a photographer. For the newspapers. I've come to say hello – to see how she's doing.' He made himself stop talking then. He looked at Vivien, hopeful she might step in and vouch for him, but she didn't.

A clock ticked somewhere, a plane flew overhead, and at length the receptionist released a slow considering sigh. 'I see,' she said, as if it were against her better judgement to admit him. 'A photographer. For the newspapers. And what did you say your name was?'

'Jimmy,' he said, glancing again at Vivien. She looked away. 'Jimmy Metcalfe.' He could have lied – he probably should have – but he didn't think of it in time. He hadn't had much practice with duplicity. 'I just wanted to see how Nella's getting on.'

The woman regarded him, lips fixed neatly together, and then she nodded briefly. 'All right then, Mr Metcalfe, follow me. But I warn you, I won't have my hospital or my charges upset. Any sign of trouble and you're out.'

Jimmy smiled gratefully. A little fearfully, too.

She pushed her chair in neatly beneath the desk, straightened the gold cross that hung on a fine chain around her neck, and then, without a backwards glance, started up the sweeping stairs with a clarity of purpose that demanded he follow. Jimmy did. He was halfway up when he realized Vivien hadn't come with them. He turned back and saw her standing by a doorway on the far wall, tidying her hair in an oval mirror.

'You're not coming?' he said. It was meant to be a whisper, but the shape of the room, the dome in the ceiling, made it echo terribly.

She shook her head. 'I have something else to do –

somebody to see.' She flushed. 'Go – go! I can't keep talking, I'm already late.'

Jimmy stayed in the dormitory for about an hour, watching the little girl tap-dance, and then a bell sounded and Nella said, 'That's lunch,' and he figured it was time to say good-bye. She held his hand as they walked together down the corridor, and when they reached the stairs she looked up at him. 'When are you coming to visit me again?' she said. Jimmy hesitated – he hadn't thought that far ahead – but when he looked at her open earnest face, he had a sudden pressing memory of his mother leaving, followed by a lightning-bright flash of awareness that came too fast to pin down but which had something to do with the innocence of children, the willingness with which they trusted, and how little it took for them to put their small soft hand in yours and presume you wouldn't let them down. He said, 'How about in a couple of days' time?' and then she smiled and waved and tapped her way happily along the corridor to the dining room.

'That was the very perfect thing to do,' said Doll later that evening, when he was telling her all about it. She'd listened avidly to his entire account, eyes widening when he mentioned the mirror outside the doctor's room, the way Vivien had blushed – guiltily, they agreed – when she realized Jimmy had seen her fixing herself up ('I told you, Jimmy, didn't I? She's seeing that doctor behind her husband's back'). Now Doll smiled. 'Oh, Jimmy, we're getting so close!'

Jimmy didn't feel so certain. He lit a cigarette. 'I don't know, Doll. It's complicated – I promised Vivien I wouldn't go back to the hospital . . .'

'Yes, and you promised Nella that you would.'

'Then you see my problem.'

'What problem? You're hardly going to break your promise to a child, are you? An orphan at that.'

He wasn't, of course he wasn't, but he obviously hadn't made Doll understand just how caustic Vivien had been.

'Jimmy?' she said again. 'You're not going to disappoint Nella?'

'No, no,' he waved the hand that was holding his cigarette, 'I'll go back. Vivien won't be happy though. She was quite clear about it.'

'You'll bring her round.' Dolly took his face gently between her hands. 'I don't think you realize, Jimmy, how people warm to you.' She brought her face close to his so that her lips were touching his ear. She said playfully, 'Just look how I'm warming to you now.'

Jimmy smiled, but distractedly, as she kissed him. He was busy envisaging Vivien Jenkins's disapproving face when she saw him again at the hospital, defying her direct orders. He was still trying to work out how he would explain his re-appearance – was it enough just to say that Nella had asked him to come? – when Dolly sat back and said, 'It really is the best way.'

Jimmy nodded. She was right; he knew she was.

'Visit Nella, bump into Vivien, set a time and a place and leave the rest to me.' She tilted her head and smiled at him; she looked younger when she did. 'Simple?'

Jimmy managed a faint smile in return. 'Simple.'

And so it had seemed, except that Jimmy didn't bump into Vivien. He went to the hospital every chance he had over the next fortnight, squeezing in visits to Nella between his responsibilities at work, and to his dad, and to Doll. But although he saw Vivien twice from a distance, neither occasion gave him the opportunity to reverse her ill opinion of him and somehow convince her to meet him again. The first time, she'd been leaving the hospital at the same time as Jimmy turned the corner into Highbury Street. She had stopped on the doorstep, glancing in either direction as she lifted up a scarf to hide her face from anyone who might recognize her. He'd picked up pace, but by the time he got near the hospital it was too late and she'd stalked off in the opposite direction, head down against prying eyes.

The second time she hadn't been so careful. Jimmy had just arrived in the hospital reception and was waiting to let Myra (the pewter-haired receptionist – they'd become quite friendly) know that he was heading up to see Nella, when he'd noticed that the door behind the desk stood ajar. He'd been able to see into Dr Tomalin's office, and there he'd glimpsed Vivien, laughing softly at someone hidden behind the door. As he watched, a man's hand came to rest on her bare forearm, and Jimmy felt his stomach start to churn.

He wished he'd brought his camera. He couldn't make out much of the doctor, but he could see Vivien clearly enough: the man's hand on her arm, the happy expression on her face . . .

Of all the days not to have his equipment with him – it would've been all they needed. Jimmy was still berating himself when Myra appeared from nowhere, closed the door, and asked him how his day was treating him.

Then, finally, at the beginning of the third week, as

Jimmy rounded the top of the stairs and started down the corridor towards Nella's dormitory, he saw a familiar figure walking ahead of him. Jimmy lingered where he was, paying fierce and undue attention to the 'Dig for Victory' poster on the wall, taking in the pigeon-toed child with his hoe and spade, while keeping both ears trained on her retreating footsteps. When Vivien had turned the corner he scurried after her, heart beginning to thump as he watched her progress from a distance. She reached a door in the wall, a small door Jimmy had never noticed before, and pulled it open. He followed, surprised when he found a flight of narrow stairs behind, leading upwards. He climbed, quickly but quietly, until a sliver of light ahead revealed the doorway she'd left by. He did the same, finding himself on a floor of the old house with lower ceilings than those below, and with less of a hospital feel. He could hear her distant footsteps but wasn't sure which way she'd gone, until he glanced left and saw her shadow slide across the faded blue and gold wallpaper. He smiled to himself – the boy in him was rather enjoying the chase – and went after her.

Jimmy had a feeling he knew where she was going; she was sneaking off to a secret meeting with Dr Tomalin, high in the quiet private attics of the old house, hidden away where no one would ever think to look for them. Except Jimmy. He poked his head around the corner and watched as Vivien stopped. This time he *did* have his camera with him. Far better to take a genuinely incriminating photograph than go through the rigmarole of setting up a false meeting that might, on photographic paper, seem compromising. This way, too, Vivien would be guilty of an actual indiscretion, and somehow that made Jimmy feel a whole lot easier. There remained the issue of sending the letter (blackmail, wasn't it? Call a spade a spade); Jimmy still found the idea pretty unpalatable, but he hardened his heart.

He watched as she opened the door, and when she made her way inside he crept forwards, removing his camera's lens cap. He stuck his foot in the doorway, just in time to keep it from closing. And then Jimmy lifted his camera to take the shot.

What he saw through the viewfinder, though, made him put it right back down.

Twenty-four

Greenacres, 2011

The Nicolson sisters (minus Daphne, who was in LA to shoot a new network promo but promised to catch the red-eye back to London 'just as soon as they can spare me') brought Dorothy home to Greenacres on Saturday morning. Rose was concerned because she hadn't been able to contact Gerry, but Iris – who always liked to be an authority – declared that she'd already telephoned his college and been told he was away on 'very important' business; the office had promised to get a message to him. Laurel had reached unconsciously for her phone while Iris was making her proclamation, turning it over in her palm, wondering why she still hadn't heard a word about Dr Rufus, but she resisted calling. Gerry worked in his own way, at his own pace, and she knew from experience there was no joy to be had by ringing his office number.

By lunchtime Dorothy was settled in her bedroom, fast asleep, with her white hair resting like a halo on the burgundy pillowcase. The sisters looked at one another and reached a tacit agreement to leave her to it. The weather had cleared up and turned unseasonably warm, and they headed outside to sit on the swing seat beneath the tree and eat the bread rolls Iris had insisted on making solo, swatting away flies and enjoying what must surely be the last hot burst of the year.

The weekend passed smoothly. They installed themselves around Dorothy's bed, reading silently or chatting together in low voices, even attempting Scrabble at one stage (though not for long – Iris never could play a full round without blowing up in the face of Rose's phenomenal knowledge of tricky two-letter words), but most of the time they took turns just sitting in quiet company with their sleeping mother. It was right, Laurel thought, that they'd brought Ma home. Greenacres was where Dorothy belonged, this funny old big-hearted house she'd discovered by chance and recognized immediately as one she must inhabit and possess. 'I always dreamed of a house like this,' she used to tell them, a broad smile spreading across her face as they walked in from the garden. 'For a time I thought I'd lost my chance, but it all came right in the end. As soon as I saw her, I knew she was the one . . .'

Laurel wondered if her mother had been thinking of that long-ago day as they drove her up the driveway on Saturday; whether she'd seen in her mind's eye the old farmer who'd made tea for her and Daddy when they knocked on his door in 1947, the birds that had watched them from behind the boarded-up fireplace, and the young woman she'd been back then, holding firm to her second chance as she looked to the future and tried to escape whatever it was she'd done before. Or had Dorothy been thinking rather, as they wound up the drive, of events that had unfolded that summer's day in 1961 and about the impossibility of ever truly escaping one's past? Or was Laurel being sentimental, and had the tears her mother shed in the passenger seat of Rose's car, the soft soundless tears, been simply the effect of great age and faulty plumbing?

Whatever the case, the move from the hospital had evidently tired her and she slept most of the weekend, eating little and saying even less. Laurel, when it was her turn at the bedside, willed her mother to stir, to open her tired eyes and recognize her eldest daughter, to resume their conversation of the other day. She needed to know what her mother had taken from Vivien Jenkins – it was the crux of the mystery. Henry had been right all along, insisting there was more to his wife's death than met the eye, that she'd been the target of shady con artists. (Con artists plural, Laurel noted – was it merely a turn of phrase, or had her mother acted with someone else? Could it have been Jimmy, the man she'd loved and lost? Was that perhaps *why* they'd been driven apart?) She would have to wait until Monday, though, because Dorothy wasn't talking. In fact, it seemed to Laurel, watching as the old woman slept so peacefully and the curtains fluttered in the light breeze, that her mother had passed through some invisible doorway into that place where ghosts from the past could no longer touch her.

Only once, in the wee hours of Monday morning, was she visited by the terrors that had nipped at her heels in recent weeks. Rose and Iris had both gone back to their own homes for the night, so it was Laurel who woke in the dark with a start and stumbled along the corridor, feeling about the wall for light switches as she went. The thought came to her of the many nights her mother had done the same thing for her: been woken from her sleep by a cry in the dark, and rushed down the hall to chase her daughter's monsters away, to stroke her hair and hum in her ear, 'Hush,

little wing ... there now, hush.' No matter Laurel's con-
flicted feelings towards her mother these days, it seemed
there was a privilege in being able to do the same in return,
particularly for Laurel, who'd left the family home in such a
fraught way, who hadn't been there when her father died,
who'd spent her whole life beholden to no one but herself
and her art.

Laurel climbed into bed with her mother, holding the
old woman firmly but gently. The cotton of Dorothy's long
white nightdress was damp with the labours of her nightmare, and her thin frame trembled. 'It was my fault, Laurel,'
she was saying. 'It was my fault.'

'Hush, hush,' Laurel comforted. 'There now, everything's all right.'

'It was my fault she died.'

'I know, I know it was.' Henry Jenkins came again to
Laurel's mind; his insistence that Vivien had died because
she'd been led to a place she'd otherwise never have gone,
led there by someone she trusted. 'There, there, Ma. It's over
now.'

Dorothy's breathing settled into a slow steady rhythm,
and Laurel thought about the nature of love. That she could
continue to feel it so intensely, despite the things she was
learning about her mother, was remarkable. It seemed that
ugly deeds did not make love disappear; but oh, the disappointment if Laurel let it could have crushed her. It was
an anodyne word, disappointment, but the shame and help-
lessness intrinsic to it were breathtaking. It wasn't that
Laurel expected perfection. She wasn't a child. And she
didn't share Gerry's blind faith that just because Dorothy
Nicolson was their mother she would somehow be found

miraculously innocent of all wrongdoing. Not at all. Laurel was a realist, she understood her mother was a human being and had naturally done things in her life that weren't saintly; she'd hated and wanted and made mistakes that never went away – just as Laurel had herself. But the picture Laurel was beginning to form of precisely what had happened in Dorothy's past, what she'd seen her mother do . . .

'He came to find me.'

Laurel had been drifting off with her thoughts and her mother's faded voice startled her. 'What's that, Ma?'

'I tried to hide, but he found me.'

She was speaking of Henry Jenkins, Laurel realized. It seemed they were drawing ever closer to what had happened on that day in 1961. 'He's gone now, Ma, he's not coming back.'

A whisper: 'I killed him, Laurel.'

Laurel's breath caught. She whispered back, 'I know you did.'

'Can you forgive me, Laurel?'

It was a question Laurel hadn't asked herself, let alone answered. Faced with it in that instant, in the dark quiet of her mother's room, all she could say was, 'Hush now. Everything's going to be all right, Ma. I love you.'

Some hours later, when the sun was just beginning to rise above the treetops, Laurel handed the baton to Rose and headed for the green Mini.

'London again?' said Rose, walking with her along the garden path.

'Oxford today.'

'Oh, Oxford.' Rose twisted her beads. 'More research, is it?'

'It is.'

'Getting close to what you're looking for?'

'You know, Rosie,' said Laurel, sitting in the driver's seat, reaching to pull the door shut behind her, 'I think I am.' She smiled and waved and put the car into reverse, glad to escape before Rose could ask anything that required heavy-duty obfuscation.

The fellow at the desk in the British Library Reading Room had seemed pleased on Friday by her request to locate 'a rather obscure memoir', even more so when Laurel mused as to how one might go about finding what happened to Miss Katy Ellis's correspondence after she died. He'd frowned determination at his computer screen, pausing every so often to jot things down on his notepad, and Laurel's hopes had risen and fallen with his brows, until evidently her rapt attention became a hindrance and he suggested it might take some time and he'd be very happy to continue the search while she got on with something else. Laurel had taken the hint, ducking outside for a quick cigarette (all right, three) and a bit of neurotic pacing, before rushing back to the Reading Room to see how he'd got on.

He'd got on rather well, as it turned out. He slid the piece of paper across the desk with a marathon runner's smile of satisfied exhaustion on his face and said, 'Found her.' The cache of her private papers, at any rate. It turned out they were located in the archives of New College Library, Oxford; Katy Ellis had studied there as a doctoral candidate and her papers had been donated after her death in September 1983. There was a copy of the memoir available, too, but Laurel figured she'd be far more likely to find what she was looking for within the primary documents.

Laurel left her green Mini at the Park and Ride site in Thornhill, and caught the bus into Oxford. The driver directed her to hop off on the High Street, which she did, right opposite Queen's College; she followed directions a short walk past the Bodleian Library, and along Holywell Street, to arrive at the main entrance of New College. She never tired of the university's extraordinary beauty – every stone, every turret and spindle pointing towards the heavens, grated and settled with the weight of the past – but Laurel didn't have time today for sightseeing; she put her hands in her trouser pockets, head down against the chill, and hurried across the grass quadrangle towards the library.

She was greeted inside by a young man with shaggy blue-black hair. Laurel explained who she was and why she'd come, mentioning that the librarian from the British Library had called ahead on Friday to make an appointment.

'Yes, yes,' said the young man (whose name, it transpired, was Ben, and who was – enthusiastically, it had to be said – serving a one-year traineeship in the library), 'I spoke to him myself. You're here to look at one of our alumni collections.'

'The papers belonging to Katy Ellis.'

'That's right. I've brought the archive over from the muniments tower for you.'

'Super. Thank you very much.'

'Don't mention it – any excuse to climb the tower.' He smiled and leaned a little closer, exhibiting an air of conspiracy. 'It's up a spiral staircase, you know, accessed through a door hidden in the panelling of the hall. Like something out of Hogwarts.'

Laurel had read *Harry Potter*, of course, and was no less immune to the charms of old buildings than anyone else, but opening hours were limited, and Katy Ellis's letters were within shouting distance, and the combination of those two facts left her rather panicked at the thought of spending another minute discussing either architecture or fiction with Ben. She smiled with a feigned lack of comprehension (Hogwarts?), he met it with one of sympathetic realization (Muggle), and they both moved on.

'The collection's waiting for you in the archive reading room,' he said. 'I'll take you over there myself, shall I? It's a bit of a maze if you haven't been here before.'

Laurel followed him along a stone corridor, Ben talking happily all the while about the history of New College, until finally they arrived, a great many twists and turns later, in a room with tables laid out and windows overlooking a magnificent medieval wall overgrown with ivy.

'Here you are,' he said, stopping at a table with twenty or so matching boxes stacked on top. 'Are you happy to work here?'

'I'm sure this will be fine.'

'Excellent. There are gloves near the boxes. Please wear them while you're touching the materials. I'll be right over there if you need me – ' he indicated a pile of papers on a desk in the far corner – 'transcribing,' he added, by way of explanation. Laurel didn't ask what for fear he'd tell her, and so, with a nod, Ben left.

Laurel waited for a moment and then whistled quietly

into the stony library silence. Finally she was alone with
Katy Ellis's letters. She fronted up to the desk and cracked
her knuckles – not metaphorically, but literally; it seemed
the right thing to do – and then she donned her reading
glasses and the pair of white gloves and started the hunt for
answers.

The boxes were identical – brown cardboard, acid-
free, each about the size of an encyclopedia. They were
named and numbered with a code Laurel didn't entirely
comprehend but which seemed to indicate a complex catalogue of items. She considered asking Ben for an explanation, but feared a fervid lecture on the history of records
management might result if she did. It appeared the boxes
had been arranged in chronological order . . . Laurel decided
to take a chance that it would all make sense once she got
going.

She opened the lid of box number one and found
several envelopes inside. The first contained twenty or so
letters bound with white tape and supported with a stiff
piece of board. Laurel eyed the large pile of boxes. It seemed
Katy Ellis had been a prolific correspondent, but with
whom had she corresponded? By the looks of it, the letters
were arranged in order of receipt, but there had to be a
better method of finding what she needed than simple trial
and error.

Laurel drummed her fingers, thinking, and then looked
over the top of her glasses at the table. She smiled as she
spied what she'd been missing – the index card – taking it
up quickly and glancing over the whole to check that it contained, as she'd hoped, a list of senders and recipients. It
did. Holding her breath, Laurel ran her finger down the

sender column, hesitating first at J for Jenkins, next at L for
Longmeyer, and finally V for Vivien.

None of the options was listed.

Laurel looked again, more carefully this time. Still she
came up blank. There was no reference in the index list to
any letters from Vivien Longmeyer or Vivien Jenkins. And
yet Katy Ellis had referred to such letters in the snippet of
Born to Teach quoted in Henry Jenkins's biography. Laurel
pulled out the photocopy she'd taken in the British Library.
There – it said so in black and white: *Over the course of our
long sea voyage, I was able to gain Vivien's trust sufficiently
to establish a relationship that continued over many years.
We corresponded by letter with warm regularity until her
tragic and untimely death during the Second World War . . .*
Laurel gritted her teeth and checked the list one final time.

Nothing.

It made no sense. Katy Ellis said there were letters – a
lifetime of them, *warmly regular*. Where were they? Laurel
glanced over at Ben's hunched back and decided there was
nothing for it.

'That's all the letters we received,' he said when she'd
explained. Laurel pointed out the lines from the memoir and
Ben wrinkled his nose and agreed that it was odd, but then
he brightened. 'Perhaps she destroyed the letters before she
died?' He wasn't to know that he was crushing Laurel's
dreams like a dried leaf between his fingers. 'That happens
sometimes,' he continued, 'particularly in the case of people
who intend to donate their correspondence. They make sure
anything they don't want seen is no longer part of the collection. Is there any reason she might have done that, do
you know?'

Laurel thought about it. It was possible, she supposed. Vivien's letters might have contained something Katy Ellis considered sensitive or incriminating – God, anything was possible at this point. Laurel's brain hurt. She said, 'Could they be stored somewhere else?'

Ben shook his head. 'New College Library was the sole beneficiary of Katy Ellis's records. Everything she left is here.'

Laurel could have thrown the neat file boxes around the room, given poor Ben a real show. To have come so close only to be thwarted at this point – it was demoralizing. Ben smiled sympathetically and Laurel was about to slump back to her desk when she thought of something. 'Journals,' she said quickly.

'What's that?'

'Journals. Katy Ellis kept journals – she mentions them in the memoir. Do you know if they're part of the collection?'

'I do, and they are,' he said. 'I brought them down for you.'

He indicated a stack of books on the floor by the table and Laurel could have kissed him. She refrained, taking her seat instead and seizing up the first leather-bound volume. It was dated 1929, the year, Laurel remembered, that Katy Ellis had accompanied Vivien Longmeyer on the long sea voyage from Australia to England. The first page held a black and white photograph, inserted neatly using gold document corners, speckled now with age. It was the portrait of a young woman in long skirts and a prim blouse, her hair – hard to tell, but Laurel had a feeling it was red – parted on one side and then pressed into neat crimped curls. Everything about her attire was modest and bluestocking-demure, but her eyes were lit with determination. She'd lifted her chin at the camera and she wasn't smiling so much as looking pleased with herself. Laurel decided that she liked Miss Katy Ellis, even more so when she read the small annotation at the bottom of the page: *A small and impudent vanity, but the author encloses here this photograph, taken at Hunter & Gould Studios, Brisbane, as a record of a young woman on the verge of her great adventure in the year of our Lord, nineteen hundred and twenty-nine.*

Laurel turned to the first page of neat penmanship, an entry dated 18 May 1929 and headed 'Week One – New Beginnings'. She smiled at Katy Ellis's slightly pompous tone, and then drew breath as the name Vivien leapt out at her. In amongst a perfunctory description of the ship – the accommodations, the other passengers and (in most detail of all) the meals, Laurel read the following:

My travelling companion is a girl, aged eight, by the name of Vivien Longmeyer. She is a most unusual child, quite perplexing. Pleasant enough to look at – dark hair, parted in the middle and kept (by me) in plaits down her back, very large brown eyes, and full lips of a deep cherry colour that she holds together with a firmness giving the impression either of petulance or strength of mind – I have yet to decide which. She is of a proud and wilful nature, I can tell that by the way those dark eyes bore directly into mine, and certainly the aunt fashioned me with all manner of reports as to the sharpness of the girl's tongue and the readiness of her fists; thus far, however, I have seen no evidence

*of her rumoured physicality, nor has she uttered more than
five words, sharp or otherwise, in my hearing. Disobedient,
she is certainly; ill-mannered, there is no doubt; and yet
somehow, in one of those inexplicable kinks of human personality, the child is oddly likeable. She draws me to her;
even when she is doing nothing more than sitting on the
deck and following the passing sea; it is not mere physical
beauty, although there is undoubtedly much that is pleasing
in her dark features – it is an aspect of herself that comes
from deep within and communicates itself quite unwittingly
so that one cannot help but watch.*

*I should add that there is an uncanny quiet about her.
She chooses, when other children might be running and
larking about the decks, to hide herself away and sit almost
entirely still. It is an* unnatural *stillness, and one for which I
had not been prepared.*

Apparently Vivien Longmeyer continued to fascinate
Katy Ellis, for along with further comments about the journey and notes for lesson plans she intended to use when she
arrived in England, the journal entries over the next few
weeks contained similar reports. Katy Ellis observed Vivien
from a distance, interacting only insofar as it was necessary
for the two of them in their shared travels, until finally, in
an entry dated 5 July 1929 and titled 'Week Seven', there
appeared to come a breakthrough.

*It was hot this morning, and a mild breeze blew from the
north. We were sitting together on the front deck after
breakfast when a most peculiar thing happened. I told
Vivien to go back to the cabin and fetch her exercise book*

so that we might run through some lessons – I'd promised her aunt before we left that Vivien's lessons would not be neglected while we were on the seas (she fears, I think, that if the girl's intellect is deemed unsatisfactory by the English uncle, she will be sent straight back to Australia). Our lessons are an interesting charade and always the same: I draw and point to the book, explaining various principles until my brain aches with the eternal quest for clarity of explanation; and Vivien stares with blank boredom at the fruits of my labours.

Still, I made a promise and so I persist. This morning, not for the first time, Vivien failed to do as I'd asked. She didn't so much as deign to meet my eyes, and I was forced to repeat myself, not twice but thrice, and in increasingly stern tones. Still the child ignored me, until finally (the urge to tears pressing in my throat) I begged to know why she so often behaves as if she cannot hear me.

Perhaps my loss of control moved the child, for she sighed then, and told me the reason. She looked me in the eye and explained that seeing as I was merely a part of her dream, a figment of her own imagination, she didn't see any point in listening, unless the subject of my 'chatter' (her word) was of interest.

Another child might have been suspected of cheek and clipped about the ears for giving such a response, but Vivien is not another child. For one thing, she does not lie – her aunt, for all her eager criticism of the child, conceded I would never hear an untruth from the girl's mouth ('Frank to the point of rudeness, that one') – and so I was intrigued. I tried to keep my voice steady, asking as nonchalantly as if I were enquiring the time of day what she meant by *saying I was part of a dream. She blinked those wide brown eyes and said, 'I fell asleep beside the creek back home and I haven't woken up yet.' Everything that had happened since, she told me – the news of her family's motorcar accident, her removal like an unwanted package to England, this long sea voyage with only a teacher for company – was nothing more than a great big bad dream.*

I asked her why she didn't wake up, how it was possible that someone could sleep for such a very long time, and she responded that it was bush magic. That she'd fallen asleep beneath some ferns on the edge of the enchanted creek (the one with the little lights, she said, and the tunnel that leads through a great engine room, right to the other side of the world) – that's why she didn't wake up as she otherwise might. I asked her, then, how she would know when she had finally woken up, and she tilted her head as if I might be simple: 'When I open my eyes and see that I'm home again.' Of course, her firm little face added.

Laurel flicked through the journals until, two weeks later, Katy Ellis revisited the subject.

I have been probing – delicately – about this dream world of Vivien's, for it interests me greatly that a child might choose to comprehend a traumatic event in such a way. I gather, from the titbits she feeds me, that she has conjured a shadow land around her, a place of darkness through which she must quest in order to get back to her sleeping self in the 'real world' of the creek bank in Australia. She told me she believes that sometimes she comes close to waking; if she sits very, very still, she says she can glimpse beyond the veil; she can see and hear her family going about their usual business, oblivious to her standing on the other side, watching them. At least now I understand why the child exhibits such a profound quiet and stillness.

The girl's theory of her waking dream is one thing. I can well understand the instinct a person might have to retreat into a safe imaginary world. What disturbs me more is Vivien's seeming gladness in the face of punishment. Or if not gladness, because that is not it precisely, her resignation, almost relief, when met with reprimand. I witnessed a brief incident the other day in which she was wrongly accused of having taken an elderly woman's hat from the top deck. She was innocent of the crime, a fact of which I was certain, having seen the ghastly cloche take up with the breeze and dance right overboard. As I watched, though – stunned for a moment into silence – Vivien presented herself for punishment, receiving a fierce tongue-lashing; when threatened with a strapping, the girl seemed quite prepared to accept it. The expression in her eyes as she was scolded was one almost of relief. I found my brio then, and stepped in to stop the miscarriage of justice, informing them in the chilliest of tones as to the hat's true fate, before directing Vivien to safety. But the look I'd seen in the girl's eyes troubled me long after. Why, I wondered, would a child willingly accept punishment, particularly for a crime they hadn't committed?

A few pages later, Laurel found the following:

I believe I have answered one of my own most pressing questions. I have sometimes heard Vivien shouting out in her sleep; the episodes are usually short-lived, ending just as soon as the girl rolls over, but the other night the situation reached a peak and I rushed from my bed to soothe her. She was speaking very quickly as she clung to my arms – it is the most effusive I have seen her – and I was able to gather from what she said that she has come to believe the death of her family was her fault in some way. A ridiculous notion, when held up to the yardstick of adult perception, for as I understand it they were killed in a motorcar accident while she was many miles away, but childhood is not a place of logic and measuring sticks, and somehow (I cannot help but think the girl's aunt might have helped it on its way) the idea has stuck.

Laurel looked up from Katy Ellis's journal. Ben was making packing-up noises and she glanced, dismayed, at her watch. It was ten minutes to one – damn; she'd been warned the library shut for an hour over lunch. Laurel was clinging to any reference to Vivien, feeling she was getting somewhere, but there wasn't time to read everything. She skimmed through the rest of the sea voyage, until finally she reached an entry written in shakier handwriting than those previous – written, Laurel gathered, as Katy Ellis took the train to York, where she was to be employed as a governess.

The conductor is coming now, so I will record quickly, before I forget, the strange behaviour of my young charge as we disembarked in London yesterday. No sooner had we cleared the gangplank, and I was looking this way and that in an attempt to discern where we ought to go next, than she hopped down on all fours – never mind the dress I'd specially hand-sponged and prepared for her to wear when meeting her uncle – and pressed her ear to the ground. I am not one to embarrass easily, so it was no such paltry emotion that made me shriek when I saw her, rather concern that the child would find herself trampled by the crowds of foot traffic, or the hoofs of a rearing horse.

I couldn't help myself, I shouted with alarm: 'What are you doing? Get up!'

To which – one should hardly be surprised – there came no answer.

'What are you doing, child?' I demanded.

She shook her head and said quickly, 'I can't hear it.'

'Hear what?' I replied.

'The sound of the wheels turning.'

I remembered then what she had told me about the engine room in the centre of the earth, the tunnel that would lead her home.

'I can't hear them any more.'

She was beginning to realize, of course, the finality of her situation, for like me she will not see her homeland again for many years, if at all, and certainly not the version of it to which she longs to return. Though my heart broke for the stubborn sapling, I did not offer her words of meaningless encouragement, for it is best, surely, that she comes in time to escape the grip of her fantasies. Indeed, it seemed there was nothing for me to say or do but to take her hand kindly and shepherd her along to where I'd spotted the meeting place her aunt had agreed upon with the English uncle. Vivien's pronouncement troubled me, though, because I knew the turmoil it would be causing within the child, and I knew too that the moment fast approached when I must bid her farewell and send her on her way.

Perhaps I would be feeling less disquieted now if I'd sensed more warmth from the uncle. Alas, I did not. Her new guardian is headmaster of the Nordstrom School in Oxfordshire, and possibly it was some aspect of professional (male?) pride that erected a barrier between us, for he seemed determined not to notice my presence, stopping only to inspect the child, before telling her to come along, they hadn't a second to spare.

No, he did not strike me as the sort of fellow to open his home with the warmth and understanding a sensitive little girl whose recent history is filled with so much distress will need.

I have written to the Australian aunt with my misgivings, but I do not hold out high hopes she will leap to the girl's aid and demand her immediate return. In the meantime, I have promised to write regularly to Vivien in Oxfordshire, and I intend to do so. Would that my new position didn't take me to the other side of the country – I would gladly tuck the girl under my wing and keep her safe from harm. Despite myself, and against the best theories of my chosen career – to observe but not absorb – I have developed strong personal feelings for her. I dearly hope that time and circumstance – perhaps the cultivation of a good friend nearby? – will conspire to mend the deep wound rent inside the child by her recent suffering. It may be that strong emotion causes me to overstate and overthink the future, to fall victim to my worst imaginings, but I fear otherwise. Vivien is at risk of disappearing deep inside the safety of the dream world she's created, remaining a stranger to the real world of human beings, and thus becoming easy prey, as she grows to adulthood, to those who would look to gain by *her ill-treatment. One wonders (suspicious-mindedly per-haps) as to the uncle's reason for accepting the child as his ward. Duty? It is possible. A fondness for children? Afearedly not. With the beauty she is sure to attain, and the vast wealth I have learned she will inherit at maturity, I worry there is much she will possess that others may seek to take.*

Laurel sat back and stared unseeing at the medieval wall on the other side of the window. She bit her thumbnail as the words went round and round inside her head: *I worry there is much she will possess that others may seek to take.* Vivien Jenkins had an inheritance. It changed everything. She was a wealthy woman with the sort of character, or so her confidante had worried, that made her the perfect victim for those who might wish to profit by her.

Laurel took off her glasses, closing her eyes as she rubbed the tender patches on the sides of her nose. Money. It was one of the oldest motivators, wasn't it? She sighed. It was so base, so predictable, but that had to be it. Her mother didn't seem at all the type to desire more than she had, let alone to make plans to take it from someone else, but that was now. The Dorothy Nicolson Laurel knew was removed by decades from the hungry young girl she'd once been, a nineteen-year-old girl who'd lost her family in the Coventry Blitz and had to fend for herself in wartime London.

Certainly, the regrets her mother was expressing now, her talk of mistakes and second chances and forgiveness, fitted the theory. And what was it she'd used to say to Iris – nobody likes a girl who expects more than the others?

Might that have been a lesson she learned from her own experience? The more Laurel thought about it, the more unavoidable the conclusion seemed. It was money her mother had needed, money she'd tried to take from Vivien Jenkins, but it had all gone terribly wrong. She wondered again whether Jimmy had been involved; whether it was the plan's failure that had seen their relationship founder. And she wondered what part exactly the plan had played in Vivien's death. Henry had held Dorothy responsible for his wife's death: she might have fled to a life of atonement, but Vivien's grieving husband had refused to give up his search, and he'd found her eventually. Laurel had seen what happened next with her own eyes.

Ben was behind her now, making small throat-clearing noises as the wall clock's minute hand slipped past the hour. Laurel pretended not to hear him, wondering what had gone wrong with her mother's plan. Had Vivien realized what was happening and put a stop to it, or was it something else, something worse that made it all blow up? She eyed the stack of journals, scanning the spines for the year 1941.

'I'd leave you here, really I would,' Ben said, 'only the head archivist is the sort to string me up by my toes.' He gulped. 'Or worse.'

Oh, bugger. Bloody hell. Laurel's heart was heavy, there was a sick swirling in the pit of her stomach, and now she was going to have to cool her heels for fifty-seven minutes while the very book that might contain the answers she needed languished here in a locked room.

Twenty-five

London, April 1941

Jimmy stood with his foot pressed against the door of the hospital attic, staring through the crack after Vivien. He was puzzled. This was not the illicit scene of an extra-marital rendezvous he'd expected. There were children everywhere, playing with puzzles on the floor, jumping round in circles, one standing on her hands. He was in the old nursery, Jimmy realized; these children, presumably, Dr Tomalin's orphaned patients. Through some unspoken awareness, their collective attention was caught and they looked up to see that Vivien was among them. As Jimmy watched, they all rushed towards her, arms out like aeroplanes. She was beaming, too, an enormous smile on her face as she dropped to her knees and held out her own arms to catch as many as she could.

They all started talking then, rapidly and with some agitation, about flying and ships and ropes and fairies, and Jimmy knew that he was witnessing a conversation with its roots in an earlier time. Vivien seemed to know what they were on about though, she was nodding thoughtfully, and not in that pretend way adults have when they're interacting with children – she was listening and considering, and the slight frown she wore made it clear that she was trying to find solutions. She was different now from the way she'd been when she spoke to him in the street; more at ease, not so on guard. When they'd all said their piece and the noise fell away – as it sometimes seems to, all at once – she held up her hands and said, 'Why don't we just start and we'll address each problem as we get to it?'

They agreed, or at least Jimmy presumed that's what had happened, for without a word of complaint they dispersed again, all industry as they dragged chairs and other seemingly random objects – blankets, broomsticks, dolls with eye patches – into the cleared section at the centre of the room and began assembling them into some sort of carefully worked-out structure. He realized then, and it made him laugh to himself with unexpected pleasure. A ship was forming before his very eyes – there was the prow, and the mast, and a plank propped up at one end by a footstool, the other by a wooden bench. As Jimmy watched, a sail went up, a bed sheet folded into a triangle with fine ropes holding each corner firm and proud.

Vivien had seated herself on an upturned crate and drawn a book from somewhere – her handbag, Jimmy supposed. She opened it and ran her fingers along the middle margins, creasing it flat, and then said, 'Let's start with Captain Hook and the Lost Boys – now, where's Wendy?'

'Here I am,' said a girl of about eleven, her arm in a sling.

'Good,' said Vivien. 'Make sure you're ready for your entrance. It won't be long.'

A boy with a hand-made parrot on his shoulder and a hook made from some sort of shiny cardboard in his hand, began to walk towards Vivien in a rollicking way that made her laugh.

They were rehearsing a play, Jimmy realized, *Peter Pan*. His mother had taken him to see it once when he was a boy. They'd made the trip to London and then had tea afterwards at Liberty's, a fancy tea it had been, during which Jimmy had sat silent and out of place, stealing glances at his mother's tight wistful expression as she peered over her shoulder at the clothing racks. There'd been a fight between his parents later over money (what else?) and Jimmy had listened from his bedroom as something smashed into pieces on the floor. He'd closed his eyes and thought back to the play; his favourite moment was when Peter had flung out his arms and addressed all in the audience who might be dreaming of Neverland: 'Do you believe in fairies, girls and boys?' he'd shouted. 'If you believe, clap your hands; don't let Tink die.' And Jimmy had been moved to stand up from his seat, thin legs trembling hopefully as he brought his hands together and shouted back, 'Yes!' with all the emphatic trust that in doing so he was bringing Tinkerbell back to life and saving everything that was more and magical in the world.

'Nathan, have you got the torch?'

Jimmy blinked back to the present.

'Nathan?' Vivien said. 'We need the torch now.'

'I'm shining it already,' said a small boy with curly red hair and his foot in a brace. He was sitting on the floor, aiming his torch at the sail.

'Oh yes,' said Vivien. 'So you are. Well, that's – good.'

'But we can hardly see it,' said another boy, standing

with his hands on his hips. He was craning up at the sail, squinting through his glasses at the spread of feeble light.

'It's not much use if we can't see Tinkerbell,' said the boy playing Captain Hook. 'It won't work at all.'

'Yes it will,' Vivien said determinedly. 'Of course it will. The power of suggestion is a tremendous thing. If we all say we can see the fairy, then the audience will, too.'

'But we can't see her.'

'Well, no, but if we *say* we can—'

'You mean lie?'

Vivien glanced towards the ceiling, searching for the words to explain, and the children began to bicker amongst themselves.

'Excuse me,' said Jimmy from where he stood in the doorway. Nobody seemed to hear him so he said it again, louder this time. 'Excuse me?'

They all turned then. Vivien drew breath when she saw him, and then she scowled. Jimmy admitted to taking a certain pleasure in upsetting her, in showing her things didn't always go her way.

'I was just wondering,' he said. 'What if you used a photographer's light? It's similar to a torch but far more powerful.'

Children being what they were, not one reacted with suspicion or even surprise that a stranger had joined them in the attic nursery and weighed in on this most specific of conversations. Instead, there was silence as they all considered his suggestion, light whispery noise as they discussed it, and then: 'Yes!' shouted one of the boys, jumping to his feet with excitement.

'Perfect!' said another.

'But we don't have one,' said the gloomy boy in the glasses.

'I could get you one,' Jimmy said. 'I work at a newspaper; we have a studio filled with lights.'

More excited cheering and chatter came from the children.

'But how would we make it look like a fairy, flying about and whatnot?' said the same doleful chap, piping up over the top of the others.

Jimmy left his doorjamb and entered the room. All the children had swivelled now to face him; Vivien was glowering, her copy of *Peter Pan* closed on her lap. Jimmy ignored her. 'I guess you'd have to shine it from somewhere high. Yes, that would work, and if you made sure it was always angling down towards the stage, it would focus a smaller light, rather than a wide, general brightness, and maybe if you fashioned a sort of funnel . . .'

'But none of us is tall enough to operate it.' The kid in the glasses again. 'Not from up there.' Orphan or not, Jimmy was starting to dislike him.

Vivien had been watching the exchange with a firm expression on her face, willing Jimmy, he knew, to remember what she'd said – to let the suggestion go and just disappear – but he couldn't do it. He could picture how brilliant it was going to look, and he could think of a hundred ways to make it work. If they put a ladder in the corner, or else attached it to a broom – reinforced somehow – and wielded it like a fishing rod, or else – 'I'll do it,' he said suddenly. 'I'll operate the light.'

'No!' Vivien said, standing.

'Yes!' cried the children.

'You couldn't.' She gave him a flinty look – 'You *won't*.'

'He could!' 'He will!' 'He *must*!' shouted the mass of children.

Jimmy spotted Nella then, sitting on the floor; she waved at him and then glanced around at the others, a glimmer of unmistakable pride and ownership in her eyes. How could he say no? Jimmy raised his palms at Vivien in a gesture of not entirely genuine apology, and then he grinned at the kids. 'That does it,' he said. 'I'm in. You've found yourselves a new Tinkerbell.'

It was hard to believe later, but when Jimmy offered to play Tinkerbell in the hospital play, he hadn't been thinking – even remotely – of the meeting he was supposed to be setting up with Vivien Jenkins. He'd merely become swept up in his grand vision for how they'd be able to represent the fairy with his photographer's light. Dolly didn't mind either way: 'Oh, Jimmy, you clever thing,' she said, drawing excitedly on her cigarette. 'I knew you'd think of something.'

Jimmy took the praise and let her believe it was all part of his plan. She was so happy lately, and it was such a relief to have his old Doll back. 'I've been thinking about the seaside,' she'd say some evenings when she smuggled him through Mrs White's larder window and they lay together in that narrow sink-in-the-middle bed of hers. 'Can't you just picture us, Jimmy? Growing old together, our children around us, grandchildren one day, visiting in their flying cars. We could get one of those swing seats for two – what do you say to that, lovely boy?'

Jimmy said yes please. And then he kissed her again on

her bare neck and made her laugh and thanked God for this new intimacy and warmth they were sharing. Yes, he wanted what she described; he wanted it so badly it hurt. If it pleased her to think he and Vivien were working together and growing closer, then it was a fiction he was glad enough to go along with.

The reality, as he knew only too well, was rather different. Over the next couple of weeks, as Jimmy fronted up to every scheduled rehearsal he could manage, Vivien's hostility astonished him. He couldn't believe she was the same person he'd met in the canteen that night, who'd seen his photograph of Nella and told him about her work at the hospital; now it was as if it were beneath her to exchange more than a few words with him. Jimmy was pretty sure she'd have ignored him entirely if she could have. He'd expected coldness to a degree – Doll had prepared him for how cruel Vivien Jenkins could be when she took against a person; what caught him by surprise was how personal her hatred was. They hardly knew each other, and furthermore she had no way of suspecting his connection to Dolly.

One day they were both laughing at something funny one of the children had done, and Jimmy glanced over, as one adult might to another, wanting nothing more than to share the moment. She sensed his gaze and met it, but the minute she saw him smiling, she let her own happy expression drop away. Vivien's animosity put Jimmy between a rock and a hard place. In some respects it suited him to be so loathed – the idea of blackmail didn't sit well with Jimmy, but he felt easier and more justified about the plan when Vivien treated him like nothing; yet without gaining her trust, if not her affection, he wasn't going to be able to make the plan work.

So Jimmy kept trying. He forced aside the resentment he felt at Vivien's hostility, her disloyalty towards Doll, the way she'd cast off his glittering girl and brought her so low, and he focused instead on how she was with the hospital orphans. The way she created a world into which they could disappear when they came through the door, their real problems left behind in the downstairs dormitories and wards of the hospital. The way they all watched her, staring spellbound when rehearsal was over and she wove stories for them about tunnels through the centre of the earth, and dark magical creeks without bottoms, and tiny lights beneath the water that called to children to come just a little closer . . .

And eventually, as rehearsals continued, Jimmy began to suspect that Vivien Jenkins's antipathy was fading; that she no longer hated him quite so much as she had at first. She continued to avoid conversation, acknowledging his contributions with no more than the barest of nods, but sometimes Jimmy caught her looking at him when she thought he didn't know, and it seemed to him that the expression on her face was not angry so much as it was thoughtful, even curious. Perhaps that's why he made his mistake. He'd started to perceive a growing – well, not a warmth, but at least an increasing thaw between them, and one day in mid-April, when the children had run off to lunch and he and Vivien were left packing up the ship, he'd asked her whether she had any of her own.

It was supposed to be the start of a light exchange, but Vivien's whole body had seemed to freeze, and Jimmy had known right away that he'd made an error – if not exactly how – and that it was too late to take it back.

'No.' The word when it came was as sharp as a stone in his shoe. She cleared her throat. 'I can't have children.'

Jimmy had wished right about then for a deep tunnel through the centre of the earth into which he could fall and fall and fall. He muttered a 'Sorry', which elicited a slight nod from Vivien, and then she finished wrapping up the sail and left the attic, letting the door shut reproachfully behind her.

He'd felt like an insensitive buffoon. It wasn't that he'd forgotten why he was really there – the kind of person she was, what she'd done to Dolly – it was only that, well, Jimmy didn't like hurting anyone. Remembering how she'd stiffened when he said it made him wince, so he brought it to mind over and over, punishing himself for being so tactless. That night when he was out photographing the latest bomb damage, pointing his camera at the newest souls to join the ranks of the homeless and bereaved, half of his brain kept turning over ways he could make it up to her.

He arrived at the hospital early the next day and waited for her across the street, smoking nervously. He'd have sat on the front steps only he had a feeling she'd turn and walk the other way if she saw him there.

When she came hurrying down the street, he got rid of his cigarette and went to meet her. He handed her a photograph.

'What's this?' she said.

'Nothing, really,' he said, watching as she turned it over

in her hands. 'I took it for you – last night. It reminded me of your story, you know, the creek with the lights at the very bottom, and the people – the family on the other side of the veil.'

She looked at the picture.

He'd taken it as dawn was breaking; sunlight had made shards of glass in the ruins glitter and sparkle, and beyond the rising smoke you could make out the shadowy forms of the family who'd just emerged from the Anderson shelter that had saved their lives. Jimmy hadn't slept after he took it, he'd headed straight over to the newspaper offices to develop the print for Vivien.

She didn't say anything, and the look on her face made Jimmy think she might be going to cry.

'I feel terrible,' he said. Vivien glanced at him. 'What I said yesterday. I upset you. I'm sorry.'

'You weren't to know.' She put the photograph carefully in her bag.

'Still—'

'You weren't to know.' And then she almost smiled, at least he thought she did; it was hard to tell because she turned quickly towards the door and hurried inside.

The rehearsal that day flew by. The children barrelled into the room and filled it with light and noise, and then the lunch bell rang and they disappeared as quickly as they'd come; a part of Jimmy had been tempted to go with them, to avoid the awkwardness of being alone with Vivien, but he'd have hated himself for his weakness if he had, so he stayed to help dismantle the ship.

He felt her watching him while he was stacking chairs, but he didn't look over; he didn't know what he'd see in her face and he didn't want to feel worse than he already did. Her voice, when she spoke, sounded different. 'Why were you in the canteen that night, Jimmy Metcalfe?'

At that, Jimmy did glance sideways; she'd turned her attention to the backdrop she was painting with palm trees and sand for the play. There was a strange formality in her use of his full name, and for some reason it sent a not-unpleasant shudder down his spine. He couldn't tell her about Dolly, he knew that, but Jimmy wasn't a liar. He said, 'I was meeting someone.'

She looked over at him and the faintest of smiles animated her lips.

Jimmy never did know when to stop talking. 'We were supposed to meet somewhere else,' he said, 'only I went to the canteen instead.'

'Why?'

'Why?'

'Why didn't you stick to your original plan?'

'I don't know. It just felt like the right thing to do.'

Vivien was still studying him, her face giving no hint as to her thoughts, and then she turned back to the frond she was working on. 'I'm glad,' she said, an edge to her other-wise clear voice. 'I'm really glad you did.'

Things changed that day. It wasn't what she said, though that was nice enough, it was an inexplicable feeling that had come over Jimmy when she looked at him, a sense of connection between them that came flooding back when he thought about the exchange afterwards. None of it had

been particularly meaningful, yet the whole thing had meant
something. Jimmy knew that at the time, and he knew it
later when Dolly asked for her usual report of the day's
progress and he didn't mention that part. It would have
made Doll glad, he knew – she'd have seen it as evidence
that he was getting closer to winning Vivien's trust – but
Jimmy said nothing. The conversation with Vivien was his;
it felt like progress of some kind and not of the sort Dolly
would have wanted. He didn't want to share it; he didn't
want it spoiled.

The next day Jimmy turned up at the hospital with
a spring in his step. But when he opened the door and
delivered the gift of a glorious ripe orange to Myra (whose
birthday it was), she told him Vivien wasn't there. 'She's not
well. She telephoned this morning and said she wasn't able
to get out of bed. She wondered if you'd take over the
rehearsal.'

'I can do that,' said Jimmy, wondering, suddenly,
whether Vivien's absence had anything to do with what had
happened between them; whether perhaps she'd regretted
letting down her guard. He frowned at the floor and then
looked up at Myra from beneath his hair. 'Sick, did you
say?'

'She didn't sound well at all, poor lamb. No need to
look so glum, though – she'll mend. She always does.' Myra
held up the orange. 'I'll save her half, shall I? Give it to her
at the next rehearsal.'

Only Vivien wasn't there at the next rehearsal either.

'Still in bed,' Myra told Jimmy when he came through
the door later in the week. 'Best thing for it, too.'

'Is it serious?'

'I shouldn't think so. She does seem to have bad luck, poor dear, but she'll be back on her feet soon enough – she never can stand being away from the children too long.'

'This has happened before?'

Myra smiled, but the gesture was restrained by something else, an element of realization, and almost of kindly concern. 'Everybody's poorly sometimes, Mr Metcalfe. Mrs Jenkins has her share of setbacks, but don't we all?' She hesitated, and when she spoke again her voice was soft but firm. 'Listen, Jimmy dear, I can see you care for her, and that's very kind of you. Heaven knows she's an angel, all she does for the children here. But I'm sure it's nothing to worry about and that her husband will be taking good care of her.' She smiled again, in a motherly way. 'Put her out of your mind now, won't you?'

Jimmy said he would and then started up the stairs, but Myra's advice gave him pause. Vivien was unwell, surely to think of her would seem natural – why then was Myra so intent on Jimmy putting her out of his mind? The way Myra said 'her husband' had been pointed, too. It was the sort of thing she might have said to someone like Dr Tomalin, a fellow who had designs on another man's wife.

He didn't have a copy of the play, but Jimmy gave the rehearsal his best shot. The kids went easy on him, running through their parts, arguing rarely, and all was going well. He was even beginning to feel a little pleased with himself, until they finished packing away the set, and gathered on the floor by his upturned crate to beg a story of him. Jimmy told them he didn't know any, and when they refused to believe him, he made a failed attempt to retell one of Vivien's, before remembering – just in time to avoid a revolt – the *Nightingale Star*. They listened wide-eyed, and Jimmy realized, as he hadn't before, how much he had in common with the patients of Dr Tomalin's hospital.

With all the activity, he forgot about Myra's comments, and it wasn't until he'd said goodbye to the kids and was heading back downstairs that Jimmy started to muse on how best to reassure her she was imagining things. He fronted up to her desk when he reached the foyer, but before he could say a word, reassuring or otherwise, Myra said, 'There you are, Jimmy. Dr Tomalin wants to say hello,' with just the sort of reverence she might have used if the king himself had decided to drop by for the afternoon and expressed an interest in meeting him. She reached to brush a piece of lint from his collar.

Jimmy waited, aware of a rising bitterness in his throat, the same feeling he used to get as a boy when he imagined confronting the man who'd stolen his mum away from them. The minutes felt interminable until finally the door near the desk opened and a dignified gentleman emerged. Jimmy's antagonism dissolved, leaving him mightily confused. The other man had white hair, neatly cropped, and glasses so thick his light blue eyes were saucers behind them; he was eighty years old if he was a day.

'So. You're Jimmy Metcalfe,' the doctor said, as he reached to shake Jimmy's hand. 'I trust you're getting on all right?'

'Yes, thank you, sir. Very well.' Jimmy was fumbling, trying to grasp the meaning of it all. The man's age didn't preclude him from a love affair with Vivien Jenkins, not entirely, but still . . .

'On something of a tight leash, I'd imagine,' the doctor continued, 'between Myra here and Mrs Jenkins. Granddaughter of an old friend of mine, you know, young Vivien.'

'I didn't know.'

'No? Well. Now you do.'

Jimmy nodded and attempted a smile.

'Anyway. Tremendous work you're doing, helping out with the children. Very kind. Much obliged.' And with that he nodded stiffly and retreated to his office, a slight limp in his left leg.

'He likes you,' Myra said, eyes wide as the door closed.

Jimmy's thoughts were circling as he tried to sort his certainties from his suspicions. 'Really?'

'Oh yes.'

'How could you tell?'

'He acknowledged your existence. He doesn't have time for many adults. Prefers children, always has.'

'You've known him a long time?'

'I've worked for him these past thirty years.' She puffed out proudly, straightening her cross so it sat flat in the V of her blouse. 'I tell you,' she said, eyeing Jimmy over the top of her half-spectacles, 'he doesn't tolerate many adults in his hospital. You're the only one I've ever seen him make an effort with.'

'Except Vivien, of course.' Jimmy was digging. Myra, surely, would be able to set the record straight. 'Mrs Jenkins, I should say.'

'Oh yes,' Myra twirled her hand, 'of course. But then

he's known her since she was a child herself – it's hardly the same thing. He's like a grandfather to her. In fact, I'd wager you've her to thank for him giving you the time of day just now. Must've put in a good word for you.' Myra caught herself then. 'Anyway, he likes you. That's lovely. Now – don't you have photographs to take for my newspaper tomorrow morning?'

Jimmy gave a mock salute that made her smile and then he started on his way.

His head was spinning as he walked home.

Dolly had been wrong – no matter how positive she'd been, she'd got it wrong. There was no affair between Dr Tomalin and Vivien; the old man was 'like a grandfather' to her. And she – Jimmy shook his head, horrified at the things he'd thought, the way he'd judged her – she was no adulteress, she was just a woman, a *good* woman at that, who'd given up her time to bring a bit of happiness to a group of orphans who'd lost everything.

It was strange, perhaps, when everything he'd believed so strongly had been proved a lie, but Jimmy felt oddly buoyant. He couldn't wait to tell Doll; there was no need now to go through with the plan – Vivien was guilty of nothing.

'Except being nasty to me,' Dolly replied when he said as much to her. 'But I suppose that counts for nothing now you're such good friends.'

'Stop it, Doll,' Jimmy said. 'It's not like that at all. Look—' He reached across the table to take her hands, adopting the sort of light gentle voice that suggested the whole thing had been a bit of a lark but it was time now to call it off. 'I know she treated you unkindly, and I think the worse of her for that. But this plan . . . it's not going to work. She's not guilty – she'd read the letter and laugh if you sent it. She'd probably show it to her husband and he'd have a good laugh too.'

'No she won't.' Dolly pulled her hands back and crossed her arms. She was stubborn, or perhaps just desperate, it could be hard to spot the difference sometimes. 'No woman wants her husband to even suspect she's having an affair with another man. She'll still give us the money.'

Jimmy took out a cigarette and lit it, studying Doll from behind the flame. Once upon a time he'd have moved to cajole her, his adoration would have blinded him to her faults. Now, though, things were different. There was a fracture that ran right the way across Jimmy's heart, a fine line that had appeared the night Dolly told him she wouldn't marry him and then left him on that restaurant floor. The break had been mended since then, and most of the time it couldn't be seen; but just like the vase his mother had dashed to the ground the day they went to Liberty's and which his dad had glued back together, the fault lines would always show up under certain lights. Jimmy loved Dolly, that would never change – for Jimmy, loyalty was like breathing – but as he looked across the table at her, he thought that he didn't really like her much right then.

Vivien came back. She'd been gone just under a week and when Jimmy turned the attic corner, opened the door and saw her in the centre of a horde of fast-talking children, something rather unexpected happened. He was glad to see her. Not just glad; the world seemed a little brighter than it had only the moment before.

He stopped where he was. 'Vivien Jenkins,' he said, causing her to look up and meet his eyes.

She smiled at him and Jimmy smiled back, and he knew then that he was in a bit of trouble.

Twenty-six

New College Library, Oxford, 2011

Laurel spent the next fifty-seven minutes, each of them excruciating, pacing New College gardens. When the doors were finally unlocked, she all but set a library record, reminding herself of a shopper at the Boxing Day sales as she jostled past other people in her hurry to get back to her desk; certainly Ben seemed impressed. 'Cool,' he said, and joked, 'I didn't leave you in here by mistake, did I?'

Laurel assured him he hadn't, and got busy skimming through Katy's first journal for 1941 in search of anything that might tell her how her mother's plan had turned pear-shaped. There wasn't much mention of Vivien in the first few months of the year, other than occasional notations advising that Katy had written or received a letter, and discreet statements along the lines of 'all seems to go the same for Mrs Jenkins', but then, on 5 April 1941, things started to liven up.

Today's post brought word from my young friend Vivien. It was a long letter by her standards, and I was alert immediately to the fact that something in her tone was changed. At first I was pleased, as it seemed that a flush of her former spirit had returned, and I wondered that a new peace might have dawned on her affairs. But alas, no, for the letter did not describe a renewed commitment to home and hearth; rather, she wrote in lengthy and profuse details about the volunteer work she's been doing at Dr Tomalin's London hospital for orphaned children, entreating me, as always, to destroy her letter afterwards and refrain from making reference to her work in my response.

I will of course comply, but I intend to implore her again, in the strongest possible terms, to cease all involvement with the place, at least until I can work out a lasting solution to her problems. Is it not enough she insists on making donations to the hospital's running costs? Does she care nothing for her own health? She won't stop, I know that; twenty years old now, but Vivien is still that stubborn child I first knew on our ship, refusing to heed my advice if it doesn't suit her. I will write anyway. I could never forgive myself if the worst were to happen and I hadn't done my best to steer her right.

Laurel frowned. What worst? Clearly she was missing something – why on earth would Katy Ellis, teacher and friend to small traumatized people everywhere, have felt so strongly that Vivien should cease volunteering at Dr Tomalin's hospital for war orphans? Unless Dr Tomalin himself was a danger. Was that it? Or was the hospital perhaps located in an area that drew a lot of German bombers? Laurel pondered the question for a minute before deciding it was impossible to know exactly what Katy feared without embarking on a tangential line of research that threatened to absorb what little time she had left. The question was intriguing, but irrelevant, she suspected, to the mission she was on to learn more about her mother's plan. She continued reading.

The cause of Vivien's improved spirits was revealed to me on the second page of her letter. It appears she has met someone, a young man, and although she is at pains to mention him in only the most casual terms – 'I am joined in my project with the children by another volunteer, a man who seems to know as little about boundaries as I know about turning lights into fairies' – I know my young friend well, and I suspect that her breezy veneer is a performance for my sake, designed to conceal something deeper. What precisely that something might be, I do not know, only that it is unlike her to devote so many lines to the discussion of an individual whose acquaintance she has just made. I am wary. My instincts have never let me down before, and I plan to write at once to urge appropriate caution.

Katy Ellis must have done just that, for her next journal entry contained a lengthy direct quote from a letter written by Vivien Jenkins, evidently in response to her concerns.

'How I miss you, Katy dear – it's been over a year since last we met; it feels like ten. Your letter made me wish that we were sitting together beneath that tree at Nordstrom, the one by the lake where we used to picnic when you came to visit. Do you remember the night we crept from the great house and hung paper lanterns from the trees in the grove? We told my uncle that it must have been gypsies and he spent the whole of the next day stalking the grounds with that shotgun on his

shoulder and his poor arthritic dog at his heels – darling old Dewey. Such a faithful hound.

'You lectured me later for causing mischief, but I seem to remember, Katy, that you were the one to describe in great detail at the breakfast table the 'fearsome' noises you'd heard in the night, when the gypsy folk must've been 'descending' on the hallowed grounds of Nordstrom. Oh, but wasn't it something, swimming by the light of the great silver moon? How I love to swim – it is to drop right over the edge of the world, isn't it? I don't think I've ever stopped believing I might just discover the hole on the stream floor that will lead me back.

'Ah, Katy – I wonder what age I will need to attain before you release me from your worries. What a burden I must be. Do you think you will still be minding me to keep my skirts clean and my nose dry when I am an old woman, clacking my knitting needles and rocking in my chair? How well you've looked out for me over the years, how difficult I've made that task for you at times, and how fortunate I am that it was you who met me that horrible day at the railway station.

'You are wise as ever in your advice, and please, dearest, be reassured that I am equally wise in my actions. I am not a child any more, and know too well my responsibilities – you're not reassured, are you? Even as you read this, you are shaking your head and thinking what an imprudent person I am. To allay your fears, let me promise you that I have hardly spoken to the man in question (Jimmy is his name, by the way – let's call him that, shall we – 'the man' has rather a sinister feel to it); indeed, I have at all times done my best to discourage any contact, even veering, when necessary, into the realm of rudeness. Apologies for that, Katy dear, I know you would not like to see your young charge gaining a reputation for bad manners, and I for

*my part detest doing anything that might bring your good
name into disrepute!'*

Laurel smiled. She liked Vivien; the response was
tongue-in-cheek without straying into unkindness towards
mother hen Katy and her wearying instinct towards worry.
Even Katy had written beneath the extract: *It is nice to see
my cheeky young friend returned. I've missed her these past
years.* Laurel liked less Vivien's naming of the young man
volunteering at the hospital with her. Was he the same
Jimmy her mother had been in love with? Surely. Could
it be a coincidence he was working with Vivien at Dr
Tomalin's hospital? Surely not. Laurel felt the rumblings of
foreboding as a sense of the lovers' plan began to take shape
in her mind.

Evidently Vivien had no idea of the connection between
the nice young man at the hospital and her one-time friend,
Dorothy – which wasn't surprising, Laurel supposed. Kitty
Barker had mentioned how careful Ma was to keep her
boyfriend away from Campden Grove. She'd also described
the way emotions were intensified and moral certainties
dissolved during the war, providing, it struck Laurel now,
the perfect environment in which a pair of star-crossed
lovers might become swept up in a *folie à deux*.

The next week of journal entries contained no mention
either of Vivien Jenkins or 'the matter of the young man';
Katy Ellis devoted herself instead to the immediate concerns
of divisional warden politics, and talk on the radio of invasion. On 9 April she recorded her concern that Vivien
hadn't written as expected, but then noted the next day a
telephone call from Dr Tomalin, letting her know that

Vivien was unwell. Now, that was interesting: it appeared the two were known to one another after all, and it wasn't an objection to the doctor's character that had set Katy so firmly against his hospital. Four days later, the following:

A letter today that vexes me greatly. I cannot possibly cap-ture the tone in summary and I wouldn't know where to begin or end in quoting the parts that trouble me. Thus, I am going against the wishes of my dear (infuriating!) young friend, just this once, and will not toss the letter on this evening's fire.

Laurel had never turned a page faster. There it was, on fine white paper and in rather messy handwriting – written in great haste, it would seem – the letter from Vivien Jenkins to Katy Ellis dated 23 April 1941. A month before she died, Laurel noted grimly.

I am writing to you from a railway restaurant, darling Katy, because I was gripped by a fear that if I didn't record it all without delay, the whole thing would disappear and I would wake up tomorrow and discover it a figment of my imagina-tion. None of what I write will please you, but you are the only person I can tell, and I must tell somebody. Forgive me, then, dear Katy, and accept my deepest apologies in advance for the anxiety I know this confidence will cause you. Only, if you must think badly of me, think it softly and remember that I am still your own Little Shipmate.
Something happened today. I was leaving Dr Tomalin's hospital and had paused on the step to straighten my scarf – I swear to you, Katy, and you know me not to be a liar, that I did

not hesitate on purpose; still, when I heard the door open behind me I knew, without turning, that it was the young man (I believe I've mentioned him once or twice in my letters – Jimmy?) who was standing there.

Katy Ellis had underlined this sentence and made an annotation in the margin, the note written in such a tiny neat script that Laurel could just picture the tight disapproving moue of its writer: *Mentioned once or twice! The delusions of the love-struck never cease to amaze one.* Love-struck. Laurel's stomach balled with concern as she concentrated her attention back on Vivien's letter. Had Vivien fallen in love with Jimmy? Was that what had turned the 'harmless' plan on its head?

Sure enough, it was him; Jimmy joined me on the front step and we exchanged there a few words about a humorous incident that had occurred between the children. He made me laugh – he is funny, Katy – I do like funny people, don't you? – my father was a very funny man, he always had us laughing – and then he asked, quite naturally, whether we might walk home together, seeing as we were both headed in the same direction, to which, against every sensible dictate, I answered, 'Yes.'

Now, while you're shaking your head, Katy (I can picture you at that little desk you told me about, beneath the window – do you have fresh primroses in a vase on the corner? You do, I know it), let me tell you why I responded that way. For weeks now, I have done as you advised and gone out of my way to ignore him, but the other day he gave me something – a gift of apology, the reason for which I won't go into, after we had a

*small misunderstanding. The gift was a photograph. I will not
describe it here other than to say that in its depiction it was as
if he had somehow seen inside my soul to the world I've kept
contained there since I was small.*

*I took that photograph home with me, and I guarded it
like a jealous child, taking it out at every opportunity, poring
over each small detail, before locking it away in the concealed
wall cabinet behind my grandmother's portrait in the bedroom
– just as a child might hide a precious object, for no other
reason than that by concealing it, by keeping it for myself, the
value was somehow magnified. He has heard me tell stories to
the hospital children, of course, and I am not suggesting there
was anything more 'magical' in his choosing such a gift, but
still it moved me.*

The word 'magical' was underlined and subject to
another annotation from Katy Ellis:

It is precisely *what she is suggesting: I know Vivien, and I
know how deeply she believes. One of the things I have
come to know most surely in my work is that the belief
system acquired in childhood is never fully escaped; it may
submerge itself for a while, but it always returns in times of
need to lay claim to the soul it shaped.*

Laurel thought of her own childhood, wondering
whether it was true what Katy said. Above any other theis-
tic system, her parents had preached the values of family;
her mother, in particular, had held the line – she'd realized
too late, she told them sadly, the value of family. And Laurel
had to concede that if she looked beyond the good-natured

bickering, the Nicolsons did come together in times of need, just as they'd been taught to do as children.

Perhaps, too, my recent indisposition has made me more reckless than usual – after a week in the dark of my bedroom, German planes thrumming overhead, Henry sitting by the bedside of an evening clutching my hand and willing me to mend, it is quite something to be out again, drinking in the fresh air of London in springtime. (As a side note, don't you find it remarkable, Katy, that the whole world can be involved in this madness we call war, and all the while the flowers and the bees and the seasons keep on doing what they must, wise but never weary in their wait for humanity to come to its senses and remember the beauty of life? It is queer, but my love and longing for the world are always deepened by my absence from it; it's wondrous, don't you think, that a person can swing from despair to gleeful hunger, and that even during these dark days there is happiness to be found in the smallest things?)

Anyway, whatever the reason, he asked me to walk with him and I said yes, and so we walked, and I let myself laugh. I laughed because he told me funny stories and it was so easy and light. I realized how long it has been since I've enjoyed that most simple of pleasures: company and conversation on a sunny afternoon. I am impatient for such pleasures, Katy. I am a woman now, and I want certain things; things that I will not have; but it is human, is it not, to long for that from which we are barred?

What things? What was Vivien barred from? Not for the first time, Laurel had the feeling she was missing an important part of the puzzle. She skimmed through the next fortnight's journal entries until Vivien was mentioned again, hoping all would be made clear.

She continues to see him – at the hospital, which is bad enough, but elsewhere, too, when she is supposed to be working at the WVS canteen or running household errands. She tells me that I must not worry, that 'he is a friend, and nothing more'. She submits as evidence a reference to the young man's fiancée: 'He is engaged to be married, Katy, they are very much in love and have plans to move to the country when the war is over; they're going to find a big old house and fill it with children; so you see, I am not in danger of breaking my own wedding vows, as you seem to fear.'

At this, Laurel felt the dizziness of recognition. It was Dorothy Vivien was writing about – Ma. The intersection of then and now, learned history and lived experience, was briefly overwhelming. She removed her glasses and rubbed her forehead, focusing on the stone wall outside the window for a moment.

And then she let Katy continue:

She knows that is not all I fear; the girl is wilfully misreading my concerns. I am no innocent, either; I know that this young man's engagement is no impediment to the human heart. I cannot know his feelings, but I know Vivien's well enough.

More extravagant worry on Katy's behalf, yet Laurel still wasn't any closer to understanding why: Vivien intimated that Katy's fears stemmed from her rigid views as to what constituted seemly marital behaviour. Did Vivien make a habit of disloyalty? There wasn't a lot to go on, but Laurel could *almost* read into Vivien's more florid romantic musings on life, a spirit of free love . . . almost.

Then Laurel found an entry, two days later, that made her wonder whether Katy had somehow intuited all along that Jimmy posed a threat to Vivien.

Dreadful war news – Westminster Hall was hit last night, and the Abbey and the Houses of Parliament; they thought at first Big Ben had been razed! Rather than pick up the newspaper or listen to the wireless this evening I determined to clear out the sitting-room cupboard to make room for my new teaching notes. I confess to being something of a bowerbird – a trait that shames me; I would prefer to be as efficient of home as I am of mind – and I found there the most amazing collection of trifles. Amongst them, a letter received three years ago from Vivien's uncle. Along with the description of her 'pleasing compliance' (I was as riled when I read that line tonight as I was at the time – how little he ever saw of the real Vivien!) he had enclosed a photograph, still folded in with the letter. She was seventeen years old when it was taken, and such a beauty – I remembered thinking, when I saw it those years ago, that she looked like the character from a fairy tale, Red Riding Hood perhaps; wide eyes and rosebud lips; and still the direct and innocent gaze of a child. I remembered hoping, too, that there was no Big Bad Wolf waiting for her in the woods.

That the letter and its photograph should have come to light today of all days gave me pause. I was not wrong the last time I had one of my 'feelings'. I didn't act then, much to my eternal regret, but I will not stand by and let my young friend make another mistake with dire ramifications. Given that I cannot express my concerns in writing as I would wish, I will make the trip to London and see her myself.

A trip she evidently took – and promptly – for the next journal entry was written four days later:

I have been to London and it was worse than I feared. It was obvious to me that my dear Vivien has fallen in love with the young man, Jimmy. She didn't say as much, of course, she is too circumspect for that, but I have known her since she was a child and thus I could see it in every animation of her face, hear it in every unspoken phrase. Worse yet, it appears she has thrown all caution to the wind; she has been repeatedly to the young man's home, where he lives with his poorly father. She insists that 'all is innocent', to which I replied that there was no such thing, and that such distinctions would do her no favours if she were called upon to answer to these visits. She told me she wouldn't 'give him up' – stubborn child – to which I summoned every bit of steel I possessed and said, 'My dear, you are married.' I reminded her further of the promise she'd made to her husband in the Nordstrom church, that she would love, honour and obey, till death did them part, etc., etc. Oh, but I won't easily forget the way she looked at me then – the disappointment in her eyes as she told me that I didn't understand.

I understand well enough what it is to love that which is forbidden, and I told her so, but she is young, and the

young are quick to presume themselves the exclusive posses-
sors of all strong feelings. I am sorry to say that we parted
on ill terms – I made one last attempt to convince her to
give up her work at the hospital; she refused. I reminded her
she had her health to consider; she waved my concerns
aside. To disappoint a soul like hers – that face which
reveals itself as if beneath a master painter's brush – is to
feel as guilty as if one had removed all goodness from the
world. Still, I will not give up – I have one last card to play.
It risks her eternal outrage, but I decided as my train left
London that I am going to write to this Jimmy Metcalfe and
explain to him the damage he does her. Perhaps he will exer-
cise proper caution where she will not.

The sun had started to set and the reading room was
growing colder and darker by the minute; Laurel's eyes were
bleary from reading Katy Ellis's neat but tiny script without
pause for the last two hours. She leaned back and closed her
eyes, Katy's voice swirling in her head. Had she written the
letter to Jimmy? Laurel wondered. Was that what had upset
her mother's plan? Had whatever Katy included in the letter
– something she obviously thought persuasive enough to
make Jimmy give up the friendship when Vivien wouldn't –
been enough to cause ruptures between Ma and Jimmy, too?
In a book, Laurel thought, that's exactly what would
happen. There was a narrative rightness to a pair of young
lovers being torn apart by the very deed they'd contrived to
commit in order to buy their shared happiness. Was that
what her mother had been thinking about that day in the
hospital when she'd told Laurel she should marry for love,
that she shouldn't wait, that nothing else was as important?

Had Dorothy waited too long, and wanted too much, and in the meantime lost her lover to the other woman?

Laurel had guessed that it was something peculiar to Vivien Jenkins which made her the very worst person around whom Dorothy and Jimmy could make such a plan. Was it simply that Vivien was precisely the type of woman Jimmy might fall in love with? Or was it something else Laurel was intuiting? Katy Ellis – every bit the minister's daughter – was obviously worried that Vivien wasn't being mindful of her marriage vows, but there was something else at work, too. Laurel wondered whether Vivien might have been ill. Katy was a worrywart, but her concern for Vivien's health was of the type usually reserved for a friend with chronic illness, not a vital young woman of twenty. Vivien herself had referred to 'absences' from the outside world, when her husband Henry sat by her bedside and stroked her hand as she convalesced. Had Vivien Jenkins suffered with a condition that made her more vulnerable to the world than she might otherwise have been? Had she experienced a breakdown of some kind, emotional or physical, that left her susceptible to a relapse?

Or – Laurel sat bolt upright at her desk – had she perhaps endured a series of miscarriages after her marriage to Henry? It certainly explained the doting care of her husband; even, to an extent, Vivien's drive to get out of the house when she was recovered, to leave the domestic site of her unhappiness and do more than she was really able. It might even explain Katy Ellis's specific concern about Vivien working with children at the hospital. Was that it? Had Katy worried that her friend was increasing her sadness by surrounding herself with constant reminders of her barrenness? Vivien had written in her letter about it being human nature, and certainly her own, to crave the very things she knew she couldn't have. Laurel was sure she was onto something – even Katy's reliance on euphemisms was consistent with *that* subject at *that* time.

Laurel wished she knew more places to look for answers. It occurred to her that Gerry's time machine would be most helpful about now. Alas, she was stuck with Katy's journals. There were a few more entries in which Vivien's friendship with Jimmy seemed to grow despite Katy's continued misgivings, and then, all of a sudden, on 20 May, an entry reporting that Vivien had written to advise she would not see Jimmy again, that it was time for him to begin a new life, and that she'd wished him well and told him goodbye.

Laurel drew breath, wondering whether Katy had sent her letter to Jimmy, after all, and if whatever she wrote to him was at the root of this abrupt change of heart. Against the odds, she felt sorry for Vivien Jenkins: even though Laurel knew that there was more to Jimmy's friendship than met the eye, she couldn't help but pity the young woman who'd been so pleased with so little. Laurel supposed her sympathy might be influenced by her awareness of what was waiting around the corner for Vivien; but even Katy, who'd been so keen that the relationship should end, seemed ambivalent now that it had.

I was worried about Vivien and wanted the affair with the young man to stop; now I suffer the burden of having been granted my wish. I have received a letter offering very little detail but with a tone that is not remotely difficult to decipher. She writes in resignation. She says only that I was right; that the friendship is over; and that I need not worry for everything has worked out for the best. Sorrow or anger I could accept. It is the defeated tone of her letter that makes me worry. I cannot help but fear it bodes ill. I will await her next letter and hope for an improvement, and I will hold fast to my certainty that what I did was done for the very best of reasons.

But there was to be no further letter. Vivien Jenkins died three days later, a fact recorded by Katy Ellis with just the sort of grief one might imagine.

Thirty minutes later, Laurel was hurrying across the dusk-draped lawn of New College towards the bus stop, musing over everything she'd learned, when her phone started buzzing at her from her pocket. She didn't recognize the number but answered anyway.

'Lol?' came the voice.

'Gerry?' Laurel had to strain to hear through the noise on the other end of the line. 'Gerry? Where are you?'

'London. A phone booth on Fleet Street.'

'The city still has working phone booths?'

'It would appear so. Unless this is the Tardis, in which case I'm in serious trouble.'

'What are you doing in London?'

'Chasing Dr Rufus.'

'Oh?' Laurel pressed a hand against her other ear so she could hear properly. 'And? Have you caught him?'

'I have. His journals, at any rate. The doctor himself died from an infection towards the end of the war.'

Laurel's heart was thumping fast; she skipped over the doctor's untimely end. In the pursuit of answers to this mystery, there was only room for so much empathy. 'And? What have you found?'

'I don't know where to start.'

'The important bit. And do please hurry.'

'Hang on.' She heard him drop another coin into the phone. 'Still there?'

'Yes, yes.'

Laurel stopped beneath a glowing orange streetlight, as Gerry said, 'They were never friends, Lol. Ma and this Vivien Jenkins – according to Dr Rufus they were never friends.'

'What?' She figured she'd misheard.

'They hardly even knew each other.'

'Ma and Vivien Jenkins? What are you talking about? I've seen the book, the photograph – of course they were friends.'

'Ma *wanted* them to be friends – from what I read, it was almost as if she wanted to *be* Vivien Jenkins. She became obsessed with the idea that they were inseparable – "two of a kind" were his exact words, but it was all in her head.'

'But . . . I don't . . .'

'And then something happened – it wasn't clear what exactly – but Vivien Jenkins did something that made it evident to Ma that they weren't close friends at all.'

Laurel thought of the argument Kitty Barker had spoken of, something happening between the two of them that had put Dorothy in a terrible mood and spurred her desire for revenge. 'What was it, Gerry?' she said. 'Do you know what Vivien did?' Or took.

'She – hang on. Bugger, I'm out of coins.' There came the fierce sound of pockets being shaken, the phone receiver being fumbled. 'It's going to cut me off, Lol—'

'Call me back. Find some more coins and ring me back.'

'Too late, I'm out. I'll talk to you soon, though; I'm coming to Greenac—'

The tone sounded flatly and Gerry was gone.

Twenty-seven

London, May 1941

Jimmy had been embarrassed the first time he brought Vivien home to visit his dad. Their small room looked bad enough through his eyes, but seeing it through hers made the half-measures he'd taken to make it homely seem truly desperate. Had he really thought draping an old tea towel across the wooden chest made it a dining table? Apparently, he had. Vivien, for her part, did a marvellous job of acting like there was nothing remotely odd in drinking black tea out of mismatched cups while perched beside a bird on the end of an old man's bed, and it had gone off rather well, all things considered.

One of those things was his father's insistence on calling Vivien 'your young lady' the whole time, and then asking Jimmy – in the pipingly clearest of voices – when the pair of them planned on getting married. Jimmy had corrected the old man at least three times before shrugging his shoulders apologetically at Vivien and giving the whole thing up for a joke. What else could he have done? It was just an old man's mistake – he'd only met Doll once, back in Coventry before the war – and there was no harm in it. Vivien didn't seem to mind and Jimmy's dad was made happy. Exceedingly happy. He got on a treat with Vivien. In her, it seemed, he'd found the audience he'd been waiting for all his life.

There were times when Jimmy watched the pair of them laughing together at some anecdote of his dad's, trying to teach Finchie a new trick or arguing cheerfully over the best way to bait a fish hook, and he thought his heart might burst with gratitude. It had been a long while, he realized – years – since he'd seen his father without the worry line that pulled between his brows when he was trying to remember who and where he was.

Occasionally, Jimmy caught himself attempting to picture Doll in Vivien's place, imagining it was her fetching a fresh cup of tea for his dad, stirring in the condensed milk just the way he liked, telling stories that made the old man shake his head with surprise and pleasure . . . but he couldn't envisage it somehow. He chided himself even for trying. Comparisons were irrelevant, he knew, and unfair to both women. Doll would have come to visit if she could. She wasn't a lady of leisure; her hours at the munitions factory were long and she was always so tired afterwards – it was only natural she'd choose to fill her rare free evenings catching up with friends.

Vivien, on the other hand, seemed genuinely to relish the time she spent in their small room. Jimmy had made the mistake of thanking her once, as if she did him a great personal favour, but she'd only looked at him like he'd lost his mind and said, 'For what?' He'd felt foolish in the face of her perplexity, and changed the subject by making a joke, but he found himself considering later that perhaps he'd got it all wrong and it was only for the old man's company that

Vivien kept up his acquaintance. It seemed as likely an explanation as any.

He still reflected on it sometimes, wondering why she'd said yes that day at the hospital when he'd asked her to walk with him. He didn't need to wonder why he'd asked her: it was having her back after she'd been ill, the brightening of everything when he'd opened the attic door and seen her there unexpectedly. He'd hurried to catch up with her when she left, opening the front door so quickly she'd still been standing on the step, tying her scarf. He hadn't expected her to say yes; he knew only that he'd been thinking about it all through the rehearsal. He wanted to spend time with her, not because Dolly had told him to, but because he liked her; he liked being with her.

'Do you have children, Jimmy?' she'd asked him as they walked together. She was moving more slowly than usual, still delicate after the illness that had kept her at home. He'd noticed a certain reticence all day – she'd laughed with the kids as usual, but there'd been a look in her eyes, a caution or reserve he wasn't used to. Jimmy had felt sad for her, though he didn't know why exactly.

He'd shaken his head, 'No.' And he'd felt his face colour, remembering how he'd upset her when he'd asked the same question.

This time, though, she was steering the conversation and she pressed on. 'But you want them one day.'

'Yes.'

'Just one or two?'

'For starters. Then the other six.'

She'd smiled at that.

'I was an only child,' he said by way of explanation. 'It was lonely.'

'I was one of four. It was noisy.'

Jimmy had laughed then, and he was still smiling when he realized what he hadn't before. 'The stories you tell at the hospital,' he said, as they turned the corner, thinking of the photograph he'd taken for her, 'the ones about the wooden house on stilts, the enchanted forest, the family through the veil – that's your family, isn't it?'

Vivien nodded.

Jimmy wasn't sure what had made him tell her about his dad that day – something in the way she'd looked when she spoke about her own family, the stories he'd heard her tell that crackled with magic and longing and made time disappear, the need he suddenly felt to let somebody in. Whatever the case, he *had* told her, and Vivien had asked questions and Jimmy was reminded of the day he'd first seen her with the children, that quality he'd noticed in the way she listened to them. When she said she'd like to meet the old man, Jimmy assumed it was just one of those things people say when they're really thinking about the train they've got to catch and wondering if they'll get to the station in time. But at the next rehearsal she said it again. 'I've brought something for him,' she added. 'Something I think he might like.'

She had, too. And the following week, when Jimmy finally agreed to take her to meet his dad, she'd presented the old man with a fine piece of cuttlefish, 'For Finchie.' She'd found it on the beach, she said, when she and Henry were visiting his publisher's family.

'She's a lovely one, Jim-boy,' Jimmy's dad had said

loudly. 'Very pretty – like something out of a painting. Kind, too. Will you wait and have your wedding when we get to the seaside, do you think?'

'I don't know, Dad,' Jimmy said, glancing at Vivien, who was pretending great interest in some of his photographs pinned to the wall. 'Let's just wait and see, eh?'

'Don't wait too long, Jimmy. Your mum and me, we're not getting any younger.'

'Right-o, Dad. You'll be first to know – promise.'

Later, when he was walking Vivien back to the underground station, he explained about his dad's confusion, hoping she hadn't been too embarrassed.

She seemed surprised. 'You mustn't apologize for your father, Jimmy.'

'No, I know. I just – I didn't want you to feel uncomfortable.'

'On the contrary. I haven't felt so comfortable in a long time.'

They walked a bit further without conversation, and then Vivien said, 'Are you really going to live at the seaside?'

'That's the plan.' Jimmy flinched. *Plan.* He'd said the word without thinking and he cursed himself. There was something enormously awkward in outlining for Vivien the selfsame future scenario that had become bound up in his mind with Dolly's scheme.

'And you're going to be married.'

He nodded.

'That's wonderful, Jimmy. I'm pleased for you. Is she a nice girl? – No, of course she is. Silly question.'

Jimmy smiled faintly, hoping that was an end to the subject, but then Vivien said, 'Well?'

'Well?'

She laughed. 'Tell me about her.'

'What do you want to know?'

'I'm not sure . . . the usual sorts of things, I suppose – how did you two meet?'

Jimmy's mind went back to the cafe in Coventry. 'I was carrying a sack of flour.'

'And she was powerless to resist,' Vivien teased him gently. 'So evidently she's partial to flour. What else does she like? What's *she* like?'

'Playful,' Jimmy said, his throat tight. 'Full of life, full of dreams.' He wasn't enjoying the conversation one bit, but he found his mind drawn to thoughts of Doll; the girl she'd been, the woman she was now. 'She lost her family in the Blitz.'

'Oh, Jimmy.' Vivien's face fell. 'The poor girl. She must be devastated.'

Her sympathy was deep and sincere, and Jimmy couldn't bear it. His shame at the deceit, the part he'd already played; his heartsickness at the duplicity: all drove him now to honesty. Perhaps, in the back of his mind, he even hoped the truth might sabotage Doll's plan in some way. 'I think you might know her, actually.'

'What?' She shot him a glance, seemingly alarmed by the idea. 'How?'

'Her name's Dolly.' He held his breath, remembering how badly things had gone between the two of them. 'Dolly Smitham.'

'No.' Vivien was visibly relieved. 'No, I don't think I know anybody by that name.'

Now Jimmy was confused. He knew they were friends – that they had been once; Dolly had told him all about it.

'You worked at the WVS together. She used to live across the road from you in Campden Grove. Lady Gwendolyn's companion.'

'Oh!' Realization dawned on Vivien's face and, 'Oh, Jimmy,' she said, stopping to grip his arm, her dark eyes wide with panic. 'Does she know we've been working together at the hospital?'

'No,' Jimmy lied, hating himself.

Her relief was palpable; a smile tried to form only to be dimmed quickly by renewed concern. She sighed with regret, pressing her fingers lightly to her lips. 'God, Jimmy, she must hate me.' Her eyes scanned his. 'It was the most awful thing – I don't know if she mentioned it to you – she did me a great favour once, returning my locket when I'd lost it, but I – I'm afraid I was rather rude to her. I'd had a bad day, something unexpected had happened; I wasn't feeling well and I was unkind. I went to see her, to apologize and explain; I knocked on the door of number 7, but nobody answered. Then the old woman died and everyone moved away; it all happened very quickly.' Vivien's fingers had fallen to her locket as she spoke; she was twisting it, turning it over in the hollow of her throat. 'Will you tell her, Jimmy? Will you tell her I didn't mean to treat her so unkindly?'

Jimmy said that he would. Hearing Vivien's explanation had made him unaccountably pleased. It confirmed Dolly's account; but it also proved that the whole thing, Vivien's seeming coldness, had been a huge misunderstanding.

They walked a little further in silence, each of them alone with their thoughts, until Vivien said, 'Why are you waiting to get married, Jimmy? You're in love, aren't you? You and Dolly?'

His gladness fell away. He wished to God she'd drop the subject. 'Yes.'

'Then why not do it now?'

The words he found to mask the lie were trite. 'We want it to be perfect.'

She nodded, considering, and then she said, 'What could be more perfect than marrying the person you love?'

Perhaps it was the haze of shame he was feeling that made him leap to justify himself; perhaps it was the latent memories of his dad waiting in vain for his mother to return, but Jimmy echoed her question – 'What could be more perfect than love?' – and then he laughed bitterly. 'Knowing you can provide enough to keep your loved one happy, for starters. That you can keep a roof over your head, put food on the table, pay for heating. For those of us with nothing to spare that's no small matter. Not as romantic as your idea, I admit, but that's life, isn't it?'

Vivien's face had paled; he'd hurt her, he could tell, but Jimmy's own temper was flashing red-hot by then, and although he was upset with himself and not with her at all, he didn't apologize. 'You're right,' she said finally. 'I'm sorry, Jimmy. I spoke out of turn; it was insensitive of me. It's none of my business anyway. You just paint such a vivid picture – the farmhouse, the seaside – it's all so wonderful. I was caught up vicariously in your plans.'

Jimmy didn't answer; he'd been looking at her as she spoke but now he turned away. Something about her face as he watched her had inspired a clear and focused image in his mind of the two of them, him and her, running off to the seaside together, that made him want to stop her, right there in the street, cup her face in his hands and kiss her long and hard. Christ. What was the matter with him?

Jimmy lit a cigarette and smoked as he walked. 'What about you?' he muttered, ashamed, and trying to make amends. 'What's in your future? What do you dream of?'

'Oh.' She waved a hand. 'I don't spend too much time thinking about the future.'

They reached the underground station and enacted an awkward goodbye. Jimmy felt uncomfortable, not to mention guilty, especially because he was going to have to hurry to meet Dolly at Lyons as they'd planned. All the same—

'Let me go with you to Kensington,' he called after Vivien. 'Make sure you get home safely.'

She glanced back at him. 'You're going to catch the bomb with my number on it?'

'I'll give it a good try.'

'No,' she said. 'No, thanks. I prefer to go alone.' And with that a flash of the old Vivien was back, the one who'd walked ahead of him in the street and refused even to smile.

Dolly sat smoking as she watched for Jimmy from the window of the restaurant. Every so often she turned away from the glass, brushing at the white fur of her coat sleeve. It was too warm, really, to be wearing fur, but Dolly didn't like to take it off. It made her feel important – powerful even – and she needed that now more than ever. Lately she'd had the terrible feeling that the strings were slipping through her fingers and she was beginning to lose control. The fear made her sick to the stomach – worst of all was the creeping uncertainty that came upon her in the night.

The plan, when she'd conceived it, had seemed faultless – a simple way of teaching Vivien Jenkins a lesson, while making things right for Jimmy and herself – but as time went on and Jimmy got no closer to setting up a meeting to take the photograph, as Dolly noticed the distance growing between them, the trouble he had meeting her eyes, she was beginning to realize she'd made a huge mistake; that she should never have asked Jimmy to do it. At her lowest moments, Dolly had even started to wonder that he might not love her in quite the same way, that he might not think she was exceptional any more. And that thought made her truly frightened.

They'd quarrelled terribly the other night. It had started over nothing, some comment she'd made about her friend, Caitlin, the way she'd behaved when they went out dancing together recently with Kitty and the others. It was the sort of thing she'd said a hundred times before, but somehow this time it turned into a full-blown argument. She'd been shocked at the sharp way he'd spoken to her, the things he'd said – he'd told her she ought to choose better friends if her old ones were such a disappointment; that she might even think about coming to visit him and his father next time instead of going out with people she clearly didn't like – and it had seemed so uncalled-for, so unkind, she'd started crying in the street. Usually when Dolly cried, Jimmy realized how hurt she was and moved to make things better, but not this time. He'd only shouted, 'Christ!', and walked away, fists balled by his side.

Dolly had swallowed her sobs then, listening and waiting in the dark, and for a minute she'd heard nothing. She'd thought she was truly alone, that somehow she'd pushed him too far and he really had left her this time.

He hadn't, he'd come back, but instead of saying sorry as she expected, he'd said, in a voice she almost didn't recognize, 'You should have married me, Doll. You should have bloody well married me when I asked.'

Dolly had felt a whimper rise painfully in her throat when he said it, and she'd heard herself cry, 'No, Jimmy, you should have asked me sooner!'

They'd made up afterwards on the steps of Mrs White's boarding house. They'd kissed each other goodnight, carefully, politely, and agreed that emotion had got the better of them, that was all. But Dolly knew it was more than that. She'd stayed awake for hours afterwards, thinking back over the past weeks, remembering each time she'd seen him, the things he'd said, the way he'd behaved, and as she did, as it all played out across her mind, she'd known. It was the plan, the thing she'd asked him to do. Rather than fixing matters between them as she'd hoped, her clever plan ran the risk of spoiling everything . . .

Now, in the restaurant, Dolly extinguished her cigarette and took the letter from her bag. She shucked it from its envelope and read it again. A job offer from a boarding house called Sea Blue. It was Jimmy who'd found the advert in the newspaper and clipped it out for her. 'It sounds great, Doll,' he'd said. 'Glorious spot on the coast – seagulls, salt on the air, ice cream . . . And I can get work doing . . . well, I'll find something.' Dolly hadn't really been able to picture herself sweeping up after pale, sandy holidaymakers, but Jimmy had stood over her until she wrote the letter, and there'd been a part of her that quite liked seeing him all forceful like that. In the end, she'd decided, why not? It would keep Jimmy sweet, and if she was offered the job she could always write back privately and turn it down. At the time, Dolly had reasoned that she wouldn't need a position

like that one, not when they finally got the photograph of
Vivien—

The door to the restaurant opened and Jimmy came
through. He'd been running, she could tell – eager to see her,
she hoped. Dolly waved and watched him as he crossed to
the table; his dark hair had fallen over his face, making him
look handsome and dishevelled in a dangerous sort of way.
'Hey, Doll,' he said, kissing her on the cheek. 'Bit too warm
for fur, isn't it?'

Dolly smiled and shook her head. 'I'm all right.' She
moved across on the booth seat, but he sat down opposite,
lifting his hand to call the waitress.

Dolly waited until they'd ordered tea and then she
could stand it no longer. She took a deep breath and said,
'I've had an idea.' His face tensed and she felt a stab of self-
reproach, realizing how wary he'd become. She reached
gently to stroke his hand. 'Oh, Jimmy, it's nothing like
that – ' She broke off, chewing her lip. 'In fact – ' she lowered her voice – 'I've been thinking about the other thing,
the plan.'

He lifted his chin defensively and she continued in a
hurry, 'Only, I thought maybe you ought to forget about it –
setting up the meeting, the photograph.'

'Really?'

She nodded, and by the look on Jimmy's face Dolly
knew she'd made the right decision. 'I should never have
asked you – ' her words were tumbling together now –
'I wasn't thinking straight. The whole thing with Lady
Gwendolyn, my family . . . it made me a bit crazy, I think,
Jimmy.'

He came to sit beside her and took her face in his

hands. His dark eyes searched hers. 'Of course it did, my poor girl.'

'I should never have asked you,' she said again as he kissed her. 'It wasn't fair. I'm sor—'

'Shh,' he said, relief warming his voice. 'Never mind about that. It's in the past. You and I need to put all that behind us and look forwards.'

'I'd like that.'

He pulled back to consider her, then he shook his head and laughed with a mixture of surprise and pleasure. It was a lovely sound that sent tingles down Dolly's spine. 'I'd like that, too,' he said. 'Let's start with your idea. You were going to tell me something when I first arrived?'

'Oh, yes,' said Dolly excitedly. 'The show you're putting on – I'm supposed to work, but I thought I'd play hookey and come with you to the performance instead.'

'Really?'

'Of course. I'd love to meet Nella and the others, and when else am I going to get the chance to see my boy play Tinkerbell?'

The first and final performance of *Peter Pan* by the young thespians of Dr Tomalin's Hospital for War Orphans was an unmitigated success. The children flew and fought and made magic out of the dusty attic and a few old sheets; those too ill to take part shouted and clapped and cheered from where they'd been carried up to form the audience; and Tinkerbell, under Jimmy's steady hands, acquitted herself admirably. The kids surprised Jimmy afterwards by taking down the painted *Jolly Roger* sign, replacing it with one that read *Nightingale Star*, and then performing a version of the story he'd told them, an act they'd been practising for weeks in secret. After the cast had made (yet another) final curtain call, Dr Tomalin gave a speech and gestured for Vivien and Jimmy to take a bow, too. Jimmy eyed Doll in the audience, waving at him; he smiled back and gave her a wink.

He'd been nervous about bringing her today, though now he wasn't sure why. He supposed when she suggested it he'd felt a surge of guilt over his closeness to Vivien, an anxiety that things might turn out badly between them. The second it became clear he wasn't going to be able to talk her out of coming, Jimmy had gone into damage-control mode. He hadn't confessed his friendship with Vivien; instead, he'd concentrated on explaining the way he'd taken her to task for treating Dolly so unkindly when she returned the locket.

'You told her about me?'

'Of course,' Jimmy said, reaching to hold Doll's hand as they left the restaurant and headed out into the blackout. 'You're my girl. How could I not talk about you?'

'What did she say? Did she admit it? Did she tell you how ghastly she was?'

'She did.' Jimmy stopped walking while Doll lit a cigarette. 'She felt horrible about it. She said she'd suffered some sort of shock that day, but that it didn't excuse her behaviour.'

In the moonlight, he saw Dolly's bottom lip trembling with emotion. 'It was awful, Jimmy,' she said in a whisper. 'The things she said. The way they made me feel.'

He threaded her hair behind her ear. 'She wanted to apologize to you; she tried to, apparently, but when she went to Lady Gwendolyn's house no one was there.'

'She came to see *me*?'

Jimmy nodded, and he noticed her face soften. Just like that, all the bitterness was gone. The transition was breathtaking, and yet he shouldn't have been surprised. Doll's emotions were kites with long strings: no sooner did one dip than another brilliant colour caught the breeze.

They'd gone dancing afterwards and for the first time in weeks, without that bloody plan hanging over their heads, Jimmy and Dolly had had a good time together, just like they used to. They'd laughed and joked with one another, and by the time he kissed her goodnight and sneaked back out of Mrs White's lower window, Jimmy had started to think it wasn't such a bad idea after all to bring Doll with him to the play.

And he'd been right. After a shaky start the day had gone off better than he could have dreamed. Vivien had been fixing the sail to the ship when they first arrived. He'd seen the surprise on her face when she turned and saw him with Doll, the way her smile had started to slide before she caught it, and he'd felt an initial stab of misgiving. She'd climbed down carefully as Jimmy was hanging up Doll's white coat, and when the two of them said hello, Jimmy had held his breath. But the greeting had gone smoothly. He'd been pleased and proud at the way Dolly handled herself. She'd gone out of her way to put the past behind her and be friendly towards Vivien. He could see that Vivien was relieved, too, though quieter than usual, and perhaps less warm. When he asked whether Henry was coming to watch the performance, she'd looked at him as if he'd just insulted her, before reminding him that her husband had a very important job with the Ministry.

Thank God for Dolly, who'd always had a knack of knowing how to lighten the mood. 'Come on, Jimmy,' she'd said, linking her arm through Vivien's as the children began to arrive. 'Take a photograph, why don't you? Something to remember the day by.'

Vivien had started to demur, saying she didn't enjoy having her picture taken, but Doll was trying so hard and Jimmy didn't want to throw her efforts back in her face. 'Promise it won't hurt,' he'd said with a smile, and eventually Vivien had nodded faint agreement . . .

The applause finally died down, and Dr Tomalin told the children that Jimmy had something for all of them. The announcement was met with another round of cheering. Jimmy waved at them and started handing out copies of a photograph. He'd taken it when Vivien was away sick: It showed the whole cast in costume, standing together on the ship set.

Jimmy had printed one for Vivien, too. He spied her over in the far corner of the attic, gathering discarded costumes into a woven basket. Dr Tomalin and Myra were talking to Dolly so he took it over to her.

'So,' he said, arriving at her side.

'So.'

'Rave reviews in tomorrow's newspaper, I should think.'

She laughed. 'Without doubt.'

He handed her a print. 'This is for you.'

She took it, smiling at the children's faces. She leaned to put down the basket, and as she did so her blouse gaped slightly and Jimmy glimpsed a bruise stretching from her shoulder to her chest bone.

'It's nothing,' she said, noticing the direction of his glance, fingers moving quickly to adjust the fabric. 'I fell, in the blackout, on my way to the shelter. A postbox got in my way – so much for paint that shows up in the dark.'

'Are you sure? It looks bad.'

'I bruise easily.' Her eyes met his, and for a fraction of a second Jimmy thought he saw something there, but then she smiled. 'Not to mention I go too fast. I'm always bumping into things – people too, sometimes.'

Jimmy smiled back, remembering the day they'd met; but, as one of the children took Vivien's hand and pulled her away, his thoughts shifted to her recurring illness and her inability to have children and what he knew of people who bruised easily, and Jimmy felt a knot of worry tighten in his stomach.

Twenty-eight

Vivien sat down on the side of the bed and picked up the photograph Jimmy had given her, the one taken in the Blitz, with the smoke and the glittering glass and the family behind. She smiled as she looked at it, and then lay back, closing her eyes and willing her mind to slip over the edge, into her shadow land. The veil, the sparkling lights in the deep of the watery tunnel, and beyond these her family, waiting for her in the house.

She lay there, and she tried to see them, and then she tried harder still.

It was no use. She opened her eyes. Lately, all Vivien saw when she closed them was Jimmy Metcalfe. The spill of dark hair across his forehead, the twitch of his lips when he was about to say something funny, the way his brows knotted together when he spoke about his father . . .

She stood up briskly and went to the window, leaving the photograph behind her on the bedspread. It had been a week since the play and Vivien was restless. She missed rehearsals with the children, and Jimmy, and she couldn't stand the endless days split between the canteen and this big quiet house. It *was* quiet, too: awfully quiet. It ought to have children running up the stairs, sliding down the banisters, stomping in the attics. Even Sarah, the maid, was gone now – Henry had insisted they let her go after what had happened, but Vivien wouldn't have minded had Sarah stayed. She hadn't realized how much she'd grown used to the thumping of the vacuum machine against the skirting boards, the creaking of the old floors, the intangible knowledge that there was somebody else breathing, moving, watching, in the same space as she was.

A man riding an old bicycle wobbled by on the street below, his handlebar basket filled with dirty gardening tools, and Vivien let the sheer day-curtain fall against the crisscrossed glass. She sat on the edge of the nearby armchair and tried again to order her thoughts. She'd been writing to Katy on and off in her mind for days; Vivien had felt a distance since her friend's recent visit to London and was keen to put things right between them. Not to concede – Vivien had never been one to apologize where she knew herself to be right – but rather to explain.

She wanted to make Katy understand, as she hadn't when they'd met, that her friendship with Jimmy was good and true; most of all, that it was innocent. That she had no intention of leaving her marriage or jeopardizing her health or any of the other dire scenarios Katy warned against. She wanted to explain about old Mr Metcalfe and the way she was able to make him laugh, about the easiness she felt with Jimmy when they talked or looked over his photographs, about the way he believed the best of people and the sense he gave her that he would never be unkind. She wanted to convince Katy that her feelings for Jimmy were simply those of one friend for another.

Even if it wasn't exactly true.

Vivien knew the moment that she'd realized she was in love with Jimmy Metcalfe. It was when she was sitting at

the breakfast table downstairs and Henry was telling her of
some work he was doing at the Ministry, and she was nodding along but thinking about an incident at the hospital –
something funny Jimmy had done when he was trying to
cheer up their newest patient – and then she'd laughed,
despite herself, and thank God it must've been at a point in
Henry's story that he found amusing, because he smiled at
her, and came to kiss her, and said, 'I knew you'd think so,
too, darling.'

Vivien also knew that the affair was one-sided and that
her feelings were not something she would ever share with
him. Even if by some chance he felt the same way, there was
no future for Jimmy with Vivien. She couldn't offer him
that. Vivien's fate was sealed. Her condition didn't cause her
angst or upset, not any more; she'd accepted for some time
the life she had remaining, and she certainly didn't need
illicit whispered confessions or physical expressions of love
to make her whole.

Quite the contrary. Vivien had learned early, as a child
in a crowded railway station, on her way to board a ship to
a faraway country, that she could only ever control the life
she led inside her mind. When she was in the house on
Campden Grove, when she could hear Henry whistling in
his bathroom, trimming his moustache and admiring his
profile, it was enough to know that what she had inside was
hers alone.

Even so, seeing Jimmy together with Dolly Smitham at
the play had been a shock. They'd spoken once or twice
about his fiancée, but Jimmy had always closed up when the
topic surfaced and so Vivien had stopped asking. She'd
become used to thinking of him as someone who hadn't a

life outside the hospital, or family aside from his father. Watching him with Dolly, though – the tenderness with which he held her hand, the way he kept his eyes trained on her – Vivien had been forced to confront the truth. Vivien might have loved Jimmy, but Jimmy loved Dolly. Moreover, Vivien could see why. Dolly was pretty and funny, and filled with a sort of zest and fearlessness that drew people to her. Jimmy had described her once as sparkling, and Vivien knew just what he meant. Of course he loved her; no wonder he was so intent on providing the mast for her glorious, billowing sail – she was just the sort of person to inspire devotion from a man like Jimmy.

And that's exactly what Vivien planned to tell Katy: that Jimmy was engaged to be married, his fiancée was a charming woman, and there was no reason he and Vivien shouldn't still—

The telephone rang on the table beside her and Vivien glanced at it, surprised. People didn't call 25 Campden Grove during the day; Henry's colleagues telephoned him at work, and Vivien didn't have many friends, not the sort who made phone calls. She picked up the receiver uncertainly.

The voice on the other end was male and unfamiliar. She didn't catch the gentleman's name, he said it too quickly. 'Hello?' she said again. 'Who did you say is calling?'

'Dr Lionel Rufus.'

Vivien couldn't think that she knew anyone by that name and wondered whether perhaps he was an associate of Dr Tomalin's. 'How may I help you, Dr Rufus?' It struck Vivien sometimes that her voice was like her mother's now, here in this other life; her mother's voice when she'd read stories to them and it had become clipped and perfect and faraway, not her real voice at all.

'Is this Mrs Vivien Jenkins?'

'Yes?'

'Mrs Jenkins, I wonder if I might speak to you on a delicate matter. It concerns a young woman I believe you've met once or twice. She lived across the road from you for a time, working as a companion to Lady Gwendolyn.'

'Do you mean Dolly Smitham?'

'Yes. Now, what I have to tell you is not something I would usually discuss – there are issues of confidentiality to consider – however in this case I feel it's in your best inter-est. You might want to sit down, Mrs Jenkins.'

Vivien was already sitting down, so she made a small noise of assent, and then she listened closely as a doctor she'd never met told her a story she could hardly believe.

She listened, and she said very little, and when Dr Rufus finally rang off, Vivien sat with the telephone receiver in her hand for a very long time. She played his words over in her mind, trying to plait each strand together in a way that made sense. He'd spoken of Dolly ('A good girl, at the whim sometimes of a grand imagination') and her young man ('Jimmy, I think – never met the fellow myself'); and he'd told her of their desire to be together, their perceived need for money so they could start again. And then he'd set out the plan they'd come up with, the part they'd cast her in, and when Vivien wondered aloud why they'd chosen her, he'd explained Dolly's despair at finding herself 'disowned' by someone she so admired.

The conversation left Vivien numb at first – and thank goodness, for the hurt at what she'd learned, the lie it made of things she'd believed fine and true, might otherwise have been crushing. She told herself the man was wrong, that it was a cruel practical joke, or else a mistake – but then she remembered the bitterness she'd seen in Jimmy's face when she'd asked why he and Dolly didn't marry and move away at once; the way he'd upbraided her, reminding her that romantic ideals were the luxury of those who could afford them; and she'd known.

She sat very still as all her hopes dissolved around her. Vivien was very good at disappearing behind the storm of her emotions – she'd had a lot of practice – but this was different; it made her ache in a part of herself she'd long ago put away for safekeeping. Vivien saw clearly then, as she hadn't before, that it wasn't Jimmy alone she'd craved, it was what he'd represented. A different life; freedom and the future she'd stopped herself from imagining, a future that rolled on ahead without impediments. Also, in some strange way, the past – not the past of her nightmares, but rather the opportunity to come to peace with the events of before . . .

It wasn't until she heard the hall clock chiming downstairs that Vivien remembered where she was. The room had grown colder and her cheeks were damp with tears she hadn't known she was crying. A draught crept from somewhere and Jimmy's photograph drifted off the bed and onto the floor. Vivien watched, wondering dully whether even that special gift had all been part of the plan, a ruse to gain her trust so the rest of the scheme might be enacted: the photograph taken, the letter sent— Vivien straightened. There was a twisting in her stomach. Suddenly she realized there was more at stake than her own grievous disappointment. Much more. A terrible train was about to be set in motion and she was the only one who could stop it. She hooked the telephone receiver back in place and looked at her wrist-watch. Two o'clock. Which meant she had three hours before she needed to be home to get ready for Henry's dinner engagement.

There was no time now to lament her losses; Vivien went to the writing desk and did what she had to do. She faltered on her way towards the door, the only outward sign of her inner torment, her rising fear, and then hurried back to retrieve the book. She scribbled her message across the frontispiece, recapped her pen, and then, without another minute's hesitation, she hurried downstairs and set off on her way.

Mrs Hamblin, the woman who came in to sit with Mr Metcalfe when Jimmy was working, answered the door. She smiled when she saw Vivien and said, 'Oh good, it's you, dear. I'll just pop down to the grocer, if you don't mind, seeing as you're here to watch him.' She fed a string bag over her arm and tapped the side of her nose as she hurried out the door. 'I've heard tell there's bananas under the counter for those that know how to ask nice for them.'

Vivien had grown enormously fond of Jimmy's dad. She thought sometimes that her own father might have been just like him, had he been given the chance to attain such an age. Mr Metcalfe had grown up on a farm, one of a great gaggle of children, and many of the stories he told were of the sort Vivien could relate to; certainly they'd influenced Jimmy's ideas about the life he wanted to lead. Today, though, was not one of his father's good days. 'The wedding,' he said, clutching her hand in alarm. 'We haven't missed the wedding, have we?'

'You most definitely have not,' she said gently. 'A wedding without you? What are you thinking – there's no chance of such a thing happening.' Vivien's heart ached for him. To be old and confused and frightened; she just wished there were more she could do to ease his way. 'How about a cup of tea?' she said.

'Yes,' he said. 'Oh yes, please.' As grateful as if she'd offered him his life's desire. 'That sounds lovely.'

When Vivien was stirring in the drop of condensed milk, just as he liked it, there was the sound of a key in the lock.

Jimmy came through the door and if he were surprised to see her there, he didn't show it. He smiled warmly, and Vivien smiled back, aware of the steel band tightening around her chest.

She stayed for a time, talking with the two of them, drawing out the visit as long as she dared. Finally, though, she had to go; Henry would be expecting her.

Jimmy walked her to the station as he always did, but when they reached the underground she didn't go straight through the entrance as was usual.

'I have something for you,' she said, reaching into her purse. She took out her copy of *Peter Pan* and gave it to him.

'You want me to have this?'

She nodded. He was touched, but also, she saw, confused. 'I wrote in the front,' she added.

He opened it and read aloud what she'd written. '"A true friend is a light in the dark."' He smiled at the book, and then, from beneath his hair, at her. 'Vivien Jenkins, this is the nicest gift I've ever received.'

'Good.' Her chest ached. 'Now we're even.' She hesitated, knowing that what she was about to do would change everything. Then she reminded herself that it had already changed: the telephone call from Dr Rufus had done that; his dispassionate voice was still in her head, the things he'd told her so plainly. 'I have something else for you, too.'

'It's not my birthday. You know that, right?'

She handed him the slip of paper.

Jimmy turned it over, reading what was written, and then he looked at her, shocked. 'What's this?'

'I should think that's self-explanatory.'

Jimmy glanced over his shoulder; he lowered his voice. 'I mean, what's it *for*?'

'Payment. For all your tremendous work at the hospital.'

He handed the cheque back as if it were poison. 'I didn't ask to be paid; I wanted to help. I don't want your money.'

For a split second, doubt flared like hope in her chest; but she'd come to know him well and she saw the way his eyes darted from hers. Vivien didn't feel vindicated by his shame, she only felt sadder. 'I know you did, Jimmy, and I know you've never asked for payment. But I want you to have it. I'm sure you'll find something to do with it. Use it to help your father,' she said. 'Or your lovely Dolly – if it makes you feel any easier, think of it as my way of repaying her for the great kindness she did me in returning my locket. Use it to get married, to make things perfect, just the way you both want, to move away and start again – the seaside, the children, the whole pretty future.'

His voice was expressionless. 'I thought you said you didn't think about the future.'

'I meant my own.'

'Why are you doing this?'

'Because I like you.' She took his hands, holding them firmly. They were warm, clever, kind hands. 'I think you're a fine man, Jimmy, one of the best, and I want you to have a happy life.'

'That sounds a lot like goodbye.'

'Does it?'

He nodded.

'I suppose that's because it is.' She came closer then and, after the merest hesitation, she kissed him, right there in the middle of the street; she kissed him softly, barely, finally, and then she held onto his shirt, with her forehead against his chest, committing the splendid moment to her memory. 'Goodbye, Jimmy Metcalfe,' she said at last. 'And this time . . . this time we really won't meet again.'

Jimmy sat in the station for a long time afterwards staring at the cheque. He felt betrayed, angry with her, even as he knew he was being utterly unfair. Only – why would she have given him such a thing? And why now, when Doll's plan was forgotten and they were becoming real friends? Was it to do with her mysterious illness? There'd been something final in the way she spoke; it had worried him.

Day after day, as he fielded his dad's questions as to when his lovely girl was coming back, Jimmy looked at the cheque and wondered what he was going to do. There was a part of him that wanted to rip the hateful thing into a hundred tiny pieces; but he didn't. He wasn't stupid; he knew it was the answer to all his prayers, even if it did make him burn with shame and frustration and a strange unnameable grief.

The afternoon he was due to meet Dolly again for tea at Lyons, he debated whether or not to take the cheque with him. He went back and forth on the subject: taking it from inside the copy of *Peter Pan*, putting it in his pocket, and then replacing it in the book and hiding the damn thing out of sight. He looked at his watch. And then he did the same thing over again. He was running late. He knew Dolly would be waiting for him; she'd telephoned him at the newspaper office and said she had something important to show him. She'd be staring at the door, eyes wide and bright, and he'd never be able to explain to her that he'd lost something rare and precious.

Feeling as if all the world's shadows were closing in around him, Jimmy pocketed *Peter Pan* and went to meet his fiancée.

Dolly was waiting in the same seat she'd sat in when she proposed the plan. He noticed her at once because she was wearing that horrible white coat of hers; it wasn't cold enough any more to wear fur, but Dolly refused to take it off. The coat had become so entangled in Jimmy's mind with the whole awful scheme that even a glimpse of it was enough to send a sick feeling surging through his body.

'Sorry I'm late, Doll. I—'

'Jimmy.' Her eyes were shining. 'I've done it.'

'Done what?'

'Here.' She was holding an envelope between the fingers of both hands and now she pulled a square piece of photographic paper from inside. 'I even had it developed myself.' She slid the picture across the table.

Jimmy picked it up and briefly, before he could stop himself, he felt a surge of tenderness. It had been taken at the hospital on the day of the play. Vivien could be made out clearly, and Jimmy, too, standing close, his hand reaching to touch her arm. They were looking at one another; he remembered the moment, it was when he'd noticed that bruise ... And then he realized what he was looking at. 'Doll—'

'It's perfect, isn't it?' She was smiling at him broadly, proudly, as if she'd done him a huge favour – almost as if she expected him to thank her.

Louder than he'd intended, Jimmy said, 'But we decided not to do it – you said it was a mistake, that you never should have asked.'

'*You*, Jimmy. I never should have asked *you*.'

Jimmy glanced again at the photograph and then back to Doll. His gaze was an unforgiving light that showed up all the cracks in his beautiful vase. She hadn't lied; he'd simply misunderstood. She'd never been interested in the children or the play or making amends with Vivien. She'd merely seen an opportunity.

'I should've just –' Her face fell. 'But why do you look that way? I thought you'd be happy. You haven't changed your mind, have you? I wrote the letter so nicely, Jimmy, not at all unkindly, and she's the only one who'll ever see the pho—'

'No.' Jimmy found his voice then. 'No, she won't.'

'Jimmy?'

'That's what I wanted to talk to you about.' He forced

the photograph back into the envelope and pushed it towards her. 'Get rid of it, Doll. There's no need for any of that, not any more.'

'What do you mean?' Her eyes narrowed suspiciously.

Jimmy took *Peter Pan* from his pocket, retrieved the cheque and slid it across the table. Dolly turned it over cautiously.

Her cheeks flushed. 'What's this for?'

'She gave it to me – to us. For help with the hospital play, and to thank you for returning her locket.'

'She did?' Tears came into Dolly's eyes, not of sadness but relief. 'But Jimmy – it's for ten thousand pounds.'

'Yes.' He lit a cigarette while she stared dazedly at the cheque.

'More than I ever would have thought to ask for.'

'Yes.'

Dolly leapt up to kiss him then, and Jimmy felt nothing.

He walked around London for a long time that afternoon. Doll had his copy of *Peter Pan* – he'd been loath to part with it, but she'd snatched it up and pleaded with him to let her take it home, and what reason could he have given to explain his reluctance to let it go? The cheque he *had* retained, and it sat like a weight in his pocket as he roamed down street after battered street. Without his camera he didn't see the small poetic vignettes of war, he saw the whole God-awful mess. One thing he knew for certain: he could never use a penny of that money, and he didn't think he'd be able to look at Doll ever again if she did.

He was crying when he got back to his room, hot angry tears that he swiped away with the heel of his hand, because everything was wrong and he didn't know how to begin setting it right. His father noticed he was upset, and asked whether one of the other neighbourhood children had been giving him a hard time at school – did he need his dad to go and sort them out? Jimmy's heart lurched then for the impossible yearning he felt at the idea of going back, of being a child again. He gave his father a kiss on the top of his head and told him he'd be all right, and when he did, he noticed the letter on the table, addressed in small precise handwriting to Mr J. Metcalfe.

The sender was a woman called Miss Katy Ellis, and she was writing to Jimmy, she said, about Mrs Vivien Jenkins. As Jimmy read it, his heart began to pound with anger, love and finally determination. Katy Ellis had some rather compelling reasons for wanting Jimmy to stay away from Vivien, but all Jimmy saw was how desperately he needed to go to her. At last, he understood everything that had previously confused him.

As to the letter Dolly Smitham wrote to Vivien Jenkins, and the photograph tucked inside its envelope: they were forgotten. Dolly had no need now for either so she didn't go looking for the envelope and therefore didn't notice it was missing. But it was. Swept aside by the sleeve of her thick white coat when she clutched the cheque and leaned ecstatically to kiss Jimmy, it had skidded to a halt on the edge of the table, teetered a few seconds, before tipping, finally, and falling deep into the thin crevice where the bench seat met the wall.

The envelope was completely hidden from sight, and perhaps it might have stayed that way, gathering dust, being nibbled at by cockroaches, disintegrating over the continuous ebb and flow of seasons until long after the names inside it were nothing more than the echoes of lives once lived. But fate has a funny way about it, and that's not what happened.

Late that night, while Dolly slept, curled up in her narrow bed at Rillington Place, dreaming of Mrs White's face when Dolly announced that she was leaving the boarding house, a Luftwaffe Heinkel III on its way back to Berlin dropped a time bomb that fell quietly through the warm night sky. The pilot would've preferred to hit Marble Arch, but he was tired and his aim was off, and so the bomb landed where the iron railing used to stand, right out the front of the nearby Lyons Corner House. It went off at four o'clock the next morning, just as Dolly, who'd woken early, far too excited to keep sleeping, was sitting up in bed, looking over the copy of *Peter Pan* she'd brought home from the restaurant, and copying her name – Dorothy – very carefully at the top of the inscription. So sweet of Vivien to give it to her – it made Dolly sad to think how she'd misjudged her, especially when Jimmy's photograph, the two of them together at the play, slipped from where it had been tucked between the pages. She was glad they were friends now. The bomb took the restaurant and half the house next door with it. There were casualties, but not as many as there might have been, and the ambulance team from Station 39 responded promptly, combing the ruins for survivors. A kindly officer named Sue, whose husband Don had come home shell-shocked from Dunkirk, and whose only boy had been evacuated to a place in Wales with a name she couldn't pronounce, was nearing the end of her shift when she spied something in the debris.

Sue rubbed her eyes and yawned, thought about leaving it, but then reached down to pick it up. It was a letter, she saw, addressed and stamped, but not yet sent. Naturally, she didn't read it, but the envelope wasn't sealed and a photograph slipped out into the palm of her hand. She could see quite clearly now, as dawn broke brilliantly over proud smouldering London: the photograph was of a man and a woman, lovers – she could tell that just by looking at them. The way the fellow had his eyes trained on the pretty young woman; he couldn't take his eyes off her. He wasn't smiling as she was, but everything in his face told Sue that the man in the picture loved that woman with all his heart.

She smiled to herself, a little sadly, remembering the way she and Don had used to gaze at one another, and then she sealed up the letter and tucked it in her pocket. She jumped into the trusty brown Daimler beside her shift partner, Vera, and they drove back to the station. Sue believed in staying optimistic, and in helping others; sending the lovers' note on its way was to be her first good deed of the breaking day. She popped the envelope in the postbox as she walked home, and for the rest of her long, largely happy life, she thought about those lovers sometimes and hoped things had turned out well for them.

Twenty-nine

Another day of Indian summer, and a golden heat haze hovered above the fields. After sitting all morning with her mother, Laurel had handed over to Rose and left the pair of them with the pedestal fan turning slowly on the dressing table while she ventured outside. She'd intended to take a walk down to the stream to stretch her legs, but the tree house had caught her eye, and she decided to climb up the ladder instead. It would be the first time she'd done so in fifty years.

Lord, but the doorway was much lower than she remembered. Laurel clambered through, bottom cocked at an unfortunate angle, and then sat with her legs crossed, surveying the room itself. She smiled when she saw Daphne's mirror still set on its side along the crossbeam. Time had caused the mercury backing to rupture and flake so that when Laurel looked at her reflection, the image was mottled as if through water. It was strange indeed to find herself within this place of childhood memories and see her grown-up wrinkled face staring back at her. Like Alice falling through the rabbit hole; or else falling through it *again*, fifty years on, only to find herself the only thing changed.

Laurel put the mirror back and allowed herself to glance out of the window, just as she had that day; she could almost hear Barnaby barking, see the one-winged hen turning circles in the dust, feel the stretched summer glare sheering off the driveway stones. She was just about convinced that if she peeked back at the house she might see Iris's hula hoop rocking against its leaning post when the hot breeze grazed it. And so she didn't look. Sometimes the distance of years – all that was contained within its concertina folds – was a physical ache. Laurel turned away from the window instead.

She'd brought the photograph of Dorothy and Vivien into the tree house with her, the one Rose had found inside *Peter Pan*, and now Laurel took it out of her pocket. Along with the play script itself, she'd been carrying it around with her ever since she'd got back from Oxford; it had become a talisman of sorts, the starting point to this mystery she was trying to unravel, and – God, she hoped – with any luck, the key to its solution. The two women hadn't been friends, Gerry said, and yet they must have been, for what else explained this picture?

Determined to find a clue, Laurel stared hard at them, their arms linked as they smiled at the photographer. Where had it been taken? she wondered. In a room somewhere, that much was clear; a room with a slanting roof – an attic maybe? There was no one else in the photo, but a small dark smudge behind the women might have been another person moving very quickly – Laurel looked closer – a small person, unless there was something tricky going on with the perspective. A child? Perhaps. Though that didn't help especially, there were children everywhere. (Or were there, in

London during the war? A lot were evacuated, particularly during the first years when London was being blitzed.)

Laurel sighed frustratedly. It was no use; no matter how hard she tried, it was still a guessing game – one option was as plausible as the next and nothing she'd discovered so far gave any real hint as to the circumstances that had led to this picture being taken. Except perhaps the book it had been nestled inside all these decades. Did that mean something? Had the two objects always been a pair? Had her mother and Vivien been in a play together? Or was it just another infuriating coincidence?

She focused her attention on Dorothy, slipping on her glasses and angling the photograph towards the light coming through the open window, all the better to see each grain of detail. It struck Laurel that there was something not quite right about her mother's face; it was strained, as if the extreme good humour she'd found for the photographer wasn't entirely genuine. It wasn't antipathy – certainly not; there was no sense that she didn't like the person behind the camera – rather that the happiness was in part a performance. That it was driven by some emotion other than pure simple joy.

'Hey!'

Laurel jumped and made an owl-like whoop. She glanced at the tree-house entrance. Gerry was standing at the top of the ladder, laughing. 'Oh, Lol,' he said, shaking his head. 'You should have seen your face.'

'Yes. Very funny, I'm sure.'

'It really was.'

Laurel's heart was still pounding. 'To a child perhaps.'

She looked out onto the empty driveway. 'How did you get here? I didn't hear a car.'

'We've been working on teleporting – you know, dissolving matter into nothing and then transmitting it. Going pretty well so far, though I think I might've left half my brain in Cambridge.'

Laurel smiled with exaggerated patience. Delighted though she was to see her brother, she was in no mood for humour.

'No? Oh, all right. I caught the bus and walked up from the village.' He climbed in and sat down next to her. He looked like a lanky shaggy giant, craning his long neck to take in every angle of the tree house. 'God, it's been a while since I've been up here. I really like what you've done with the place.'

'Gerry.'

'I mean. I like your flat in London, but this is less pretentious, isn't it? More natural.'

'Are you finished?' Laurel blinked sternly at him.

He pretended to consider, tapping his chin, and then pushed his unruly hair back from his forehead. 'You know, I think I am.'

'Good. Then would you kindly tell me what you found in London? I don't mean to be rude, but I'm trying to solve a rather significant family mystery here.'

'Right, well. When you put it like that . . .' He was wearing a green canvas satchel across his body and he lifted the strap over his head, long fingers feeling about inside to draw out a small notebook. Laurel felt a surge of dismay when she saw it, but she bit her tongue and didn't remark on how tatty the book was – scraps of paper coming out at all angles, curling Post-it notes at top and bottom, a coffee ring on the front. The man had a doctorate and more besides, presumably he knew how to take good notes, hopefully he'd be a dab hand at finding them again.

'While you're riffling,' she said with determined cheerfulness. 'I've been wondering about what you said the other day, on the phone.'

'Mm?' He continued searching through a clutch of papers.

'You said Dorothy and Vivien weren't friends, that they hardly knew each other.'

'That's right.'

'I just – I'm sorry, but I just don't understand how that can be. Do you think you might've got it wrong somehow? I mean – ' she held up the photograph, the two young women, arms linked, smiling at the camera – 'what do you say to that?'

He took it from her. 'I say they're both very pretty young ladies. Film quality's come a long way since then. Black and white's a far more moody finish than col—'

'Gerry,' Laurel warned.

'And,' he handed it back, 'I say all this photo tells me is that for a moment in time, seventy years ago, our mother linked arms with another woman and smiled at a camera.'

Damned, dry science logic. Laurel grimaced. 'What about this then?' She took up the old copy of *Peter Pan* and opened it to the frontispiece. 'It's inscribed,' she said, pointing her finger at the handwritten lines. 'Look.'

Gerry set his papers in his lap and took the book from her. He read the message. '"For Dorothy, A true friend is a light in the dark. Vivien."'

It was small of her, she knew, but Laurel felt just a wee bit triumphant then. 'That's a little harder to dispute, isn't it?'

He stuck the pad of his thumb in his chin dimple and frowned, still staring at the page. 'That, I grant you, is a tad trickier.' He brought the book closer, lifted his brows as if he were trying to focus, and then he leaned it more towards the light. As Laurel watched, a smile brightened her brother's face.

'What?' she demanded. 'What is it?'

'Well, I wouldn't expect you to notice, of course – you humanities types are never big on detail.'

'The point, Gerry?'

He handed the book back to her. 'Have a closer look. It strikes me that the body of the message is written in a different pen from the name above it.'

Laurel moved to beneath the tree-house window and let sunlight stream directly onto the page. She adjusted her reading glasses and stared hard at the inscription.

Well, some detective she'd turned out to be. Laurel couldn't believe she hadn't noticed before. The message about friendship was written in one pen, and the words *For Dorothy*, at the top, though also in black ink, had been written with another, slightly finer. It was possible Vivien had started writing with one and then switched to a second – the ink of the first might have been running low – but it was unlikely, wasn't it?

Laurel had the dispiriting sense she was grasping at straws, particularly when, as she continued to look, she started to perceive slight variations in the two handwriting styles. Her voice was low and clipped. 'You're suggesting

Ma might have written her own name in the book, aren't you? Made it look as if it were a gift from Vivien?'

'I'm not suggesting anything. I'm just saying two different pens have been used. But yeah, that's a distinct possibility, especially in light of what Dr Rufus observed.'

'Yes,' said Laurel, closing the book. 'Dr Rufus – tell me everything you found, Gerry. Everything he wrote about this – ' she waved her fingers – 'obsessive condition of Ma's.'

'First up, it wasn't an obsessive condition, it was just your garden-variety obsession.'

'There's a difference?'

'Well, yes. One is a clinical definition, the other is a single trait. Dr Rufus certainly thought she had some issues – I'll get to those – but she was never actually his patient. Dr Rufus had known her as a child – his daughter had been friends with Ma when they were growing up in Coventry. He liked her, I gather, and he took an interest in her life.'

Laurel glanced at the photograph in her hand, her beautiful young mother. 'I'll bet he did.'

'They met regularly for lunch and – '

' – and he just happened to write down most of what she told him? Some friend he turned out to be.'

'Just as well, for our purposes.'

Laurel had to concede the point.

Gerry had closed his notebook and he glanced at the Post-it note stuck to its cover. 'So, according to Lionel Rufus, she'd always been an outgoing sort of girl, playful, fun and very imaginative – all the things we know Ma to be. Her origins were ordinary enough, but she was desperate to lead a fabulous life. He first became interested in her because he was researching narcissism—'

'*Narcissism?*'

'In particular the role of fantasy as a defence mechanism. He noticed that some of the things Ma said and did as a teenager tallied with the list of traits he was working on. Nothing over the top, just a certain level of self-absorption, a need to be admired, a tendency to see herself as exceptional, dreams of being successful and popular—'

'Sounds like every teenager I've met.'

'Exactly, and it's all a sliding scale. Some narcissistic traits are common and normal, other people parlay the same traits into forms for which society generously rewards them—'

'Like who?'

'Oh, I don't know – actors . . .' He gave her a crinkly smile. 'Seriously, though, despite what Caravaggio would have us believe, it's not all about staring into mirrors all day.'

'I should think not. Daphne would be in trouble if it were.'

'But people with a bent towards narcissistic personality types *are* susceptible to obsessive ideas and fantasies.'

'Like imagined friendships with people they admire?'

'Yes, precisely. Many times it's a harmless delusion that fades eventually, leaving the object of the ardour none the wiser; other times, though, if the person is forced to confront the fact that their fantasy isn't real – if something happens to crack the mirror, so to speak – well, let's just say they're the type to feel rejection rather deeply.'

'And to seek revenge?'

'I should say so. Though they'd more likely see it as justice than revenge.'

Laurel lit a cigarette.

'Rufus's notes don't go into enormous detail, but it seems that in the early 1940s, when Ma was around nineteen years old, she developed two major fantasies: the first with regards to her employer – she was convinced the old aristocrat looked upon her as a daughter and was going to leave her the bulk of the ancestral estate—'

'Which she didn't?'

Gerry inclined his head and waited patiently for Laurel to say, 'No, of course she didn't. Go on . . .'

'The second was her imagined friendship with Vivien. They *knew* each other, they just weren't as close as Ma believed them to be.'

'And then something happened to spoil the fantasy?'

Gerry nodded. 'I couldn't find a lot of details, but Rufus wrote that Ma was "slighted" by Vivien Jenkins; the circumstances weren't clear, but I gather Vivien openly denied knowing her. Ma was hurt and embarrassed, angry too, but – he thought – until a month or so later he was advised she'd come up with some sort of plan to "put things right".'

'Ma told him that?'

'No, I don't think so . . .' Gerry scanned the Post-it note. 'He didn't specify how he knew, but I got the impression – something in the way it was worded – that the information didn't come directly from Ma.'

Laurel drew in the corner of her mouth, considering. The words 'put things right' made her mind cast back to her visit with Kitty Barker, in particular the old woman's account of the night she and Ma went out dancing. Dolly's wild behaviour, the 'plan' she kept on about, the friend she'd brought with her – a girl she'd grown up with in Coventry. Laurel smoked thoughtfully. Dr Rufus's daughter, it had to be, who'd later told her father what she'd heard.

Laurel felt sorry for her mother then – denied by one friend, reported on by another. She could well remember the hot intensity of her own teenage daydreams and imaginings; it had been a relief when she became an actress and was able to funnel them into artistic creations. Dorothy, though, hadn't had that opportunity . . .

'So what happened, Gerry?' she said. 'Ma just let her fantasies go, snapped out of it?' The word 'snapped', and Laurel remembered her mother's crocodile story. That sort of change was exactly what she'd been suggesting in the tale, wasn't it? A transition from the young Dolly of Kitty Barker's London memories to Dorothy Nicolson of Greenacres.

'Yes.'

'That can happen?'

He shrugged. 'It *can* happen because it *did* happen. Ma's the proof.'

Laurel shook her head at him in wonder. 'You scientists really do believe whatever your proofs tell you.'

'Of course. That's why they're called proofs.'

'How, though, Gerry . . .' Laurel needed more than that. 'How did she shake off these . . . traits?'

'Well, if we consult the theories of our good friend Lionel Rufus here, it would appear that although some people go on to develop a full-blown personality disorder, many simply outgrow the narcissistic traits of adolescence when they reach adulthood. Of most relevance to Ma's situation, though, is his theory that a major traumatic event

– you know, shock or loss or grief – something outside the direct personal sphere of the narcissistic person, can, in some cases, "cure" them.'

'Put them back in touch with reality, you mean? Make them look outwards rather than inwards?'

'Exactly.'

It was what they'd posited when they met that night in Cambridge: that Ma had been involved in something that turned out terribly, and she became a better person for it.

Gerry said, 'I guess it's the same as the rest of us – we grow and change depending on what life throws at us.'

Laurel nodded pensively and finished her cigarette. Gerry was putting away his notebook and it seemed they'd reached the end of the road, but then something occurred to her. 'You said before that Dr Rufus was studying fantasy as a defence mechanism. Defence against what, Gerry?'

'Lots of things, though most notably Dr Rufus believed children who felt out of place within their families – you know, those who were held at a distance by their parents, made to feel odd or different – were susceptible to developing narcissistic traits as a form of self-protection.'

Laurel considered their mother's reluctance to speak in detail about her past in Coventry, her family. She'd always accepted it was because Ma was too grief-stricken by their loss; now, though, she wondered if her silence hadn't been due in part to something else. *I used to get in trouble when I was young*, Laurel could remember her mother saying (usually when Laurel herself had misbehaved); *I always felt different from my parents – I'm not sure they knew quite what to make of me.* What if young Dorothy Smitham had never been happy at home? What if she'd felt an outsider all her life, and her loneliness had driven her to generate grand fantasies in a desperate attempt to fill the hole of need inside? What if it had all gone terribly wrong, and her dreams had come crashing down, and she'd had to live with the fact, until finally she was permitted a second chance, an opportunity to put the past behind her and start again, to become, this time, the person she'd always wanted to be, within a family who adored her?

No wonder she'd been so stricken when Henry Jenkins, after all that time, had walked up the drive. She must have seen him as the author of her dream's demise, his arrival bringing the past into collision with the present in a nightmarish way. Maybe it was shock that made her lift the knife. Shock mixed with fear that she might lose the family she'd created and that she adored. It didn't make Laurel feel any easier about what she'd seen, but it certainly went some way towards explaining it.

But what was the 'major traumatic event' that so changed her? It was something to do with Vivien, with Ma's plan, Laurel would have staked her life on that. But what exactly? Was there any way of finding out more than what they knew already? Anywhere else she might look?

Laurel thought again about the locked trunk in the attic, the place Ma had hidden the playbook and photograph. There'd been very little else inside, only the old white coat, the carved Mr Punch, and the thank-you card. The coat was part of the story – the ticket dated 1941 must surely have been the one Ma bought when she fled London – the provenance of the figurine was impossible to know . . . But what about the card with the Coronation stamp on its envelope? Something about that card had given Laurel a flutter of déjà vu when she found it – she wondered if it might not be worth her while to take another look.

Later that evening, when the day's heat had begun to roll away and night was falling, Laurel left the others looking through photo albums and disappeared up to the attic. She'd taken the key from her mother's bedside-table drawer without even a twinge of conscience. Perhaps knowing precisely what she'd find inside the trunk took some of the sting out of her prying. That, or her moral compass was now completely moribund. Whatever the case, she didn't linger, merely took what she'd come for and hurried back downstairs.

Dorothy was still sleeping when Laurel returned the key, the sheet drawn high on her body, and her face wan against the pillow. The nurse had been and gone an hour before, and Laurel had helped to bathe her mother. As she'd drawn the flannel down Ma's arm, she'd thought: *These are the arms that nursed me*; as she held the old, old hand, she'd found herself trying to remember the reverse sensation, of her small fingers wrapped inside the safety of her mother's palm. Even the weather, the unseasonal warmth, the bursts of sun-shot air that came down the chimney, made Laurel feel unaccountably nostalgic. *Nothing unaccountable about it,* said a voice in Laurel's head. *Your mother's dying – of course you feel nostalgic.* Laurel did not like that voice and shooed it away.

Rose stuck her head around the door and said, quietly, 'Daphne just called. Her plane gets in to Heathrow at midday tomorrow.'

Laurel nodded. It was just as well. When the nurse was

leaving earlier, she'd told them, with a delicacy Laurel appreciated, that it was time to call the family home. 'She hasn't far to walk now,' the nurse had said. 'Her long journey's almost done.' And it *was* a long journey – Dorothy had lived a whole other life before Laurel had even been born; a life that Laurel was only now beginning to glimpse.

'Need anything?' said Rose, tilting her head so that silvery ripples of hair fell over one shoulder. 'Fancy a cup of tea?'

Laurel said, 'No thanks,' and Rose left. Sounds of movement started up in the kitchen downstairs: the hum of the kettle, cups being laid out on the bench top, the cutlery clattering in the drawer. They were comforting noises of family life, and Laurel was glad her mother was home to hear them. She went closer to the bed and sat down on a chair, stroking Dorothy's cheek lightly with the back of her fingers.

There was something soothing in watching the gentle rise and fall of her mother's chest. Laurel wondered whether even in her sleep she could hear what was happening; whether she was thinking, *My children are down there, my grown-up children, happy and healthy and enjoying one another's company.* It was hard to know. Certainly Ma slept more calmly now; there'd been no nightmares since the other evening, and although her moments of wakeful lucidity were rare, they were radiant when they came. She seemed to have let go of the restlessness – the guilt, Laurel supposed – that had plagued her over the past few weeks, and was moving beyond the place where contrition ruled.

Laurel was glad for her; no matter what had occurred in the past, it was insupportable to think of her mother, so much of her life led in kindness and love (repentance, perhaps?), engulfed by guilt at the very end. Yet there was a selfish part of Laurel that wanted to know more; that *needed* to talk to Ma before she passed away. She couldn't bear to think that Dorothy Nicolson might die without them having spoken about what happened that day in 1961, and what happened before that in 1941, the 'traumatic event' that changed her. For surely at this point it was only by asking outright that Laurel was going to find the answers she needed. *Ask me again one day, when you're older*, her mother had said when Laurel wondered how she'd turned from a crocodile into a person; well, Laurel wanted to ask now. For herself, but more than that so she could give Ma the comfort and true forgiveness she so surely craved.

'Tell me about your friend, Ma,' Laurel said softly to the dim, silent room.

Dorothy stirred and Laurel said it again, a little louder. 'Tell me about Vivien.'

She didn't expect an answer – the nurse had administered morphine before she left – and none came. Laurel leaned back in her chair and slipped the old card from its envelope instead.

The message hadn't changed; it still read only *Thank you*. No more words had appeared since last she'd looked, no clue as to the sender's identity, no answers to the riddle she sought to solve.

Laurel turned the card over and over again, wondering whether it was only a lack of other options that made her think it was important. She put it back into its envelope, and as she did so, the stamp caught her eye.

She felt the same frisson of memory as last time.

Something was definitely eluding her, something to do with that stamp.

Laurel brought it closer, taking in the young queen's face, her coronation robes ... It was hard to believe it had been almost sixty years. She rattled the envelope thoughtfully. Perhaps her sense of the card's importance was less to do with Ma's mystery and more to do with its representation of an event that had loomed so large in Laurel's eight-year-old mind. She could still remember watching it on the television set her parents had borrowed specially for the occasion; they'd all gathered around and—

'Laurel?' The old voice was as thin as a drift of smoke.

Laurel put the card aside and leaned her elbows on the mattress as she took her mother's hand. 'I'm here, Ma.'

Dorothy smiled faintly. Her eyes were glazed as she blinked at her eldest daughter. 'You're here,' she echoed. 'I thought I heard ... I thought you said ...'

Ask me again one day, when you're older. Laurel felt herself at a precipice; she'd always believed in crossroad moments: this, she knew, was one of them. 'I was asking about your friend, Ma,' she said. 'In London, during the war.'

'Jimmy.' The name came quickly, and with it a look of panic and loss. 'He ... I didn't ...'

Ma's face was a mask of anguish, and Laurel hurried to soothe her. 'Not Jimmy, Ma – I meant Vivien.'

Dorothy didn't say a word. Laurel could see her jaw twitching with unsaid things.

'Ma, please.'

And perhaps Dorothy perceived the note of desperation in her eldest daughter's voice, because she sighed with ancient sorrow, her eyelids fluttered, and she said, 'Vivien . . . was weak. A victim.'

Every hair on Laurel's neck stood alert. Vivien was a victim, she was Dorothy's victim – this felt like a confession. 'What happened to Vivien, Ma?'

'Henry was a brute . . .'

'Henry Jenkins?'

'A vicious man . . . he beat . . .' Dorothy's old hand gripped Laurel's, her gnarled fingers trembling.

Laurel's face heated as realization fired. She thought of the questions raised by what she'd read in Katy Ellis's journals. Vivien wasn't ill or infertile – she was married to a violent man. A charming brute who abused his wife behind closed doors and then smiled at the world; who did the sort of damage that kept Vivien in bed for days at a time recovering while he maintained a vigil at her side.

'It was a secret. No one knew . . .'

That wasn't quite true though, was it? Katy Ellis had known: the euphemistic references to Vivien's health and well-being; the excessive concern over Vivien's friendship with Jimmy; the letter she intended to write, telling him why he had to stay away. Katy had been desperate that Vivien not do anything to draw her husband's ire. Was that why she'd counselled her young friend away from Dr Tomalin's hospital? Had Henry been envious of the other man's place in his wife's affections?

'Henry . . . I was scared . . .'

Laurel glanced at her mother's pale face. Katy had been Vivien's friend and confidante – it was understandable that she might know such a dirty marital secret; how though did Ma know such a thing? Had Henry's violence spilled over?

Was that what had gone wrong with the young lovers' plan?

And then Laurel was seized by a sudden, awful idea. Henry had killed Jimmy. He'd found out about Jimmy's friendship with Vivien and killed him. That was why Ma hadn't married the man she loved. The answers fell like dominoes: that was how she knew about Henry's violence, that was why she was scared.

'*That's* why,' Laurel said quickly. 'You killed Henry because of what he did to Jimmy.'

The answer came so softly it might have been the current of the white moth's wings as it flew through the open window and soared towards the light. But Laurel heard it. 'Yes.'

Just a single word, but to Laurel it was music. Caught within its three simple letters was the answer to a lifetime's question.

'You were frightened when he came here, to Greenacres, that he'd come to hurt you, because everything went wrong and Vivien died.'

'Yes.'

'You thought he might hurt Gerry, too.'

'He said . . .' Ma's eyes shot open; her grip tightened on Laurel's hand. 'He said he was going to destroy everything I loved—'

'Oh, Ma.'

'Just as I . . . just as I'd done to him.'

As her mother released her grip, exhausted, Laurel could have wept; she was overwhelmed by an almost crushing sense of relief. Finally, after weeks of searching, after years and years of wondering, everything was explained: what she'd seen; the menace she'd felt as she watched the man in the black hat walking up the driveway; the secrecy afterwards that she couldn't understand.

Dorothy Nicolson killed Henry Jenkins when he came to Greenacres in 1961 because he was a violent monster who used to beat his wife; he'd killed Dorothy's lover; and spent two decades trying to track her down. When he found her, he'd threatened to destroy the family she loved.

'Laurel . . .'

'Yes, Ma?'

But Dorothy didn't say more. Her lips moved soundlessly as she searched the dusty corners of her mind, grasping at lost threads she might never catch.

'There now, Ma.' Laurel stroked her mother's forehead. 'Everything's all right. Everything's all right now.'

Laurel fixed the sheets, and stood for a time watching her mother's face, peaceful now, asleep. All this time, she realized, this whole hunt she'd been on had been driven by a yearning need to know that her happy family, her entire childhood, the way her mother and father had looked at one another with such rare abiding love, was not a lie. And now she did.

Her chest ached with a complex blend of burning love, and awe, and yes, finally, acceptance. 'I love you, Ma,' she whispered, close by Dorothy's ear, feeling, as she did, the end to her search. 'And I forgive you, too.'

Iris's voice was growing typically heated in the kitchen and Laurel itched, suddenly, to join her brother and sisters. She gathered Ma's blankets up smoothly and placed a kiss on her forehead.

The thank-you card was sitting on the chair behind her and Laurel picked it up, intending to stow it in her bedroom. Her mind was already downstairs fixing a cup of tea, so she couldn't have said later what it was that made her notice then the small black marks on the envelope.

But notice them she did. Her steps faltered halfway across Ma's room and she stopped. She went to where the lamplight was brightest, slipped on her reading glasses and brought the envelope close. And then she smiled, slowly, wonderingly.

She'd been so distracted by the stamp that she'd nearly missed the real clue staring her in the face. It had been franked. The cancellation mark was decades old and it wasn't easy to read, but it was clear enough to make out the date the card had been posted – 3 June 1953 – and, better yet, where it had been sent from: Kensington, London.

Laurel glanced back towards her mother's sleeping form. It was the very place Ma had lived during the war, in a house on Campden Grove. But who had sent her a thank-you card over a decade later, and why?

Thirty

Vivien glanced at her wristwatch, the cafe door, and finally the street outside. Jimmy had said two, but it was almost half past and there was still no sign of him. He might have run into trouble at work, or maybe with his dad, but Vivien didn't think so. His message had been urgent – he *needed* to see her – and he'd delivered it by such cryptic methods; Vivien couldn't believe he'd have let himself get caught up. She bit her bottom lip and checked her watch again. Her gaze shifted to the full cup of tea she'd poured fifteen minutes ago, the chip on the saucer's rim, the dried tea in the dip of the spoon. She glimpsed outside the window again, saw no one she knew, and then tilted her hat to hide her face.

His message had been a surprise, a wonderful, terrible heart-pounding surprise. Vivien had truly believed when she gave Jimmy the cheque that she wouldn't see him again. It hadn't been a trick, a way to bluff him into making fevered contact; Vivien valued his life, if not her own, too much for that. Her intention had been the opposite. After hearing Dr Rufus's story, after realizing the repercussions – for all of them – should Henry learn of the friendship she'd formed with Jimmy, the work she'd been doing at Dr Tomalin's hospital, it had seemed the only way. The perfect way, in fact. It delivered money to Dolly, and the sort of insult to Jimmy that would most offend a man like him, an honourable man, a kind one, and thereby be sufficient to keep him away – to keep him safe – forever. She'd been reckless in letting him get so close, she ought to have known better; Vivien knew she had brought this whole situation on herself.

In some way, giving the cheque to Jimmy had also delivered to Vivien what she most wanted in the world. She smiled now, just a little, thinking of it. Her love for Jimmy was selfless: not because she was a good person but because it had to be. Henry would never ever allow them to be anything to one another, and so she let her love take the form of wanting for Jimmy the best life he could have, even if she couldn't be a part of it. Jimmy and Dolly were free now to do everything he dreamed of: to leave London, to be married, to live happily ever after. And by giving away money Henry guarded so jealously, Vivien was striking at him, too, in the only way she could. He would find out, of course. The strict rules of her inheritance weren't easily circumvented, but Vivien had no great interest in money and what it could buy – she signed over whatever amount Henry demanded and needed very little for herself. Nonetheless, he made it his business to know precisely what was spent and where; she would pay a hefty price, just as she had over the donation to Dr Tomalin's hospital, but it would be worth it. Oh yes, it pleased her greatly to know the money he craved so dearly would go elsewhere.

Which wasn't to say telling Jimmy goodbye hadn't been one of the most agonizing things Vivien had ever done, because it had been. Faced with seeing him now, the joy that pulsed beneath her skin when she pictured him arriving through that door, the fall of dark hair over his eyes, the smile that suggested secret things, that made her feel understood – recognized, before he said a single word – she couldn't believe she'd found the strength to go through with it.

Now, in the cafe, she looked up as one of the waitresses arrived at the edge of her table and asked if she'd like to order food. Vivien told her no, that she was fine with tea at the moment. It occurred to her that Jimmy might've come and gone already, that perhaps she'd just missed him – Henry had been unusually tense over the past few days, it hadn't been easy getting away – but when she asked the waitress, the girl shook her head. 'I know the fellow you're talking about,' she said. 'Handsome man with the camera.' Vivien nodded. 'Haven't seen him in a couple of days – sorry.'

The waitress left and Vivien turned and looked out the window again, checking up and down the street for Jimmy, and for anybody else who might be watching too. She'd been shocked initially by what Dr Rufus had told her on the telephone, but as she'd made her way to Jimmy's place, Vivien had thought she understood: Dolly's hurt when she imagined herself rejected, her impulse for revenge, her burning desire to reinvent herself and start again. There were people, Vivien was sure, who'd find such a scheme inconceivable, but she wasn't one of them. She found nothing particularly difficult in believing that a person might go to such lengths if they thought the ends made possible an escape; especially someone like Dolly, who'd been cut adrift by the loss of her family.

The aspect of Dr Rufus's story that cut like a knife was

Jimmy's part in it. Vivien refused to believe that everything they'd shared had been pretend. She knew it hadn't. No matter what had brought Jimmy to her on the street that day, the feelings between them were real. She knew it in her heart, and Vivien's heart was never wrong. She'd known it that very first night in the canteen, when she'd seen the photograph of Nella and exclaimed, and Jimmy had looked up and their eyes had met. She knew it, too, because he hadn't stayed away. She'd given him the cheque – everything Dolly wanted and more – but he hadn't walked away. He'd refused to let her go.

Jimmy had sent word with a woman Vivien didn't know, a funny little thing who'd knocked on the front door at 25 Campden Grove with a tin in her hand for donations to the Soldiers' Hospital Fund. Vivien had been about to collect her purse, when the woman shook her head and whispered that Jimmy *needed* to see her, that he'd meet her here in this railway cafe at two o'clock on Friday. And then the woman had gone and Vivien had felt hope flicker inside her before she knew how to stop it.

But – Vivien checked her watch – it was almost three now; he wasn't coming. She knew it. She'd known it for the past thirty minutes.

Henry would be home in an hour and there were things she had to take care of before he arrived, things that he expected. Vivien stood and tucked the chair beneath the table. Her disappointment now was a hundred times worse than it had been the last time she'd left him. But she couldn't wait longer; she'd already stayed beyond what was safe. Vivien paid for her pot of tea, and with a last glance around the cafe, she pushed her hat down low and hurried back towards Campden Grove.

'Been out for a walk, have you?'

Vivien stiffened in the entrance hall; she glanced over her shoulder, through the open door to the sitting room. Henry was in the armchair, legs crossed, black shoes gleaming, as he watched her over the top of a thick Ministry report.

'I . . .' Her thoughts swam. He was early. She was supposed to greet him at the door when he arrived home, hand him his whisky and ask about his day. 'It's such lovely weather. I couldn't resist.'

'Go through the park?'

'Yes.' She smiled, trying to still the rabbit in her chest. 'The tulips are in bloom.'

'Are they?'

'Yes.'

He raised his report again, covering his face, and Vivien let herself breathe again. She remained where she was, but only for a second, only to be sure. Careful not to move too quickly, she set her hat down on the stand, removed her scarf, and walked as smoothly as she could, away.

'See any friends while you were out?' Henry's voice stopped her as she reached the bottom step.

Vivien turned slowly; he was leaning, casually, against the sitting-room doorjamb, smoothing his moustache. He'd been drinking; there was something in his manner, a looseness that she recognized, that made her stomach swoop with dread. Other women, she knew, found Henry attractive, that dark, almost sneering expression, the way his eyes refused to let theirs go; but Vivien didn't. She never had. Ever since the night they met, when she'd thought herself alone by the lake at Nordstrom and looked up to find him leaning against the pool house, staring at her while he smoked. There'd been something in his eyes as he watched her; lust, of course, but something else besides. It had made her skin crawl. She saw it in them now.

'Why, Henry, no,' she said, as lightly as she could, 'of course not. You know I haven't time for friends, not with my canteen work.'

The house was still and silent, no cook downstairs rolling out pastry for the dinner pie, no maid wrestling with the vacuum cord. Vivien missed Sarah; the poor girl had cried, embarrassed and ashamed, when Vivien came across the two of them together that afternoon. Henry had been livid, his pleasure spoiled and his dignity wrinkled. He'd punished Sarah's compliance by letting her go; he'd punished Vivien's timing by making her stay.

And so here they were, just the two of them. Henry and Vivien Jenkins, a man and his wife. *Henry was one of my brightest students*, her uncle had said when he told her what the two men had discussed in his smoke-filled study. *He's a distinguished gentleman. You're very lucky that he's interested in you.*

'I think I'll go upstairs and lie down,' she said, after a pause that seemed interminable.

'Tired, darling?'

'Yes.' Vivien tried to smile. 'The raids. The whole of London's tired, I suppose.'

'Yes.' He came towards her with lips that smiled and eyes that didn't. 'I suppose they probably are.'

*

Henry's fist hit her left ear first and the ringing was deafening. The force of the blow sent her face into the entrance-
hall wall and she fell to the floor. He was on top of her then,
grabbing at her dress, shaking her, his handsome face twisting with anger as he hit her. He was shouting, too, spittle
coming from his mouth, landing on her face, her neck, his
eyes glinting as he told her over and over that she belonged
to him and she always would, she was his prize, that he'd
never let another man touch her, he'd sooner see her dead
than let her go.

Vivien closed her eyes; she knew it drove him wild with
rage when she refused to look at him. Sure enough, he
shook her harder, gripped her by the throat, shouted closer
to her ear.

*In the black of her mind, Vivien looked for the creek,
the shining lights . . .*

She never fought back, even when her fists clenched
hard at her sides, and that balled-up part of her, the essence
of Vivien Longmeyer that she'd tucked away so long ago,
wrestled for release. Her uncle might have struck the deal in
his smoky study, but Vivien had had her own reasons for
being so traceable. Katy had tried her best to change her
mind, but Vivien had always been stubborn. This was her
penance, she knew, it was what she deserved. Her fists were
the reason she'd been punished in the first place; the reason
she'd been left at home; the reason her family had hurried
back from the picnic and been lost.

*Her mind was liquid now; she was in the tunnel, swim-
ming down and down, her arms and legs strong as they
pulled her through the water towards home . . .*

Vivien didn't mind being punished; she just wondered

when it would end. When he would put an end to her. Because he would one day, of that she was certain. Vivien held her breath, waiting, hoping, this might be it. For each time she woke and found herself still here in the house on Campden Grove, the well of despair inside her deepened.

The water was warmer now; she was getting closer. In the distance, the first twinkling lights. Vivien swam towards them . . .

What would happen, she wondered, when he did kill her? Knowing Henry he'd have the wherewithal to make sure someone else took the blame. Or else he'd have it seem she'd died by accident – an unfortunate fall, bad luck in the air raids. Wrong place, wrong time, people would say, shaking their heads, and Henry would be cast evermore as the devoted, grieving husband. He'd probably write a book about it, about her, a fantasy version of Vivien, just like the other one, *The Reluctant Muse*, about that horrid pliable girl she didn't recognize, who worshipped her author husband and dreamed of dresses and parties.

The lights were bright now, nearer, and Vivien could make out shimmering patterns. She looked beyond them, though; it was what lay beyond that she had come to find . . .

The room tilted. Henry was finished. He picked her up and she felt her body slump like a rag doll, limp in his arms. *She ought to do it herself.* Take rocks, or bricks – something heavy – and put them in her pockets; walk into the Serpentine, one step at a time, until she saw the lights.

He was kissing her face, smothering it with wet kisses. His ragged breaths, his smell of hair grease and alcohol turned to sweat. 'There now,' he was saying. 'I love you, you know I do, but you make me so angry – you shouldn't get me angry like that.'

Tiny lights, so many lights, and on the other side, Pippin. He turned towards her, and for the first time it seemed he could see her . . .

Henry carried her up the stairs, a ghastly groom with his bride, and then he laid her gently on the bed. *She could do it herself.* It was so clear to her now. She, Vivien, was the final thing she could take from him. He peeled off her shoes and fixed her hair so it fell evenly over each shoulder. 'Your face,' he said sadly, 'your beautiful face.' He kissed the back of her hand and set it down. 'Have a rest now,' he said. 'You'll feel better when you wake up.' He leaned close, his lips against her ear. 'And don't you worry about Jimmy Metcalfe. I've had him taken care of; he's dead now, rotting at the bottom of the Thames. He won't come between us any more.' Heavy footsteps; the door closing; the key being turned in the lock.

Pippin lifted his hand, half a wave, half a beckoning motion, and Vivien went towards him . . .

She woke an hour later, in her bedroom at 25 Campden Grove, with afternoon sunlight streaming through the window onto her face. Immediately Vivien closed her eyes again. She had a throbbing headache behind her temples, in the back of her eye sockets, at the base of her neck. Her whole head felt like a ripe plum that had fallen onto tiles from somewhere high. She lay as still as a plank, trying to remember what had happened and why she ached so terribly.

It came back to her in waves, the whole episode, mixed,

as always, with impressions from the watery salvation of her mind. Those were the hardest memories to bear – the shadowy sensations of supreme well-being, of eternal longing, more febrile than real memories, and yet so much more potent.

Vivien winced as slowly she shifted each part of her body, trying to ascertain the damage. It was part of the process; Henry would expect her to be 'neatened up' by the time he got home; he didn't like it when she took too long to heal. Her legs seemed unharmed – that was good, limping prompted awkward questions; her arms were bruised but not broken. It was her jaw that throbbed, while her ear was still ringing and the side of her face burned. That was unusual. Henry didn't normally touch her face; he was careful, keeping the blows always below the neckline. She was his prize, nothing should mark her but him, and he didn't like to be confronted by the evidence; it reminded him of how angry she'd made him, how disappointing she could be. He liked her injuries to remain safely beneath her clothing, there for only her to see, to remind her how much he loved her – he would never hit a woman if he didn't care so damned much.

Vivien cleared her mind of Henry. Something else had been trying to get to the surface, something important; she could hear it like a lone mosquito in the dead of night, buzzing close before skirting away, but she couldn't catch it. She stayed very still as the hum came near, and then – Vivien gasped for air; she remembered, and she reeled. Her own suffering paled. *Don't you worry about Jimmy Metcalfe. I've had him taken care of; he's dead now, rotting at the bottom of the Thames. He won't come between us any more.*

She couldn't breathe. Jimmy – he hadn't come to meet her today. She'd waited but he hadn't come. Jimmy wouldn't have left her there; he'd have come if he could.

Henry knew his name. He'd found out somehow, had Jimmy 'taken care of'. There'd been others before, people who'd dared get between Henry and the things he wanted. He never did it himself, it wouldn't have been seemly – Vivien was the only one who knew the cruelty of Henry's fists. But Henry had his men, and Jimmy hadn't come.

A keening noise rose up, the terrible sound of an animal in pain, and Vivien realized it was her. She curled onto her side and pressed her hands against her skull to ease the ache, and she didn't think she'd ever move again.

The next time she woke, the sun had lost its bite and the room had taken on the blue of early evening. Vivien's eyes stung. She'd been crying in her sleep, but she didn't cry now. She was empty inside, desolate. All that was good in the world had gone, Henry had seen to that.

How had he known? He had his spies, she knew, but Vivien had been careful. She'd gone to Dr Tomalin's hospital for five months without incident; she'd broken off contact with Jimmy so this exact thing wouldn't happen; as soon as Dr Rufus told her about Dolly's intentions, she'd known—

Dolly.

Of course, it was Dolly. Vivien forced her mind back to the details of her conversation with Dr Rufus, straining to remember; he'd told her Dolly planned to send a photograph of Vivien and Jimmy with a letter saying she'd tell

Vivien's husband all about the 'affair' unless Vivien paid for her silence.

Vivien had thought the cheque would be enough, but no, Dolly must have sent the letter after all, and in it, along with the photograph, she'd named Jimmy. The foolish, foolish girl. She'd imagined herself the inventor of a clever scheme; Dr Rufus said she'd thought it was harmless, she'd been convinced that no one would get hurt; but she hadn't known with whom she was dealing. Henry, who got jealous if Vivien stopped to say good morning to the old man who sold newspapers on the street corner; Henry, who wouldn't allow her to make friends or have children for fear they'd take her time away from him; Henry, who had contacts in the Ministry and could find out anything about anybody; who'd used her money to have others 'taken care of' in the past.

Vivien sat up gingerly – shooting stars of pain behind her eyeballs, inside her ear, in the crown of her head. She took a breath and pushed herself to standing, relieved to find she could still walk. She caught sight of her face in the mirror and stared: there was dried blood down one side and her eye had started to swell. She turned her head gently to the other side, everything hurting as she did so. The tender spots were not yet purple; she would look worse tomorrow.

The longer she spent on her feet, the better she was able to stand the pain. The bedroom door was locked, but Vivien had a secret key. She went slowly to the hidey-hole behind her grandmother's portrait, struggled a moment to remember the combination, and then turned the dial. A hazy memory came of the day some weeks before her wedding when Vivien's uncle had brought her to London to visit the family lawyers and, afterwards, the house. The caretaker had pulled her aside when they were alone in the bedroom and pointed out the portrait, the safe behind. 'A lady needs a place for her secrets,' she'd whispered, and although Vivien hadn't liked the sly look on the old woman's face, she'd always craved a place of her own and had remembered the advice.

The safe door sprung open and she retrieved the key she'd had cut last time. She took the photograph Jimmy had given her, too; it was strange, but she felt better for having it near her. As carefully as she could, Vivien closed the door and hung the painting straight.

She found the envelope on Henry's desk. He hadn't even bothered to hide it. It was addressed to Vivien, postmarked two days before, and had been sliced open. Henry always opened her post – and therein lay the terrible flaw in Dolly's great scheme.

Vivien knew what the letter would say, but her heart still pounded as she skimmed its contents. All was as she'd expected; the letter written almost in a kindly tone; Vivien just thanked God the silly girl hadn't signed her name, that she'd written only *A Friend*, at the bottom.

Tears threatened when Vivien looked at the photograph but she forced them back. And when her memory tossed up tantalizing echoes of precious moments in Dr Tomalin's attic, of Jimmy, of the way he'd made her feel as if she just might have a future to look forward to, she quashed them. She knew better than anyone that there was no going back.

Vivien turned the envelope over and she could have

wept tears of despair. For there, Dolly had written: *A Friend, 24 Rillington Place, Notting Hill.*

Vivien tried to run, but her head thumped and her thoughts swam and she had to stop at each looming lamp post, steadying herself as she made her way through the navy-dark streets towards Notting Hill. She'd stayed in Campden Grove long enough only to rinse her face, hide the incriminating photograph, and scratch out a hurried letter. She dropped it in the first postbox she passed and continued on her way. There was a single thing left she had to do, her final act of penance before everything was set right.

Once she'd realized that fact, everything else had come into glorious focus. Vivien shed desolation like an unwanted coat, and stepped towards the shining lights. It was all so simple really. She had brought about her family's death, she had brought about Jimmy's death, but now she was going to make sure Dolly Smitham was saved. Then, and only then, she would go to the Serpentine and make her pockets heavy with stones. Vivien could see the end and it was beautiful.

Speed of light and limb, her father used to say, and although her head throbbed, although she had to clutch the railings sometimes to stop from falling, Vivien was a good runner, and she refused to stop. She imagined herself a wallaby, scooting through the bush; a dingo, slinking in the shadows; a lizard, sneaking in the dark . . .

There were planes in the distance and Vivien glanced at the black sky every so often, stumbling when she did. A part of her willed them to fly overhead, to drop their load if they dared; but not yet, not yet, she still had work to do.

*

Night had fallen when she reached Rillington Place, and Vivien hadn't brought a torch. She was struggling to find the right number when a door slammed shut behind her; she glimpsed a figure coming down the steps of the nearby house.

Vivien called, 'Excuse me?'

'Yes?' A woman's voice.

'Please – can you help me? I'm looking for number 24.'

'You're in luck. It's right here. No rooms free at the moment, I'm afraid, but there will be soon.' The woman struck a match then and brought it to her cigarette so that Vivien saw her face.

She couldn't believe her luck, and thought at first she must be seeing things. 'Dolly?' she said, rushing towards the pretty woman in the white coat. 'It *is* you, thank God. It's me, Dolly. It's—'

'Vivien?' Dolly's voice was filled with surprise.

'I thought I might've missed you, that I was too late.'

Dolly was immediately suspicious. 'Too late for what? What is it?'

'Nothing.' Vivien laughed suddenly. Her head was spinning and she faltered. 'That is, everything.'

Dolly drew on her cigarette. 'Have you been drinking?'

Something moved in the dark beyond; there were footsteps. Vivien whispered, 'We have to talk – *quickly*.'

'I can't. I was just—'

'Dolly, *please*.' Vivien glanced over her shoulder, terrified she'd see one of Henry's men coming towards her. 'It's important.'

The other woman didn't answer at once, wary perhaps

of this unexpected visit. Finally, grudgingly, she took Vivien's arm and said, 'Come on, let's go back inside.'

Vivien breathed a tentative sigh of relief as the door shut behind them; she ignored the curious glance of an elderly woman in glasses, and followed Dolly up the stairs, along a corridor that smelled of old food. The room at its end was small, dark and stuffy.

When they were inside, Dolly flicked the light switch and a bare bulb fired above them. 'Sorry it's so hot in here,' she said, taking off the heavy white fur she'd been wearing. She hung it on a hook on the back of the door. 'No windows, more's the pity – makes the blackout easier but it's not so handy for ventilation. No chair, either, I'm afraid.' She turned and saw Vivien's face in the light. 'My God. What happened to you?'

'Nothing.' Vivien had forgotten how ghastly she must look. 'An accident on the way. I ran into a lamp post. Stupid of me, rushing as usual.'

Dolly looked unconvinced, but she didn't press the subject, indicating instead that Vivien should sit on the bed. It was narrow and low, and the bedspread was marked with the general creeping stains of age and overuse. Vivien wasn't fussy, though; to sit was a welcome respite. She collapsed onto the thin mattress, just as the air-raid siren began to wail.

'Ignore it,' she said quickly, when Dolly moved to go. 'Stay. This is more important.'

Dolly dragged nervously on her cigarette, and then folded her arms defensively across her chest. Her voice tightened. 'Is it the money? Do you need it back?'

'No, no, forget about the money.' Vivien's thoughts had

scattered and she fought to gather them back, to find the clarity she needed; everything had seemed so straightforward before, but now her head was heavy, her temples an agony, and the siren kept on with its caterwauling.

Dolly said, 'Jimmy and I—'

'Yes,' Vivien said quickly, and her mind suddenly cleared. 'Yes, Jimmy.' She stopped then, struggling to find the words she needed to say the terrible truth out loud. Dolly, watching her closely, began to shake her head, almost as if she'd guessed somehow what Vivien had come to tell her. The gesture gave Vivien courage and she said, 'Jimmy, Dolly – ' just as the siren stopped its cry – 'he's gone.' The word echoed in the room's new quiet.

Gone.

A hasty knock on the door, and a shout of, 'Doll – are you in there? We're going down to the Andy.' Dolly didn't answer; her eyes searched Vivien's; she brought her cigarette to her mouth, smoking feverishly, fingers shaking. The person knocked again, but when there was still no response, ran along the corridor and down the stairs.

A smile wavered, hopefully, uncertainly, on Dolly's face as she sank down next to Vivien. 'You've got it mixed up. I saw him yesterday, and I'm seeing him again tonight. We're going together, he wouldn't have gone without me . . .'

She hadn't understood and Vivien said nothing further for a moment, held captive by the well of deep sympathy that had opened up inside her. Of course Dolly didn't understand; the words would be like chips of ice, melting in the face of her hot disbelief. Vivien knew only too well what it was to receive such awful news, to learn from nowhere that one's most treasured loves were dead.

But then a plane chugged overhead, a bomber, and Vivien knew there was no time to waste in pity, that she had to keep explaining, to make Dolly see she was telling the truth, to make her understand that she had to leave now if she wanted to save herself. 'Henry,' Vivien began, 'my husband – I know he might not seem it, but he's a jealous man, a violent man. That's why I had to get you out of there that day, Dolly, when you brought back my locket; he doesn't let me have friends—' There was a tremendous explosion somewhere not so far away, and a swishing sound went through the air above them. Vivien paused a second, every muscle in her body tensed and aching, and then she continued, faster now, more purposefully, sticking to the bare essentials. 'He received the letter and photograph and they humiliated him. You made him seem a cuckold, Dolly, so he sent his men to put things right – that's how he sees it; he sent his men to punish you and Jimmy both.'

Dolly's face had turned as white as chalk. She was in shock, that was clear, but Vivien knew she was listening because tears had begun to stream down her cheeks. Vivien continued, 'I was supposed to meet Jimmy in a cafe today but he didn't come. You know Jimmy, Dolly, he never would have stayed away, not when he said he'd be there – so I went home and Henry was there, and he was angry, Dolly, so angry.' Her hand went absently to her throbbing jaw. 'He told me what had happened, that his men had killed Jimmy for getting close to me. I wasn't sure how he knew, but then I found your envelope. He opened it – he always opens my letters – and he saw us together in the photograph. It all went wrong, do you see – your plan all went terribly wrong.'

When Vivien mentioned the plan, Dolly clutched her arm; her eyes were wild and her voice a whisper. 'But I don't know how – the photograph – we agreed not to, that there wasn't any need, not any more.' She met Vivien's eyes and shook her head frantically. 'None of this was meant to happen, and now Jimmy—'

Vivien waved further explanation aside. Whether or not Dolly meant to send the photograph was neither here nor there as far as she was concerned; she hadn't come here to rub Dolly's nose in her own mistake. There was no time now for guilt; God willing, Dolly would have plenty of time to reproach herself later. 'Listen to me,' she said. 'It's very important that you listen. They know where you live and they *will* come after you.'

Tears slipped down Dolly's face. 'It's my fault,' she was saying. 'It's all my fault.'

Vivien seized the other woman's thin hands. Dolly's grief was natural, it was raw, but it wasn't helpful. 'Dolly, please. It's as much my fault as yours.' She raised her voice to be heard over the bombers. 'None of that matters now anyway. They're coming. They're probably on their way already. That's why I'm here.'

'But I—'

'You need to leave London, you need to do it now, and you mustn't come back. They won't stop looking for you. Not ever—' There came a blast and the whole building shuddered; it was closer than the one before, and despite the room's lack of windows an uncanny light flooded through every tiny pore in the building's skin. Dolly's eyes were wide with fear. The noise was relentless; the whistling as bombs fell, the blast when they landed, the anti-aircraft guns firing back. Vivien had to shout to be heard as she asked about Dolly's family, her friends, whether there was anywhere at all that she could safely go. But Dolly didn't answer. She shook her head and continued to cry helplessly, her palms pressed now to her face. Vivien remembered then what Jimmy had told her about Dolly's family; it had warmed her to the other woman at the time, knowing that she, too, had suffered such a crippling loss.

The house rattled and shook, the plug just about leapt out of the horrid little sink, and Vivien felt her panic rise. 'Think, Dolly,' she implored, at the same time as a deafening explosion. 'You have to think.'

There were more planes now, fighters as well as bombers, and the guns were chattering fiercely. Vivien's head throbbed with the noise, and she imagined the bodies of the aircraft passing over the roof of the house; even with the ceiling and the attic above, she could all but see their whale-like bellies. 'Dolly?' she shouted.

Dolly's eyes were closed. Despite the clamour of bombs and guns, the roar of the planes, for a moment her face brightened, seeming almost peaceful, and then she lifted her head with a start and said, 'I applied for a job a few weeks ago. It was Jimmy who found it . . .' She took a sheet of paper from the small table beside her bed and handed it to Vivien.

Vivien scanned the letter, a job offer for Miss Dorothy Smitham at a boarding house called Sea Blue. 'Yes,' she said, 'perfect. That's where you must go.'

'I don't want to go by myself. We—'

'Dolly—'

'We were supposed to go *together*. It wasn't meant to be like this, he was going to wait for me—'

And then she was crying again. Fleetingly, Vivien allowed herself to sink inside the other woman's pain; it was so tempting just to let herself collapse, to give up and let go, to be submerged . . . But it didn't do any good, she knew she had to be brave; Jimmy was already dead and Dolly would be too if she didn't start listening. Henry would not waste too much time. His thugs would be on their way already. Gripped by urgency, she slapped the other woman's cheek, not hard, but sharply. It worked, for Dolly swallowed her next sob, holding her face and hiccuping. 'Dorothy Smitham,' said Vivien sternly. 'You need to leave London and you need to go quickly.'

Dolly was shaking her head. 'I don't think I can.'

'I *know* you can. You're a survivor.'

'But Jimmy—'

'That's enough.' She took Dolly by the chin and forced her gaze. 'You loved Jimmy, I know that – ' *I loved him too* – 'and he loved you – my God, I know that. But you have to listen to me.'

Dolly gulped and nodded tearfully.

'Go to the railway station tonight and buy yourself a ticket. You're to—' The light bulb flickered as another bomb landed close with a thundering crump; Dolly's eyes widened, but Vivien stayed calm, refusing to let her go. 'Get on that train and ride it all the way to the very end of the line. Don't look back. Take the job, move again, live a good life.'

Dolly's eyes had changed as Vivien was speaking; they'd focused, and Vivien could tell that she was listening now, that she was hearing each and every word, and more than that, she was starting to understand.

'You have to go. Seize this second chance, Dolly: think of it as an opportunity. After everything you've been through, after everything you've lost.'

'I will,' Dolly said quickly. 'I'll do it.' She got up, pulled a small suitcase from beneath her bed and began filling it with clothing.

Vivien was so tired now; her own eyes had begun to water with utter exhaustion. She was ready for it all to end. She'd been ready for a long, long time. Outside, planes were everywhere; the ack-acks were firing and spotlights sliced through the night sky. Bombs fell and the earth trembled so they could feel it through the foundations under their feet.

'What about you?' said Dolly, sealing her case and standing up. She held out her hand to take back the boarding-house letter.

Vivien smiled; her face ached and she was bone-tired; she felt herself sinking under the water, towards the lights. 'Don't worry about me. I'm going to be fine. I'm going home.'

As she said it, an enormous explosion sounded and light was everywhere. Everything seemed to slow down. Dolly's face lit up, her features frozen in shock; Vivien glanced upwards. As the bomb fell through the roof of 24 Rillington Place, and the roof fell through the ceiling, and the bulb in Dolly's room shattered into a million tiny shards, Vivien closed her eyes and rejoiced. Her prayers had been answered at last. There would be no need for the Serpentine tonight. She saw the twinkling lights in the darkness, the bottom of the creek, the tunnel to the middle of the world.

And she was in and swimming, deeper and deeper, and the veil was right before her, and Pippin was there, waving, and she could see them all. They could see her, too, and Vivien Longmeyer smiled. After such a long, long time, she'd reached the end. She'd done what she had to do. Finally, she was going home.

Part Four

DOROTHY

Thirty-one

Laurel had come to Campden Grove first thing; she wasn't sure why exactly, only she'd had a conviction it was what she must do. In her heart of hearts, she supposed she'd hoped to knock on the door and find the person who'd sent Ma the thank-you card still living inside. It had seemed logical at the time; now, though, standing in the foyer of number 7 – an apartment block of short-term holiday lets these days – breathing in the scent of lemon deodorizer and weary travellers, she felt rather foolish. The woman working in the small cluttered reception area looked up from behind her telephone again to ask if she was still all right, and Laurel assured her that she was. She went back to eyeing the dirty carpet and tying her thoughts in knots.

Laurel wasn't remotely all right; in fact, she was exceedingly dismayed. She'd felt so exhilarated the night before when Ma told her about Henry Jenkins, about the kind of man he'd been. Everything had made sense and she'd felt sure they'd reached the end; that finally she understood what had happened that day. Then she'd noticed the cancellation mark on the stamp and her heart had turned a cartwheel; she'd been sure it was important – more than that, the discovery had felt personal, as if she, Laurel, was the only person who could unravel this final knot. But now here she was, standing in the middle of three-star accommodation, at the end of a wild goose chase, with nowhere to look, nothing to look for, and no one to speak to who'd lived there during the war. What did the card mean? Who'd sent it? Did any of it really matter? Laurel was beginning to think it did not.

She waved at the receptionist, who mouthed, 'Bye-bye,' over the phone receiver, and then Laurel went outside. She lit a cigarette and smoked it tetchily. She was fetching Daphne from Heathrow later; at least the journey wouldn't be a complete loss. She glanced at her watch. Still a couple of hours to kill. It was lovely and warm, the sky was blue and clear, scarred only by the perfect jet streams of people going places – Laurel figured she ought just to pick up a sandwich and walk in the park by the Serpentine. As she drew on her cigarette she remembered the last time she'd come to Campden Grove. The day she'd stood outside number 25 and seen the little boy.

Laurel eyed the house now. Vivien and Henry's house: the site of his secret abuse; the place in which Vivien had endured. In a funny way, with all she'd read in Katy Ellis's journals, Laurel knew more of life in that house than she did of the one behind her. She finished her cigarette, considering, and bent to drop the butt into the ashtray by the apartment entrance. By the time she'd straightened, Laurel was decided.

She knocked on the door to 25 Campden Grove and waited. The Halloween decorations were gone from the window and there were painted cutouts of children's hands – at least four different sizes – hanging in their place. That was nice. It was nice that a family lived there now. That ugly memories from the past were being written over by new ones. She could hear noises inside – someone was definitely home – but no one had come to the door so she knocked again. She turned around on the tiled landing and looked across the street to number 7, trying to picture her mother as a young woman, a lady's maid, climbing those stairs.

The door opened behind her and the pretty woman Laurel had seen the last time she came was standing there, a baby slung over one shoulder. 'Oh my God,' she said, blinking her wide blue eyes. 'It's – *you*.'

Laurel was used to being recognized but there was something different in the way this woman said it. She smiled and the woman blushed, wiping her hand on her blue jeans and then holding it out to Laurel. 'I'm so sorry,' she said. 'Where are my manners? I'm Karen, and this is Humphrey – ' she patted the child's padded bottom and a mop of blond curls shifted slightly on her shoulder, one sky-blue eye regarding Laurel shyly – 'and of course I know who you are. It's such a huge honour to meet you, Ms Nicolson.'

'Laurel, please.'

'Laurel.' Karen bit down gently on her bottom lip, a nervous, pleased gesture, and then she shook her head in a disbelieving way. 'Julian mentioned seeing you, but I thought ... Sometimes he ...' She smiled. 'Never mind – you're here. My husband is going to be *beside* himself when he meets you.'

You're Daddy's lady. Laurel had an unshakeable sense that there was more going on than she knew.

'You know, he didn't even tell me you were coming.'

Laurel didn't mention that she hadn't called ahead; she still didn't know how she'd explain why she'd come. She smiled instead.

'Come in, please. I'll just call Marty down from the attic.'

Laurel followed Karen into the cluttered entrance hall, around the lunar-module pram, through a sea of balls and kites and mismatched tiny shoes, and into a warm bright sitting room. There were white bookcases from floor to ceiling, books lying every which way, children's paintings on the wall beside family photographs of happy smiling people. Laurel almost tripped over a small body on the floor; it was the boy she'd seen last time, now lying on his back with his knees bent. He had one arm in the air above him animating a Lego plane, and was making low engine noises, lost completely in the veracity of his plane's flight. 'Julian,' his mother said, 'Juju – run upstairs, little love, and tell Daddy we have a visitor.'

The boy looked up then, blinking back to reality; he saw Laurel and the light of recognition appeared in his eyes. Without a word, without so much as a faltering pause in the engine noise he was making, he set his plane on a new course, scrambled to his feet, and followed it up the carpeted stairs.

Karen insisted on putting the kettle on to boil, and so Laurel sat on a comfortable sofa with felt-pen marks on its red and white gingham cover, and smiled at the baby, who was sitting now on a floor rug, kicking a rattle with his fat little foot.

A hurried creaking came from the stairs and a tall man, handsome in a dishevelled sort of way with his longish brown hair and black-rimmed glasses, appeared in the sitting-room doorway. His pilot son followed him into the room. The man held out a large hand and grinned when he saw Laurel, shaking his head wonderingly, as if she might just be an apparition materialized in his home. 'My goodness,' he said, as their palms touched and she proved herself to be flesh and blood. 'I thought Julian might have been pulling my leg, but here you are.'

'Here I am.'

'I'm Martin,' he said. 'Call me Marty. And you'll have to forgive my incredulity, only – I teach theatre studies at Queen Mary College, you see, and I wrote my doctoral thesis on you.'

'You did?' *You're Daddy's lady.* Well, that explained it.

'*Contemporary Interpretations of Shakespeare's Tragedies.* It was a lot less dry than it sounds.'

'I imagine it was.'

'And now – here you are.' He smiled and then frowned slightly and then smiled again. He laughed, a lovely sound. 'Sorry. This is just such an extraordinary coincidence.'

'Did you tell Ms Nicolson – Laurel – ' Karen flushed, as she re-entered the room, 'about Gramps?' She slid a tray of tea things onto the coffee table, cutting a swathe through a forest of children's craft materials, and sat beside her husband on the sofa. Without so much as a sideways glance, she handed a biscuit to a little girl with brown ringlets who'd sensed the arrival of sweets and appeared from nowhere.

'My grandfather,' Marty explained. 'He's the one who got me hooked on your work. I'm a fan, but he was religious. He never missed a single one of your plays.'

Laurel smiled, pleased and trying not to seem it; she was charmed by this family and their delightful scruffy home. 'Surely he must have missed one.'

'Never.'

'Tell Laurel about his foot,' said Karen, rubbing gently at her husband's arm.

Marty laughed. 'He broke his foot one year and made them release him from hospital early so he could see you in *As You Like It*. He used to take me with him when I was still small enough to need three cushions just to see over the seat in front of me.'

'He sounds like a man of splendid taste.' Laurel was flirting, not just with Marty, but with all of them; she felt rather appreciated. It was a good thing Iris wasn't there to witness it.

'He was,' Marty said with a smile. 'I loved him dearly. We lost him ten years ago, but not a day goes by that I don't miss him.' He pushed his black frames higher on his nose and said, 'But enough about us. Forgive me – I blame the surprise of seeing you – we haven't even asked yet why you've come to see us. Presumably it wasn't to hear about Gramps.'

'It's a rather long story, actually,' Laurel said, taking the cup of tea she was offered, stirring in some milk. 'I've been researching my family history, in particular my mother's side, and it turns out she was once –' Laurel hesitated – 'friendly, with the people who lived in this house.'

'When would that have been, do you know?'

'The late 1930s and the early years of the war.'

A nerve pulled at Marty's eyebrow. 'How extraordinary.'

'What was your mother's friend's name?' Karen asked.

'Vivien,' said Laurel. 'Vivien Jenkins.'

Marty and Karen exchanged a glance, and Laurel looked between them. She said, 'Did I say something odd?'

'No, not odd, only – ' Marty smiled at his hands as he collected his thoughts – 'we know that name rather well here.'

'You do?' Laurel's heart had begun to thump rather loudly. They were Vivien's descendants, of course they were. A child Laurel hadn't learned about, a nephew—

'It's rather a peculiar story, actually, one of those that's entered family legend.'

Laurel nodded eagerly, willing him to continue as she took a sip of tea.

'My great-grandfather Bertie inherited this house, you see, during the Second World War. He was unwell, the story goes, and very poor: he'd worked all his life but times were tough – there was a war on, after all – and he was living in a tiny flat near Stepney, being looked after by an old neighbour, when one day, out of the blue, he received a visit from a fancy lawyer who told him he'd been left this place.'

'I don't understand,' Laurel said.

'Neither did he,' said Marty. 'But the lawyer was quite clear on the matter. A woman named Vivien Jenkins, whom my great-grandfather had never heard of, had made him the sole beneficiary of her will.'

'He didn't know her?'

'Never heard of her.'

'But that's so strange.'

'I agree. And he didn't want to come here at first. He suffered with dementia; he didn't like change; you can imagine how much of a shock it was – so he stayed where he was and the house sat empty, until his son, my grandfather, came back from the war and was able to convince the old man that it wasn't a trick.'

'Your grandfather had known Vivien, then?'

'He had, but he never talked about her. He was pretty open, my gramps, but there were a couple of subjects on which he'd never be drawn. She was one of them; the other was the war.'

'I believe that's not uncommon,' Laurel said. 'All the horrors those poor men saw.'

'Yes.' His face fell into a sad frown. 'But it was more than that for Gramps.'

'Oh?'

'He was drafted into service from prison.'

'Oh, I see.'

'He was rather spare with the details, but I did some checking.' Marty looked a little sheepish and lowered his voice as he continued, 'I found the police records and learned that one night in 1941 Gramps was fished out of the Thames, badly beaten.'

'By whom?'

'I'm not sure, but it was while he was in hospital that the police came round. They had it in their heads he'd been involved in some sort of blackmail attempt and took him in for questioning. A misunderstanding, he always swore, and if you knew my gramps you'd know he didn't lie, but the coppers didn't believe him. According to the records he was carrying a large cheque made out to cash when they found him, but he wouldn't say how he came by it. He was thrown into prison; he couldn't afford a lawyer, of course, and in the end the police didn't have enough evidence so they joined him up. It's funny, but he used to say they saved his life.'

'*Saved* his life? How?'

'I don't know, I could never work that out. Maybe it was a joke – he joked around a lot, my gramps. They sent him to France in 1942.'

'He hadn't been in the army before that?'

'No, but he saw action – he was at Dunkirk, in fact – only he didn't carry a gun. He took a camera. He was a war photographer. Come and see some of his photographs.'

'My God,' Laurel said, realizing, as she studied the black and white photographs that covered the wall, 'Your grandfather was James Metcalfe.'

Marty smiled proudly. 'None other.' He straightened a photo frame.

'I recognize these. I saw an exhibition at the V&A about a decade ago.'

'That was just after he died.'

'His work is incredible. You know, my mother had one of his prints on the wall when I was a girl, just a small one – she still does, for that matter. She used to say it helped her to remember her family; what happened to them. They were killed in the Coventry Blitz.'

'I'm sorry about that,' Marty said. 'Terrible. Impossible to imagine.'

'Your grandfather's photographs go some of the way to helping with that.' Laurel looked at each photograph in turn. They really were exceptional; people who'd been bombed out of their houses, soldiers on the battlefield.

There was one of a little girl in a strange outfit, tap shoes and oversized bloomers. 'I like this one,' she said.

'That's my aunt Nella,' Marty said, smiling. 'Well, we called her that, though she wasn't really a relation. She was a war orphan. That photo was taken on the night her family was killed. Gramps stayed in touch with her, and when he got back from the war he tracked her down with her foster family. They remained friends for the rest of his life.'

'That's lovely.'

'He was like that, very loyal. You know, before he married my grandmother, he went to look up an old flame just to make sure she was doing all right. Nothing would've stopped him marrying my gran, of course – they were very much in love – but he said it was something he had to do. They were separated during the war and he'd only seen her once since he got back, and then from a distance. She'd been on the beach with her new husband and he hadn't wanted to interrupt them.'

Laurel was listening and nodding, when suddenly the pieces kaleidoscoped into order: Vivien Jenkins had left the house to the family of James Metcalfe. James Metcalfe, with his old and unwell father – why, it was Jimmy, wasn't it? It had to be. Ma's Jimmy, and the man Vivien had fallen in love with, against whom Katy had warned her, fearful of what Henry might do if he found out. Which meant Ma was the woman Jimmy had tracked down before he got married. Laurel felt faint, and not just because it was her mother Marty was talking about; there was something tugging at her very own memories.

'What is it?' said Karen, concerned. 'You look as if you've seen a ghost.'

'I-I just –' Laurel stammered, 'I just – I have an idea what might have happened to your grandfather, Marty. I think I know why he was beaten; who it was that left him for dead.'

'You do?'

She nodded, wondering where to start. There was so much to tell.

'Come back to the sitting room,' Karen said. 'I'll put the kettle on again.' She shivered, excited. 'Oh, it's silly of me, I know, but doesn't it feel wonderful to solve a mystery?'

They were turning to leave the room when Laurel saw a photograph that made her gasp.

'She's beautiful, isn't she?' Marty said, smiling as he noticed the direction of her gaze.

Laurel nodded, and it was on the tip of her tongue to say, 'That's my mother,' when Marty said instead, 'That's her, that's Vivien Jenkins. The woman who left Bertie this house.'

Thirty-two

The end of the line, May 1941

Vivien walked the last part of the journey. The train had been crammed with soldiers and tired-looking Londoners – standing room only, but she'd been offered a seat. There were advantages, she realized, to looking as if one had just been plucked from a bomb-blast site. There'd been a young boy sitting on the seat opposite, a suitcase on his lap and a jar clutched tightly in his hand. It had contained, of all things, a small red goldfish, and every time the train slowed or sped up or lurched into the sidings to wait out an alert, the water sloshed against the glass and he held it up to check his fish wasn't panicked. Did fish panic? Vivien was sure they didn't, though the idea of being trapped inside a glass jar made something inside her contract so tightly it was hard to breathe.

When he wasn't peering at his fish, the boy watched Vivien, his large sombre blue eyes taking in her injuries, her thick white coat even though it was the end of spring. She smiled slightly when their eyes met, about an hour into the journey, and he did the same, but only briefly. She wondered, among the other thoughts that flooded her mind and fought for attention, who the boy was and why he was travelling all by himself in the midst of a war, but she didn't ask – she was far too nervous to speak to anyone for fear of giving herself away.

There was a bus that ran into the town every half hour – when they drew near the station, she'd heard a couple of elderly women discussing its surprising reliability – but Vivien decided to walk. She couldn't shake off the feeling that only by keeping on moving could she stay safe.

A motorcar slowed behind her and every nerve in Vivien's body tensed. She wondered if she'd ever stop being frightened. Not until Henry was dead, she knew, for only then would she truly be free. The driver of the car was a man with a uniform she didn't recognize. She imagined how she must appear to him – a woman in a winter coat, with a bruised and sorry face, and a small suitcase, walking into town alone. 'Good afternoon,' he said.

Without turning her head, she nodded a reply. It had been almost twenty-four hours, she realized, since she'd spoken aloud. It was superstitious nonsense, but she couldn't shake the sense that once she opened her mouth the game would be up, that Henry would hear somehow, or one of his cronies would, and then he'd come to find her.

'Heading into town?' said the man in the car.

She nodded again, but she knew she was going to have to answer at some point, if only to satisfy him she wasn't a German spy. The last thing she needed was to be hauled into the local police station by some jumped-up Civil Defence Warden keen to uncover the invasion.

'I can give you a lift, if you like,' he said. 'The name's Richard Hardgreaves.'

'No.' Her voice was husky from lack of use. 'Thank you, but I enjoy the walk.'

It was his turn to nod. He glanced through the wind-screen in the direction he was heading, before turning back to Vivien. 'Are you visiting someone in town?'

'I'm starting a new job,' she said. 'At Sea Blue boarding house.'

'Ah! Mrs Nicolson's place. Well then, I'll see you around town, I'm sure, Miss—?'

'Smitham,' she said. 'Dorothy Smitham.'

'Miss Smitham,' he repeated with a smile. 'Lovely.' And then he gave her a small wave of his hand and continued on his way.

Dorothy watched until his car disappeared over the crest of the grassy hill, and then she cried tears of relief. She'd spoken and nothing terrible had happened. A whole conversation with a stranger, the giving of a new name, and the sky hadn't fallen in; the earth hadn't opened and swallowed her. Taking a deep cautious breath, she let herself entertain the smallest sliver of hope that perhaps it really was going to be all right. That she was to be allowed this second chance. The air smelled of salt and the sea, and a group of gulls circled in the distant sky. Dorothy Smitham picked up her suitcase and kept on moving forwards.

In the end, it was the poor-sighted old woman at Rillington Place who'd given her the idea. When Vivien opened her eyes in the middle of the dust-filled bombsite and realized she was still, unfathomably, alive, she'd started to weep. There were sirens, and the voices of brave kind men and women arriving at the site to put out fires, and patch up wounds, and take away the dead. Why, she wondered, couldn't she be one of them – why couldn't life just have let her go?

She wasn't even badly injured – Vivien was practised at assessing the severity of her wounds. Something had fallen across her, a door she thought, but there was a gap and she was able to work herself free. She sat, dizzy in the dark. It was cold, freezing cold now, and she was shivering. She didn't know the room well, but she felt something furry beneath her hand – a coat! – and pulled it free from where it had been pinned by the door. She found a torch in the coat pocket, and when she pointed its fine beam she saw that Dolly was dead. More than dead, she'd been crushed by bricks and ceiling plaster and a large metal chest that had fallen from the attic above.

Vivien was sick, with shock and pain and the churning disappointment of having failed at her task; she clambered to her feet. The ceiling had gone and she could see stars in the sky; she was gazing at them, swaying unsteadily, wondering how long it would take Henry to find her, when she heard the old woman call, 'Miss Smitham, Miss Smitham is alive!'

Vivien turned towards the voice, dazed because she knew Dolly was most certainly not alive. She was about to say so, pointing her arm aimlessly in Dolly's direction, but she couldn't find any words inside her throat, just a hoarse, airy sound, and the old woman was still shouting that Miss Smitham was alive, and pointing at Vivien, and that was when she realized the landlady's mistake.

It was an opportunity. Vivien's head hammered and her thoughts were clouded, but she saw at once she'd been given a chance. In fact, within the startling aftermath of a direct bomb strike, the whole thing seemed remarkably simple. The new identity, the new life, was as easily acquired as the coat she'd slipped on in the dark. No one would be harmed; there was no one left to be harmed – Jimmy was gone, she'd done what she could for Mr Metcalfe, Dolly Smitham had no family, and there was no one to mourn Vivien – and so she took the chance. She pulled off her wedding ring and crouched in the dark, pushing it onto Dolly's finger. There was noise everywhere, people shouting, ambulances coming and going, rubble still heaving and settling in the smoking dark, but Vivien heard only her own heart pounding – not with fear, but with determination. The offer of employment was still clenched in Dolly's other hand, and Vivien steadied her nerves, taking Mrs Nicolson's letter for herself and slipping it inside the pocket of the white coat. There were other things in there already, a small hard object, and a book, she could tell, when her fingers brushed against it, but she didn't look to see which one.

'Miss Smitham?' A man wearing a helmet had leaned his ladder against the edge of the broken floor, and climbed so his face was level with where she was standing. 'Don't worry, miss, we're going to get you down from here. Everything's going to be all right.'

Vivien looked at him, and for once she wondered if it might be true. 'My friend,' she said in a hoarse voice, using her torch to indicate the body on the floor. 'Is she . . . ?'

The man glanced at Dolly, her head crushed beneath the metal chest, her limbs splayed in directions that made no sense. 'Bloody hell,' he said, 'I should say she is. Can you tell me her name? Is there anyone we ought to call?'

Vivien nodded. 'Her name is Vivien. Vivien Jenkins, and

she has a husband who ought to know she won't be coming home.'

Dorothy Smitham spent the rest of the war years making beds and cleaning up after Mrs Nicolson's boarding-house guests. She kept her head down, she tried not to do anything that might bring undue attention, she never accepted invitations to dances. She polished and laundered and swept, and at night, when she closed her eyes to go to sleep, she tried not to see Henry's eyes, staring at her in the dark.

By day, she kept her own eyes peeled. At first she saw him everywhere: the familiar strutting walk of a man coming down the jetty, a set of ripe, brutish features on a passing stranger, a raised voice in the crowd that made her skin creep. Over time she saw him less, and she was glad, but she never stopped watching, because Dorothy knew that some day he would find her – it was only a matter of when and where – and she intended to be ready for him.

She sent only one postcard. When she'd been at Sea Blue boarding house six months or so, she picked the prettiest picture she could find – a great big passenger ship, the sort people boarded to travel from one side of the world to the other – and she wrote on the back: *The weather's glorious here. Everybody well. Please destroy upon receipt*, and addressed it to her dear friend – her only friend – Miss Katy Ellis of Yorkshire.

Life gained a rhythm. Mrs Nicolson ran a tight ship, which suited Dorothy fine: there was something deeply therapeutic in being held to military standards of housekeeping excellence and she was freed from her dark memories by the pressing need to buff as much oil as possible ('without wasting it, Dorothy – there's a war on, didn't you know?') into the stair rails.

And then one July day in 1944, a month or so after the D-Day landings, she came home from the grocery store to find a man in uniform sitting at the kitchen table. He was older, of course, and a little the worse for wear, but she recognized him instantly from the eager boyish photograph his mother kept enshrined on her mantelpiece in the dining room. Dorothy had polished the glass many times before, and knew his earnest eyes, the angles of his cheekbones, the dimple in his chin so well, she blushed when she saw him sitting there, just as surely as if she'd been peeking through his keyhole all these years.

'You're Stephen,' she said.

'I am.' He leapt up to help her with the paper bag of groceries.

'I'm Dorothy Smitham. I work for your mother. Does she know you're here?'

'No,' he said. 'The side door was open so I let myself in.'

'She's upstairs; I'll just go—'

'No—' He'd spoken quickly, and his face crinkled into an embarrassed smile. 'That is, it's kind of you, Miss Smitham, and I don't want to give you the wrong idea. I love my mother – she gave me life – but if it's all right by you I'm just going to sit a few moments and enjoy the peace and quiet, before my real military service begins.'

Dorothy laughed then and the sensation took her by surprise. She realized it was the first time she'd laughed since she'd arrived from London. Many years later, when their children asked for the story (again!) of how they fell in love, Stephen and Dorothy Nicolson would tell them about the night they stole along the broken pier to dance at its very end. Stephen had brought his old gramophone and they'd put it on, dodging holes in the boards to the strains of 'By the Light of the Silvery Moon'. Later, Dorothy had slipped and fallen when she was trying to balance her way along the railing (pause for parental instruction: 'You must never try to balance on high railings, darlings'), and Stephen hadn't even taken off his shoes, he'd dived straight over the edge and fished her right back out – 'And that's how I caught your mother,' Stephen would say, which always made the children laugh with the image it conjured of Mummy at the end of a fishing line – and the pair had sat on the sand afterwards, because it was summer and the night was warm, and they'd eaten cockles out of a paper cup and talked for hours until the sun broke pink across the horizon and they strolled back to Sea Blue and knew, without either saying another word, they were in love. It was one of the children's favourite stories, the picture it painted of their parents walking along the pier in saturated clothing, their mother as a free spirit, their father as a hero – but in her own heart, Dorothy knew it was, in part, a fiction. She'd loved her husband long before that. She fell for him that first day in the kitchen when he'd made her laugh.

The list of Stephen's attributes, had she ever been called upon to write it, would have been long. He was brave and protective; he was funny; he was patient with his mother, even though she was the sort of woman whose most amiable chatter contained acid enough to strip paint from the walls. He had strong hands and he did clever things with them: he could fix just about anything, and he could draw (though not as well as he'd have liked). He was handsome, and had a way of looking at her that made Dorothy's skin heat with desire; he was a dreamer, but not so that he lost himself inside his fancies. He loved music and played the clarinet, jazz songs that Dorothy adored but which drove his mother wild. Sometimes, while Dorothy sat crosslegged in the window seat in his room watching him play, Mrs Nicolson would take up her broom downstairs and hammer the end of it against the ceiling, which made Stephen play louder and jazzier, and made Dorothy laugh so hard she had to clap both hands across her mouth. He made her feel safe.

At the top of her list, though, the thing she valued high above the rest, was his strength of character. Stephen Nicolson had the courage of his convictions: he would never let his lover bend his will and Dorothy liked that; there was a danger, she thought, in the sort of loving that made people act against type.

He also had a great respect for secrets. 'You don't talk much about your past,' he'd said to her one night as they sat together on the sand.

'No.'

A silence stretched between them in the shape of a question mark, but she didn't say more.

'Why not?'

She sighed but it caught the night sea breeze and drifted away silently. She knew his mother had been whispering in his ear; terrible lies about her past, aimed to convince him that he ought to wait a while, see other women, think about settling down with a nice local girl instead, someone who didn't have 'London ways' about her. She knew, too, that

Stephen had told his mother that he liked mysteries, that life was rather dull if you knew all there was to know about a person before you'd crossed the street to say hello. Dorothy said, 'For the same reason, I suspect, that you don't talk much about the war.'

He took her hand and kissed it. 'Makes sense to me.'

She knew she'd tell him all about it one day, but she had to be careful. Stephen was the sort of man who'd want to march right up to London and take care of Henry himself. And Dorothy wasn't about to lose anyone else she loved to Henry Jenkins. 'You're a good man, Stephen Nicolson.'

He was shaking his head; she could feel his forehead shifting against hers. 'No,' he insisted. 'Just a man.'

Dorothy didn't argue, but she took his hand in hers and leaned her cheek gently on his shoulder in the dark. She'd known men before, good men and bad, and Stephen Nicolson was a good man. The best of men. He reminded her of someone else she used to know.

Dorothy thought about Jimmy, of course, in the same way she continued to think of her brothers and sister, her mother and father. He'd taken up residence with them in that weatherboard house in the subtropics, welcomed by the Longmeyers of her mind. It wasn't difficult to imagine him there, beyond the veil; he'd always reminded her of the men in her family. His friendship had been a light in the dark, it had given her hope, and maybe if they'd had the chance to know one another longer and better, it would have deepened into the sort of love that was written about in books, the sort of love she'd found with Stephen. But Jimmy belonged to Vivien, and Vivien was dead.

Just once she thought she saw him. It was a few days after her wedding and she and Stephen were walking hand in hand along the water's edge when he leaned to kiss her neck. She laughed and wriggled free, skipping ahead before glancing over her shoulder to call something teasing back to him. And that's when she noticed a figure on the strand, way in the distance, watching them. Her breath caught in recognition as Stephen reached her and swept her off her feet. But it was just her mind playing tricks on her, for when she turned around to look again he was gone.

Thirty-three

Greenacres, 2011

Their mother had requested the song and she wanted to listen to it in the sitting room. Laurel offered to bring a CD player into the bedroom so she didn't have to move, but the suggestion was quickly dismissed and Laurel knew better than to argue. Not with Ma, not this morning when she had that otherworldly look in her eyes. She'd been like it for two days now, ever since Laurel got back from Campden Grove and told her mother what she'd found.

The long slow drive from London, even with Daphne talking about Daphne the whole way, had done nothing to diminish Laurel's exhilaration, and she'd gone in to sit with her mother as soon as they could be alone. They'd spoken, finally, of everything that had happened, of Jimmy, and Dolly, and Vivien, and the Longmeyer family in Australia too; her mother told Laurel of the guilt she'd always harboured about having gone to see Dolly on the night of the bombing and urging her back inside the house. 'She wouldn't have died there if not for me. She was on her way out when I arrived.' Laurel reminded her mother that she'd been trying to save Dolly's life, that she'd been delivering a warning and she couldn't possibly blame herself for the random landing places of German bombs.

Ma had asked Laurel to bring in Jimmy's photograph – not a print at all, but the original – one of the few vestiges of the past she hadn't locked away. Sitting there beside her mother, Laurel had looked at it afresh: the dawn light after a raid, the broken glass in the foreground shining like little lights, the group of people emerging from their shelter in the background, through the smoke. 'It was a gift,' Ma said softly. 'It meant such a lot when he gave it to me. I couldn't have borne to part with it.'

They'd both wept as they talked, and Laurel had wondered at times, as her mother found a reserve of energy and managed to speak – haltingly but with intent – about the things she'd seen and felt, if the strain of old memories, some of them desperately painful, would prove too much; but, whether it was gladness at hearing Laurel's news of Jimmy and his family, or relief at finally having let go of her secrets, she seemed to have rallied. The nurse warned them that it wouldn't last, that they weren't to be misled, and that the decline when it came would be swift; but she smiled, too, and told them to enjoy their mother while they could. And they did; they surrounded her with love and noise and all the happy, fractious crush of family life that Dorothy Nicolson had always loved best.

Now, while Gerry carried Ma to the sofa, Laurel thumbed through the vinyls in the rack, looking for the right album. She went quickly, but paused a moment when she reached Chris Barber's Jazz Band, a smile settling on her face. The record had belonged to her father; Laurel could still remember the day he'd brought it home. He'd got out his own clarinet and played along with Monty Sunshine's solo for hours, standing right there in the middle of the rug, pausing every so often to shake his head in wonder at the sheer virtuosity of Monty's skill. All through dinner that night he'd kept to himself, the noise of his daughters washing over him as he sat at the head of the table with a glow of perfect satisfaction lighting his face.

Infused by the memory's lovely emotion, Laurel pushed Monty Sunshine aside and continued flipping through the records until she found what she was after, Ray Noble and Snooky Lanson's 'By the Light of the Silvery Moon'. She looked back to where Gerry was settling their mother, pulling the light rug so gently to cover her frail body, and she waited, thinking what a boon it was to have had him back at Greenacres these past days. He was the only one in whom she'd confided the truth of the past. They'd sat up together the night before, drinking red wine in the tree house and listening to a London rockabilly station Gerry found on the Internet and talking nonsense about first love and old age and everything in between.

When they spoke of their mother's secret, Gerry said he didn't see there was any reason to tell the others. 'We were there that day, Lol; it's a part of our history. Rose, Daphne and Iris . . .' He'd shrugged then and had a sip of wine. 'Well, it might just upset them, and for what?' Laurel wasn't so sure. Certainly, there were easier stories to tell; it was a lot to cope with, especially for someone like Rose. But at the same time, Laurel had been thinking a lot lately about secrets, about how difficult they were to keep, and the habit they had of lurking quietly beneath the surface before sneaking all of a sudden through a crack in their keeper's resolve. She supposed she'd just have to wait a while and see how things turned out.

Gerry glanced up at her now and smiled, nodding from where he'd perched near Ma's head that she should start the song. Laurel slid the record out of its paper sheath and put it on the player, setting the needle on the outer rim. The swell of the piano opening filled the room's silent pockets and Laurel sat back on the other end of the sofa, laying her hand on her mother's feet and closing her eyes.

Suddenly, she was nine years old again. It was 1954 and a summer's night. Laurel was wearing a nightie with short sleeves and the window above her bed was open in the hopes of luring in the night's cool breeze. Her head was on the pillow, long straight hair splayed out behind her like a fan, and her feet were resting on the sill. Mummy and Daddy had friends over for dinner and Laurel had been lying in the dark like that for hours, listening to the gentle tides of conversation and laughter that rose sometimes over the mumbled sighs of her sleeping sisters. Periodically the scent of tobacco smoke drifted up the stairs and through the open door; glasses chinked together in the dining room, and Laurel basked in the knowledge that the adult world was warm and light and spinning still beyond her bedroom walls.

After a time there came the sound of chairs scraping back beneath the table and footsteps in the hall and Laurel could imagine the men shaking hands, and the women kissing one another's cheeks as they said, 'Goodbye,' and, 'Oh! What a lovely night,' and made promises to do it all again. Car doors clunked, engines purred down the moonlit driveway; and finally, silence and stillness returned to Greenacres.

Laurel waited for her parents' footsteps on the stairs as they went to bed, but they didn't come and she teetered on the rim of sleep, unable quite to release herself and fall. And then, through the floorboards, a woman's laugh, cool and quenching, like a drink of water when you're thirsty, and Laurel was wide awake. She sat up and listened as there came more laughter, Daddy's this time, followed quickly by the sound of something heavy being moved. Laurel wasn't supposed to get up this late at night, not unless she was ill or needed to use the toilet or had been woken by a bad dream, but she couldn't just close her eyes and go to sleep, not now. Something was happening downstairs and she needed to know what it was. Curiosity might have killed the cat, but little girls usually fared much better.

She slid out of bed and tiptoed along the carpeted corridor, nightie fluttering against her bare knees. Quiet as a mouse, she sneaked down the stairs, pausing on the landing when she heard music, faint strains coming from behind the sitting-room door. Laurel hurried the rest of the way down and knelt as carefully as she could, pressing first one hand and then her eye hard against the door. She blinked against the keyhole and then drew breath. Daddy's armchair had been moved back into the corner, leaving a large clear space in the centre of the room, and he and Mummy were standing together on the rug, their bodies clasped together in an embrace. Daddy's hand was large and firm against Mummy's back, and his cheek rested against hers as they swayed in time to the music. His eyes were closed and the look on his face made Laurel swallow and her cheeks heat. It was almost as if he were in pain, and yet somehow the opposite of that, too. He was Daddy, and yet he wasn't, and to see him that way made Laurel feel uncertain and even a little envious, which she couldn't understand at all.

The music kicked into a faster rhythm and her parents' bodies drew apart as Laurel watched. They were dancing, really dancing, like something from a film, with clasped hands and shuffling shoes and Mummy spinning round and round beneath Daddy's arm. Mummy's cheeks were pink and her curls fell looser than usual, the strap of her oyster-coloured dress had slipped a little from one shoulder, and nine-year-old Laurel knew that if she lived to be a hundred she'd never see anyone more beautiful.

'Lol.'

Laurel opened her eyes. The song had ended and the record was turning by itself on the table. Gerry was standing over their mother, who'd drifted off to sleep, stroking her hair lightly.

'Lol,' he said again, and there was something in his voice, an urgency that brought her attention to him.

'What is it?'

He was looking intently at Mummy's face, and Laurel followed his gaze. When she did, she knew. Dorothy wasn't sleeping; she'd gone.

Laurel was sitting on the swing seat beneath the tree, rocking it slowly with her foot. The Nicolsons had spent most of the morning discussing funeral arrangements with the local minister, and Laurel was now polishing the locket her mother had always worn. They'd decided – unanimously – to bury it with Ma; she'd never been one for material possessions, but had valued the locket especially, refusing ever to take it off. 'It holds my dearest treasures,' she used to say, whenever it was mentioned, opening it to show the photographs of her children inside. As a girl, Laurel had loved the way the tiny hinges worked, and the pleasing click of the clasp when it caught.

She opened it and closed it, looking at the smiling young faces of her sisters and brother and herself, pictures she'd seen a hundred times before; and, as she did, she noticed that one of the pieces of oval glass had a chip in its side. Laurel frowned, running her thumb over the flaw. The edge of her nail caught it, and the glass shifted – it was looser than she'd thought – falling out onto Laurel's lap. Without its seal, the fine photographic paper lost its taut-ness, lifting in the centre so that Laurel could see beneath it. She looked closer, slid her finger under and pulled the photograph out.

It was as she'd thought. There was another photo beneath, of other children, children from longer ago. She checked the other side too, hurrying now, as she drove out the glass and pulled the picture of Iris and Rose free. Another old photo: two more children. Laurel looked at the four of them together and gasped: the vintage of the cloth-ing they were wearing, the suggestion of immense heat in the way they were all squinting at the camera, the particular stubborn impatience on the littlest girl's face – Laurel knew who these children were. They were the Longmeyers of Tamborine Mountain, Ma's brothers and sister, before they were lost in the terrible accident that saw her packed up on that ship to England, tucked beneath Katy Ellis's wing.

Laurel was so distracted by her find, wondering how she could go about tracking down more information about this distant family she'd only just discovered, that she didn't notice the car on the driveway until it was almost at the fence. They'd had visitors all day, popping in to pay respects, each of them offering up yet another story about Dorothy that made her children smile, and Rose cry even harder into the large supply of tissues they'd had to buy in specially. As Laurel watched the red car approach, though, she saw this time it was the postman.

She walked over to greet him; he'd heard the news, of course, and passed on his condolences. Laurel thanked him and smiled as he told her a tale of Dorothy Nicolson's surprising abilities with a hammer. 'You wouldn't have credited it,' he said, 'a pretty lady like her nailing fence palings into place, but she knew just what to do.' Laurel shook her head along with his wonder, but her thoughts were with the one-time cedar-getters of Tamborine Mountain as she took the post back with her to the swing seat.

Among the mail there was an electricity bill, a leaflet about a local council election, and another largish envelope besides. Laurel raised her eyebrows when she saw it was addressed to her. She couldn't think there were many people who knew she was at Greenacres, only Claire, who never sent a letter when a phone call would do. She turned the envelope over and saw that the sender was Martin Metcalfe of 25 Campden Grove.

Intrigued, Laurel tore it open, pulling out the contents. It was a booklet, the official museum guide from his grandfather James Metcalfe's exhibition at the V&A ten years earlier. *Thought you might like this. Regards, Marty*, read the note pinned to its cover. *P.S. Come and see us next time you're in London?* Laurel had a good idea she might: she liked Karen and Marty and their kids, the little boy with the Lego plane and the faraway look in his eyes; they felt like family in a strange, muddled-up way, all of them joined together by those fateful events of 1941.

She flicked through the booklet, admiring once again the glorious talent of James Metcalfe, the way he'd succeeded somehow in capturing more than a mere image with his camera, managing to tell an entire story out of the disparate elements of a single moment. And such important stories, too – they were a record, these photographs, of a historical experience that would be almost impossible to conceive of without them. She wondered if Jimmy had known that at the time; if, as he captured small instances of individual grief and loss on film, he'd realized the tremendous memorial he was sending forwards into the future.

Laurel smiled at the photograph of Nella, and then paused when she came to a loose photo, pinned at the back, a copy of the one she'd noticed in Campden Grove, the picture of Ma. Laurel detached it, holding it close and taking in each of her mother's beautiful features. She was putting it back when she noticed the final photograph in the booklet, a self-portrait of James Metcalfe, taken, it said, in 1954.

It gave her a strange feeling, that picture, and at first she put it down to the crucial part Jimmy had played in her mother's life, the things Ma had told her about his kindness and the way he'd made her happy when there was little other light in her life. But then, as she looked longer, Laurel became more certain that it was something else making her feel this way, something stronger, more personal.

And then, suddenly, she remembered.

Laurel fell back against the seat and gazed at the sky, a smile spreading wide and disbelieving across her face. Everything was illuminated. She knew why the name Vivien had struck her so strongly when she heard it from Rose in the hospital; she knew how Jimmy had known to send the anonymous thank-you card for Vivien to Dorothy Nicolson at Greenacres Farm; she knew why she'd been experiencing little jolts of déjà vu every time she looked at that Coronation stamp.

God help her – Laurel couldn't help but laugh – she even understood the riddle of the man at the stage door. The mysterious quote, so familiar yet impossible to place. It wasn't from a play at all; that's why she'd had so much trouble – she'd been racking the wrong part of her brain. The quote was from a long-ago day, a conversation she'd completely forgotten until now . . .

Thirty-four

The best thing about being eight years old was that Laurel could finally turn proper cartwheels. She'd been doing them all summer long, and her record so far was three hundred and twenty-six in a row, all the way from the top of the driveway to where Daddy's old tractor stood. This morning, though, she'd set herself a new challenge: she was going to see how many it took to go all the way around the house, *and* she was going to do it as quickly as she could.

The problem was the side gate. Every time she got to it (forty-seven – sometimes forty-eight – cartwheels in), she marked her spot in the dust where the hens had pecked away the grass, ran to pin it open and then hurried back to her mark. But by the time she raised her hands, preparing to turn herself over, the gate had creaked itself back shut. She thought about propping something against it, but the hens were a naughty bunch and would be just as likely to flap their way into the vegetable patch if she gave them half the chance.

Still, she couldn't think that there was any other way she was going to complete her cartwheel lap. She cleared her throat like her teacher Miss Plimpton did whenever she had a grave announcement to make, and said, 'Now, listen here, you lot – ' pointing her finger for good measure – 'I'm going to leave this gate open, but only for a minute. If any of you has any bright ideas about sneaking out when I turn my back, especially into Daddy's garden, I'd like to remind you that Mummy's making Coronation Chicken this afternoon and may be looking for volunteers.'

Mummy wouldn't have *dreamed* of putting any of her girls in the pot – hens were all guaranteed death from old age when they had the good fortune of being born onto the Nicolson farm – but Laurel saw no reason to tell them that.

She fetched Daddy's work boots from beside the front door, and carried them over, leaning them one by one against the open gate. Constable the cat, who'd been watching proceedings from the front doorstep, miaowed now to register reservations with the plan, but Laurel pretended not to notice. Satisfied that the gate would stay put, she reiterated her warning to the hens and, with a final check of her watch, waited for the second hand to hit the twelve, shouted, 'Go!' and started turning cartwheels.

The plan worked a treat. Round and round she went, long plaits dragging in the dust and then flicking against her back like a horse's tail: across the hen enclosure, through the open gate (hurrah!) and back to where she'd started. Eighty-nine cartwheels, three minutes and four seconds exactly.

Laurel felt triumphant – right up until she noticed those naughty girls had done *exactly* what she'd told them not to. They were running amok now in her father's vegetable patch, pulling down the heads of corn and pecking like they didn't get a good three square meals a day.

'Hey!' Laurel shouted. 'You lot, get back in your pen.'

They ignored her, and she marched over, waving her arms and stomping her feet, being met with nothing but continued disdain.

Laurel didn't see the man at first. Not until he said, 'Hi there,' and she looked up and saw him standing near where Daddy's Morris was usually parked.

'Hello,' she said.

'You look a little cross.'

'I *am* cross. The girls have escaped and they're eating all my daddy's corn and I'm going to get the blame.'

'Goodness,' he said. 'That sounds serious.'

'It is.' Her bottom lip threatened to quiver, but she didn't let it.

'Well now – it's a little-known fact, but I happen to speak hen rather well. Why don't we just see what we can do to get them back?'

Laurel agreed, and together they chased the hens all around the patch, the man making clucking noises, and Laurel watching over her shoulder with wonder. When every last bird was present and accounted for, safely shut behind the gate, he even helped her remove the evidence from Daddy's corn stems.

'Are you here to see my parents?' said Laurel, suddenly realizing that the man might have a purpose other than to help her.

'That's right,' he said. 'I used to know your mother, a long time ago. We were friends.' He smiled, the sort of smile that made Laurel think that she liked him, and not just because of the hens.

The realization made her a little shy, and she said, 'You

can come inside and wait if you like. I'm supposed to be tidying up.'

'OK.' He followed her into the house, slipping off his hat when they went through the door. He glanced around the room, noticing, Laurel was sure, the brand-new coat of paint Daddy had given the walls. 'Your parents aren't home?'

'Daddy's down in the field, and Mummy's gone to borrow a television set for the coronation.'

'Ah. Of course. Well, I should be fine here, if you need to get on with that tidying.'

Laurel nodded but she didn't move. 'I'm going to be an actress, you know.' She was overcome by a sudden urge to tell the man all about herself.

'Are you now?'

She nodded again.

'Well then, I'm going to have to look out for you. Will you play the London theatres, do you think?'

'Oh yes,' said Laurel, pursing her lips in that considering way grown-ups did. 'I should say that I probably will.'

The man had been smiling but his face changed then, and at first Laurel thought it was something she'd said or done. But then she realized that he wasn't looking at her any more, he was staring beyond her at the wedding photograph of Mummy and Daddy, the one they kept on the hall table.

'Do you like it?' she said.

He didn't answer. He'd gone to the table and was holding the frame now, staring at it as if he couldn't quite believe what he was seeing. 'Vivien,' he said softly, touching Mummy's face.

Laurel frowned, wondering what he meant. 'That's my Mummy,' she said. 'Her name's Dorothy.'

The man looked at Laurel and his mouth opened as if he was going to say something, but he didn't. It closed again and a smile came on his face, a funny smile as if he'd just worked out the answer to a puzzle and what he'd found made him happy and sad all at the same time. He put his hat back on his head and Laurel saw that he was going to leave.

'Mummy won't be long,' she said, confused. 'She's only gone to the next village.'

He didn't change his mind, though, walking back to the door and stepping out into the bright sunshine beneath the wisteria arbour. He held out his hand and said to Laurel, 'Well, fellow hen-wrangler, it's been lovely to meet you. Enjoy the coronation, won't you.'

'I will.'

'My name's Jimmy, by the way, and I'm going to look out for you on those London stages.'

'I'm Laurel,' she said, shaking his hand. 'And I'll see you there.'

He laughed. 'I've little doubt of that. You strike me as just the sort who knows how to listen with her ears, her eyes and her heart all at once.'

Laurel nodded importantly.

The man had started to leave when he stopped mid-pace and turned back one last time. 'Before I go, Laurel, can you tell me – your mum and dad, are they happy?'

Laurel wrinkled her nose, not sure what he meant.

He said, 'Do they make jokes together, and laugh and dance and play?'

Laurel rolled her eyes. 'Oh yes,' she said, '*always*.'

'And is your daddy kind?'

She scratched her head and nodded. 'And funny. He makes her laugh, and he always makes her tea, and did you know he saved her life? That's how they fell in love – Mummy dropped off the side of a big deep cliff, and she was frightened and alone and probably in mortal danger, until my daddy dived in, even though there were sharks and crocodiles and certainly pirates, too, and he rescued her.'

'Did he?'

'He did. And they ate cockles afterwards.'

'Well then, Laurel,' the man, Jimmy, said, 'I think your dad sounds like just the sort of fellow your mum deserves.'

And then he looked at his boots, in that sad-happy way of his, and waved goodbye. Laurel watched him go, but only for a little while, and then she started wondering how many cartwheels it would take to get all the way down to the stream. And by the time her mother got home, and her sisters too – the television set in a box in the boot – she'd all but forgotten the kind man who'd come that day and helped her with the hens.

Acknowledgements

Thanks are due to an invaluable trio of early readers, Julia Kretschmer, Davin Patterson and Catherine Milne; my brilliant and inexhaustible editorial team, including my publisher, Maria Rejt, Sophie Orme, Liz Cowen and Ali Blackburn at Pan Macmillan, UK; Christa Munns and Clara Finlay at Allen & Unwin, Australia; Judith Curr, Lisa Keim, Kim Goldstein and Isolde Sauer at Atria, US; test-reader extraordinaire, Lisa Patterson; and to my publisher and great friend, Annette Barlow, who merrily went beyond the edge of reason with me.

I'm enormously grateful to my publishers around the world for their ongoing support, and to all the talented people who help turn my stories into books and send them on their way. Thanks to every bookseller, librarian and reader who continues to keep the faith; to Wenona Byrne for the many extra things she does; to Ruth Hayden, artist and inspiration; and to my family and friends for letting me disappear inside my imaginary world and return to them later as if nothing's happened. Special thanks, as always, must go to my agent, Selwa Anthony, my precious boys, Oliver and Louis, and most of all, for everything and more, to my husband, Davin.

I consulted many sources while researching and writing *The Secret Keeper*. Among the most useful were: the BBC's online archive *WW2 People's War*; the Imperial War Museum, London; the British Postal Museum and Archive; *Black Diamonds: The Rise and Fall of an English Dynasty* by Catherine Bailey; *Nella Last's War: The Second World War Diaries of 'Housewife, 49'*, edited by Richard Broad and Suzie Fleming; *Debs at War: How Wartime Changed Their Lives, 1939–1945*, by Anne De Courcy; *Wartime Britain 1939–1945* by Juliet Gardiner; *The Thirties: An Intimate History* by Juliet Gardiner; *Walking the London Blitz* by Clive Harris; *Having It So Good: Britain in the Fifties* by Peter Hennessy; *Few Eggs and No Oranges: The Diaries of Vere Hodgson 1940–45*; *How We Lived Then: A History of Everyday Life during the Second World War* by Norman Longmate; *Never Had It So Good: A History of Britain from Suez to the Beatles* by Dominic Sandbrook; *The Fortnight in September* by R. C. Sherriff; *Our Longest Days: A People's History of the Second World War* by the writers of Mass Observation, edited by Sandra Koa Wing; *London at War 1939–1945* by Philip Ziegler.

Thanks also to Penny McMahon at the British Postal Museum & Archive for answering my questions on cancellation marks; the good people at Transport for London who let me glimpse what a 1940s Tube station was like; John Welham for sharing his remarkable knowledge on a variety of historical topics; Isobel Long for furnishing me with information about the fascinating world of archives and record management; Clive Harris, who continues to provide insightful answers to my every wartime-query, and whose walking tour of Blitz-time London first inspired the world of this story; and Herbert and Rita, from whom I caught my love of theatre.

If you enjoyed
The Secret Keeper
you'll love Kate Morton's
The Distant Hours

It started with a letter . . .

Edie Burchill and her mother have never been close, but
when a long lost letter arrives with the return address of
Milderhurst Castle, Kent, printed on its envelope, Edie
begins to suspect that her mother's emotional distance
masks an old secret.

Evacuated from London as a thirteen-year-old girl, Edie's
mother is chosen by the mysterious Juniper Blythe, and taken
to live at Milderhurst Castle with the Blythe family.

Fifty years later, Edie too is drawn to Milderhurst and
the eccentric Sisters Blythe. Old ladies now, the three still
live together, the twins nursing Juniper, whose abandonment
by her fiancé in 1941 plunged her into madness.

Inside the decaying castle, Edie begins to unravel her
mother's past. But there are other secrets hidden in the
stones of Milderhurst Castle, and Edie is about to learn
more than she expected. The truth of what happened in the
distant hours has been waiting a long time for someone to
find it . . .

Out now in paperback

An extract follows here . . .

A Lost Letter Finds Its Way

1992

It started with a letter. A letter that had been lost a long time, waiting out half a century in a forgotten postal bag in the dim attic of a nondescript house in Bermondsey. I think about it sometimes, that mailbag: of the hundreds of love letters, grocery bills, birthday cards, notes from children to their parents, that lay together, swelling and sighing as their thwarted messages whispered in the dark. Waiting, waiting, for someone to realize they were there. For it is said, you know, that a letter will always seek a reader; that sooner or later, like it or not, words have a way of finding the light, of making their secrets known.

Forgive me, I'm being romantic – a habit acquired from the years spent reading nineteenth-century novels with a torch when my parents thought I was asleep. What I mean to say is that it's odd to think that if Arthur Tyrell had been a little more responsible, if he hadn't had one too many rum toddies that Christmas Eve in 1941 and gone home and fallen into a drunken slumber instead of finishing his mail delivery, if the bag hadn't then been tucked in his attic and hidden until his death some fifty years later when one of his daughters unearthed it and called the *Daily Mail*, the whole thing might have turned out differently. For my mum, for me, and especially for Juniper Blythe.

You probably read about it when it happened; it was in all the newspapers, and on the TV news. Channel 4 even ran a special where they invited some of the recipients to talk about their letter, their particular voice from the past that had come back to surprise them. There was a woman whose sweetheart had been in the RAF, and the man with the birthday card his evacuated son had sent, the little boy who was killed by a piece of falling shrapnel a week or so later. It was a very good programme, I thought: moving in parts, happy and sad stories interspersed with old footage of the war. I cried a couple of times, but that's not saying much: I'm rather disposed to weep.

Mum didn't go on the show, though. The producers contacted her and asked whether there was anything special in her letter that she'd like to share with the nation, but she said no, that it was just an ordinary old clothing order from a shop that had long ago gone out of business. But that wasn't the truth. I know this because I was there when the letter arrived. I saw her reaction to that lost letter and it was anything but ordinary.

It was a morning in late February, winter still had us by the throat, the flowerbeds were icy, and I'd come over to help with the Sunday roast. I do that sometimes because my parents like it, even though I'm a vegetarian and I know that at some point during the course of the meal my mother will start to look worried, then agonized, until finally she can stand it no longer and statistics about protein and anaemia will begin to fly.

I was peeling potatoes in the sink when the letter dropped through the slot in the door. The post doesn't usually come on Sundays so that should have tipped us off, but it didn't. For my part, I was too busy wondering how I was going to tell my parents that Jamie and I had broken up. It had been two months since it happened and I knew I had to say something eventually, but the longer I took to utter the words, the more calcified they became. And I had my reasons for staying silent: my parents had been suspicious of Jamie from the start, they didn't take kindly to upsets, and Mum would worry even more than usual if she knew that I was living in the flat alone. Most of all, though, I was dreading the inevitable, awkward conversation that would follow my announcement. To see first bewilderment, then alarm, then resignation, cross Mum's face as she realized the maternal code required her to provide some sort of consolation . . . But back to the post. The sound of something dropping softly through the letterbox.

'Edie, can you get that?'

This was my mother. (Edie is me: I'm sorry, I should have said so earlier.) She nodded towards the hallway and gestured with the hand that wasn't stuck up the inside of the chicken.

I put down the potato, wiped my hands on a tea towel and went to fetch the post. There was only one letter lying on the welcome mat: an official Post Office envelope declaring the contents to be 'redirected mail'. I read the label to Mum as I brought it into the kitchen.

She'd finished stuffing the chicken by then and was drying her own hands. Frowning a little, from habit rather than any particular expectation, she took the letter from me and plucked her reading glasses from on top of the pineapple in the fruit bowl. She skimmed the post office notice and with a flicker of her eyebrows began to open the outer envelope.

I'd turned back to the potatoes by now, a task that was arguably more engaging than watching my mum open mail, so I'm sorry to say I didn't see her face as she fished the smaller envelope from inside, as she registered the frail austerity paper and the old stamp, as she turned the letter over and read the name written on the back. I've imagined it many times since, though, the colour draining instantly from her cheeks, her fingers beginning to tremble so that it took minutes before she was able to slit the envelope open.

What I don't have to imagine is the sound. The horrid, guttural gasp, followed quickly by a series of rasping sobs that swamped the air and made me slip with the peeler so that I cut my finger.

'Mum?' I went to her, draping my arm around her shoulders, careful not to bleed on her dress. But she didn't say anything. She couldn't, she told me later, not then. She stood rigidly as tears spilled down her cheeks and she clutched the strange little envelope, its paper so thin I could make out the corner of the folded letter inside, hard against her bosom. Then she disappeared upstairs to her bedroom leaving a fraying wake of instructions about the bird and the oven and the potatoes.

The kitchen settled in a bruised silence around her absence and I stayed very quiet, moved very slowly so as not to disturb it further. My mother is not a crier, but this moment – her upset and the shock of it – felt oddly familiar, as if we'd been here before. After fifteen minutes in which I variously peeled potatoes, turned over possibilities as to whom the letter might be from, and wondered how to proceed, I finally knocked on her door and asked whether she'd like a cup of tea. She'd composed herself by then and we sat opposite one another at the small Formica-covered table in the kitchen. As I pretended not to notice she'd been crying, she began to talk about the envelope's contents.

'A letter,' she said, 'from someone I used to know a long time ago. When I was just a girl, twelve, thirteen.'

A picture came into my mind, a hazy memory of a photograph that had sat on my gran's bedside when she was old and dying. Three children, the youngest of whom was my mum, a girl with short dark hair, perched on something in the foreground. It was odd; I'd sat with Gran a hundred times or more but I couldn't bring that girl's features into focus now. Perhaps children are never really interested in who their parents were before they were born; not unless something particular happens to shine a light on the past. I sipped my tea, waiting for Mum to continue.

'I don't know that I've told you much about that time, have I? During the war, the Second World War. It was a terrible time, such confusion, so many things were broken. It seemed...' She sighed. 'Well, it seemed as if the world would never return to normal. As if it had been tipped off its axis and nothing would ever set it to rights.' She cupped her hands around the steaming rim of her mug and stared down at it.

'My family – Mum and Dad, Rita and Ed and I – we all lived in a small house together in Barlow Street, near the Elephant and Castle, and the day after war broke out we were rounded up at school, marched over to the railway station and put into train carriages. I'll never forget it, all of us with our tags on and our masks and our packs, and the mothers, who'd had second thoughts because they came running down the road towards the station, shouting at the guard to let their kids off; then shouting at older siblings to look after the little ones, not to let them out of their sight.'

She sat for a moment, biting her bottom lip as the scene played out in her memory.

'You must've been frightened,' I said quietly. We're not really hand-holders in our family or else I'd have reached out and taken hers.

'I was, at first.' She removed her glasses and rubbed her eyes. Her face had a vulnerable, unfinished look without her frames, like a small nocturnal animal confused by the daylight. I was glad when she put them on again and continued. 'I'd never been away from home before, never spent a night apart from my mother. But I had my older brother and sister with me, and as the trip went on and one of the teachers handed round bars of chocolate, everybody started to cheer up and look upon the experience almost like an adventure. Can you imagine? War had been declared but we were all singing songs and eating tinned pears and looking out of the window playing I-spy. Children are very resilient, you know; callous in some cases.

'We arrived eventually in a town called Cranbrook, only to be split into groups and loaded onto various coaches. The one I was on with Ed and Rita took us to the village of Milderhurst, where we were walked in lines to a hall. A group of local women were waiting for us there, smiles fixed on their faces, lists in hand, and we were made to stand in rows as people milled about, making their selection.

'The little ones went fast, especially the pretty ones. People supposed they'd be less work, I expect, that they'd have less of the whiff of London about them.'

She smiled crookedly. 'They soon learned. My brother

was picked early. He was a strong boy, tall for his age, and the farmers were desperate for help. Rita went a short while after with her friend from school.'

Well, that was it. I reached out and laid my hand on hers. 'Oh, Mum.'

'Never mind.' She pulled free and gave my fingers a tap. 'I wasn't the last to go. There were a few others, a little boy with a terrible skin condition. I don't know what happened to him, but he was still standing there in that hall when I left.'

'You know, for a long time afterwards, years and years, I forced myself to buy bruised fruit if that's what I picked up first at the greengrocer's. None of this checking it over and putting it back on the shelf if it didn't measure up.'

'But you were chosen eventually.'

'Yes, I was chosen eventually.' She lowered her voice, fiddling with something in her lap, and I had to lean close. 'She came in late. The room was almost clear, most of the children had gone and the ladies from the Women's Voluntary Service were putting away the tea things. I'd started to cry a little, though I did so very discreetly. Then all of a sudden, *she* swept in and the room, the very air, seemed to alter.'

'Alter?' I wrinkled my nose, thinking of that scene in *Carrie* when the light explodes.

'It's hard to explain. Have you ever met a person who seems to bring their own atmosphere with them when they arrive somewhere?'

Maybe. I lifted my shoulders, uncertain. My friend Sarah has a habit of turning heads wherever she goes; not exactly an atmospheric phenomenon, but still...

'No, of course you haven't. It sounds so silly to say it like that. What I mean is that she was different from other people, more ... Oh, I don't know. Just *more*. Beautiful in an odd way, long hair, big eyes, rather wild looking, but it wasn't that alone which set her apart. She was only seventeen at the time, in September 1939, but the other women all seemed to fold into themselves when she arrived.'

'They were deferential?'

'Yes, that's the word, deferential. Surprised to see her and uncertain how to behave. Finally, one of them spoke up, asking whether she could help, but the girl merely waved her long fingers and announced that she'd come for her evacuee. That's what she said; not *an* evacuee, *her* evacuee. And then she came straight over to where I was sitting on the floor. "What's your name?" she said, and when I told her she smiled and said that I must be tired, having travelled such a long way. "Would you like to come and stay with me?" I nodded, I must have, for she turned then to the bossiest woman, the one with the list, and said that she would take me home with her.'

'What was her name?'

'Blythe,' said my mother, suppressing the faintest of shivers. 'Juniper Blythe.'

'And was it she who sent you the letter?'

Mum nodded. 'She led me to the fanciest car I'd ever seen and drove me back to the place where she and her older twin sisters lived, through a set of iron gates, along a winding driveway, until we reached an enormous stone edifice surrounded by thick woods. Milderhurst Castle.'

The name was straight out of a gothic novel and I tingled a little, remembering Mum's sob when she'd read the woman's name and address on the back of the envelope. I'd heard stories about the evacuees, about some of the things that went on, and I said on a breath, 'Was it ghastly?'

'Oh no, nothing like that. Not ghastly at all. Quite the opposite.'

'But the letter . . . It made you—'

'The letter was a surprise, that's all. A memory from a long time ago.'

She fell silent then and I thought about the enormity of evacuation, how frightening, how odd it must have been for her as a child to be sent to a strange place where everyone and everything was vastly different. I could still touch my own childhood experiences, the horror of being thrust into new, unnerving situations, the furious bonds that were forged of necessity – to buildings, to sympathetic adults, to special friends – in order to survive. Remembering those urgent friendships, something struck me: 'Did you ever go back, Mum, after the war? To Milderhurst?'

She looked up sharply. 'Of course not. Why would I?'

'I don't know. To catch up, to say hello. To see your friend.'

'No.' She said it firmly. 'I had my own family in London, my mother couldn't spare me, and besides, there was work to be done, cleaning up after the war. Real life went on.' And with that, the familiar veil came down between us and I knew the conversation was over.

We didn't have the roast in the end. Mum said she didn't feel like it and asked whether I minded terribly giving it a miss this weekend. It seemed unkind to remind her that I don't eat meat anyway and that my attendance was more in the order of daughterly service, so I told her it was fine and suggested that she have a lie-down. She agreed, and as I gathered my things into my bag she was already swallowing two paracetamol in preparation, reminding me to keep my ears covered in the wind.

My dad, as it turns out, slept through the whole thing. He's older than Mum and had retired from his work a few months before. Retirement hasn't been good for him: he roams the house during the week, looking for things to fix and tidy, driving Mum mad, then on Sunday he rests in his armchair. The God-given right of the man of the house, he says to anyone who'll listen.

I gave him a kiss on the cheek and left the house, braving the chill air as I made my way to the tube, tired and unsettled and somewhat subdued to be heading back alone to the fiendishly expensive flat I'd shared until recently with Jamie. It wasn't until somewhere between High Street Kensington and Notting Hill Gate that I realized Mum hadn't told me what the letter said.